# THE MAILMAN

# THE MAILMAN

## ANDREW WELSH-HUGGINS

THE MYSTERIOUS PRESS
NEW YORK

THE MAILMAN

Mysterious Press
An Imprint of Penzler Publishers
58 Warren Street
New York, N.Y. 10007

Library of Congress Control Number: 2024945700

ISBN: 978-1-61316-610-9
eBook: 978-1-61316-611-6

10 9 8 7 6 5 4 3 2 1

Printed in the United States of America
Distributed by W. W. Norton & Company

*For Pam, who always answered my letters*

"The pony express enterprise continued for about two years, at the end of which time telegraph service between the Atlantic and Pacific oceans was established. Few men remember those days of excitement and interest. The danger surrounding the riders can not be told. Not only were they remarkable for lightness of weight and energy, but their service required continual vigilance, bravery, and agility. Among their number were skillful guides, scouts, and couriers, accustomed to adventures and hardships on the plains—men of strong wills and wonderful powers of endurance."

—*Seventy Years on the Frontier,* Alexander Majors

# ONE

Rachel Stanfield paused, not sure she heard her husband correctly, but wanting as always to give him the benefit of the doubt. Grateful for the distraction of a sound outside, she peered through the kitchen window but saw nothing. Another stray cat, maybe, the second prowling around in two days if so. She hoped that wasn't going to become a thing, a concern to raise with the neighbors they still barely knew.

At least it was Thursday, she thought with a sigh, studying the bag of power greens on the counter. The week had felt impossibly long. And now this: what seemed like the prelude to an argument when all she wanted to do was relax, chat about their days over dinner, and burrow into *The Crown*.

Composing herself and trying not to frown, she turned her attention to Glenn. She knew he hated it when she frowned. It was something she was working on as a show of good faith. Despite how much he frowned, nearly every hour of every day. Especially, for whatever reason, these days.

"Not to nitpick here," Rachel said. "But did you just say, 'Going through a phase'?"

Glenn, seated on a light oak stool at the kitchen island, studied her before taking a sip of his Dewar's neat. His second of the evening if you were counting. Which Rachel was, if only because she was so desperate for a drink of her own.

"I did. Because that's what I think it is."

Cautiously, Rachel said, "Really? You think four Ds and an F are a 'phase'? One of the Ds is in Spanish, by the way, which is a little ironic."

"Yeah, that one's a head-scratcher. But that's Abby. You know how she gets. Once she sets her mind to something, there's nothing stopping her."

Rachel reached under the counter for a colander and placed it in the sink. She dumped the greens in and ran them under water for a count of ten. Finished, she bounced them up and down, shaking off the loose drops, then placed them between two paper towels to soak up the rest of the moisture.

"Yeah, but," she said.

"But what?"

"Well, that whole 'setting her mind to something' deal? That's a phrase usually associated with an accomplishment of some kind. As in, 'Once she set her mind to making the team, there was nothing stopping her.'" She hesitated, then plunged ahead. "I'm not as familiar with it as an excuse for trashing grades. Especially at . . ."

Glenn frowned and gulped from his glass. "Go ahead. Say it. *Especially at these prices?* I assume that's the direction you're going?"

"It crossed my mind, yes," she said, immediately regretting the comment. Before Glenn could respond, she rose on her tiptoes to retrieve the wooden salad bowl from the cabinet. She gave the greens a last pat, spilled them into the bowl, and retrieved a yellow pepper and waxy red tomato from the refrigerator. She cut the pepper in half, dug out the seeds, began slicing, and said, quietly, "For the record, I don't begrudge the tuition—"

"Really?"

She paused, taken aback. "You know, there's no need to raise your voice."

"I'm not raising my voice."

She took a breath. "But—you're doing it right now. I don't appreciate it. I'm on your side here, in case you've forgotten."

"I'm not—" He stopped, voice still elevated. Rachel looked at him with both curiosity and concern, feeling her heart go out to him despite her annoyance at his tone. The look on his face was troubling—a combination of worry, anger, and something else, amorphous and ever-shifting, like an undefined illness—that nothing she did or said recently seemed to ameliorate. A look that more and more came and went like black clouds crowding out the sun, spoiling his handsome, still boyish face.

"Hey. Are you all right?"

"I'm fine," he said.

"It just seems like something's on your mind."

"I said I'm fine."

"Okay, then," Rachel said, not convinced. "In that case, back to Bellbrook real quick. I just want you to understand where I'm coming from. I don't mind the tuition. I really don't. It's worth every penny. The teachers alone. And the resources there. My God. I guess all I'm suggesting is that there's such a thing as a two-way street, and I'm not sure Abby always gets that. And if she's so unhappy, we already live in a perfectly good school district."

"Meaning?"

"Meaning there's other options if she's miserable. We can work with her." She hesitated. "I can work with her. I'd like that."

Glenn steepled his fingers on either side of his glass as if examining a religious artifact. "Who says she's miserable?"

"I just assumed. All those texts she's been sending?" Rachel slid the diced peppers into the salad bowl with her knife—pausing again, sure she heard a sound; stupid cats—and turned to the tomato. "How much she hates Bellbrook? Begging to come home? And now, I mean, these grades? It's just natural, isn't it? If she's unhappy, what incentive does she have to do well?"

"Well, you . . ."

Rachel pulled up. "I what?"

"Nothing."

"No—go ahead." She put the knife down. "I'm listening."

"I said it's nothing." Almost, but not quite, shouting.

"Glenn?"

He lowered his voice. "I'm sorry. I didn't mean anything. I shouldn't have—"

She folded her arms. "You shouldn't have implied that I'm successful but not happy?"

"I'm sorry," he repeated.

"For what? Speaking the truth?"

"Rachel—"

Eyes brightening, she waved Glenn off from further conversation, sliced the tomato loudly—the knife *clack-clack-clack*ing on the cutting board—slid the segments into the salad bowl, and set the bowl on the island. She sighed. Leave it to Glenn to see straight through to her heart, to put his finger on the crux of the matter keeping her up at night. Maybe not in the most tender fashion, but attentive to her inner turmoil even as he brushed off whatever was weighing him down these days.

She turned away, distressed by the look on Glenn's face as it dawned on him how much he'd hurt her. She grabbed the wooden tongs they brought home from last summer's trip to Mexico and set them into the bowl. She went to the refrigerator and pulled out the steaks, the sight of the marbled red meat turning her stomach for a moment. She knew Glenn would work his usual magic on the grill and in a few minutes—assuming his nightly moodiness faded and they moved past this . . . discussion? Disagreement? Argument?—she'd soon be enjoying a better-than-restaurant-quality porterhouse. Things were better now that she was into the second trimester. Still: there was just something about the texture of raw meat.

She pushed the salad bowl to the side, placed the plastic-wrapped plate of steaks beside her husband, and said, "I'm sorry. I overreacted. That's a fair observation. It still feels like I made the right decision, but I know I'm not always a happy camper. You shouldn't have to put up with that."

"Rachel—"

"It's just that I'm worried about Abby and I took my concerns about her out on you—not cool."

"And I shouldn't have said what I said. I know things have been hard. You know if you ever want to go back—"

She waved him off once more. Despite the job challenges she faced, there was no point going down that path again. What was done, was done. For good reason. She poured herself a glass of water, and said, "In my defense, all I was trying to say—my own situation notwithstanding—is sometimes you have to work hard in spite of how much you dislike the process. A lot of the time, if I'm being honest about it, and that was true even before I took this job."

"Really?"

"Yes, really," she said, wondering if in fact that were true.

"You don't sound convinced."

"There's no need to patronize me."

"I'm not patronizing you."

"Sorry," she said, retreating. "I know you're trying to help." The stove timer sounded just then and she welcomed the distraction, sliding over to turn off the heat under the potatoes boiling in the copper-clad Williams Sonoma pot, part of a wedding-gift set from Glenn's mother. Donning oven mitts and grabbing the pot—ignoring Glen's offer of help—Rachel said, "I'm only saying that sometimes it feels as if Abby doesn't understand how the world works. That she equates being happy with doing well, to her detriment."

She emptied the potato water into the sink as she stepped back to avoid the billow of steam, and then replaced the pot on the stove. Then, against her better judgment, she blurted out, "And sometimes I think we're to blame for that."

"What are you talking about?"

"How easy we've made it for her. She sees this"—Rachel swung her arm in an arc around the kitchen—"and everything else around here, and she takes it for granted. She doesn't see the effort it requires to maintain what we have. It's no wonder she doesn't care about her grades."

"In other words, we haven't made her feel guilty about wealth?" Anger back in Glenn's voice, like a toxic chemical drifting into a formerly pristine stream.

"That's not what I'm saying. And please stop shouting."

"I'm not shouting," Glenn said, nearly shouting. "And isn't what you're saying is *I've* made things too easy for her? *I* haven't explained the way things work?"

"No," Rachel said, mind awhirl, wondering how they arrived at this moment, the precipice of a fight, and whether Glenn's moodiness or her uncertainty about, well, about everything, was more to blame. "That's not what I mean."

"Sure about that? She's my daughter, after all."

That stung, after everything they'd been through. "Our daughter," Rachel said. "Ours. You know that's how I feel."

"Sometimes I have my doubts."

*And that's my fault?* Rachel thought, suddenly furious. She found herself on the cusp of voicing those words aloud, the fate of their restaurant-quality meal be damned. She never got the chance. One moment Rachel was pondering the complications of life as a stepmother, her concerns about Glenn, a gnawing sense that things would never be the same again at work—her mind racing—and the next she stood, transfixed, as the back door opened and four masked men walked in off the deck, dressed from head to toe in black.

"The hell are you—" Glenn managed, rising from his stool before the tallest and widest-shouldered of the four swung a gun against his head. He collapsed, folded onto the island, and fell to the floor.

Despite the terror flooding her insides, Rachel rushed to Glenn's side. "Who are you?" she screamed. "Get out. Get out."

The thinnest of the four pulled off his mask and stared emotionlessly at her. She looked at him, recognition striking like an electric shock, and thought she might throw up.

"You."

"Don't say I didn't warn you."

# TWO

They were seated on the black leather living room sectional, hands zip-tied behind them. Finn, the man who'd pulled off his mask in the kitchen, had drawn the curtains closed, presumably to shield them from their neighbors' prying eyes. Though that was a bit of a joke, Rachel thought as the horror of their situation sank in, considering how spread out the houses were here, each on its own half-acre of lawn and gardens. Just the kind of privacy they sought when they upsized thanks to Rachel's new salary.

Two men stood behind Rachel and Glenn respectively, guns held loosely at their sides. Finn sat in Glenn's wingback on the other side of the glass-top coffee table, face neutral, his own gun resting on his right thigh. The fourth man, the one who hit Glenn, stood behind Finn. The remaining three men had also removed their masks. Which Rachel knew instinctively was a very bad sign.

"Who are you?" Glenn said for what must have been the fifth time since coming to with a moan. Finn had repeatedly ignored Rachel's pleas to dress his wound and give him something for the pain.

Finn said nothing. Just stared.

Glenn said, "Is this about Xeneconn? If it is, you've made a big mistake."

Finn didn't speak. After a moment, Rachel said, "Glenn—it's not about Xeneconn."

"What?" Glenn said, turning his head with difficulty.

"I said, it's not about Xeneconn."

"How do you know that?"

"I just know."

"But how—"

"You should listen to your wife."

They looked up. Finn had spoken at last.

"Tell us what's going on," Glenn mumbled, still struggling to form words. "If it's not about Xeneconn, why are you here?"

His phrasing, the way he posed the question, caught Rachel's attention. As if something about Glenn's company would give these thugs a reason to be in their house. But that didn't make any sense—

Before she could finish her thought, Finn, said, "Why not ask Rachel? Or should I say, Attorney Stanfield? She and I both know why I'm here."

"She what?" Glenn turned to Rachel. "Do you know this man?"

Hesitantly, she nodded. "Sort of."

"Sort of? What's that supposed to mean?"

"He's the one I told you—"

"It means it's time to get down to business," Finn said. He shifted in his chair and studied Rachel with a frown. She summoned all her remaining courage and faced him, taking in the short-cropped black hair, the scar on his left cheek, and the slightly weak chin, as if a sculptor crafting a bust had run out of clay at the last minute. The face that had so unnerved her the first time she saw it, two days earlier.

"To review," Finn said. "You conducted a deposition within the last six weeks with a woman named Stella Wolford. I have asked you repeatedly, and professionally, for a copy of that deposition. You in turn have refused my request."

Rachel couldn't help herself. "Professionally?"

"Way I see it, yes."

Rachel recalled the multiple phone calls and emails and texts that she received from Finn in recent days, each more demanding than the last, culminating in his appearance by her side in the cereal aisle at Whole Foods Sunday morning. Making his case in person, he called it. She called it stalking and told him to go to hell.

But quibbling seemed a fool's errand at this point. Her only focus now was hoping she could see her and Glenn through this without further injury.

"As I've explained," Rachel said, forcing herself to keep her voice calm, "it's a proprietary document that I can't release because it hasn't been filed."

"And as I've explained, who cares? I still want it."

Rachel persisted. "A lawyer with a legitimate connection to the case could file a motion with the court to participate in the litigation. It's possible that—"

"Yes, yes," Finn said. "I already told you there's no such lawyer on my end. And having asked repeatedly, and professionally, you've forced my hand and now, with regrets, I have to make other arrangements. Namely—you have sixty seconds to produce the document or we're going remove your husband's fingers. One for every minute of delay." He nodded at the man behind Rachel, who responded by pulling a pair of pruning shears from his pocket and opening and closing them three times. *Slice. Slice. Slice.*

"At least tell me why you want it?" Rachel said, voice rising. "What possible interest is it to you?"

"Fifty-five seconds."

Rachel's mind raced, trying to discern why this brute, this lunatic, could possibly want the deposition of a low-level employee at a health-care company who had been fired for poor performance and for some reason believed she had cause for a wrongful termination lawsuit. What the hell was she missing here?

"Forty-five seconds." Finn gestured at Pruning Shears, who walked around to the front of the couch, sat beside Glenn, and reached behind his back for his bound hands.

"Rachel," her husband said weakly.

Rachel felt tears well up. Not for her or Glenn or even their unborn child. But for Glenn's daughter. *Their* daughter. She imagined a school counselor walking into a classroom and searching out Abby—obstinate, mouthy, opinionated, brilliant, beautiful Abby—and gesturing with a grim look to follow her into the hall. *Honey, I'm afraid I have some bad news.* No, not her daughter. But yes, goddammit. Her daughter.

"Thirty-five seconds."

"All right, all right," Rachel said. "I mean, this is insane. And so illegal. But okay."

"Thirty."

"I'll need my laptop," she shouted. "It's in my black briefcase, in the office off the kitchen."

"The deposition is on it?" Finn said.

"Not on the laptop. It's on a company server I can access remotely. It'll just take a minute to get through the firewall."

"I'll need a copy."

"I can download it for you. Or print it out. Whichever is easiest."

"Both, please. And just to be clear, if there's a trick involved, like a silent electronic trigger, something that alerts someone—the same punishment applies. Understood?"

"Yes," Rachel said, perspiration pouring down her back, dampening her blouse. "No tricks. I promise."

Finn nodded at the big man, the one who hit Glenn, and he left the room. A minute passed. Rachel heard what sounded like furniture being overturned. She snuck a glance at Glenn and the look they shared, the mutual understanding that they might not survive the night—all four men unmasked, so their IDs were of no concern—tore her heart in half. After two long additional minutes the man returned. He handed the laptop to Finn.

"Also, I found this." His voice deep and rough, like a longtime smoker with a heavy cold. Rachel looked in disbelief at the gun in the man's hand.

"Interesting," Finn said, taking the weapon. He turned to Rachel. "This doesn't seem like the kind of neighborhood where you need a gun. What's it for?"

Rachel looked at Glenn. "I have no idea. I've never seen it before."

"Is that right?" He pointed it at her and then at Glenn. "So it just magically appeared?"

"Unless you put it there."

"Why would I do that? I have plenty of guns already."

"Well, it's certainly not mine."

"Is it yours?" Finn said, directing the question at Glenn.

"Go to hell."

Rachel flinched at Glenn's response. Was he saying that—

"I'll take that as a yes," Finn said. He handed the weapon back to the big man. "We'll talk more about that later. Right now, I need that deposition." He looked at the man with the pruning shears. The man nodded, approached Rachel, reached behind her, and cut the ties binding her hands as she involuntarily yelped. While she flexed her numb fingers in relief, Finn handed her the laptop.

"Make it fast."

Hands trembling, Rachel opened the computer and powered it up. Beside her, Glenn watched, suppressing an occasional groan.

"Well?" Finn said.

*Jesus*, Rachel thought, smelling the rank odor of fear rising on her. She clicked in vain on the wireless icon. This was all they needed.

"There's something wrong. I can't log on."

She expected Finn to lash out at her, or worse. Instead, to her surprise, he swore under his breath and nodded at the big man. He disappeared around the corner. A moment later the connection reappeared.

"Working?"

"Yes," Rachel said. "What did you—"

"Deposition. Now."

In less than five minutes, Finn eying her every move, Rachel was in her firm's document bank and clicking on Stella Wolford's interview.

"There."

Finn picked up the laptop and read for a full minute, scrolling down three screens as he did. Finished, he handed Rachel the laptop and gave her a flash drive. "Save it, and print it."

Ten minutes later, Finn pocketed the drive and scanned the sheaf of papers that Rachel's home office printer spat out.

"Satisfied?" Rachel said.

"Not really. This would have been so much easier if you cooperated from the beginning. The delay makes me think you're hiding something."

"There's no delay," Rachel protested. "I'm not hiding anything. Like I told you a million times, it's proprietary information you're not entitled to in the first place."

"Regardless, my suspicions now require more questions. Starting with—where is Stella Wolford?"

"I have no idea. I'm not even sure where she lives."

"Well, I am. In fact, it just so happens that the address here"—Finn waved the print-out at Rachel—"matches our records. Yet she can't be found. Why is that?"

Rachel blinked away tears. "How should I know?"

"Interestingly enough, her lawyer said the same thing. And look what happened to him."

Rachel's stomach contracted. "What are you talking about? What happened to her lawyer?"

"Next question," Finn said, ignoring her. "What do the numbers 'twenty-two seven' mean to you?"

"'Twenty-two seven'?"

"You heard me."

"Nothing. What do they have to do with anything?"

"What about you?" The question directed at Glenn.

"Nothing," he mumbled.

Finn sat back, glancing through the sheaf of papers once more, before raising his eyes to Rachel.

"Why do I think you're lying?"

"I'm not lying. I have no idea what those numbers mean."

"A neutral observer might suggest you have every incentive to lie. Especially about those particular numbers."

"But I'm not. *We're* not." Despite everything they were going through, Rachel was growing angrier and angrier at Finn and his unwillingness to believe her. Like she'd lie in a situation like this. "You've got the deposition now, not that I have any idea why you'd need it. There's no 'twenty-two seven' in it, except a page number or something. If you could tell me more about what you're looking for, maybe I could help."

Instead of answering her, Finn said to Pruning Shears, "Bag."

The man lifted a black nylon duffel bag off his left shoulder and placed it on the coffee table with a loud clunk.

"Open it."

The man—gaunt face, dimpled chin, blond buzz cut—stepped forward and unzipped the bag. Without instruction, he removed a series of smaller cloth bags. After a minute, Rachel found herself looking at several items spread across the coffee table. A set of gleaming scalpels. Two spools of black wire. A small butane torch. Three pairs of pliers—parrot nose, needle, and diagonal—and a power drill fitted with a bit almost as wide as a finger. As she watched, the man set the pruning shears alongside the tools.

"My associate here"—Finn nodded at the man—"has made a study of using tools like this to extract information. He is very good at what he does. Gifted, I might say. So—this is your last opportunity to tell me the truth before he takes over. Stella Wolford's whereabouts. And 'twenty-two seven.' Simple enough."

"I don't know anything about Stella Wolford and I don't know anything about those numbers," Rachel said, enunciating each word as she struggled to keep it together. When Finn arched his eyebrows, she said, "I'm telling you the truth."

"Please don't hurt her," Glenn said. "Take me but leave Rachel alone. She's pregnant, for God's sake. I'm begging you."

"I'm sorry to hear that," Finn said. "But at this juncture that would be a matter of water under the bridge."

Rachel turned to Glenn, meeting his eyes again. Wishing he hadn't revealed that particular piece of information. Ready to chastise him. But the look on his face stopped her, and she felt her stomach shrink at the sight of his wound, the blood and the bruises, and at the love—and fear—she had for him at that moment.

Finn rose from the chair. "Basement," he said to the trio. "Him first. Make her watch—duct tape her head in place if you have to. Whatever. You know the drill."

"No," Rachel shouted. "I swear. I'm telling you the truth—we don't know what you're talking about. Please—"

She stopped midsentence as the man who remained behind them reached over her head in one smooth motion and gagged her, knotting the cloth so tightly and painfully she thought for a moment she might pass out.

"Wait," Glenn shouted. "I have money. Lots of it. Millions. Anything you want."

Even in her terror, Rachel stared at her husband in disbelief. Millions? What was he talking about?

An instant later Glenn's voice was also cut short, his own gag pulling his bruised face into a terrified rictus.

"Move it," Finn said. "We don't have all night. I'll be down in a second. Everything they know—understand?"

The man with the bag nodded, unable to disguise a smirk.

"Oh, and?" Finn said.

The man waited.

"See if he's telling the truth about the money. If he is, get all the bank information. That might come in handy."

The man nodded, a look of almost blissful contentment coming over him.

Screaming through her gag, Rachel struggled in vain as the man who hit Glenn yanked her roughly to her feet, gripped her upper arms in his huge hands, and pushed her toward the door to the furnished basement below. Soundproofed, in case they ever played loud music. She watched the second man, a big redhead, yank Glenn off the couch, then stared in terror as the man with the nylon duffel bag gathered up his tools. *God,* she thought, eyes filling with tears. *How the hell could this be happening?*

"Hup-hup," Finn said.

Rachel tried to escape from her captor's iron grip, but it was hopeless. She might as well free herself from the crumpled remains of a wrecked car.

All at once, she felt her will to fight drain away as surely as water flowing down a storm grate. She prayed that—whatever else happened, for their sakes but also for what Abby would come to learn—that their deaths would be swift.

Why struggle? It was no use.

It was over.

At that moment, the doorbell rang.

# THREE

"Hold it," Finn said.

Stone and Paddy, on Rachel and Glenn respectively, paused in their movements as quickly and smoothly as if he'd depressed an off switch. You could always tell good training, Finn thought. They waited, eyes not on the door but on Finn. Good dogs. Which was funny in a dark way, if you thought about it.

"Are you expecting someone?" Finn said.

Rachel shook her head.

"You're sure?"

She nodded, maybe a little too fast. She could be lying. Or she could be losing it from the fear, which Finn knew from experience was likely flooding her gut like poison. He crossed the room.

"Listen carefully," he said, making no effort to disguise the irritation he felt at the interruption. "If you raise your voice, cry for help, whatever, I'm going to spill Glenn's intestines across the floor. Understand?"

She nodded again. He signaled Vlad, who retrieved a screwdriver from his duffel bag of goodies, and, ignoring Rachel's whimper of terror, used it to undo the gag's knot. Finn frowned at the relief filling her eyes after the restriction was removed, but he didn't have long to dwell on the fact.

The doorbell rang again.

"Who is that?" Finn said.

"I don't know," she whispered.

"You're lying. Like you did about Stella Wolford. And the numbers. And the gun in the office."

"Please. I'm telling the truth. I have no idea what the hell 'twenty-two seven' is or means." She glanced at the door. "And I have no idea who that is. We don't know the neighbors. We get all our packages at our offices. We never order food."

"Liar."

"No—" she said, then stopped as he held up a warning finger.

The problem was, Finn wasn't so sure this time. Something in Rachel's eyes told him she was as startled by the bell as he was. That she really didn't know who was at the door. Whether she was telling the truth about Stella Wolford's whereabouts or 22/7—he had his doubts—was another matter. The difference now, of course, was he was seeing hope on Rachel's face for the first time since he walked in from the deck, while all he felt was annoyance at a complication.

Either way, it was an unwelcome interruption at the worst possible moment. Not that Jason would care either way. Finn could bank on that.

Because Jason cared about one thing only, as Finn knew all too well.

The doorbell rang again, a deep gong that was starting to grate on Finn's nerves.

*Who rings a doorbell three times?*

"Basement," Finn said, making his decision. "Vlad and Paddy. Park them—don't do anything yet. Not a fucking sound, understood?" He turned to Stone. "You're with me."

As Vlad and Paddy disappeared around the corner with their prisoners, Finn gestured to Stone to position himself just out of sight in the dining room. Finn jammed his gun into his waistband and slowly opened the door.

"There you are," the man standing before him said. "Was starting to think no one was home."

Finn stared at the figure in front of him.

"May I help you?" he said at last.

"Hopefully. Delivery for Rachel Stanfield?"

The man was slight, no more than five ten, with a thin, spare frame. Wire-rimmed eyeglasses, brown eyes, wearing, of all things, a Rochester Red Wings ball cap. His expression halfway between boredom and complacency. The man had on gray nylon hiking shoes, faded beige cargo shorts, and a black T-shirt under a tan utility vest equipped with multiple pockets. In his left hand he grasped a clipboard holding a single sheet of paper. Finn looked past him and saw a large white SUV, emergency lights blinking. An older model Suburban, if Finn had to guess, though in the fading light of the central Indiana dusk he couldn't be certain. The car was parked nose first in the direction of the main road, which—it occurred to Finn—raised two concerns.

First, the man had turned around after reaching the house so he was facing the road, making it easier to drive off when he was done with his delivery. Not totally strange but—unusual. Second—and this was more striking—he had driven *onto* the lawn to get around their van which they had parked halfway up the long asphalt drive before disembarking and sneaking around back. Odd, for sure. Why not park behind the van and walk up?

Not liking what he was seeing, Finn returned his attention to the stranger.

"Ms. Stanfield isn't home at the moment. I'd be happy to sign for whatever you have."

"Appreciate it. But delivery has to go to the name on the invoice."

"I don't expect her for a while."

"I understand. Rules are rules."

Frustrated, Finn considered his options. Starting with dropping the man where he stood. Tough luck for the guy, but oh well. One to the head and one to the neck, let Stone deal with the mess while Finn oversaw the basement interrogation. It would complicate matters, obviously, but there was more at stake here than the disappearance of a shrimpy delivery guy. Though Finn's eyes tended to glaze over at Jason's apocalyptic monologuing, he still embraced Jason's message like any good red-blooded American would. Should.

What stayed Finn's hand in the moment was the blinking of the SUV's lights. It made him wonder if the man was alone. It also spoke, somehow, to a schedule, to the notion that the man was part of an interconnected delivery system and his vanishing might set off alarms sooner than Finn would like.

"Sorry," Finn said. "Who do you work for? Like, Amazon?"

"Oh gosh, nobody that big. I'm independent, actually."

"Independent?"

"That's right. I work for myself."

"And Rachel—Ms. Stanfield—is expecting you?"

"Not really sure."

"What?"

"I said, I'm not sure. Whether she's expecting me, I mean."

"Why not?"

The man furrowed his brows at the question. Raising his right hand—Finn flinched at the gesture—he adjusted his ball cap. "I just deliver stuff. In this case I suppose it's possible she's expecting me, but I'm not a hundred percent sure."

Finn felt his blood pressure rising. Nothing about this felt right, yet the slight deliveryman could scarcely be deemed a threat. Bottom line, though, was that Finn didn't like all the time he was wasting just standing here.

He said, "Well, who's it from, if I may ask."

"You can't."

"I'm sorry?"

"I said, you can't ask. Not being rude or anything, but the origin of deliveries is confidential. Rules again."

Finn squeezed his right fist open and shut as he fought the temptation to reach for his gun. "You said you were independent?"

"That's right. I'm a freelance courier."

"So these rules—whose are they?"

The man deliberated a moment. "Mine, I guess."

"Can you at least tell me your name—so I can tell Ms. Stanfield when she's available," he added.

"Sure. It's Merc. Merc Carter."

"Okay. So, listen, Mark—"

"Sorry. It's Merc. Not Mark. Short for Mercury. Don't worry. I get that all the time."

"All right, *Merc*. Where is it, then?"

"Where's what?"

"The delivery. All I see is a clipboard."

Instead of answering, Carter said, "Any idea what time Ms. Stanfield might be home? I'm on a bit of a tight schedule. I'm supposed to be in Louisville later tonight."

*What. The fuck.* Like he needed this shit right now, Finn thought.

"I don't actually know when she'll be back," he said, casting a quick glance behind him. "You're welcome to come inside and wait if you want."

"Kind of you. But no thanks."

As Finn turned back around, he saw to his surprise that Carter was three feet farther from the door than a couple of seconds earlier. He had backed up without a sound in the instant Finn took his eyes off him. So quickly and silently it didn't seem natural, as if three or four frames were missing from a movie reel of the scene.

*Weird*, Finn thought.

"You're sure? Make you a cup of coffee while you wait? Or something stronger?"

"Appreciate it, but I'm sure," Carter said. "I'll just sit in the car and get some paperwork done, if it's all the same to you. You're sure you can't ballpark when she might be here? In case I have to adjust things on my end? Other deliveries, I mean."

"I really can't say. You could leave me your number if you want and I can have her call when she arrives."

"I'll just give it a few minutes, thanks." Carter turned and walked back to the SUV before Finn could say anything else.

Finn stood on the door's threshold and watched Carter climb inside the car. He half expected Carter to start the engine and drive off, which would have been both a relief and possibly a further complication. But, true to the strange little guy's word, the vehicle stayed put, emergency blinkers flashing steadily on-off, on-off. As far as Finn could discern, Carter was just sitting there, examining his clipboard.

"Everything okay?" Stone growled when Finn was back inside, standing in the living room with a puzzled look on his face.

"I'm not sure."

"Not sure why? Sounds like he's just a guy in the wrong place at the wrong time."

"Maybe."

"Maybe?"

"I don't know. I don't like it." He told Stone about the positioning of Carter's vehicle.

"Okay then," Stone said. "So, what now?"

Finn weighed his options. He thought about Stella Wolford and 22/7 and Jason's geeky but lethal instructions—*no muss, no fuss, no witnesses*—and the couple in the basement, awaiting a fate no one—except Finn, and Vlad, of course—would wish on their worst enemy. He thought about what Carter said, that he was on a tight schedule. Well, Finn was on a tight schedule, too. One that didn't have room for unexpected developments, no matter how minor. Especially ones involving a freelance delivery guy who—assuming that's what he really was—seemed like he was making those bullshit rules up on the spot.

Finn pulled the curtain aside and glanced out the window at the SUV. Was it his imagination or was Carter staring at the house? He made up his mind in that moment.

"Go ahead and handle it," Finn said to Stone, tipping his head toward the door. "I'm pretty sure he's alone but be careful, just in case. There should be room in the garage for his car. If not, park it in the back. It's not going to matter either way."

"Got it," Stone said, approaching the door, gun at his side. "Anything I need to know? About the guy, I mean?"

"Well, he's got that funny name," Finn said, reviewing the Merc/Mark thing.

"Anything else?"

"Nothing," Finn said, distracted, mind already on the basement. "Absolutely nothing at all."

# FOUR

Carter sat in the Suburban, the second game in a three-game Jays-Mets series on the radio, and massaged his forehead with two fingers. Fortunately, the headaches were rarer and rarer, mostly triggered these days by interruptions to his routine. His personal canary in a coal mine. Which meant, like tonight, paying special attention to the precipitating event. In fact, he thought about calling in the episode with the guy at the front door to his uncle but determined he probably didn't have time. He was right, although he ended up with an extra minute he hadn't counted on.

Right, because initially he assumed the guy who answered the door, the one with the Iowa-shaped scar on the left side of his face and the gun concealed in his waistband, would have made the move himself. He seemed like the kind of guy in charge—and there was no question he was in charge of whatever Carter had stumbled upon—who would want to take care of loose ends himself. The kind of perfectionist Carter could appreciate under different circumstances.

Instead, he earned the extra minute after the guy in charge delegated the job to the gorilla currently walking down the drive and toward the Suburban. Carter decided that was less a miscalculation on his part than a testament to the fact that a lot was going on inside that house. At least as far as Carter could infer. Because good managers, perfectionists or not, handed things off to subordinates when things got busy.

The gorilla arrived at the driver's side door. Carter watched out of the corner of his eye as the man—features suggesting Nordic ancestry, icy blue eyes, pitted face that hinted at a bad case of childhood acne or a brush with a powerful accelerant—tapped on the window with a gun. Carter ignored him and instead dipped his right hand into the lower right-hand pocket of his utility vest and gripped the item inside. Another tap, a little louder this time. Carter continued to ignore him. A third tap, pretty forceful, the kind that made him worry the glass might shatter à la one of those emergency glass breakers you saw on YouTube. Like the one on Carter's key ring, in point of fact.

The tap was followed by a summons in the hoarse voice of someone who apparently ate gravel for breakfast, washed down by sand.

"You. Open the door."

Carter turned up the radio as the count went to 3-2 at the bottom of the first inning with two on base. Man. The Jays' pitching this year. They'd better—

"Hey," the man said.

*Oh well*, Carter thought. He depressed the power button, lowered the window, shouted "Boo," squeezed his eyes shut, and emptied the canister of Mace in his hand into the man's face. The effect would have been funny if the situation weren't so serious. Caught off guard by Carter's shout, the man gasped involuntarily and in so doing increased by upwards of twenty percent the amount of capsaicin-infused particles driven into his lungs. Happened every time. Carter wasn't exactly sure why. He was sure it was explained back in his BIT days, but obviously that had been a while. It was something to do with reflexes, or fight-or-flight, or nerve impulses. Something like that. Nothing to dwell on now.

Wrapping his fingers around the canister, Carter opened his eyes and drove his right hand into the man's nose, wincing as he felt bone break and cartilage tear. But not his. In almost the same motion he shoved the door open hard and fast, slamming it into the man's head, now bowed as he struggled with the combined effects of the spray and a broken nose.

Carter hopped out and kicked the guy where it counted, waited for him to involuntarily fold in half—they always folded in half—and kneed him in the head. As the man crumpled, Carter planted his right foot between the man's shoulder blades, pushed him flat onto the asphalt, flipped around and straddled him. In the same motion he pulled the man's gun free from his right hand where, impressively, it remained despite what had just happened to him.

"Gah," the man groaned.

Carter tossed the gun into the grass and retrieved a pair of heavy-duty twenty-four-inch zip ties from a pocket on the left side of his utility vest. Moving fast, he bound the man's hands behind him, pulling tightly enough that he could see the skin on his wrists pinch white. Next, he yanked off the man's thick boots and repeated the drill on his feet, joining two zip ties together to be sure they circled around fully. The guy had really thick ankles.

Working quickly as the man emerged from the pepper spray haze and the blows to the head and began to struggle, Carter undid the laces on the right boot and then reached for a pair of latex gloves from an upper vest pocket. Snapping them on, he used the thick leather lace as a gag, wrapping it across the man's mouth three times. It was good quality leather; they were nice boots. Carter was glad for the gloves as a gush of tears and snot continued unabated while he worked.

Satisfied, he knelt and examined the man, who despite everything was squirming and making angry, guttural noises.

Carter leaned in.

"Listen."

The man turned his head and stared at Carter through bloodshot eyes that held rage and the threat of violent death.

"If you don't stop moving I'm going to kick you in the head."

The man growled a threat indecipherable through the gag, though the intent was clear enough.

"I don't think you're following here," Carter continued. "I said, I'm going to kick you in the head if you don't stop moving. What I'm trying to convey is you'll probably lose an eye, but that's not the worst part. The problem with orbital socket fractures is sometimes a splinter of bone dislodges into the brain and then you're drinking dinner through a straw for the rest of your life. Do you understand?"

After a moment the man stilled. Carter nodded to himself in appreciation. One nice thing about professionals is they weren't into maverick behavior. They understood where you were coming from. Of course, the problem with professionals in a situation like this is they were a lot like silverfish. Where you had one, you usually had more. Which meant that whatever was going on in the house, whatever he had walked into, wasn't over yet. He was sure of it.

"Okay then." Carter returned his attention to his captive. "I'm going to ask you some questions. While I do, focus on the concept of socket fractures. Understood?"

No response. But the man, head resting at an angle on the cool asphalt, never took those icy blue eyes off Carter, committing every inch of his face to memory. It would have been a disconcerting feeling if Carter weren't so accustomed to it.

"Question one. Is Rachel Stanfield alive?"

Slowly, the man nodded.

"You thinking about those fractures?"

Nod.

"Sticking with that answer?"

Another nod.

"The thing is, I have a delivery for her and she's the only one who can take possession. It would screw up everything if she couldn't. Also, I've never missed a delivery, so it's a point-of-pride thing. Long story short, it's important that she's in a position to sign for it herself. You following?"

The man didn't move for a moment. Finally, he nodded once more.

"All right then." Carter knew the man might be lying, uncertain of what the reaction would be if he acknowledged that the intended recipient of Carter's delivery was dead. But Carter was banking on the fact that this guy was not somebody accustomed to approaching a target as soft as a deliveryman and a moment later finding himself trussed like a hog on slaughtering day. It was an unexpected turning of the tables which probably, at least for the moment, highlighted the consequences of not telling the truth.

"Question two. How many others?"

No reaction for a moment. Carter watched indecision flicker across a pair of merciless blue eyes. Asking about a victim's status was one thing. Revealing your strength to an enemy was another thing altogether. *I get it*, Carter thought. *Been there.* Finally, the man blinked twice, slowly, so as not to confuse his meaning.

"Two others, besides you?"

The man nodded decisively, to show he was cooperating.

"Good man. So Rachel Stanfield's alive, and there are two other guys besides you inside. Armed, I assume?"

Another nod.

"Anyone else?"

A hint of confusion clouded the man's face.

"Anyone else in the house besides Rachel Stanfield and your two colleagues."

Slowly, the man nodded.

"Husband?"

Nod.

"Any kids?"

A shake of his head.

"Any pets? A dog? Anything like that?"

He shook his head again, though Carter detected something different in the man's eyes this time. Something about the question of a dog had triggered a reaction, a flickering of the eyes, though Carter couldn't read it.

"Sure about that?"

Nod.

"Rachel Stanfield, her husband, your two guys, and that's it."

Nod.

"I appreciate your forthrightness," Carter said, retrieving his blackjack from a right-hand side vest pocket and lightly bludgeoning the back of the man's head. Once certain he was out but not, you know, *out*, he walked around to the man's feet, grabbed the zip ties binding them, and dragged him away from the Suburban and onto the lawn. Weighing his options, Carter positioned his prisoner behind a landscaped plot of ornamental grass and mums. Satisfied the man was safely hidden, at least for the time being, he picked up the man's gun—an efficient Ruger—removed the magazine, and unchambered the live round. He returned to the Suburban's driver's side door, opened it, and set the weapon and ammunition on the passenger seat.

And took a breath. And glanced at his watch. Five minutes had passed since the first tap on the glass window with the gun. He looked at the front door of the house. He had, he figured, under a minute before it opened again. Before the next guy up came through. The next guy of at least three, he was guessing, since there was no question the man sent to kill him—the man now lying unconscious on the lawn—had lied about the number of accomplices inside. Carter didn't blame him; he would have done the same thing himself. Had done, in fact.

The only question was whether Carter waited for the next guy to emerge or just barged inside himself. He needed to decide fast because he had a couple of things to do first. Also, because he figured that if Rachel Stanfield really was alive, she probably didn't have much longer if something didn't happen quickly.

Because: professionals.

# FIVE

**M**om? What's wrong? I couldn't understand your message.
Mom?

*Your father, she whispered.*

*Mom . . . ?*

As a kid, Carter had it all figured out. Finish high school, wait for the scouts to call, put in his time in the minors—first choice the Red Wings, obviously, but he wouldn't be choosy. Lots of options. Durham Bulls, of course, because who didn't love the movie? Columbus Clippers also sounded good, mainly because his mom's brother, Uncle Bill, was a big fan and always treated him to a game on their annual summer visits. Or maybe the Pawtucket Red Sox, mostly because he loved saying the name of the city. Pawtucket. Pawtucket. Pawtucket. Heck, even the Iowa Cubs would do as a start. He'd only spend a year or two in the minors anyway. After that, he'd be in the big dance, with his choices (in reverse order): the Mets, the Indians, the Reds, the Brewers, and the Blue Jays. People raised their eyebrows at the Toronto option until he explained his father was born there and that, after the Rochester Red Wings, it was practically Carter's hometown team.

Yeah, Carter had it all figured out. Except for the part about breaking his left ankle his junior year as he tried to stretch a single to a double and collided with a beefy second baseman from McQuaid High who was no more willing to cede the plate to a scrappy bantamweight like Carter than a concrete pillar might yield to a speeding bicycle.

*The irony, that Carter was known for his baserunning. Mercury had turned out to be a perfect name for a speedster. The fact that his mailman father, in a fit of uncharacteristic ebullience, named his son after the original mailman—the messenger of the gods—paying dividends on ball fields.*

*Until the accident.*

*So that was that.*

*The consolation prize—second-string shortstop at SUNY Geneseo, the only school that would even look at him—didn't bear thinking about most days. Sure, he was probably stronger physically in the aftermath, especially after his father and his uncle, fed up with Carter's moping, marched him into the basement, forced gloves onto his hands, and started him on the punching bag they went in on together. Nevertheless, he nearly quit the team the week before his sophomore season until his father talked a bit of sense into him.*

*"Remember what I always say, Merc."*

*"Which is what?" Cupping his flip phone to shield it from the breeze on a mild March morning as he trudged to class.*

*"There's only two kinds of baseball. Playing baseball and—"*

*"And not playing baseball," Carter said, finishing the thought. "Yeah, I get it."*

*And he did, though he didn't credit his father for the good advice in the moment.*

*Which was too bad, since it wasn't long after that that he lost the chance to credit his father for anything ever again.*

"Hang on," Finn said, eyeing the scalpel in Vlad's right hand.

"What?" Vlad said impatiently, hunched over Rachel.

Finn listened but upstairs was quiet. Which was the problem.

"I said, hang on."

"What's wrong?" Paddy chimed in.

*"Shut the fuck up and hang on."*

It wasn't the lack of gunshots. Stone would have used his suppressor, or wrestled the delivery guy inside the garage and done it there, out of earshot. That wasn't the issue. It was how much time elapsed since Finn had dispatched Stone to deal with the interruption. Finn prided himself on his internal clock, an ability to measure almost to the second the passage of minutes or hours, a gift going back to childhood—what there was of it. After their last firefight, Vlad let down his guard long enough to remark, "Only four minutes? Felt like twenty."

Wrong. Three minutes and forty-seven seconds.

Now, almost exactly seven minutes had passed. But where was Stone? He was not a man prone to delays. That was one of many reasons Finn tapped him for this job.

"What's going on?" Finn said to Rachel.

Bound tightly to a chair, hands behind her, eyes bright, she moved her head back and forth, the motion almost imperceptible.

"One more time. The guy. What's he delivering?"

She shook her head again.

"You're lying. Delivery guys don't just show up like that."

Another shake of her head, more vigorously, like trying to rid herself of a bothersome fly. Those bright eyes berating him. Finn glanced at Glenn. He sat bound in his own chair opposite his wife, eyes dull with pain from the untreated wound on his face. Eyes that remained unwaveringly fixed on Rachel. Finn saw in that expression an unusual devotion. A caring that he planned to exploit if he could ever get to the task at hand. But he still faced the same problem as before.

On the one hand, he was convinced that Rachel knew more about Stella Wolford and the secrets she was hiding than she was letting on.

22/7, etc. Yet he also felt certain, thanks to an internal compass almost as accurate as his timekeeping ability, that she was telling the truth about the deliveryman's appearance.

He made his decision and spoke to Paddy.

"Go see what's going on."

"Now?"

"No. Three days from now. Yes, now. Make sure everything's all right up there."

Paddy hesitated for a moment, looking at Rachel and Glenn. The expression on his face clear as day: he didn't want to miss anything down here.

"Got it," he said after a beat too long. "Anything to watch out for?"

Finn recalled Stone's own query along those lines. He replayed the way Carter retreated those three steps when Finn's back was turned. Not a very delivery guy–type move, if you thought about it.

"Be careful. There's something off about him."

"Off how?"

"I'm not sure. Keep your eyes open."

"Always," Paddy said, and headed for the stairs.

Finn turned to Vlad, who waited expectantly, scalpel in hand, his opened duffel bag beside him on a footstool.

"Let's change things up," Finn said.

"Change?"

"Tick tick."

"Really?"

"Just in case."

"Kind of hard to go back if we do."

"A risk we'll have to take." Vlad nodded, keeping his face blank, and reached into the bag.

The cutout was all Tomeka. Classic move on her part. But keeping it in the Suburban—Carter had his uncle to thank for that.

It really was an amazing likeness, even for a life-size, blown-up, cardboard-mounted photograph. But however they worked it, the image remained clear, the color separations intact, his features hardly blurred at all. Certainly, at a distance the resemblance was overwhelming. A gag that Tomeka came up with for Carter's fortieth birthday party, greeting people as they walked into the house, and which ended up in more selfies than the real Carter. Afterward, it stayed in the living room for a week until he had to decide what to do with it. That's when his uncle stepped in. He was the one who suggested a notch by the beltline to allow the cutout to be folded in half for easy storage in the rear of the Suburban. Since then, it had come in handy more than once. And again tonight, propped by the back of the SUV, a facsimile Carter standing with his hands on his hips and a rare smile on his face.

It was the first thing the next guy out the door saw. Also, for the time being, the last.

Carter knew that normal protocol—that engaged by professionals, anyway—would call for the guy—a tall, stocky redhead—to take a disciplined approach. Look around, assess the periphery, go one step at a time. The caution in the man's stance as the door opened suggested he had that exact intention. Then he glanced up and saw the cutout. As Carter hoped, the visual trick short-circuited his environmental review and he raised his gun without taking the usual precautions. Which was all the time needed by Carter, flattened against the house by the door. He swung the blackjack fast and hard and the man fell without a sound into Carter's arms. It was a good thing he braced himself; this was not a small individual.

There'd be no line of questioning this time. The redhead was out cold. Carter dragged the unconscious man across the driveway, zip-tied and gagged him, and relieved him of weapons, which included the gun and a nasty-looking switchblade. The former went onto the passenger seat of the Suburban, the latter into an upper right-hand pocket on Carter's utility vest. All very quickly, because Carter figured he had almost no time to waste. The second guy's absence would set off more alarm bells than the first, and faster.

Carter pulled out his own gun, a Beretta 92D, standard issue from the old days, and approached the front door of the house. It was time to make a move before it was too late.

# SIX

F inn watched Rachel as she watched Vlad work. He appreciated the look of horror on her face as the implication of the situation sank in. Despite the hiccup presented by the delivery guy, things were still unfolding more or less to plan. If anything, the circumstances that Rachel's husband now found himself in would only aid in the extraction of information that Finn believed in his heart Rachel was withholding. Then Finn, a type of delivery person himself, if you thought about it, could finish this assignment, hand that information over to Jason, wait for the headlines from Jason's plan, and move on to his next undertaking.

At that moment, Finn heard the creak of a floorboard overhead and realized they had a new problem.

What was it with this job?

*Irony, if you could call it that: Carter rarely drank if at all. Yet that's what he was doing the fateful night the call came about his father. Which was why he missed the news at first.*

*Any predisposition to hoisting a few—what kid didn't in those days?— dried up in high school the day their starting pitcher on the 16U summer league showed up hungover for the district semis in Canandaigua and they were shellacked 12-2. Making matters worse, the guy—the pitcher—laughed it off afterward.*

You'd have thought Carter's broken ankle the following spring would have provided an excuse to open the floodgates, so to speak, but the opposite was true. Carter was so focused on rehab, on weightlifting and hitting the boxing bag and spending hours in the batting cage, that he pretty much swore off the stuff, even after he got to Geneseo, where binge drinking was practically a varsity sport.

Nevertheless, the Thursday night the call came, Carter was in a bar on Main Street with his two roommates and his one roommate's sister eating pizza and drinking Genny Cream from plastic pitchers, his phone buried at the bottom of his backpack under his business and sociology textbooks, meaning he never heard the ring. Even if he had, it's possible he would have ignored it, being so focused on—and so flustered by—the sudden presence of his roommate's sister's left hand on his right knee under the table. A miraculous development, considering the crush from afar he'd had on her—on Mindy—since she arrived on campus the previous fall, a transfer from SUNY Brockport. He'd actually been working up the nerve to ask her out when his roommate suggested the beers.

"I'm going to the library—if you're headed in that direction?" Mindy said as they left the bar an hour later, sun starting to set.

"Sure," he said, scarcely believing his luck.

It was as they walked, Carter listening to Mindy talk about her upcoming psych exam, shyly glancing at her thick but still pretty waist, her freckled face and severe bangs, that he remembered his phone and unconsciously dug into his backpack for it. And stared at the string of missed calls from his mother. When he played the most recent message, it was impossible to understand her through the sobs.

"Everything all right?" Mindy said as he stopped.

"I'm not sure," he said, pressing dial.

*"Mom? What's wrong?" Carter said when she picked up. "I couldn't understand your message."*

*"Your father," she whispered.*

*"Mom?"*

*"He's . . . someone shot him. He's . . . he's . . ."*

*Dead. Shot in his mail truck on his regular rounds off Clinton Avenue near the end of his route.*

*His father dead. Murdered.*

*And the killer nowhere to be found.*

As soon as Carter entered Rachel Stanfield's house and determined the living room was empty, he assumed he was dealing with a basement situation. Whatever was going on with Stanfield, whatever the guy with the scar on his face was up to, it probably wasn't the sort of thing enhanced by windows, curtained or not.

He moved across the light gray carpet, taking in smudges of blood on the couch and on a throw rug, and stepped lightly until he reached the kitchen. He processed the signs of a meal interrupted midpreparation—a plate of raw steaks on the marble-topped island, a copper-clad pot of potatoes cooling on the six-burner stovetop—and synced the information with the pool of blood on the floor beside an overturned stool. Peering through the opened basement door, Carter had just put his foot onto the first step when he heard a voice.

"Is that you, Paddy? We don't have all day."

Paddy. The redhead. Irish fellow—made sense. The speaker—it sounded like Scar Guy—thought he was hearing the return of the man he sent after the first guy. Meaning Carter had the element of surprise. Except after a second he realized maybe he didn't.

The fact that Scar Guy didn't immediately inquire after the fate of the first man, which was the whole reason Paddy had entered the outside fray, was a giveaway. Scar Guy wanted Carter to think he wasn't expecting trouble. Which was trouble in and of itself. Craptastic. At this rate, Carter wasn't liking his chances of hitting Louisville on schedule tonight. It was always something. *All right then*, he thought, *here goes nothing.*

Beretta in hand, he crept down three beige-carpeted steps, then paused above the landing where the stairs turned to the right. On his left hung a framed lithograph of a 1909 Art Deco rendering of the Indianapolis Motor Speedway. Carter was more a NASCAR man himself on the few occasions he caught himself watching auto racing on TV, but you had to appreciate the Brickyard either way.

"Hey," he said. "Listen up."

Silence.

"It's Mercury Carter. I'm hoping we can work something out here." Raising his voice to be sure Scar Guy heard him. "With my delivery, I mean. Like I said, I'm on a tight schedule."

More silence.

"Also, I'm alone. Just FYI."

Carter let that sink in for a second. He was about to speak again when a voice interrupted.

"You come down here, I'm going to kill her."

Scar Guy.

Carter gripped his gun tighter as he rested his left hand on a shelf below the Indy 500 poster that held a family photo triptych, including Stanfield, a man he assumed was her husband, and a black-haired teenage girl.

"That's fine," he said, weighing the next words out of his mouth. He wasn't a gambler, but sometimes it paid to pretend. "All I ask is that you let me make my delivery to Ms. Stanfield first. Shouldn't take more than five minutes. That'll square things on my end and I can close out the job and get going. After that, she's all yours."

Five seconds passed.

"I'm serious," Scar Guy said at last. "I'll kill her."

"I believe you, trust me. I'm just asking for five minutes. I miss the delivery, the paperwork's a bear."

"What's the delivery?"

"I already told you, that's between Ms. Stanfield and me. Those rules and stuff."

"Bullshit. Who the hell are you, anyway? Not a mailman, that's for damn sure."

Carter glanced at the lithograph. *Greatest Race Course in the World.* Well, no arguing with that.

"Just a guy trying to make a living. A living making deliveries, as it turns out. And I don't necessarily disagree with you about the rules." He thought about what else to say to keep Scar Guy guessing. "One thing I hate is bureaucracy. But sometimes regs have their place, you know? Like the net in tennis or rhymes in poems."

"You're out of your mind, you know that? Last chance."

"Tell you what. Maybe we could keep it simple. Do a trade, like."

Even this far up the stairs, Carter heard Scar Guy react to his offer with a dismissive intake of breath. "A trade? What could you possibly have that I want?"

"How about your car keys, for starters?"

Another moment of silence. Carter imagined him trading glances with whoever else was with him.

"What the hell are you talking about?"

"Take a normal driver," Carter said, clearing his throat. "He's usually got two sets of keys. Standard operating procedure. One for him, one for his wife, business partner, adult child. Whoever. Three sets is rare, in my experience. And the thing is, I've got two sets of keys to your van at the moment. Well, not on me. But I know where they are. One from the pocket of the first gentleman you sent and one from the second. The first set was on a keychain with a miniature Viking short sword. Pretty cool. The second set—I'm guessing that's Paddy's—has a dyed green rabbit's foot. Not quite as cool, in my opinion. Just so you know I know what I'm talking about. So how about this? I make my delivery, you get your keys back."

Scar Guy said, "How about you give me the keys or I shoot Rachel Stanfield on the count of three?"

Carter took a long, deep breath, trying to slow the beating of his heart. He raised the gun in his right hand and braced himself to leap down the remaining stairs.

He said, "If that's how you want to play it, be my guest. Only problem is I also have physics on my side. I'll be back up the stairs locking the door the minute I hear gunfire. Fingers hitting 911 a second later. As a courtesy, I'll suggest you won't make it through the door before the cops show up. I mentioned I'm alone, right? Just feels like with my way, there's less mess."

Carter heard what sounded like the guttural whispers of two men having a conversation.

"All right," Scar Guy said at last. "Come down. Slowly."

*Right*, Carter thought.

"I think upstairs is better," he said. "Maybe the living room? More comfortable for everyone."

"Don't push it, Carter."

"Car keys," he replied.

Several more seconds passed. At last, Scar Guy said, "All right. I'm bringing Stanfield up."

"Appreciate it. Just one other thing first." He took a deep breath. "I need you to prove you actually have her."

"What?"

"Prove she's alive. That it's her you're bringing upstairs. It's a paperwork thing, sorry. But I need to be sure."

"You're not serious."

"Rules are rules."

"If I don't?"

"Well, like I said, the keys and stuff."

Almost half a minute passed. At last, Carter heard a woman's voice, weak and tremulous. "It's me. It's Rachel."

"It's Merc Carter, Ms. Stanfield. Glad to hear you're okay. Hopefully, we can get this delivery thing worked out and I'll be on my way and out of your hair. Just one thing, if you don't mind. If you could tell me what city your stepdaughter's mother was born in."

"The fuck do you need to know that for?" Scar Guy said.

"I'm waiting."

After a moment, Rachel said, a quaver in her voice, "Morelia. She was born in Morelia, in Michoacán."

"See you upstairs," Carter said.

Without waiting for a response Carter bounded up the steps and dashed through the kitchen. Once in the living room, he tucked himself behind the left side of the alcove wall leading from the dining room. Carefully, he used his foot to push a wicker basket piled high with catalogs and magazines across the gray carpet to make more room. The basket was topped by the June issue of *Attorney at Law Magazine Indianapolis*. He held his breath and listened to the sound of footsteps on the basement stairs and then the passage of people through the kitchen.

Second bites of the apple were rare in Carter's experience. He only tried it because he figured he had nothing to lose when it came to keeping Rachel Stanfield alive. It was true that he'd never missed a delivery. But he had to admit to more than a little surprise that Rachel Stanfield was still aboveground, given the two guys he'd danced with outside. He decided to risk it and was glad he did. A gaunt guy with a hollowed-out face was first around the corner and didn't hesitate when he saw the cutout of Carter by the front door. He sighted and fired, *click-click-click*, the suppressed shots like pennies dropping into an empty coffee can. So much for Tomeka's handiwork, Carter thought gloomily, watching the cutout fall to the floor. Which was all he had time for.

He brought his gun down on Gaunt Guy's gun hand, knocking the weapon to the floor, and simultaneously used his left hand to deliver a pair of rabbit punches to the man's kidneys. The blows sent him to his knees, and then with a groan onto his chest, ass in the air, like a sleeping baby, or a running back not rising from the gridiron anytime soon.

"Don't move."

Scar Guy appeared on Carter's right, pushing a stumbling Rachel Stanfield before him, his gun barrel against the base of her skull.

"Ready when you are," Carter said.

"New deal," Scar Guy said, frowning at the sight of the guy on the floor.

"Oh?"

"It goes like this." He used his left hand to pull out his phone. "There's a bomb strapped to Rachel's husband downstairs. I dial a number"—he raised the phone—"and he's stew meat."

"Wow. So not cool."

"Like you're playing fair," Scar Guy said, casting a glance at the ruined cutout.

"Fine," Carter said. "What's the deal?" Keeping his expression neutral, as if watching a nature documentary he'd already seen twice, Carter took stock of the terror on Rachel's exhausted face.

"The deal is, I walk out of here with her. You wait ten minutes and when I'm sure I'm not being followed, I text a code that deactivates the device. Otherwise, boom."

"I can't let you do that," Carter said.

"Please," Rachel whispered.

Carter and Scar Guy both looked at her.

"Do as he says. I can't—please don't kill Glenn. Please."

"There you have it," Scar Guy said.

"What about my delivery?"

"You can't be fucking serious."

"Plus," Carter said, ignoring the observation, "what guarantees do I have you won't set that thing off as soon as you're gone?" As he spoke the man on the floor moaned and tried to rise to his knees. Carter ground his right heel into the man's back, causing him to collapse onto the floor with a yelp.

"You have my word," Scar Guy said. "What more could you need?"

"I need to make my delivery."

"Last chance," Scar Guy said, raising the phone again.

"Please," Rachel Stanfield said, her voice catching.

*Hoo boy*, Carter thought.

# SEVEN

*F*or better or worse, it only took a few days to figure out what happened to Danny Carter, Carter's father. Or rather, why.

Turns out that the number of shrink-wrapped bundles of pure Colombian blow hidden in cardboard boxes and shipped via US mail to addresses up and down Rochester and across Monroe County had tripled in recent months. As it had everywhere. And why not? "Neither snow nor rain nor heat nor gloom of night" was the kind of delivery model that drug dealers banked on. Inspectors caught some of the boxes, a few here, a few there, but putting a serious dent in the volume of shipments coursing through the system was equivalent to slowing the flow of the Niagara River over the falls.

Compounding the problem—as Carter and his family, numb with shock, learned in the ensuing days—US Postal Inspection Service agents weren't the only ones trying to intercept the packages. The Crips and the Bloods and "all the cockroaches in between" (in the words of Earl Madden, Danny Carter's supervisor at the central post office) had their eyes on everyone else's packages and worked relentlessly to lift the goods from rivals A and B and on down the line as often as possible. Without asking nicely. Without giving two shits about the side effects of grabbing the boxes, in the form of mail carriers coldcocked, pistol-whipped, pepper-sprayed, and, in more than one case, shot in cold blood.

Like Danny Carter.

"What a waste," Madden said on more than one occasion in the following days. "What a complete fucking waste."

*It was Madden, in fact, who protested the loudest when the inevitable questions arose: Was Danny Carter the architect of his own demise? Had he turned a blind eye to suspicious boxes on his route or, worse, been compensated to ensure their safe delivery?*

*"It's standard operating procedure," an apologetic Marcus Washington—the USPIS inspector handling the investigation—explained to Carter's mother, Marcy, and Danny's brother, Carter's uncle Dean, defending the line of inquiry. "We can't rule anything out."*

*"Bullshit," was Madden's response, hand wrapped around a bottle of Bud Light at the open house following the family-only burial service a week after Danny Carter's murder. "Classic US-PISS," he continued. "Smear one of us to cover the fact they couldn't find their own dick in the shower."*

*Carter's uncle agreed and suggested hiring a lawyer and suing to stop the allegations in their tracks. Carter was still too young to know what to do, though he burned at the aspersions leveled at his father, remembering him trudging out the door day after day, week after week, the epitome of a hard-working civil servant who still always had time for Carter's ball games.*

*In the end, there'd been no need for a lawyer. In a tense meeting with Carter, his mother, and his uncle ten days after the funeral, Marcus Washington explained that upon further investigation, no evidence was found linking Danny Carter to the drugs he'd been delivering—unwittingly— along his route. Furthermore, a suspect had been identified. Antoine Hairston, a Crips sublieutenant, was reliably determined to be the triggerman, the shooting the result of a botched robbery of a rival gang's drug box. An indictment was handed down and a federal arrest warrant issued.*

*Exactly one month after Danny Carter's death, a US Marshals' fugitive task force team consisting of USPIS inspectors, FBI agents, Rochester cops, and Monroe County deputies descended on Hairston's apartment in a decaying Victorian off Monroe Avenue. According to several neighbors who*

*witnessed what happened, Hairston appeared to be complying with the team's*
*orders to surrender as he stood in his doorway when he suddenly pulled a gun.*

*Hairston's own funeral was held three days later.*

*"Pest control," Earl Madden said at a ceremony a few weeks after that,*
*where a plaque commemorating Danny Carter was unveiled in the post*
*office lobby.*

*"Damn straight," Dean Carter said, his arm around Carter.*

*For Carter's part, he said hardly anything at all other than the single line*
*that had become his mantra: "I'm headed to the gym for a while."*

*But six weeks later, he filled out the paperwork to apply to USPIS upon*
*graduation. It was impossible to escape the irony that his father's death had*
*paved the way for Carter—his baseball dreams dead—finally having an*
*idea of what he wanted to do with his life.*

*But at this point, he would take what he could get.*

First things first, Finn thought.

He dragged Stanfield down the driveway to the van, ignoring her
whimpers, and shoved her into the back seat. He warned her not to
move, speak, or even breathe loudly. As he did, he tried to decide
whether Carter was being clever or just an asshole by securing the van
keys in a bowl of potpourri by the front door, next to where they positioned the jammer. Either way, the smell was going to linger for a while.

Next, he walked over and freed Stone, the prone man blinking in
confusion as he came to, while Vlad, still gasping in pain from the
blows to his kidneys, sliced through Paddy's bindings. Finn didn't
bother searching for their guns. More where those came from.
He and Vlad had to practically carry both men into the van, which he
wasn't thrilled about. Because it raised an unpleasant thought, one
he wasn't accustomed to. Namely: What kind of guy takes out not

Stone, not Paddy, not Vlad, but all three? The trio the best of the worst, as he liked to say. Who can do that?

Delivery guy my fucking foot.

Not that it would matter either way.

"Where are we going?" Rachel said three minutes later as the van raced in near darkness down the narrow street toward the subdivision entrance, the distant lights of the other McMansions winking through the trees.

"That's up to you," Finn said, keeping his eyes on the road. In the passenger seat, Stone gingerly rubbed the back of his head.

"What do you mean?"

"You need to give me something, right now. Tell me the truth about Stella Wolford. Or boom." He held the phone up.

"You promised you wouldn't hurt him."

"And I won't, as long as you come clean."

Finn watched in the rearview mirror as Rachel wrestled with her thoughts. It was just as he imagined. It was clear as day from the look on her face that she hadn't been completely forthcoming. He knew it. When five seconds turned to ten, then fifteen, and she bit her lower lip, Finn raised the phone again.

"Last chance."

"Art Wheeler," she said.

"Who?"

"Summa ProHealth. He's the general counsel."

"What about him?"

"He might know something. It's his company. They're the ones being sued. I'm outside counsel—it's possible he's not telling me everything."

"Where can I find Art Wheeler?"

"Chicago. That's where the company's based."

"Where in Chicago?"

"I'm not sure. Downtown someplace. I've only been there once."

"What about Wheeler? Where's he live?"

Rachel turned her head in the direction of her house. "I have no idea. Someplace up there I assume."

"You think he knows something about this?"

"I have no idea. But if anyone does, he would."

"All right," Finn said. "Chicago it is." He handed the phone to Stone. At the main road, Finn turned left and then nodded. Stone lifted the phone and punched in a number.

"What are you doing?" Rachel said, panic in her voice.

"Taking care of business," Finn said. "I don't know who that Carter guy is, or what he's playing at, but he's caused way too much trouble to leave your house in one piece. Glenn's collateral damage, I'm afraid."

"No—you promised. You promised!"

"Sorry," Finn said, as Stone depressed the green call button.

Carter worked quickly, squeezing the pliers he retrieved from a utility vest pocket. It was tough going. It seemed in character that Scar Guy would have wrapped the chain binding the bomb to Glenn's chest three times around, because why not? It was pointless to try to disarm the explosive itself. Carter had a vague idea of which wire did what, but one false move and, well. If they taught that stuff in BIT, he didn't remember. As it was, he figured he had just seconds to spare. And he'd need at least five of those to get them up the basement stairs since, if the shrapnel didn't shred them, the concussive force of the detonation would reduce them to skin-covered sacks of jelly.

"Ohhh," Glenn moaned.

"Hang on," Carter said, sweat beading on his forehead as he pinched down and broke the second strand of chain.

To his credit, especially given the state of his ravaged face, Glenn was performing admirably. Both hands gripped the copper-clad pot positioned over the explosive, despite how slippery the aluminum foil the pot was wrapped in had become thanks to the blood dripping from his cheek. The foil Carter hastily wrapped the pot in after racing through the kitchen, finding the foil, and grabbing the pot from the stove on his way downstairs. The potatoes a pulpy mess strewn along the steps. The copper and aluminum trick—he hadn't learned that in BIT—would buy them no more than a few moments as the combo temporarily confounded the signal from Scar Guy's incoming call. Which Carter knew was coming. Hopefully, a few moments were all they needed.

"There," Carter said, the pliers snapping the last of the chain lengths with a dull *chink*. He took the pot from Glenn and lifted the contraption free, the severed chain clinking as he set the bomb on the floor. Carter wrapped his right arm around Glenn's waist and helped him to his feet, ignoring his gasp through the gag as he hauled him across the floor and onto the stairs. He had to hurry. Rounding the corner and making it up the first set of steps wouldn't be enough. The only thing shielding them at that point was sheet rock and two-by-four framing, which might as well be plastic wrap for all the protection it provided.

Around the moment they hit the landing, Glenn's legs buckled and Carter thought, *Well, it had been worth a try.* Then Glenn's head bobbed up and he glanced at the photo triptych and focused for a moment on the picture of the girl, and somehow he moved again and they made it across the landing and up the second set of stairs and three full steps into the kitchen before the world splintered.

Afterward, Carter wasn't sure whether the force of the blast pushed him almost to the dining room or if the lift of the house's main carrying beam as it levitated upward caused him to lose his balance and trip ahead like a skater losing his bearings. All he knew was that he gained consciousness a few seconds later someplace he hadn't been moments before. He opened and shut his eyes to clear his head, checked for missing limbs and appendages, satisfied himself that surgery wasn't in his future, and rose and searched for Glenn.

He found him, improbably tucked into a ball on the far side of the kitchen island, no telling how he'd gotten there, but a good thing regardless. Carter ran the same check on Glenn's extremities and once again satisfied, helped him to his feet. He used Paddy's knife to cut the gag and walked Glenn toward the living room and the front door.

"Rachel," Glenn said.

"Gone, I'm afraid."

"Need to find her . . ."

"Let's get outside first."

With smoke pouring from floor vents and filling the living room, Carter walked Glenn through the door and straight to the Suburban. He opened the passenger door, set the confiscated guns in the back, and boosted Glenn into the seat. He did a quick tour around the SUV and noted that none of the tires had been slashed. Scar Guy hadn't bothered deploying the most obvious delay tactic because he assumed neither Carter nor Glenn would leave the house alive. A fortunate miscalculation, though one he doubted Scar Guy would repeat. Tucking that thought away, Carter slid into the driver's seat, turned off the emergency blinkers, put the car in neutral, and eased it three dozen yards down the drive toward the road.

"What are you doing?"

"Trying to avoid them."

"Who?"

Carter pointed at figures running across lawns toward the house.

"Your neighbors. They heard the noise. So what now?"

"What do you mean?"

*Good question*, Carter thought.

"Two options, basically," he said. "We go after Rachel so I can deliver my package, or we wait here for the police. I give them ten minutes tops. I'm guessing they'll be right behind the first tanker and pumper."

Glenn's eyes cleared momentarily and he looked at Carter as if seeing him for the first time.

"Who are you?"

"Just a delivery guy, like I told them inside. I can explain more in a second. Right now we have a decision to make. Rather quickly, I'm afraid. Rachel, or the police." Already in the distance, he heard sirens.

"You're not the police?"

Carter shook his head.

"Those men—how would we find them?"

"Leave that part to me."

Glenn turned with difficulty to look up the driveway. A handful of neighbors stood near the front door, peering through the smoke pouring outside.

"Rachel," Glenn said, turning around, his face stricken. "We need to save Rachel."

# EIGHT

Carter drove in silence for the next few minutes, keeping a close eye on his phone, until he saw a sign for I-465 in one mile. Now or never. He exited into a large shopping plaza that sat along the road between Fishers and Carmel and parked in the third-to-last row of a Walmart Supercenter lot. Far enough back to avoid the eyes of curious shoppers but not so far away as to raise the security guys' antennae. As Carter knew from experience.

"What are we doing?" Glenn said.

"We need to take care of your face. They did a heck of a job on you, whoever that was."

"Here?"

"It's here or a hospital. Hospital's better care but they're going to ask questions, not to mention how long it'll take to be seen. Time we don't have if we're going to rescue Rachel. We'll go in the back if that's all right."

Once he had Glenn positioned in the rear of the Suburban, Carter worked methodically but quickly, removing each item he needed from the black vinyl medical kit he kept in the locked metal box beneath the middle seat. He washed and cleaned Glenn's face, removing the smears of blood from his brow and cheeks and chin. Then he worked on the wound itself, a bloody cut about two inches long on Glenn's left cheek. At least the cut was clean and not ragged, thanks to the sharp edge of the gun used on Glenn.

Next, Carter cleansed the wound with antiseptic wipes as Glenn twitched and swore under his breath. Once Carter dried the skin on either side, he closed the wound with surgical glue, pinching the gash shut but not too tightly, to give it space to heal. He covered his work with a gauze bandage and dug around in the medical kit until he found the pill bottle he was looking for. He shook out four gel tablets, handed them to Glenn, and retrieved a bottle of water.

"How's the pain?"

"It hurts."

"The shock's wearing off. The next couple of hours will be rough. This is Tylenol. It should help. Under certain circumstances, I'd go with an opioid, but I tend to play it conservative. We can change course depending on how bad it gets."

Glenn stared at Carter. "You have opioids? Why?"

"Just in case."

"In case of what?"

"We should probably get going. If we're going to catch up to them." He returned to the driver's seat and waited for Glenn to move forward and buckle himself in.

Glenn said, "We don't even know where they are."

Carter examined the screen of his phone, which sat in its holder on the dashboard. "From the looks of it, I'd say they're headed north, but we won't be sure for another few minutes."

"How do you know that?"

"I stuck a GPS monitor on the underside of their van."

"You did what?"

"What I said. I keep a few around. You never know when you might need one."

Glenn looked at Carter as if he'd materialized behind a zoo's glass enclosure. "Jesus Christ. Enough's enough. Who are you? What the hell is going on?"

Instead of responding, Carter pulled out of the parking lot and headed for the highway. Once he was safely back on the road, he said, "My name's Mercury Carter, though I'm guessing you heard that part already. What's going on is I was in the process of making a delivery to your wife when I realized something was up and figured I'd better see what was going on."

"What kind of delivery?"

Carter hesitated. "It's a little complicated. Probably better to explain once we have Rachel back."

"Is it related to what just happened? To those men?"

"I don't think so."

"So it's just a coincidence you showed up like that?"

"I guess so."

Glenn shook his head in disbelief. "Can you at least say who it's from?"

Carter hesitated once more. It was an unusual situation, to say the least. Even though he felt confident that the delivery and the kidnapping weren't related, he was under an unorthodox NDA for reasons that only Rachel could appreciate.

Finally, he said, "Like I told the guy who answered the door, I can't reveal the source of a package. Rules and stuff. But I will, I promise, as soon as we find Rachel."

"Finn," Glenn said.

"Who?"

"That man. That's his name."

"Finn. Okay. So what happened, anyway?"

Carter listened as Glenn explained, starting with his and Rachel's conversation in the kitchen, moving on to the appearance of the men through the back door, and concluding with the terrifying few minutes in the living room as they sat bound on the couch. Glenn went over Rachel's retrieval of the deposition and, voice cracking, Finn's ratcheted-up demands about Stella Wolford's whereabouts and something called 22/7, followed by Finn's orders that the other men torture him and Rachel. Carter took it all in, keeping his expression blank. No point in letting Glenn know he could tell this was bad. Seriously bad.

"No idea why Finn cares so much about this Stella Wolford?"

"None at all."

"You said she's suing a company that Rachel represents?"

"That's right." He told Carter about Summa ProHealth and the little he knew about the lawsuit; something to do with Wolford fighting her firing over alleged poor performance.

"Summa ProHealth's in Indy? That's why Rachel's involved?"

"It's based in Chicago. Rachel's firm is assisting as outside counsel."

Carter looked at the GPS mapping app on his phone, watching the progress of Finn's van, a pulsing red light, as it traveled along the ribbon of I-65 headed north. At this rate, they were twenty minutes behind Finn, more or less.

"Rachel's firm—Donavan, Crabtree and Hamilton?"

"That's right. How do you know that?"

"I did a little research before I came." He saw Glenn's eyes widen at that comment and continued before he was interrupted. "No offense, but is it possible she knew something she wasn't telling these guys? That she was, I don't know, hiding something about this lady? Stella Wolford? Protecting information of some kind?"

"Of course not."

"You're sure?" Carter said, glancing at his passenger and the rectangle of white gauze covering his cheek.

"Of course I'm sure. She told them everything she knew, which wasn't much. And it still wasn't enough."

"What about you?"

"Me?"

"Are you hiding something?"

Glenn looked at him in disbelief. "Are you out of your mind? I'm the victim here. *We're* the victims. We were attacked. Nearly killed for something we know nothing about. How could you ask such a thing?"

"Relax, okay? It's just a question."

"An idiotic one—"

"Except it's interesting to me that you chose going after Rachel over waiting for the police. I mean, gut move, it totally makes sense. First instinct is to protect the loved one. Always. I'm married myself. I get it." He thought briefly of Tomeka and realized he'd missed their nightly check-in thanks to Finn.

"But the thing is," he continued, "most people, after going through something like that, they're opting for the cops. Not some guy they just met. So it has me thinking."

Glenn didn't say anything for a moment.

"No offense, I mean."

"Would you please tell me who you are?" Glenn said finally. "Please tell me what the hell is going on."

Changing the subject. *Interesting*, Carter thought. Deciding to roll with things, he said, "I need to make a quick call first—"

"No, you don't. You need to start talking. I'm grateful to you. You saved my life—our lives. And you're right—I picked finding Rachel over, I don't know, common sense. Because I can't lose her. I *can't*. I understand why I did, even if you can't. But—why are you in this? Why were you there, at our house? How'd you even know those men would be there?"

"I didn't. Like I said, I just happened to be delivering a package for Rachel. Right place, right time."

"But you can't say who it's from."

"Afraid not. Company rules."

"Whose company?"

"Mine."

"What's the name of it? Your company?"

"It's really just me. I'm on my own. A freelance courier, like."

"A courier."

"That's right. Like a mailman."

"A mailman delivering a package from someone you can't identify, who happens to show up at our house as four armed guys were about to torture my wife and me, and you proceed to take out three of them without even needing to catch your breath, then you pull that trick with the copper pot and the foil, and you just happen to have a GPS tracking device to stick on their van? And I'm supposed to believe it's just some big coincidence?"

"Actually, I was kind of winded—"

"Answer the damn question."

Carter glanced at his phone, watching the progress of the van in front of them. Still a good twenty minutes behind Finn. But the gap was holding and Carter wasn't pushing the speed, which meant Finn wasn't either. Which meant that whatever else was happening, the guy wasn't stupid. He knew the last thing he needed was a reason for a state trooper to pull him over. Twenty minutes, mile after mile. No more, no less.

Carter said, "I'm not sure what to say. I'm a guy who delivers stuff. Occasionally, things get complicated."

"Bullshit," Glenn said. "How'd you know where Abby's mother was born? Don't tell me that's something a regular mailman knows. Come to think of it, how'd you even know about Abby?"

"Well, there's that photo of the three of you. On the landing? Abby—that's your daughter?—was wearing a monarch pin. Morelia's famous for its monarch reserve. Looking at her, I put two and two together and figured she had some kind of roots there."

"But how'd you know she wasn't Rachel's daughter?"

Carter put his left turn signal on and slowly passed a Noble Roman's tractor trailer.

"Well," Carter said. "I knew this was a second marriage for you and Rachel, plus it's kind of obvious given that both of you are lighter-complected than Abby, but she also looks just like you."

"Why in the world would you know that? That I'd been married before? Or what either of us looked like? You'd never seen us before. Or had you?"

"You need to relax, okay? I don't want that wound to open up. Infection's the last thing we need to deal with at the moment. As for your marital status, like I said, I tend to do a little research before I make a delivery. Standard procedure, really."

"Again, bullshit. You're telling me FedEx does that? UPS?"

"I couldn't say. I don't work for them. I'm independent, remember?"

"But what if you'd been wrong?" Glenn said, hysteria causing his voice to rise. "What if Rachel had said, I don't know, Oaxaca or Guadalajara or Mexico City, or wherever? What then?"

"But she didn't, did she? Her answer confirmed her identity and I proceeded accordingly."

"Except what the hell kind of mailman asks that sort of question? Or takes out three guys like that? Or knows how to stop a bomb going off?"

"Listen," Carter said, beginning to feel annoyed. He understood where Glenn was coming from, sure. But how much plainer could he be? "You're overthinking this. I'm telling you like it is. I'll admit my methods are a little out there. But I'm on my own here. I have to take precautions other guys don't."

Glenn shook his head. "Assuming any of this is true, you're telling me it's a coincidence you showed up tonight? Just as they were about to . . ." His voice trailed off.

"That's right."

"But if you hadn't come just then. Rung the doorbell at that precise moment . . ."

"Good thing I did, right?"

"It's too much," Glenn said. "It's too unbelievable."

"You don't believe in coincidences?"

"No. Do you?"

Carter let his mind go someplace he hadn't allowed himself to venture in a long time.

"Most of the time, no," he said, exiting onto I-65 headed north as he glanced once more at this phone.

Nineteen minutes now. No more, no less.

# NINE

Carter noticed two things right away when he arrived at the USPIS Career Development Unit in Potomac, Maryland, in the summer of 2005.

First, he was accorded far more deference than he felt he deserved. But there was no getting around it. His story quickly became legend. Son of a carrier murdered on duty. Grateful to the Inspection Service for solving the crime and bringing his slain father a modicum of justice. Wanting to give back by devoting himself to that same service.

The reality was more complicated, but only just. Carter's uncle hadn't been sure about the decision. Carter's mother, still numb with grief, hadn't known what to think. Earl Madden, furious at the brief period when Danny Carter himself was under suspicion, nearly declined to give his blessing but relented during an awkward visit just before Carter left for basic training. "Your father would have been proud," he said in a gruff voice, shaking Carter's hand.

So yeah, the awe bestowed by his twenty-three fellow trainees was one surprise. The other was how few of them wanted to be there. Not be in service, exactly. But with USPIS. It turned out, at least in Carter's class, that most landed there after a shotgun application approach that had them dreaming of the FBI or the DEA or the ATF or any number of other more high-profile alphabet agencies. Apparently, USPIS was an outlier when it came to federal law enforcement. Despite being one of the country's oldest police divisions, dating to 1775, your average citizen—not to mention a lot *of local cops—assumed the agency's inspectors literally did just that, inspected mail, and were surprised to hear the agents carried guns and could arrest people "like real police officers."*

*After a while, it started to make sense to Carter why his classmates, some of them obsessed with dark jackets emblazoned with three-letter acronyms a bit more familiar than the confusing "USPIS," hoped for a different posting. He understood, but he didn't share the sentiment. He only saw himself doing one thing going forward, with one agency. For Carter, it was the Postal Inspection Service or nothing. Though he demurred when it came to discussing his personal story in any detail, he had to admit it was mostly true. He was there to honor his father and his father's profession, and to make sure the same thing didn't happen to other carriers.*

*And he stayed the course, starting by holding a gun for the first time in his life, a Beretta 92D, agency issue at the time. Surprising everyone but chiefly himself by scoring in the top tenth percentile for accuracy on the CDU's indoor range. Sweating out the monthly multiple-choice exams on everything from criminal law to postal policy to USPIS regulations. Eighty percent to pass; otherwise, you were headed home. Again to his surprise, never scoring below ninety-five. And finally, showing a remarkable aptitude for the academy's weekly officer survival and defensive tactics training given that his one and only physical encounter with another person involved the high school crash with the second baseman that tanked his baseball dreams.*

*Regardless of his reason for joining the USPIS, it turned out that Carter was well suited for the job. From building entry to room clearing; from close quarters combat to warrant service; from pressure points to subject control—he got it. Along the way, he earned the nickname that stayed with him throughout his time in uniform: Cool Carter. Unassuming, inscrutable, seemingly unflappable.*

"You're a bit of a cipher, Carter," his academy instructor told him one day after he'd scored ten out of ten on a series of virtual training simulation exercises in which he correctly decided when to fire his weapon—and when not to—every time. "Most people would be proud of a performance like that."

"I'm proud."

"You don't look it."

"I don't?"

"You don't look glad, and you don't look sad."

"What do I look like?" Carter said, genuinely interested.

"Like a guy who's perfectly happy to shuffle papers on his desk for an hour before quitting time. Not blow the top off the hardest training exercise we offer."

"Is there a problem, ma'am?"

She studied him. "No problem. I just want to be sure you understand what you accomplished."

"I understand," Carter said.

"Anything else?"

"Well, I'm headed to the gym for a while."

After those sixteen weeks of trial by fire, Cool Carter stayed the course even as many of his classmates floated résumés within days of graduating from the academy. Carter kept his head down and worked hard at post-graduation postings in Rapid City, Omaha, and Bloomington. He kept at it all the way until he returned to Rochester seven years later when an inspector's job opened up in his hometown. Bought a house not far from his mom. Split season Red Wings tickets with his uncle. Let Earl Madden buy him a cup of coffee, sat politely while Earl reminisced about his dad.

Back home. Everything well and good. Cool Carter on the job.

Until his life crashed and burned a second time.

Looking out the Suburban's passenger window, Glenn lapsed into silence. He wasn't sure he believed a word Carter said. He also wasn't sure it mattered. Whoever the guy was, it was indisputable that he and Rachel owed their lives to him, coincidental last-second arrival or not. It was also indisputable that Carter appeared committing to finishing the job—to rescuing Rachel, as improbable as that seemed.

What mattered now was trying to figure out what was going on. He didn't quite buy the whole thing about that lady's deposition. Stella Wolford. Whoever she was, was she worth killing for? As compared to the secret Glenn was hiding, which really was?

The secret that Glenn assumed was behind the attack. Felt with certainty the second he saw the strangers burst into the kitchen. The secret that scared him enough that three weeks ago he secretly purchased the gun the tall brute found during his search of their home office. Glenn's face reddening as he handed over the cash at the gun store, hating himself for hiding such a thing from Rachel because of how much they shared, but feeling—knowing—he didn't have a choice. Of course, fat lot of good it had done them sitting in a locked drawer. A hidden gun Glenn still hadn't brought himself to tell Rachel about before tonight. Because doing so would open a Pandora's box of deceit and betrayal that didn't bear thinking about.

Ironically, he'd decided not twenty-four hours earlier to change course. To confess to Rachel. To reveal the mess he made and face the consequences with or without her. He'd been leading up to it tonight, maybe over dinner, maybe afterward, before things went south because of Abby's grades and the disagreement that followed. Well, the disagreement and then the attack.

So the opportunity was lost. The only thing that mattered now was saving Rachel. Explaining everything would have to come later. If there was a later. Glenn swallowed. No. There had to be. Despite the likely destruction of their marriage and the impact that would have on Abby. He had to be able to tell Rachel, which meant they had to save her. Somehow.

He had to explain what a complete and total idiot he'd been.


Carter glanced at Glenn looking silently out the window. He knew it was a lot. The business of him showing up at exactly the right moment was a tough pill to swallow, no question. For Glenn and for Carter. Tomeka accused him more than once of being like this guy Zelig in a movie—Carter hadn't seen it—always popping up at random times in history. Carter wasn't sure he saw the connection. He just knew that, since he'd quit his old job and struck out on this new venture, odd stuff tended to happen to him. Like tonight. Which, by the way, meant he was way behind schedule, with Louisville out of the question for now. He also knew his hand hurt from breaking Blue Eye's nose, and he was annoyed this Finn guy got the drop on him at the last second and took off with Rachel, which put his delivery in jeopardy, which was all that really mattered.

He said, "I'm going to make that call now, if it's all right."

"What call?" Glenn said wearily.

Carter gave his phone an instruction. The number rang just once before the connection went through.

"Dispatch."

Despite the circumstances, Carter smiled at the formality his uncle insisted on, even though it was just the two of them.

"Hi there. I'm on speaker, just so you know. There's a passenger."

"Roger that. Status?"

"There's been a delay."

"One sec. Let me sync up." Thirty seconds passed, with no sound other than the rush of highway traffic. "Okay. Got you. I-65 North. Go ahead."

Carter explained the events of the evening beginning from the moment the man named Finn opened the door and Carter realized he had a problem. He went over Stella Wolford and the deposition and "twenty-two seven" and described each man he encountered as best he could. He repeated the name of Rachel Stanfield's downtown Indy law firm and explained that Glenn worked for a pharmaceutical company called Xeneconn. He concluded with their current speed-limit-only pursuit of the van headed northwest on I-65 out of Indianapolis and said if he had to guess they were headed to Chicago. He glanced at the phone screen while he talked. Still nineteen minutes, no more, no less.

"Twenty-two seven?" his uncle said.

"That's correct."

"And why Chicago?"

Carter told him.

"All right. Call you back."

"One sec. Can you text Tomeka, tell her I'm tied up? But I'll be in touch soon?"

"You got it."

The phone went dead. Carter looked over at Glenn, who as anticipated was staring at him once more.

"How did you know I worked for Xeneconn?"

Carter adjusted the brim of his Red Wings cap. "Research?"

"But why me? I wasn't the one getting the delivery."

"Precautionary. Notch the belt, tighten the suspenders, that kind of thing. Xeneconn—you make pharmaceuticals, right? And you're in the general counsel's office over there?"

"None of your business," Glenn said, more forcefully than Carter thought the situation warranted. "Who was that? On the phone?"

Carter ignored him. "Xeneconn's been in the news lately. Aren't you working on some kind of vaccine? For alcoholism or something?"

"Addiction," Glenn said, spitting out the word. "Please answer the question. The person on the phone?"

"Just the office."

"Office? Before you made it sound like you're a one-man band or something."

"Good point. One-man band and change, I guess."

Glenn looked about to say something but stopped suddenly, a look of affliction twisting his face as if someone had jabbed his wound with a stick.

He said, "You think they're headed to Chicago?"

"Best guess. If Stella Wolford is that important to them, and they couldn't get what they wanted from Rachel, and Chicago is where Summa ProHealth is located, stands to reason they'd head that way. Is there something—are you all right?"

Carter looked in alarm at Glenn, who seemed to be having trouble breathing.

"Glenn?"

"Abby," he gasped. "She's in Chicago. Her school's there."

"What school?"

"Bellbrook Academy. It's a boarding school. It's—well, long story. We thought it was the right choice at the time. What if they . . ."

"Calm down. Did her name come up when these guys were in the house? Did they mention her?"

Glenn hesitated.

"What?"

"It's nothing."

"Tell me. There's no 'nothing' in a situation like this. Everything matters."

Carter watched Glenn struggle over what to say next. Finally, he said, "Rachel and I were having a disagreement about her, about Abby, before it all happened. We were in the kitchen."

"What about Abby?"

"Her grades haven't been great. In the toilet, actually. I'm not sure why. She's always been a good student."

Carter pictured the layout of the kitchen. "They came in through the back door, right? Any chance they heard something beforehand?"

"Off the deck, yeah. No, I don't think so. I can't say for sure, though." He thought for a moment. "Shit—the window was open. But they never mentioned her once they were inside."

Carter recalled the photo triptych on the landing. If he saw it, they saw it.

"I should call her," Glenn said. "Make sure she's all right. Warn her."

Carter looked at his phone. Still nineteen minutes, no more, no less.

"I'm not sure about that. About warning her, I mean."

"Why in God's name not?"

Carter hesitated, thinking of the best way to explain this.

"First of all, you'd be calling from a strange number, so odds are fifty-fifty she even picks up," Carter said, choosing his words carefully. "Second, who calls their kid anymore? So that's another flag for her. Assuming you do reach her, she already has questions about why you're calling and not texting, and that's before you get around to warning her."

"But she could be in danger."

"Keyword 'could.' And remember, once you do warn her, the genie's out of the bottle. Maybe she agrees to take precautions and leaves it at that. Or maybe she tells a friend, who tells a teacher or tutor or whatever they have there, and they get involved. Maybe that person tells the school head. Maybe that person calls the police. What I'm saying is, warning her is an option—I'm not denying it. But, thinking about the task at hand, is that really what we want?"

Glenn didn't respond right away. As they sat in silence, Carter studied Glenn's face while shifting patterns of car beams and overhead road lamps painted and repainted it in darkness, like a portrait being drawn over and over again to get just the right contrast of shadow and light. Carter considered that for a man in his situation, Glenn was curiously reticent on the subject of contacting authorities. Not that Carter was complaining, exactly. In his line of work, he wasn't a fan of drawing attention from law enforcement either. It's just that that tended not to be a universally shared sentiment.

"Glenn?"

"I don't know what to do. I can't lose Abby too. But I hear what you're saying."

"For the record, we haven't lost Rachel." Carter looked at his phone. Nineteen minutes, more or less. "We're doing fine on that front. So here's a thought."

"What?"

Carter handed Glenn his phone and instructed him what to do.

"Is that legal?"

"Does it matter?"

Glenn looked at him for a few seconds and then, nodding to himself, went to work. As Glenn's fingers worked the keypad, Carter ticked the cruise control up a notch. Just one. It couldn't hurt. As he approached the rear of a Ryder truck and signaled to move around it, he thought again how lucky it was he'd arrived at Rachel's house when he did.

Then Carter thought about the fact that ten minutes before turning into Rachel and Glenn's driveway he considered stopping at Steak 'n Shake to tide him over before the push onto Louisville. Nothing like a double steakburger with cheese. Stopping and going inside, of course, because even though it took longer, Carter hated drive-throughs. But he decided not to, for no good reason, opting to get the delivery over with first.

Meaning he arrived at Rachel Stanfield's house at precisely the right time.

"Okay," Glenn said, returning the phone to its holder. "It's all good. It worked perfectly."

"And?"

"She's fine. She's on a field trip tonight—they're going to see *Hamilton* downtown. On a chartered bus, her whole class together, a bunch of chaperones, the complete deal."

"Good to hear. What did you decide about warning her?"

Glenn glanced out the window. "I didn't say anything. I just pretended to check in. You were right. Calling would have been weird. That app worked perfectly. It made it look just like I was texting from my phone."

"Comes in handy sometimes. Hang on." Carter slid his finger along his phone's incoming call bar. "Yes?"

"Not much luck, I'm afraid," his uncle said. "Still working on twenty-two seven. My working theory is it's either an address or part of a bank code. I'll keep checking. Drew a blank on Finn, too."

"What about Stella Wolford?"

"Worked up a profile on her, but it's not much. Found her address and the lawsuit you're talking about pretty easily. But it sounds like they already knew where she lived, right? Urbana? It's just that she wasn't there?"

Carter looked at Glenn, who nodded.

"That's right," Carter said.

"If it helps, there's a guy named Art Wheeler listed in the court docket. Summa ProHealth general counsel. Does that name mean anything?"

"I've heard the name," Glenn said. "Rachel mentioned it a couple of times. He's her contact there."

A brief silence. Then: "Merc?"

"It's okay," Carter said. "That's Glenn. Glenn Vaughn. He's Rachel's husband. Any contact info for Wheeler?"

"Office and home. Texting them to you now. I'll keep after Finn and company."

"Thanks."

"Oh, and Tomeka says hi. And to remind you to pick up a couple bottles of Uncle Nearest when you're in Louisville. If you can find it."

"On my to-do list."

"Figured as much."

"What now?" Glenn said after the call disconnected.

Carter thought about Steak 'n Shake. He thought about his father. He thought about coincidences. Then he looked at the ribbon of highway unspooling on his phone, at the slow pulse of the red dot of Finn's van. The gap had narrowed to eighteen minutes, more or less.

"Now you call Art Wheeler."

# TEN

Rachel rested her head against the side of the windowless van, willing herself not to cry.

To some tiny degree, the rhythm of the van's smooth passage along what she—now blindfolded—guessed was an interstate highway offered a sliver of relief from the terror gripping her insides. Terror and exhaustion and despair. As much as she fought it, she couldn't stop imagining Glenn's final seconds before the bomb went off. What he must have felt—the fear he would have experienced when in a fraction of a second he realized the end had come. Rachel squeezed her eyes tight at the thought that the discussion they were having in the kitchen, the talk on the brink of an argument, were the last words she and Glenn would share together.

She replayed the conversation over and over, always stopping at his suggestion that she could go back to her old life. Like that was going to happen, even if she wanted to. Chad Setterlin made sure of that. Then Rachel paused, remembering something else.

The gun the big man found in the office. And Glenn's bizarre claim at the last second before they were dragged to the basement.

*I have money. Lots of it. Millions.*

What the hell?

Why did Glenn have a gun? What money was he talking about? They did all right, despite the strain of Abby's tuition. But not *millions* all right. What was going on? Up until tonight, she would have considered their marriage close to ideal. No secrets that she was aware of. Then she considered Glenn's moodiness in recent weeks. He kept attributing it to work stress. But was that really it? What wasn't he telling her?

Distraught, Rachel reviewed the horror of the living room interrogation, both repulsed by the memory and drawn to it like someone who can't help reaching for the top wire of an electrified fence. The sight of the men entering their kitchen and everything that happened afterward was seared into her brain like the most unreal thing—and also the most authentic—that had ever happened to her. The night terror you awake from with relief and realize with chilling dismay was absolutely genuine. And the strange, temporary rescue, if that's what you called it, by someone named Mercury Carter. Who somehow knew that Abby's mother was from Morelia, but who didn't know enough to save her and Glenn in the end.

The van hit a bump in the road, jarring her back to reality. A thought came to her. A moment later, she sighed deeply through her gag.

Rachel sensed the man sitting beside her shift briefly before going still. A man she had heard Finn call Paddy.

"Quiet," he said

Rachel almost followed the order. She thought of Glenn, and Abby, and the child growing within her, and decided she had nothing to lose. She angled her shackled hands toward her crotch, pointed deliberately, and cried out through the gag.

Nothing happened for a moment. Then Rachel felt Paddy shift and shivered at the touch of his hands on her neck. For a terrified second, she imagined he was going to choke her into unconsciousness, or worse. Instead, he reached around the back of her neck and loosened the gag just enough that she could speak.

"I have to pee."

"Hold it," Finn said.

Rachel swallowed, focusing on her family. What was left of it. "I can't. I really have to go. Sorry about that, but it happens when you're pregnant."

"And I said hold it."

"I can't. Not for much longer, anyway," Rachel said as defiantly as she dared. "I can go sitting here if you want. But it's going to be messy. I was about to go when you showed up at the house, and that's been a while."

"Why should I believe you?"

Rachel fought to control her voice, anxious not to jeopardize the respite from the gag. "You don't have to believe me. I'm going to prove it in about two minutes whether you like it or not."

The man in the passenger seat growled, "Rest stop in two miles." Rachel had glimpsed him briefly as they piled in after she was pulled from the house and away from Glenn, the bomb strapped to his chest in the basement. A slate-faced giant with a swollen nose and red, runny eyes.

"No go," Finn said. "Cameras everywhere."

"Side of the highway?"

"Sure. Like that wouldn't attract attention."

"Please," Rachel said. "I'll be quick. I promise."

"In case you haven't noticed, you're not in a position to promise anything."

A minute passed as they traveled along the highway in silence. Rachel said a silent prayer. She really did have to pee; not as badly as she was making out, but still. What mattered more was what amounted to a test. An examination of her captors' will and how serious they were about her making it to Chicago and Art Wheeler's house alive.

"There," Finn said.

Rachel heard the distinctive tick of a turn signal and half a minute later felt the van slow and veer to the right. Her stomach flopped as they completed half a clover leaf a little too fast and then the van stopped. The turn signal ticked once more and after two or three minutes the van rolled to a halt.

"Listen up," Finn said. "Make it fast. Don't even think of trying anything. You know what happened to Glenn. You so much as move a wrong muscle and it's over. Understand?"

*And then how would you get through to Art?* Rachel thought. But all she said was, "I understand."

She heard the jingle of metal, the click of a lock, a door swinging open. A moment later rough hands pulled her from her seat. As her feet touched the ground she experienced a rush of cool, country air and heard the sound of crickets over the distant rush of highway traffic.

"Down there," Finn said. "Hurry up."

Rachel stumbled down an incline, something sharp and nettle-y brushing her ankles, a man on either side gripping her arms like giant C-clamps. The sound of crickets intensified. She thought she smelled stagnant water. A pond or stream? A moment later they stopped. As ice flooded her insides, she felt the fingers of the man on her right—Paddy, she guessed—fumbling at the front of her slacks. After a second he tugged them unceremoniously to her ankles and repeated the action with her panties.

"You heard what he said. Make it fast."

"I have to crouch," she said, and before they could protest she bent her knees, lowered herself, and steeled her mind against the ludicrous horror of her situation. An instant later she felt a wave of relief as her bladder released.

"For fuck's sake," Paddy said. "You're getting it on my shoes."

"Sorry, sorry," Rachel said. *Not sorry, asshole.*

"Are you done yet?"

"Almost."

She held the crouch until she was sure she was finished, that she'd discharged every last drop she could, aware the van might not stop again until Chicago no matter how much she begged.

"Okay." She tried to stand but as she did her knees wobbled under her weight, borne until that moment by the men supporting her. She cried out as she lost her balance and the men's grip on her arms slipped as her heft briefly overwhelmed them. She stumbled forward into the weeds, landing face down and bare ass up in the air, her humiliation complete.

"Jesus," Paddy said. "The fuck are you doing?"

"The fuck am I doing? The fuck are you doing?" the second man with Rachel said. His name unknown to her. "You're supposed to be holding her."

"The fuck you think I was doing?"

"Quit screwing around, both of you." Finn, from above them. "We need to get moving."

Any relief Rachel felt in understanding that the men were angry at each other and not her over the mishap vanished a second later as someone grabbed her hair and yanked it to pull her head out of the weeds. The iron hands returned, pinioning her arms as she was pulled roughly to her feet. She gritted her teeth as she felt thick fingers around her ankles, her calves, the stolen caresses unmistakable before whoever it was redressed her, his hands lingering moments too long on her thighs as he pulled up her garments.

"I said, move it," Finn said.

Arms pinched once more in the grip of her captors, Rachel half-stumbled and half-walked up the incline. Just as she felt the crunch of the berm's gravel beneath her shoes and guessed the van was mere inches away, she cried out.

"You're hurting me." She sagged in the men's arms, letting her weight do the work as her shackled hands drifted to her waist.

"Not again, bitch," Paddy said and pulled her to her feet.

A moment later she was in the side seat again, the gag and the blindfold retied even tighter. Doors slammed shut with the finality of prison cell closures. Rachel's stomach flipped again at the speed and sharpness of the U-turn pulled by the driver and a minute later they were back on a highway, miles once more rolling past in an unseen succession interrupted only by the occasional diesel grunt of a truck.

Rachel's knees ached from how she'd landed as she stumbled forward into the grass. She felt the itch from bits of weed and small sticks no one bothered to brush free from her legs as they righted and redressed her. But it was all right. The tumble, pure accident, had gifted her an unexpected benefit.

She tried to imagine how the object made its way into the weeds. Remnants of a long-gone farmhouse? Shaken free from a load of lumber on a flatbed whose driver just happened to travel down that road? No matter. It had been there, lying flat on the grass, when Rachel lost her balance and fell. She mistook it for a stick at first, hard and straight and unbreakable. As her fingers closed around it she realized her mistake. No stick has quite that sharp a point or such a flat head on the opposite end. She spent enough hours in her father's workshop as a child to know the feel of a carpenter's nail.

Now that nail, clenched in her closed fist as Paddy and whoever dragged her back to the van, was hers and hers alone, slipped into her waistband as she manufactured a collapse just before they shoved her back inside. Impossible to say what good it might do her. But for the first time since that terrible moment in the kitchen, Rachel felt the tiniest bit less helpless. Less helpless, and ready for whatever came next.

# ELEVEN

As Glenn placed the call to Art Wheeler, Carter saw a sign for Lafayette. About two hours to go, if he recalled travel times correctly. He hesitated and then clicked his speed up another mile per hour. Beside him, he heard Glenn clear his throat.

"Mr. Wheeler? It's Glenn Vaughn calling. I'm Rachel Stanfield's husband. Yes, that's right."

From there, the call went about as well as Carter expected. He wasn't exactly sure what Glenn did, someone who worked in the general counsel's office of a large pharmaceutical manufacturer like Xeneconn. He imagined a lot of documents on screens and meetings and Zoom calls. What it didn't entail, it quickly became obvious, was dissembling on the phone, especially under these conditions. Glenn made it okay through the first part they rehearsed, the heads-up that Rachel wasn't feeling well and wouldn't be available Friday. A little odd that Rachel herself wouldn't just text or send an email, but Carter thought Glenn could finagle his way through that irregularity. And he did, give or take.

It was the next part, trying to tease out information about the lawsuit, that didn't go so well.

"Believe me, she feels bad she's so out of it," Glenn said. "Which reminds me of something. She did ask me to check whether we'd heard from Stella Wolford yet."

If Carter had to guess, it was the "we'd" that did it. The implication, however innocent, that the three of them—Rachel, Art, and Glenn—were one big happy legal family dealing with this particular wrongful termination suit. That didn't sit well, which meant Glenn never moved on to the question of whether Wheeler had had any unusual contacts recently.

"Of course, of course," Glenn said, before lowering the phone, staring at it a moment, and replacing it in the console holder.

"Hung up?" Carter said.

"Not quite. But his tone changed. He asked why Rachel couldn't check in herself. He said to tell her he'd touch base with her tomorrow if she was feeling better. I screwed up, didn't I?"

"Not exactly. It was a fifty-fifty proposition anyway." Carter tried to decide if this were true. "Downside, he's wondering what that was all about. He might even try Rachel herself, just to be sure that was actually you. That wouldn't be good for us, assuming Finn has control of her phone. But that's on me. I should have considered that. Upside, we know he's around. We need for him to be there when Rachel shows up."

"Why?"

"Hang on."

Carter examined the screen on his phone. The blinking red light of Finn's van. Eleven minutes ahead, more or less. Something had happened. Somehow Carter had gained more than six minutes. The advantage couldn't be on Carter's end; he hadn't sped up that much. It couldn't be a traffic-driven issue, either, as the app showed a clear highway with no signs of a slow-down. Worst-case scenario, Finn had figured out that Carter was in pursuit and was reducing his speed to trigger a confrontation by drawing even with them. Carter dismissed the thought a second later. He'd run a sweep of the Suburban before pulling away from Rachel and Glenn's house and knew his own vehicle was free of tracking devices.

More to the point, he knew from experience how guys like Finn thought. People who strapped bombs to other people's chests, who promised not to detonate the devices as long as the victims cooperated, and who then detonated them anyway, were generally not the type of person who considered an alternative outcome. They were too focused on the goal of atomized flesh painting the walls of, in this case, a smartly finished basement.

Which left the only other outcome. Finn had made a pit stop. Not for gas, because Carter also knew that guys like Finn didn't run out of gas. He would have had a full tank when he arrived at Rachel and Glenn's so as not to risk stopping anywhere within two hundred miles of a crime scene afterward. It also wouldn't be for bathroom breaks for Finn or the other three; that's why God invented empty drink bottles. Carter could attest to that.

That left Rachel. Rachel, who was pregnant. Rachel, whose unexpected presence in their van Carter brought about by his arrival at her house. Finn wouldn't have bothered to provision the van with adult diapers or pads or whatever ladies on surveillance peed in because he hadn't planned on Rachel leaving her house alive. Which meant the odds were better than even that Finn had stopped the van on account of her. Which meant Finn needed Rachel once he arrived in Chicago, which meant she was still aboveground.

Carter looked at his phone. Eleven minutes, more or less.

Out of the blue, Glenn said, "You still haven't told me who Dispatch is."

"Like I said, it's an office thing."

"But who is he? He sounds just like you, only a little older. Is he your dad?"

"He's not my dad."

"Then who?"

"Don't worry about him. The only thing you need to know is he's on our side. That's all that matters."

"But—"

"You should get some rest. It could be a long night, depending on what happens at Art Wheeler's."

"You really think that's where they're going?"

Carter glanced at his phone. Ten minutes behind, no more, no less.

"Running all the numbers, yes. Guys like Finn are like rats. They always head for the cheese. We get to the cheese, we catch the rat. We catch the rat, we get Rachel back."

"Then what?"

"What do you mean?"

"What happens after we rescue Rachel from these maniacs who tried to kill us?"

"Simple," Carter said. "I deliver her package."

*If not for Confidential Human Source No. 5 it was entirely possible that Carter would still be wearing a suit and carrying a badge as he investigated mail fraud, mail carrier robbery, and the continuing problem of illegal drug shipments.*

*Carter came across Markey Snyder—CHS5—the same way as a kid he'd found centipedes and crickets and roly-poly bugs. Lift up enough rocks and eventually you'll find sneaky creatures trying their best to avoid daylight.*

*It went down like this. A homeless woman tried cashing a $500 check at a Citizens Bank branch and a suspicious teller contacted police. The cops quickly determined the woman had agreed to undertake the transaction in exchange for $20 in McDonald's coupons promised by a man she'd met outside the* *shelter a day earlier. Carter got involved when the man—Snyder—plucked off the street by a uniformed Rochester PD officer following a citywide BOLO, offered to trade information about an armed robbery for leniency. Because the robbery involved a postal carrier, Carter took the call.*

*The robbery was a priority, since masked men brandishing large handguns had relieved the carrier of his arrow key, which opened collection boxes in the Eastwood Avenue zip code where several checks had been reported missing. They'd seen a rash of arrow key robberies recently, including one involving the savage beating of a carrier. So far they'd been stymied. But now, Snyder purported to know a name.*

*Which naturally turned out to be a bust.*

*"This name you gave us," Carter said, sitting opposite Snyder in an interview room in the Monroe County Jail at their second meeting. "He's got an aunt and two cousins who swear he was sleeping on the couch at the time."*

*Snyder licked his lips and looked nervously at the door. "They're lying."*

*"Maybe. Or maybe you're grasping at straws. Either way, there's nothing here that can help you."*

*Carter stood to leave.*

*"Wait."*

*"Why?"*

*"The guy. Who was shot."*

*Carter shook his head. "What guy?"*

*"A few years ago. In his truck. The one Antoine Hairston went down for."*

*Carter froze.*

*"What about him?"*

*"Hairston had help."*

*Slowly, Carter said, "Help from who?"*

*"Some guy."*

*"Some guy who?"*

*"I don't know his name. He knew what packages were on what routes. Hairston paid him for the info."*

*"And how would he know that?"*

*"He was on the inside. I mean, like a mail guy."*

*Carter didn't say anything for a second. He focused on slowing his racing heart.*

*"Okay. How do I find this guy, assuming he even exists?"*

*"He exists," Snyder said. "There's a bar. I see him around. I can show you. If . . ."*

*"If what?"*

*"If you can help me out."*

*Cool Carter. Unflappable. Inscrutable. Calm as a guy moving paper from one side of his desk to the other.*

*"Show me the bar," Carter said.*

Finn had to hand it to Stone. Despite the beating he took from Mark-Merc-Whoever-the-Fuck-Carter, he was soldiering on. Back in the driver's seat now, handling the wheel like a champ despite the lingering effects of the Mace and the broken nose and the blow on the back of the head, for all of which he coldly refused even the suggestion of Tylenol or Advil. All that, plus the humiliation of being taken down by a guy Stone would normally have for lunch. Finn might have chalked up Carter's success to luck if it wasn't for Paddy. And, well, Vlad. Finn wasn't sure who Carter was—he sure as hell wasn't a mailman—or how he caught on to their scheme in time to screw Phase One up so badly. He was just glad to have him out of the picture. The bomb had been a good call. So that problem was taken care of.

Of course, guys like Carter, with skills like that, raised a bigger concern—that he wasn't acting alone. That he was part of an organization. Some kind of syndicate—possibly an opposing one. Finn found himself wondering if Jason had told him everything he needed to know about this operation. Whether, caught up in his latest rag-head rant, he'd left something important out. Finn placed a check mark in the "cons" side of the mental ledger he was keeping about the job, and again, just for a moment, found himself fighting off a smidgeon of panic. Tamping down worry.

His confidence won out in the end. It was okay. Carter—whoever he was—was no longer an issue. If he represented the tip of a spear, if others were involved, if a chase was on, Finn could deal with them as they came. He wouldn't be taken off guard again. Guaranteed.

Downtown Chicago traffic was about as bad as Finn feared, but they weren't planning to stay so there was that. Without instruction, Stone found a side street away from the bustle where he parked just long enough for him and Vlad to leave the van and walk up the sidewalk without turning around. Finn slid into the driver's seat and was on the road again in less than a minute.

He let Paddy navigate them north along the lake. Twenty minutes later he pulled over a block from Art Wheeler's brownstone. A cinch locating the address after Rachel gave up the name. Amazing the info you could find on people these days without breaking a sweat. He bowed his head and checked his phone. Nothing yet. It was all right. He wasn't worried. Stone and Vlad knew what they were doing.

Fifteen minutes later his phone buzzed. He read the text message and nodded at Paddy. Paddy reached behind Rachel's head and removed the blindfold. Finn examined her face in the rearview mirror. She was a pretty enough woman, especially under the circumstances—shoulder-length brown hair, intelligent eyes, strong chin. A shame, really. But it was hard to focus on that right at the moment. Because to be honest, Finn was a little taken aback by the defiance he saw in her eyes, which was not what he expected. Well, no matter. He'd douse that fire soon enough.

"Listen carefully," he said, locking eyes with her in the mirror. "This can still work out for you, as long as you start cooperating."

She stared at him without reaction.

"You and me and Paddy here are going to have a conversation with Art Wheeler. I'm assuming you can guess the topic. And assuming we get the information we need, assuming both of you are forthcoming, we'll be on our way and that's that." The lie out in the open, he relaxed and warmed to the task.

"The key, though," Finn continued, "is that we get inside without a problem. No tipping your hand when he answers the door. You have a simple but important job and I can't afford for you to screw it up."

Still staring. Still no reaction.

"Just in case that's not clear, there's an additional factor I need you to consider."

He lifted the phone and angled it in Rachel's direction, displaying the photo of Abby with the barrel of Vlad's gun against the side of her head, a thin lock of black hair draped atop the muzzle. A knockout compared to her stepmother, which was saying something, despite the terror in those big, brown eyes. As with Rachel and the fate awaiting her, awaiting both of them, it seemed like a bit of a waste.

That was more like it, Finn thought. He watched Rachel's face contort in agony as if they'd actually gotten around to jolting her with electricity. He listened as she let loose a guttural moan barely stifled by the tightly knotted gag. Then he smiled.

"Let's go," he said.

# TWELVE

*T*he bar, Tony's, sat at the far end of a Rochester strip plaza on 15A in a retail hodgepodge near the Henrietta line. Schlit, read the neon beer sign flashing in the window, the dead z flickering off and on every few seconds. Carter sat in his personal car, a beige Ford Taurus, and made CHS5 Markey Snyder repeat his description of the man for the third time in the past thirty minutes.

"You're on thin ice here. If this doesn't pan out."

"I'm telling you, he's always in there."

Carter left his car and walked across the parking lot, shrugging deeper into his parka against the cold February night air. Light snow was falling and patches of parking lot ice gleamed under the lone street lamp. He pulled the door open and walked inside, pausing a moment as his eyes adjusted to the darkness.

The bar was long but narrow. On the left, eight booths, each dimly illuminated by buttery yellow light from sconce wall lamps. On the right, a row of barstools three-quarters' occupied. No one fitting Snyder's description of the inside man. In the middle of the bar five spigots, two of them labeled Genesee. Liquor bottles stacked neatly on three lighted glass shelves behind the bar.

Carter slid onto the nearest stool, unzipping his parka but keeping it on. A minute later a bartender arrived—white haired, neatly trimmed beard, an earring in his left ear—and placed a napkin before Carter.

"Jack Daniels, on the rocks," Carter said, defaulting to his father's drink of choice since he so rarely drank himself.

"*You got it.*"

Carter casually looked around. Only two of the booths were occupied. Both male-female couples, older, hunched quietly over their drinks, neither of the men close to Snyder's mysterious guy. If he even existed.

The bartender returned with his drink. Carter thanked him and took a sip, holding it in his mouth and rolling it around in hopes of avoiding the usual burn. He looked at the TV over the bar; the Sabres were on, playing the Blue Jackets. He checked his watch. He decided to give it half an hour. Long enough to call BS on Snyder's Hail Mary, but not so long that Snyder would freeze to death in Carter's Taurus while he awaited his fate.

Ten minutes passed. Fifteen. Carter finished his Jack Daniels to blend in, ordered another with no expectation of touching it. He ate three bar nuts. He fiddled with his napkin. He watched the game. Twenty minutes. Twenty-five.

As Carter's unofficial timer hit twenty-nine minutes, he pulled out his wallet and fished for a twenty. As he did, he felt a rush of cold air as the door to the bar opened. He looked over, half expecting Snyder.

"*Mercury.*"

Carter stared at the man saying his name as he stepped inside.

"*Haven't seen you here before.*"

Carter swallowed, thinking fast. "*Happened to be down this way. Long day. Figured why not.*"

"*What are you drinking?*"

Carter told him.

The man sat down beside him. Fitting Snyder's description to a T. Big, fleshy face, gray hair, thick black glasses.

His father's supervisor.

*Earl Madden.*

On any other occasion, Finn thought, he wouldn't have minded a chance to investigate Wheeler's brownstone more thoroughly. *Investigate* as in *tag items for removal.* Because there was a lot worth removing. The jewelry in its little boxes on Mrs. Wheeler's walnut dressing table in the corner of their bedroom, for starters. Thick gold bracelets, pearl necklaces, diamond earrings—so many earrings. None of that paste shit; good for her. Next, all the paintings on the brownstone's high walls, masses of squiggles and thick brushstrokes and vibrant colors. Finn didn't know fuck all about art, but he knew those kinds of abstract-y pictures were unlikely to be copies—originals all, since who could copy crap like that?—and so came with high-dollar value. Then came the liquor cabinet in the dining room, itself a work of art with its mahogany panels polished to a high sheen, and moving on to the single-malt whiskeys inside, none of which Finn had heard of but for which a quick search on his phone turned up bottle prices that gave even him pause. For some crazy reason Jason was into whiskey, which made this encounter feel even more favorable.

Finn took a sip of something called Lagavulin from a thick cut-glass tumbler he swiped from the cabinet and imagined Jason's reaction when presented with all those bottles. He eyed Art Wheeler and his wife—Gail, it transpired. They sat on opposite ends of the upholstered living room couch the color of red wine, wood trim running across the rounded back, staring at him in terror.

Even from here, Finn heard the whimpering of the dog that had greeted them at the door, unhappy at being tossed into the backyard. And at the kick Paddy landed on its side, hurling it against the sharp edge of the stairway post where it lay a few moments, stunned, as Paddy overpowered Mrs. Wheeler and Finn went in search of Art. Finn pretended not to remember the momentary shiver he felt at seeing the animal. And got down to business.

"So," he said, "any thoughts?"

Rachel sighed. She met his warning glance with the same look of resignation he'd enjoyed since the shock settled in when she saw they had Abby. Satisfied, he looked back at the Wheelers. They were a matched set, no doubt about it. Both thickset, but not what you'd call obese. Wheeler was mostly balding, unruly salty-peppery eyebrows atop sleepy-looking eyes, with red cheeks and a chin with the slightest hint of a dimple. Gail, with collar-length white hair, had a too-small nose that momentarily distracted from the battle she'd lost fending off multiple chins. Based on the mortified expressions on each of their fleshy faces, both looked capable of keeling over at any instant.

"I have no idea what you're talking about," Art said, voice cracking.

"Think again.Twenty-two seven. What did Stella Wolford tell you about it?"

Wheeler glanced at Rachel. She returned nothing, not even a nod of encouragement.

"Nothing. I swear."

"Why should I believe you?"

"Because I'm telling the truth."

Even at this moment, one of Wheeler's last on earth, a touch of defiance. Finn could appreciate that.

"Even assuming that's true, which I doubt, it's possible you could redeem your response by at least telling me where she is."

"Who?"

"Stella Wolford."

"I already told you," Wheeler said, forehead shiny with sweat. "I don't know. You have her address, right?"

"She's not there."

"What about her attorney?"

"He's not in a position to answer the question."

"What's that supposed to mean?"

Finn dialed up the article on his phone and pushed it in front of Wheeler. At this point, Finn could recite the headline by heart.

LOCAL ATTORNEY DEAD AFTER FIERY ONE-CAR CRASH.

"Does that help jog your memory?" Finn said.

"Please," Wheeler said, raising his bound hands to brush away the droplets of perspiration rolling into his eyes. "I don't know where Stella Wolford is or what 'twenty-two seven' means. I have no idea why you'd be interested in her. Unless maybe you were her dealer." Again, a hint of defiance despite his circumstances.

"Dealer?"

"You've either read the deposition or you haven't. Stella Wolford was fired because of her drug use."

"So?"

"So she frequently missed work. When she was at work her performance was subpar because most of the time she was high. And by *subpar* I don't just mean she missed quotas, which were not unreasonable. She made errors. Mistakes that meant additional work for other departments. Despite all that, she was given multiple opportunities to redeem herself before she was terminated."

"What's your point here, Mr. Wheeler?"

"My point is, why would you want to find such an individual unless she owes you money for drugs?"

"I'm not her dealer," Finn said. "Believe me when I tell you that if I were, she wouldn't have disappeared into thin air. I'd know exactly where she is."

"And like I said, I don't. I can't help you."

"That's what her attorney said. I didn't believe him and I don't believe you. And look what happened to him."

"I'm telling you—"

Finn took a breath. "Get the dog," he said to Paddy. "Maybe that'll help him remember."

"You sure?" Paddy said.

Finn swallowed, trying to disguise his discomfort. "Of course I'm sure."

"For God's sake, leave the dog alone," Wheeler said.

"And you'll do what?" Finn said, nodding at Paddy, who rose, cracked his knuckles, and headed for the kitchen.

"Danville," Wheeler gasped.

"Danville what?"

It was too late. Before he could respond, Wheeler's hands rose to his chest at the same moment his eyes rolled into the back of his head.

*For fuck's sake*, Finn thought. *What was it with this job?*

# THIRTEEN

C arter removed his phone from the console, handed it to Glenn, and said, "If I'm not back in twenty minutes, call 911."

"I thought we weren't involving the police."

"We aren't. Emphasis on *we*. But if I'm out of the picture they're your best shot. After that, call Dispatch. He'll take it from there." He gave him his uncle's number.

"And I'm supposed to just sit here until then?"

"Yes."

Glenn started to say something but Carter shut the driver's door and walked up the sidewalk. This was a solo job; that much was clear from Glenn's stiff movements as he turned this way and that in his seat while they drove, still bearing the effects of his beating. Plus, there wasn't much time. The gap between them and Finn had been down to three minutes, no more, no less, by the time Carter watched the blinking red dot stop for the final time at what turned out to be a parking space three car lengths down from Art Wheeler's brownstone. At first, hitting the Chicagoland traffic, Carter wasn't sure they were going to make it in time. Gaining an hour by entering Central Time also meant they hit the remnants of rush hour. But the mysterious detour Finn took at the last moment, parking downtown briefly before setting out again, allowed him to make up the difference.

Coming across Finn's van, Carter stopped long enough to kneel, retie his left shoe, remove a utility knife with a three-inch retractable blade from a pocket on the left side of his utility vest, open up a hole in the rear tire, and rise again. He repeated the gesture at the front of the van as he re-tied his right shoe. Pocketing the knife, he turned down the alley in front of him and cut left down the next alley, which ran past the rear of the row of brownstones that included Art Wheeler's. Reaching the lawyer's garage, Carter found the hard plastic-shell box sheltering the number keypad for the garage door. He opened the box's door, examined the keypad inside, shut the door, and, bracing his left hand on the box, swung himself onto the garage roof and then down.

Eighteen minutes left.

Wheeler's backyard was narrow but organized nicely all the same. A paved brick walk ran from the garage to the backdoor steps. A small, vine-covered pergola to the left sheltered a farmhouse patio table, six chairs, and a polished concrete-topped outdoor bar. The furniture sat on a half circle of sunken pavers with a chiminea parked at the far edge of the curve.

On the opposite side of the yard, illuminated by an alley light, pink and red roses bloomed from bushes rising from a series of raised beds that ran the length of the fence. The highest of the blooms obscured a fish-eye lens security camera affixed to an outer brick wall. Carter wondered if Art Wheeler was aware of the gap in protection. He would mention it if he had the chance. To the left of the last garden bed, a coil of green hose encircled a reel anchored to the back of the house, just beside the backdoor stairs. Beneath the hose, a dog had tucked itself against the condo's outer brick wall. The dog—a gray schnauzer—didn't look right. It whimpered as Carter approached. Carter knelt and set his hand on the animal's head. It whimpered again. Carter saw from the way it flinched that it was in pain. Carter felt a momentary twinge of anger flare up in the back of his brain. His head began to ache right on schedule. He stayed crouched, slowly breathing in and out through his nostrils the way Tomeka taught him, until the feeling passed and the ache subsided. Which was right when he heard steps approach from inside the house.

Carter kept his right hand on the dog's head, gently stroking it, even as he reached for the end of the green hose with his left hand. The back door opened and a man stepped onto the stoop. Carter wasn't one to judge, but given the circumstances, he would have led with his gun instead of keeping it in his waistband the way Paddy was doing. A personal preference kind of thing.

Kneeling in the shadows, Carter let the redhead scan the yard for a second, getting his bearings. The way he searched made him think Paddy was looking for the dog. A moment later Carter had his answer as he felt the dog twitch beneath his hand as it spied the giant on the stairs. Carter considered the blackjack in his utility vest—it worked once on Paddy just fine—but decided against it. Paddy had had his chance, the way he looked at it. Carter gave the animal a final pat before leaping up, draping a loop of hose around Paddy's neck, and jerking back hard, like a man putting everything into starting a lawn mower. In the same moment, Carter used his right foot to kick Paddy's knee out from under him and gave the hose just enough play to allow the heavy man to fall face first onto the brick walk with a grunt. Carter jumped onto Paddy's back a second later, twisting the hose once before pulling it back as he drove his weight onto Paddy's shoulder blades. Carter pulled hard, ignoring Paddy's hands scrabbling first at the loop and then at Carter, trying to detach him.

Paddy grunted in distress as he strained for air. Once, twice, a third time.

Each time he made a noise, Carter yanked a little tighter, forearms straining with the effort. He almost lost the fight. Paddy was strong, very strong, despite the blow Carter had given him outside Rachel's house, and fought hard. At one point he half rose, knocking Carter to the side. Carter lost his grip and Paddy gained more purchase. *Crap.* This wasn't good. Paddy's right hand found Carter's elbow and gripped it with the force of an extra-large plumber's wrench. Carter fought the urge to drop the hose and fight back with his hands, took a deep breath, and instead drove his right knee into the side of Paddy's head. The blow interrupted his momentum just enough for Carter to climb back up and retighten the loop around Paddy's neck.

Carter gave it a full two minutes, at the end of which he heard the click of Paddy's hyoid bone fracturing and felt a shudder in Paddy's legs. Carter relaxed his grip on the hose and paused, listening. The yard was quiet. Even the dog was still. Out front, a car drove past with what sounded like a game on the radio. Carter waited until the car passed and then, working from experience, took a series of breaths to calm his heart rate. Relaxed, he checked Paddy for a pulse. Satisfied after a thirty-second count that nothing was there, he stood, pulled out his Beretta, cradled the whimpering dog in his left arm, and climbed the back stairs.

Thirteen minutes to go.


*Funny thing was, despite strict prohibitions against it, Carter might have been better off freelancing the Madden investigation after all. He knew that's how it would go in the movies. Aggrieved officer takes matters into his own hands and metes out justice of his own making. Personal vendetta trumps agency policy every time.*

*Not for him. This would be by the books. Would have to be. They had to get it right.*

*The day after encountering Earl Madden at Tony's, Carter arrived at the office early and requested a meeting with his supervisor. He filled him in on what he knew. No, there was no question. Snyder confirmed it after Carter left the bar ninety minutes after entering it, Madden clapping him on the back to cement their agreement to get together soon.*

*"That was the guy," Snyder squeaked, teeth clicking from the cold as Carter started the engine and cranked the heat. "I told you."*

*"Stay down."*

*"You believe me now?"*

*"I said, stay down."*

*Carter was off the case immediately. A, because he was in an ethically compromised position, and B, because the investigation was screwed if Madden caught wind of Carter sniffing around any further. It was bad enough he'd been the one to make the ID at Tony's. He might face discipline yet for taking that field trip to the bar, since Snyder's initial tip involved his father's case. For now, though, he was out of the picture. On the sidelines.*

*That was fine with Carter. Well, not really. The rage he'd felt welling inside since Madden walked into Tony's and Carter realized the depth of the betrayal by the man he considered a family friend was smoldering like unvented lava, ready to explode at a moment's notice. But he tamped it down, because that's what professionals did.* Cool Carter. *Nailing Madden was all that mattered. Whatever it took. And it was going to be complicated, because surveillance had to be set up, package traces launched, sealed search warrants for phone access applied for. This wasn't an overnight job. It was going to take patience, something Carter specialized in.*

*Which, in the end, is how he almost missed the crunch.*

*Two nights later. Two nights after Tony's. Pulling into his garage just past six thirty* P.M. *Night long fallen. A day spent on paperwork, double-checking details on an insurance fraud case in Irondequoit. Denied official access to progress on the Madden investigation but filled in on the sly by sympathetic colleagues. Not satisfied with the already glacial pace but knowing it was the right way to proceed. Preoccupied as he exited the garage and opened the door to the backyard and the walkway leading past the old maple to the back steps of his prewar bungalow.*

*Preoccupied, and so the crunch registered a second late. Under normal circumstances, that might have been it. Say what you will, a second is long enough for a lot of things to happen, many of them bad. But it wasn't a normal night. Which is to say, it was normal, but in a fashion that tipped the scales Carter's way. Because it was Rochester. It was February. It was cold and it was snowing. The air was still in the backyard. The resident squirrels asleep, the rat problem of the fall dealt with. Nothing should be crunching.*

*Carter didn't bother locating the noise. His training, his instincts, whatever, taught him that much. Look and lose time. He took two enormous strides forward and threw himself behind the oak just as the first shot went off. Then a second, then a barrage. The slightest tremors as the oak absorbed the onslaught. As the shots continued, snow being jarred from branches joined the flakes in the air to create a fine, gauzy curtain between Carter and the garage.*

*When the shots stopped, Carter paused for a split second, satisfied himself the assault was over, spun around, sighted the shooter crouched in the shadows, and returned fire. The man toppled into the snow with a groan. Carter retreated behind the tree. Five seconds passed. Ten. Twenty. The groans grew quieter, more spaced out. At last, satisfied the threat had passed, Carter inched back around the tree.*

*A boom.*

*Splintering, blinding pain.*

*Darkness.*

Inside, standing in Art Wheeler's Lincoln Park kitchen, Carter paused at the jumble of sounds coming from around the corner. Living room, he guessed. He tried to gauge what was happening. A woman sobbing and wailing. Not Rachel, though. Someone older. Then: a man's guttural gasps, not unlike gasps Carter heard outside a couple of minutes earlier. But not from Finn, as far as he could tell. Art Wheeler, probably, which wasn't good.

Carter hated to do it, but he set the dog down on the blue tile floor and nudged it forward with his right foot. The dog yelped but didn't need the prompt. It limped quickly away from Carter and toward the living room. Carter followed, gun raised.

Chaos greeted him as he rounded the corner. Finn was standing, an odd look in his eyes, staring at the dog as it nuzzled its head against the calf of an older, white-haired woman on the couch. Carter couldn't get a good look at her because she was struggling despite her bound hands to support a heavyset man leaning toward her at an angle, sweat pouring down his white face. Rachel Stanfield sat in a chair beside Finn, her face nearly as white as the man on the couch.

"The fuck," Finn said, eyes growing wide as he stared at Carter.

"You're alive," Rachel said at almost the same moment.

It was all she was able to say. Finn dragged her to her feet in a single, smooth motion, and placed the muzzle of his gun under her chin. The funny look on his scarred face was gone, but no amount of posturing could disguise the surprise in his eyes.

"Paddy," Finn said, his voice a command.

"He's not coming," Carter said.

"Glenn," Rachel said. "Is he—"

She gagged before she could finish, the skin on her throat puckering white from the warning thrust of Finn's gun.

"Please," the woman on the couch said, as the man beside her—Wheeler?—groaned and his eyelids fluttered. "Please help him."

"What the hell are you doing here?" Finn said to Carter, glancing nervously to his right as if still expecting Paddy to reappear.

"I already told you. I have a delivery to make." He gestured at Rachel with his gun. "I'm just trying to do my job here."

"Bullshit. How did you find me?"

"I didn't find you. I found her." He almost left it at that, then added: "Glenn and I found her."

Finn was speechless for a moment. Rachel's eyes widened and she looked about to speak. But Carter, aware of the situation's urgency, stared her into silence.

He glanced at his watch.

Eleven minutes to go.

"You're lying," Finn said. "You're lying about Glenn."

"Maybe," Carter said. "Maybe Glenn's dead and Paddy's the one who's going to walk back inside in a second or two. Happy to wait if you want."

"*Paddy*," Finn said.

No answer.

On the couch, Art Wheeler's mouth opened and closed like a fish on ice.

"Please," Mrs. Wheeler said.

"Thoughts?" Carter said.

"Okay," Finn said at last.

"Okay what?"

"I don't know who the fuck you are, or what you're up to. Deliveryman my ass. But I'm willing to work things out with you. Settle this once and for all. But you've got a decision to make."

"Which is?"

"Her or him."

"Him?"

"That lying tub of lard on the couch." Finn nodded at Wheeler. "I'm guessing he's got two, three minutes left, tops. Without assistance. So you can follow me and we'll work something out, or you can stay and save him. Your call."

"Please," Rachel said. "They've got Abby—"

She gagged again at the upthrust of Finn's gun.

"You took the girl?" Carter said. "Really?"

"Make up your mind."

"This is very inconvenient. I need to make this delivery."

"Then make it," Finn said, backing out of the room as Rachel coughed, choking from the pressure of the muzzle against her throat. "I'll be waiting outside."

# FOURTEEN

*D*arkness.
*Carter opened his eyes.*

*A flash of memory. Evening. Exiting his garage. Snow. A crunch. A tree. The boom of gunfire.*

*He raised his head and examined his surroundings.*

*A room bathed in gray light. A machine by Carter's side, blurred numbers and letters on screens, beeps. An opened curtain. A sink. A cart.*

*A figure in a chair in the corner.*

*More memories. Returning fire. Waiting. Waiting. Silence.*

*Glancing around the tree.*

*Boom.*

*Carter closed his eyes.*

*Darkness.*

Carter stood, frozen in place, weighing his options.

Nine minutes to go.

His first inclination was to chase after Rachel. Sorry, Mr. Wheeler, but the delivery trumped everything. He'd never missed one. He had a reputation to keep in mind, not to mention a business to run. People didn't hire him to try to deliver stuff. That wasn't why he'd gotten into the business.

Carter was also pretty sure he'd come out on top in a confrontation with Finn. He could end the threat, hand the package to Rachel, have her sign the invoice, hand her the receipt—that part was for show, but customers liked it—escort Glenn from his Suburban, and be on his way. Louisville out of the question tonight, but maybe make it back to Indy and a hotel and an early start tomorrow. Considering all that, the calculus was clearly in favor of Rachel.

"Please," the woman on the couch begged. "Do something."

Eight minutes to go.

The problem with calculus was the number of moving parts involved. Well, not parts, exactly. Formulas. Derivatives. Equations. X here, Y there. Outcomes change depending on input. Tomeka was better at math by a long shot—obviously—but he caught the drift. Up until five minutes ago, the information at hand seemed straightforward. Rescue Rachel Stanfield, deliver package, drive to Louisville. Now Carter had new data to consider.

Art Wheeler, dying on the couch. That was bad enough. But it was another piece of information that had Carter's mind turning. Rachel's strangled cry. *They have Abby.* That meant Finn had a new card to play. He had leverage. He could tell Carter, sure, take Rachel. She's all yours. I'm going to kill her stepdaughter in return, but go ahead and make your delivery.

Technically, that wasn't Carter's problem. Saving children wasn't in his prospectus. But the dilemma, if that's what you called it, raised two additional points. One, he was pretty sure his uncle would see it differently. And make his opinion known, and not quietly. And two, and more to the point, he knew Rachel wouldn't surrender to him as long as Finn had Abby. So the whole thing was moot anyway.

"Please," the woman gasped.

Seven minutes to go. Carter looked in the direction where Finn and Rachel disappeared. And swung into action.

He retrieved the utility knife from its vest pocket and cut the woman's bonds, then Wheeler's.

"Help me get him on the floor."

They worked together to ease the man off the couch and onto the thick, red-patterned area rug. Carter straddled Wheeler and began chest compressions.

"You're Mrs. Wheeler?"

She nodded, hand on her mouth.

"If he has medicine for this, get that first and bring it here, and then call 911," he said between compressions. "Call it in as a heart attack, but don't mention the men who were here."

"Why in God's name not?"

"Sorry, I wasn't clear. Don't mention the men who were here to the dispatcher. If you do, there's a chance the paramedics will wait for the police to arrive and clear the scene. Standard operating procedure. Usually a good idea. Except in this case it might be too late for your husband. For the record, you're safe now. There's no danger anymore. Of course, tell the EMTs right away about what happened. You might also suggest they check the backyard."

The woman stared at Carter as if he had materialized in the room and begun speaking to her in another language.

"Ma'am? The medicine?"

A moment later she nodded and stumbled out of the room. Carter felt the dog beside him as it tried to rest its head on Wheeler's chest. He gently brushed it away. Carter ignored the heaviness in his arms from the effort it had taken with Paddy and worked until he saw color return to Wheeler's face at the same moment the lawyer began breathing more normally. A second later, the woman reappeared, a plastic vial clutched in her left hand as she pressed a cell phone to her right ear.

"Tell them he's stable," Carter said. "I think he'll be fine."

"Who are you?"

Carter didn't respond right away, thinking she was speaking to a dispatcher. When she repeated the question, he looked up.

"Just a mailman, ma'am. I'm sorry you got caught up in this. I have to go now. I need to find Ms. Stanfield."

"What did she mean, they have Abby?"

"It means I really need to get going." At that moment, Carter realized he'd made a miscalculation a few minutes earlier. An error in judgment he was now regretting. *Shoot.* This was going to complicate things at the worst possible moment.

Four minutes to go.

"Real quick," Carter said. "Did your husband say anything about someone named Stella Wolford? Any idea where she might be?"

"They kept asking about her. Why?"

"I'm not sure. But anything he said might help me find Rachel."

Mrs. Wheeler knelt with difficulty beside her husband. She struggled with the pill bottle, her trembling hand unable to open it. Carter took the vial and twisted the lid. Carefully she reached in, found a pill, and placed it in her husband's mouth.

Carter waited what felt like an eternity, then asked, "Anything?"

"Something about Danville. That's all I know."

"Danville, Illinois?"

"I'm guessing, yes."

Carter reached the Suburban as Glenn was lifting the cell phone out of the dashboard holder. Carter opened the driver's side door and said, "Stop."

"You said twenty minutes. Time's up."

"It's not necessary now. Help's on the way." He heard the wail of a siren in the distance. At least he remembered to tell Mrs. Wheeler not to mention the home invasion over the phone. It almost made up for his mistake when they arrived on the street.

"Where's Rachel?"

"Finn took her."

"You didn't rescue her?"

"The situation evolved. Some things happened I wasn't expecting. And now Finn has a little problem we need to take care of." He started the SUV and pulled onto the street.

"Which is?"

"He and his men have your daughter."

Glenn snapped his head around to face Carter. "What?"

"Best guess, they snatched her at the theater as collateral. So next step is getting her back."

"The theater? What—how did they know she was there?"

"Not sure, but we're not dealing with amateurs here. It's the kind of thing they might make a point of knowing. It's not worth worrying about now."

Glenn reached over and grabbed Carter's right arm, and for a second it was all Carter could do to keep the steering wheel steady. "For God's sake, what are we going to do about Abby?"

"Like I said, we're going to get her back. But we have to move fast."

Glenn released Carter and rocked back and forth, saying his daughter's name over and over. He was silent for a moment and then shouted at Carter. "Why in the world would you say we have a *little* problem?"

"I didn't say that."

"You just said—"

"I didn't say *we* had a little problem. I said Finn does."

# FIFTEEN

L ike most cops, Detective Rosa Jimenez prided herself on having seen it all and then some. Take the guy whose wife got tired of all the slaps and punches, slipped him a Mickey in the hot tub one night, and cranked the temperature well past "slide off the bone" hot. *Yeah, I'll give you that one. But first, let me tell you about my double homicide with both vics decapitated and the heads switched to the opposite bodies.* So, there's that.

Still, standing on the backdoor steps, watching the forensic guys get to work, trying to put herself in the shoes of whoever had done whatever happened here, Jimenez was struggling to rank this one. It didn't come close to the top hundred messiest crime scenes she'd attended. Only one victim as far as they knew. But still. What the hell. Nothing was adding up.

Sure, a home invasion at an address like this was rare. You caught a break-in at a brownstone this tony, it tended to be a burglary, part of a pattern by a team working the area, maybe stretching their boundaries up from the Gold Coast. Generally while the homeowners were away for the night or, better yet, the weekend. Remotely hacking the wireless alarm system all the rage now. Give her three deadbolts and a German shepherd any day. All that said, a forced-entry robbery with guns wasn't unheard of, even here.

Except that hadn't happened. At least not exactly. According to the first uniform on the scene, who got it from the first EMT inside, who heard it from the wife of the man found on the floor in respiratory distress from an apparent heart attack, two men had walked in, right behind a female subject known to the victims. A lawyer, even. Only after that did the guns come out.

Easy enough to sort through, except nobody was here. The wife was with her husband at the hospital, having threatened bodily harm if she wasn't allowed inside the ambulance with him. Jimenez had the names—Art and Gail Wheeler—but not a whole lot else about them. No sign of the female subject who presented herself at the door, who-ever she was. One of the two bad guys—if that's who they were—was also gone, while the other was permanently face down in the backyard. A dog, slightly injured, was cowering on the couch in the living room. Jimenez was left with an empty brownstone—except for the dog—and ten million questions.

Starting with: Who was the dead redheaded giant with a garden hose around his neck?

Moving on to: Why was the Wheelers' dog limping?

And concluding with: Who was the third guy she was hearing about from the uniforms via the EMTs, via Gail Wheeler?

This last detail was proving especially hard to square. From what Jimenez could gather via the shards of information dumped in her lap after she arrived, the third guy somehow saved the day. Or something. Had appeared as if by magic just when things looked the most dire. As far as Jimenez could tell, his appearance coincided with the demise of the giant. The guy then chased off the remaining bad guy and saved Art Wheeler's life by doing a damn good set of chest compressions. The same mystery man also instructed Mrs. Wheeler—this particular point fascinated Jimenez—to not mention the home invasion when she called 911 to avoid a police response that might delay the arrival of medics. Who did that?

Here was the other thing. Mrs. Wheeler managed a vague description of the bad guy who seemed to be in charge, including a scar on his cheek. But what caught Jimenez's attention was the description she gave of the mystery man. Rough, admittedly, since it came to the detective from the uniform from an EMT. But also curious: "Nondescript, wearing a baseball cap, on the short side."

On the short side?

Jimenez eyeballed the body stretched along the brick walk just past the back steps. Hard to estimate height without getting on her knees with a tape measure, but she was going with six three or six four. Freckled neck wide as a bank column, arms thick as stacked two-by-fours. Not the most chiseled guy she'd ever seen, but his weight would have worked to his advantage in a fight, of which she was guessing there'd been more than a few based on the scars on his knuckles.

So if this wasn't an accident, if he didn't slip and break his neck—right—then what? Mystery man took this guy out? With a garden hose? A man described as on the short side and wearing a baseball cap got one over on someone who looked like he'd give most bouncers nightmares? Who was the guy? For that matter, who was the giant? And who was the other bad guy, the one with the scar? And what about the lawyer lady who accompanied the two bad guys in?

*I mean, what the heck is going on here?* Jimenez thought.

# SIXTEEN

Carter shifted in his wheelchair, rolling his uncle's question around in his head, curious the response it would get. He didn't have long to wait.

"Well, while there's a lot we know about TBI now, especially after Iraq and Afghanistan, everything we learned at Walter Reed, there are still unkowns. Outcomes and reactions vary widely. And, being blunt, long-term prognoses are all over the map."

Carter's brain surgeon. Dr. Priya Thakkar. Six weeks out consultation, in her sunny, houseplant-forward office at Strong Memorial. TBI: traumatic brain injury. Which Carter had, putting it mildly. Carter in the wheelchair he didn't really need anymore but tolerated for these visits. His mother and his uncle beside him.

He'd been lucky, to say the least. The bullet fired by the dying shooter passed through Carter's right frontal lobe tip, missing most brain tissue and major blood vessels. Thanks to neighbors who heard the shots and called 911, he was in the ER with an external ventricular drain helping reduce swelling inside thirty minutes. After a week of acute care, he'd been declared out of the woods. Nevertheless, Dr. Thakkar warned, he faced a long and uncertain road to neurological recovery, with some permanent deficits possible.

His uncle glanced at Carter, another question on his lips, hesitation in his eyes. Carter nodded.

"So the . . ."

He stopped.

"Yes?" Dr. Thakkar said.

*"Well, long-term, we know some damage might be permanent. The cognitive stuff you mentioned. Motor control and all that."*

*Dr. Thakkar sat patiently, waiting for a question.*

*Carter's mother jumped in. "What Dean is trying to say, is that Mercury doesn't always seem like his old self."*

*"That's to be expected. Especially so soon after the event."*

*"Beyond that, though."*

*"Beyond that how?"*

*Before his mother could reply, Carter said slowly, "What she's trying to say is that she's worried I'm becoming a Yankees fan."*

*"That would certainly be cause for concern," Dr. Thakkar said, smiling.*

*Carter's mother pressed on. "Is there anything specific we should be on the lookout for? Anything we haven't covered?"*

*"Like what?"*

*Carter cleared his throat. Slowly, focusing on each word, he said, "What my mother and my uncle want to know is whether TBI can produce autism-like symptoms. Which they think I'm exhibiting."*

*Carter's mother reddened. His uncle stared at his feet. But neither objected to the statement.*

*Dr. Thakkar laced her fingers together and propped her hands on her desk.*

*"Not to worry. It's a common enough question, so you shouldn't be afraid to ask it. The short answer is no."*

*"That's a relief," Carter's uncle said.*

*Dr. Thakkar paused a moment, then said, However, the longer answer is more complicated. There are degrees to which TBI can in fact mimic symptoms of autism, especially when it comes to attention span, speech patterns, regulation of emotions, things like that. Mimic, but not cause. There's absolutely no evidence of causation."*

*Carter's uncle and his mother exchanged glances.*

"Is there a concern?" Dr. Thakkar said.

Carter's uncle said, "His, well, affect sometimes seems different." He turned to Carter. "Sorry, Merc. I don't mean to talk about you in the third person."

"Merc says it's okay," Carter said.

"Different how?" Dr. Thakkar said.

"I'm not sure. Maybe more disassociated, if that's a word? But also, I don't know, more formal at times? Like he's always making a speech."

"My fellow Americans," Carter said.

His mother rested her hand on his left shoulder.

"Well, Mercury isn't"—Dr. Thakkar stopped and addressed Carter directly—"You may never be your old self, completely. Unfortunately. The injury you suffered, it was as bad as something can be that's still survivable, if that makes sense. The slightest difference in trajectory that night and . . ." She paused and took a breath. "Even though the outcome was positive, the recovery is still going to be long. It's possible you'll have cognitive deficits, or brain processing alterations, vision problems, or simple memory issues, for a long time, and they'll manifest themselves in different ways." She looked at Carter's uncle. "Like the disassociation or the speechmaking or"—she gave a small smile—"the Yankees. That's the bad news. The good news is that the brain is a remarkably adaptive organ. It can surprise us in a million ways. You've already surprised us, Mercury."

"You're welcome."

A few more minutes of conversation, Carter's uncle and mother offering their enthusiastic thanks to Dr. Thakkar, then off to physical therapy.

Despite the temporary awkwardness it created, Carter was glad his uncle and mother asked the question they did, because in and out of the fog of recovery, he'd wondered something along the same lines.

Something was different about him now, but exactly what was difficult to nail down. Like reaching for an object and encountering a shadow. Like *grasping for a name and finding nothing but blank space. But also like undertaking a series of rote brain-exercise tasks—memorizing playing cards, reciting US presidents—and finding the effort not just tolerable but, well, engaging.*

*It had been like that since he gained consciousness for good, a week after the surgery that saved his life.*

*A week after the shooting in his backyard.*

*A week after the shooter dispatched by Earl Madden came close to fulfilling his mission.*

*Or so the Rochester cops and the FBI and USPIS and the US Attorney's Office suspected.*

*Because when officers stormed Madden's house that evening, he was gone. Suitcase packed. Car missing. In the wind.*

*"Didn't even have the guts to kill himself and spare us the trouble of chasing him," Marcus Washington, the USPIS inspector who'd investigated Danny Carter's killing, whispered to Carter's uncle during a hospital room visit when everyone thought Carter was asleep.*

*Now, six weeks on, Carter's recovery in full swing, Madden still hadn't been found.*

*Three months in, nothing.*

*A year—radio silence.*

*A central mystery behind the death of Carter's father had been solved.*

*But to this day, the actor responsible for the killing of Danny Carter had melted away as thoroughly as the blood-stained snow in Carter's backyard the night everything changed, forever.*

"Okay," Carter said to Glenn. "Time to get real."

They were headed away from the zoo, toward DePaul, but not in a rush. He drove slowly, fighting the urge to speed, as he planned out a loop around the neighborhood. He figured Finn and Rachel had to be relatively close to the Wheelers' brownstone still, though because of the mistake he'd made he couldn't be sure. The bigger question was, where was Abby and who was she with?

"Meaning what?" Glenn said.

"The police."

"The police what?"

Carter stopped for a red light. He glanced at his passenger. "Here's how I see it. You've been home invaded, pistol whipped, nearly blown up, your house *has* been blown up, your wife's been kidnapped, your daughter's also been kidnapped, there's been a second home invasion, and yet you still haven't suggested the time has come to call the cops. So my question is, why not?"

Glenn stared out the car window, his lips twitching as he formulated a response that didn't come.

"The thing is," Carter continued, "you don't seem like a guy with warrants hanging over his head. If you had large amounts of drugs or illegal weapons hidden in your house, I didn't see them. Same with funny mounds in the backyard. So that leaves something else. Work, I'm guessing. Something about that vaccine? A way to prevent addiction? I'm thinking that would attract a lot of interested parties. Might be a heap of trouble there just based on stuff I read in the news."

The light changed. Carter drove through the intersection. Glenn nodded.

"You nodded," Carter said.

Glenn nodded again.

"What does that mean?"

What felt like an eternity passed. Carter pegged it at almost half a minute, which was close.

"It means I'm in trouble."

Relief in Glenn's voice, as if finally relaxing after carrying a great weight.

"What kind?"

"Financial."

"You owe money."

"No. That's the problem."

"The problem is you don't owe money?"

"In a manner of speaking. The problem is, I have money. So much money. That's why I can't call the cops."

Maybe Glenn could argue he'd been tricked. At least at first. That the initial requests to review the execution of a complicated trust were exactly why he worked in Xeneconn's general counsel's office. Just because a financial transaction looked unorthodox didn't make it illegal. He'd touched on that very point in a contracts class in law school. If they taught it at the University of Chicago, it must be true. Well, the unorthodox angle was accurate up to a point. It was also accurate that once Glenn figured out what was really happening, he could have raised a red flag. It would have meant his job, which in hindsight seemed preferable to his current situation.

In his defense, Glenn played along in a desperate gambit to try to fix things. Make them right. Which of course he couldn't. Because he just got in deeper and deeper. More and more entangled. And eventually, scared. Which was why he bought the gun. And hid it. And didn't tell Rachel.

Yeah, he could argue it wasn't his fault. All the way to divorce court and a prison cell.

Of course, that was assuming he made it through the night alive.

Carter took a left and headed south. He glanced at the red flashing light on his phone screen indicating Finn's van. Stationary now for ten minutes.

Dumb. Dumb. Dumb.

He turned to Glenn. "How much money?"

"I can't—"

"Don't mess around. The lives of two people you love are at stake."

Glenn's head dipped and his shoulders sagged.

"Around $20 million."

Carter did his best to hide his surprise. "You have $20 million dollars?"

"Access to it. But yes."

"That's why you're in trouble."

Glenn confirmed it.

"It's money the cops can't know about."

"That's right."

"And it's worth endangering Rachel and Abby for. It's that bad?"

"No. It's not like that. You're right—I'm not thinking straight. I would never do anything to hurt them. Ever."

Carter wondered if that were strictly true, if only from a benign neglect standpoint. But instead of raising the issue, he said, "Is that what this is all about? Finn's using Rachel to get to your money?"

"That's what I thought at first. As soon as the men came inside. I'm not so sure now. All they seemed to care about was this lady. Stella Wolford. I don't know why. And Rachel didn't either—I swear."

"Do they know you have that much money?"

"Not the specific amount. I mean, they know there's a lot. That was one of the things they . . ." He clapped his hands over his eyes. "That was one of the things they were going to do in the basement. Get my banking information."

"How did they know about it?"

Glenn explained about his last-second begging, his offer of millions for his and Rachel's lives.

"Would you have given it to them?"

"Of course. It's just at that point, the things they said, I didn't think it would make a difference. It felt like we were dead either way. Until you showed up."

"Does Rachel know about it? The money?"

Glenn hung his head again. "She does now. She didn't before."

Carter considered this development. It had been a very odd evening, with no sign of things letting up.

He said, "Why do you have $20 million dollars you couldn't tell your wife about and the cops can't know of?"

"I can't tell you."

"You're not serious."

"You don't understand. I could go to prison. We'd be ruined."

"Feels like you're choosing not going to prison over your family's well-being."

Glenn didn't get a chance to answer. Carter's uncle called at that moment.

"Everything all right, Merc?"

Carter filled him in.

"That's low, taking the girl," his uncle said. "All right. I'll check the Chicago scanners, see what's up. And see what I can find out about Danville. Hang tight."

After he disconnected, Carter said to Glenn, "This money you can't talk about. What kind of access do you have?"

"What do you mean?"

"How quickly could you get to it? Either in cash or a bank transfer."

"Not quickly. It's protected by a lot of layers." He made a face. "Thanks to me."

"So not a few minutes kind of thing."

"Definitely not. Hours, maybe. Possibly. Depending on a bunch of factors."

Carter pulled over on a residential street beside a large oak, midway between pools of light spilling from two streetlamps. He did some math in his head. He sat for nearly three minutes without speaking.

"What's going on?" Glenn said at last.

"Quiet."

Two minutes later Carter settled on it. Not perfect, not by a long shot, but it was all they had. It was risky to say the least. But the alternatives didn't bear thinking about. Without saying anything, Carter took his phone, found the number for Glenn's daughter, and hit "call."

"What are you doing?" Glenn said.

"Testing a theory."

"A theory? About what?"

Carter didn't reply. A moment later they heard a man's voice as the call went through.

"Who is this?"

"It's Mercury Carter. I need to speak to Finn. I have something I think he'll want. But first I need to hear Abby's voice."

Silence over the line. Then the man's voice again, dry and thin, like a branch scraped across the road in winter. Gaunt Guy, Carter guessed.

"What is it?"

"Something important."

"You're bluffing. You have nothing."

"Maybe. But maybe on the other hand I'm sitting here with Abby's father who's willing to do anything to get his daughter back. Absolutely anything. And I'm guessing that that anything is something Finn wants to hear. And that he's going to be upset if he finds out later he wasn't told about it."

More silence. Carter waited patiently, imagining the man weighing his options, trying to figure out what to do.

"Tell me."

Carter nodded at Gaunt Guy's response. A good sign. Glenn looked at him, puzzled, but Carter just shook his head in return.

"I might. There's a good possibility I'll do that at some point. Because you're going to be interested in it as well. From a financial perspective, I mean. You seem like a smart guy. It takes a smart guy to snatch a girl on a class field trip to a downtown Chicago theater. I appreciate the skill that must have taken. One professional to another. But first I have to speak with Finn. The girl, then Finn. Then you."

A second passed. Three. Five. Still nothing. Glenn looked at Carter, desperation in his eyes. Carter looked back at him. And blinked. Seven seconds.

Ten.

"Dad?"

A girl's voice, small and weak.

Glenn lurched toward the phone. "Abby? Are you all right?"

"Satisfied?"

Gaunt Guy, back on the line.

"I appreciate you working with me," Carter said. "Now, Finn?"

It took almost a minute. A minute was a lot longer than the ten seconds before hearing Abby's voice, and that had been a very long time indeed. Carter wouldn't have ranked the minute they waited after Gaunt Guy hung up as among the favorite minutes in his life. Then, fifty-nine seconds in, his phone rang.

"The fuck."

Finn.

"Thanks for calling. I know you're busy. Been quite the evening." Carter paused. "Especially for Paddy. As a result I'll keep it short and sweet. I believe you figured out that Glenn has money. Figured out back at his house in Indy, I mean. So here's the deal. We're willing to offer ten million dollars for the safe return of Rachel and her daughter. No strings attached. You deliver them, we deliver the money, we all walk away."

Silence.

"One thing," Carter added. "If Rachel is already dead, I'll have to reconsider. Apologies, but it's a package deal."

Carter saw Glenn stiffen in his seat.

Finn didn't say anything. Carter waited. Glenn stared at Carter's phone so intensely Carter worried it might burst into flames. A few feet in front of them, a tiger cat blip-blip-blipped across the street, something struggling in its mouth.

"I'm alive," Rachel said, voice coming over the speaker.

"Thank God," Glenn said.

A moment later, Finn was back on the line.

"I don't know who the fuck you are, Carter, or what you're up to. But you must take me for an idiot. We do a meet, next thing I've got, what, black helicopters circling over me? Yeah, let's cut that deal in your dreams. So here's my counteroffer. You ever want to see Rachel or Abby in one piece again, you leave me the hell alone. I get what I want from Rachel, maybe—"

"Twenty million," Carter said. "Ten million each. No black helicopters. Untraceable funds. You walk away, we walk away. It will be like tonight never happened."

Silence over the phone. Lot of that going around, Carter thought.

"Finn?"

Nothing.

Carter waited for ten seconds. It felt almost as long as waiting to hear Abby's voice. Not quite, but close.

"Finn?"

Another ten seconds passed. No sound on the other end of the line. Twenty seconds more. Almost half a minute. The silence stretched on so long that Carter thought the connection had been cut.

Finn finally returned. But only briefly.

"Carter?"

"Yes."

"No deal," Finn said, and ended the call.

# SEVENTEEN

Beside Carter, Glenn burst into tears.

"Jesus Christ. You've killed Abby. And Rachel. You just condemned my family to death."

Carter focused on the street, giving Glenn a minute.

"You okay?" he said at last.

"Okay? Did you hear what I said?"

"I heard."

"And?"

"I think you're overreacting."

"Overreacting?" Glenn wiped tears from the non-bandaged side of his face. "Are you fucking kidding me? Not that I know what you're playing at, or who the hell you really are, but if Finn wouldn't take that much money, what value do their lives have? Zilch. I saw what kind of man he is, back at the house. I know what he's capable of. It's only a matter of time now. Unless—"

"Unless what?"

"Let's take it to him. He's down a man, right? We head for his van and just, I don't know, attack. You seem pretty good at that kind of stuff and I'll do my best."

The moment Carter had been dreading had arrived. He said, "We can't."

"Why not? Nothing's stopped you so far."

"We can't because I don't know where Finn is."

"Aren't you tracking him? Isn't that how we ended up in Chicago in the first place?"

"It is. But I made a mistake earlier. I slashed the tires on Finn's van. I thought Art Wheeler's would be the end point. That we'd resolve things there. I wanted to pinch off Finn's escape route. Obviously not. He ditched the van and now he's in the wind."

"Oh God. Then they really are dead."

Carter did his best to rally. "First of all, they're not dead. We just heard both their voices. Secondly, we've learned some important things."

"Name one."

"First, they're not together. The guy who has Abby is in a separate vehicle. We proved that when he didn't put Finn on right away. He had to call or text Finn, who then called me."

"But we have no idea where Finn is. Or Rachel."

"Not yet we don't. He'll show himself, trust me."

Glenn didn't look convinced. "C'mon. They could be anywhere."

"Negative," Carter said. "I'll get to that in a minute. The other thing we know, the most important thing of all, is that Finn's not in charge."

Glenn stared at him. "Not in charge? What are you talking about? I told you what happened at the house, before you came. And now you've dealt with him. You know what he's like. Bullshit he's not in charge."

Carter shook his head. He'd seen this kind of thing before, investigating gang operations when he still wore a badge. He just wasn't explaining it right. He said, "He's a troop leader, is all. A pretty good one, I'd say, except for the dog thing."

"The what?"

"He's got a thing about dogs. You could see it in his eyes when the Wheelers' schnauzer came into the room. Makes me wonder about that scar on his face."

"Forget that. What do you mean he's not in charge?"

"He's not the shot caller."

Glenn groaned. "Meaning what, for God's sake?"

"Think about what just happened. How long the line went quiet after I upped the ante to $10 million apiece. That's not Finn sitting there doing the math himself. He was texting someone. Texting or calling on another phone. He definitely muted us—the street sounds went away. He was running the proposal past his boss. Finn knew enough to take the offer seriously because of the way his plans have been altered tonight. He understood he couldn't discount me after, well, after all the stuff that's happened. Twenty million is a lot of money. He told someone all that. And whoever he talked to turned it down. Turned down $20 million. Which means whatever's going on, it's about more than money. And Finn doesn't have final say."

"But—"

"Both of which facts bode well for Rachel. At least for now."

Across the street, the door of a beige Dutch Colonial opened. A man looked out, his eyes settling on Carter's Suburban. Without making eye contact, Carter pulled away from the curb.

"Where are we going?" Glenn said.

Carter looked at him as if he hadn't heard correctly.

"Where else? To get Abby."

Carter drove two streets over and parked again, this time on a small business strip across from a pizza restaurant with the lights still on.

"Okay," Carter said. "You've got $20 million dollars you can't touch without some heavy lifting. What about your checking account? Or savings? How much in those?"

"I told you, they took my wallet."

"Forget the wallet. Just answer the question."

"I'm not sure—maybe six, seven thousand. Between checking and savings."

"Does Abby have an account linked to yours? And her own bank card?"

"Yes. But only for emergencies. She has to get permission for any purchases. She has a separate school account for buying snacks, toiletries, things like that."

Carter reached behind him and retrieved a black carrying bag. He looked inside, debated, and removed one of three laptops. He handed it to Glenn.

"I need you to log into your account and transfer five thousand dollars to Abby. Can you verify your identity without them sending a text to your phone?"

"I set up security questions, so yes. But why—"

"Do it. We don't have much time." He opened the driver's side door.

"Where are you going?"

"To get dinner. I'm hungry."

Ignoring Glenn's protests, Carter crossed the street, went into the pizza place—Corrigan's Chicago-Style Pizza—and stood at the counter. While he waited to be served he read the hand-lettered cardboard sign propped against a glass bowl holding donations for Lion's Club vision care. *Driver needed. Car provided. Ask about signing bonus.*

A lady appeared from the back. "Help you?"

Carter ordered two medium deep dishes with sausage and sweet peppers to go, paid for them with cash, and said that rather than stand there and wait, he'd be right back, that he was just sitting over there parked.

"Okay," the lady said.

"Done," Glenn said, as Carter climbed into the driver's seat.

Thirty seconds later Carter had Gaunt Guy back on the line.

"Look, Carter, I told Finn to call—"

"Listen carefully. We just deposited five thousand dollars into Abby's bank account. She can use her phone to verify it. That money's yours. You want it in cash, you may have to hit a few ATMs. Or maybe Abby can Venmo it to you. I'll let the two of you work that out. But she has our permission to give it to you. Five thousand dollars, free and clear."

The slightest pause before Gaunt Guy responded, which told Carter all he needed to know.

"What the hell are you talking about?"

"Think of it as a good-faith payment, in hopes that you'll treat her well. But I want to be clear here, it's not ransom. That's not money we're offering for Abby. The money's yours whether we ever see her again." Next to Carter, Glenn gasped. Carter ignored him and said, "Yours and whoever else you're with. It's sitting in her account right now, waiting for you."

Silence filled the line. Nearly a minute passed.

"All right," Gaunt Guy said when he returned. "I see the money. I can get to it. So what?"

What was it Gaunt Guy said when Carter called back just now? *Look, Carter, I told Finn to call—*

He hadn't spoken to Finn since Carter had.

"Focus on good-faith payment," Carter said. "Your money, no strings attached. Not ransom. But here's the situation. We do have ransom money available. Ten million dollars. We offered it to Finn. He turned it down, just so you know. Actually, that's not right. He turned down $20 million, since we were offering ten each. Ten for Abby, ten for Rachel. He didn't get a good-faith payment, by the way."

Gaunt Guy didn't say anything.

"Now we have $10 million dollars for Abby that we don't know what to do with. So I'm presenting you with the option. Ten million for Abby."

"You're being serious?"

"Hundred percent. But before you respond, you need to think about a couple of things."

"Like what?"

"Like I said before, you're a smart guy. I admire how you pulled this off. As I'm sure you know, however, being smart and everything, we're not operating in a vacuum here. Teenage girls don't disappear from field trips to downtown Chicago without repercussions. Alarm bells go off. Maybe you got a head start if you grabbed her on her way to the bathroom or something. Ten, fifteen, twenty minutes and nobody paid attention. But someone's noticed by now. Someone's called the cops. Someone's checking cameras. Maybe you're good enough that you dodged the cameras. Can you be absolutely sure, though? There's a lot of cameras these days."

Nothing on the other end of the line. But the call hadn't been cut, either.

"And the thing is," Carter continued, "the world isn't fair. Not in the least. The fact is, a girl from Bellbrook Academy who goes missing on a field trip to downtown Chicago is going to attract a lot of attention. A whole lot. And that attention isn't stopping tonight. And if something happens to that girl, there's going to be consequences. Remember, I'm just a delivery guy. Nobody special. If I'm talking to you, the cops probably aren't far behind."

"What do you want, Carter?"

"Don't take this personally. But I don't want you. You can walk away from this and you'll never hear from me again. I'm not a vengeful person. I just want the opportunity to pay you $10 million dollars for Abby. Finn wouldn't take it. That's his choice. Maybe you have a different perspective. Maybe you'd like a new opportunity. Work for yourself. Be your own boss. Whatever floats your boat. You can run all this past Finn if you want. Or not. I just want you to have the option. Ten million dollars."

A long pause.

"Cash?"

"Cash tonight? Not a chance. I'm not a miracle worker. But a bank transfer that can't be tracked? Or crypto? Your choice. We meet, you give us Abby, we move eight figures into your account."

"Prove it."

"You need more proof than the five thousand dollars I just handed you?"

"Don't take me for a fool, Carter. You have five minutes to prove you have access to that amount of money. After that, I can't make any promises about the girl."

Gaunt Guy cut the call before Carter could respond. He turned to Glenn, trying to ignore the look of affliction on his face.

"Well?" Carter said.

"Well what?"

"Can you prove you have the money?"

"Of course I can't. That's the whole problem. It's shielded twelve different ways. It's—"

"Think. Any documentation. Put your mind to it. Stop thinking about yourself for a change and think about your daughter."

"How dare you—"

"Focus. A bank account number. An email. One of those, what do you call it—apostilles. A receipt. Routing digits. Anything."

"Apostilles?"

Carter thought for a second, going back to USPIS days. "It's a form of international certification. Required for signers of the 1961 Hague Convention—"

"I know what apostilles are. How do you?"

"Long story. Well?"

"It's a possibility. I can check."

"A possibility? How about, Abby could have less than five minutes to live if you don't produce."

Glenn opened his mouth and shut it just as quickly. He bowed his head over the laptop.

Carter let Glenn work. He surreptitiously glanced at his watch. Three minutes left.

Two minutes.

One.

"How's it going?"

"Almost."

Thirty seconds.

"Glenn?"

"Got it." He hesitated. "You were right. There's an apostille. I had to file one early on before before everything went south."

Carter gave Glenn instructions for sending the document to him, then dialed Gaunt Guy back on Abby's number.

"Well?"

"I'm about to send you a text."

"Of what?"

"The proof you need."

He sent the text. The phone went quiet. While they waited, Carter said to Glenn, "You have the passwords memorized for that account? Or is it all security questions?"

"Both."

"I'm impressed."

"Don't be. It's a stupid party trick. Passwords, birthdays, family cell phones. Fat lot of good any of it has done me. Rachel barely knows any of that stuff. But she's a far better person than me."

Carter let that one go. He was focusing on the time. Nearly a minute had passed.

Glenn, shifting in his seat, said, "What if he doesn't—"

"Carter?"

Gaunt Guy.

"Yes."

"There's a park. North of the zoo. Boat launch. Fifteen minutes. I'll have the girl. Be ready to make the transfer."

Glenn glanced at Carter, waiting for him to respond. Carter just stared out the window.

"Carter?" Gaunt Guy said.

Carter didn't respond.

"Did you hear what I said?"

"Ten million dollars," Carter said, and cut the line. He placed the phone in a right-hand pocket on his utility vest and opened the car door.

"What are you doing?" Glenn said.

"Picking up our pizzas."

"Are you crazy? We need to get going."

"I already paid for them. Plus, I'm starving and I bet you are too. We need our strength. To be ready."

"To get Abby?"

Carter stared at him blankly.

"For Abby? No."

"Then what?"

"For the trap they're about to set."

# EIGHTEEN

As Finn dragged Rachel down the front steps of the Wheelers' brownstone she thought about using the nail then and there. Reaching into her pants and grabbing it and gouging it into an ear or an eye or into his neck. She burned to do it. But they weren't twenty seconds down the street when Finn stopped and grabbed her shoulders and looked into her eyes. Rachel expected to be terrified. Instead, she saw something there that gave her pause.

"I know what you're thinking," Finn said, seeing the look on her face. "You're thinking this is the time to try something. To run or to scream. Your moment to turn the tables. You're free to do so. But Stone and Vlad have their instructions, and they're clear. If they don't hear from me in regular intervals, or there's the faintest hint the cops have been called, they'll kill Abby. They won't ask for permission. They'll just do it. You'll never see her again. And her body will never, ever be found. I need you to understand that. If you cooperate, she'll be fine. Otherwise . . ." Finn released his grip long enough to draw a finger across his throat.

Plunge it into his eye. Lance the vein pulsing so prominently on the left side of his neck. Tear a new scar into his face.

"Rachel?"

All of a sudden she relaxed. She felt the rage drain from her like the release of relaxing from a long plank hold. For just a moment, a sense of profound calm filled her. The last thing she expected to feel.

"Rachel?"

She looked him in the eyes.

"You're scared," she said.

"What?"

Half a block down, hidden in a locust tree whose leaves were starting to yellow, a mourning dove cooed.

"You're scared of that guy. The mailman. Mercury Carter. I can see it."

"Shut up." He gripped her tighter. "I'm not kidding about Abby—"

"He tracked us here. You thought you killed him, him and Glenn, but he escaped. And found you. Whoever he is, he won't stop chasing you. You know it. And you don't know what to do about it."

"I know I'm going to kill you if you don't stop talking."

"Go ahead. I don't expect to survive the night. But you don't either, do you?" She stood as tall and straight as her fear and exhaustion allowed her and met his angry stare. "You thought you were the hunter. At my house. And at Art's. But that's not true anymore, is it? Now you're the one being hunted."

"Shut the fuck up," he said, jerking her roughly down the street.

And so she did. She went quiet. She stayed by Finn's side. She didn't run. She didn't use the nail. Because she meant what she said about assuming she would die. But also about the fate awaiting Finn. If her compliance could at least save Abby, all the better.

Instead, she followed. Stood still a moment later as Finn swore under his breath at the sight of the van's slashed tires. Listened to him make a terse call to the men who had Abby. Waited while he unloaded three bags from the van and then strode down the street, ignoring the *whoop-whoop* of an ambulance as it rumbled past, Rachel trailing helplessly in his wake. Kept quiet when, two blocks down, he did something to the door of a minivan, opened it and shoved her inside, and zip-tied her hands back together. Stayed mum when, ten minutes later, they pulled into the parking lot of a Trader Joe's, closed for the evening, and sat there without speaking for another ten minutes. Watched silently when Finn sat up at the sight of a car's lights appearing at the far end of the parking lot and fought the urge to scream as she saw the brute called Stone exit the car and walk toward them.

Which meant Abby was in that car.

A hundred yards away. Their daughter.

Her daughter.

Rachel kept quiet until Finn's phone rang again and she heard the voice of the deliveryman on the other end. Her eyes widened at the offer he was making, and when the time came, she gasped—at Finn's unspoken command—"I'm alive." A few minutes after listening to an odd, one-sided phone conversation Finn had with someone, she despaired and tried unsuccessfully to blink back the hot tears spilling from her eyes as she heard Finn call Carter back and say, "No deal." She gasped as Stone's giant hands forced her down onto the seat, below the windows, and he gagged her once more.

Which meant all she could do was whimper as she heard another call, and then Finn's cold voice say to Stone, "Make sure we get the money first. Then do the girl. Then Glenn. Then Carter. In that order."

"Got it."

"In that order," Finn said, turning around and glaring at Rachel. "I want Carter to understand the penalty for sticking his oar in. To see it with his own eyes. You understand?"

"Yes," Stone said.


Glenn said, "How do you know about cryptocurrency?"

"I'm sorry?"

"Before—you said you could transfer my money using cryptocurrency. Even I'm not sure how to do that."

Carter took another bite of pizza and chewed for a second.

"I have no idea. I just keep hearing about crypto on the news. I'm not even sure what it is, to tell you the truth. Something to do with the Internet, I think? I always imagine those little yellow cartoon dudes with the weird voices jumping around."

"Minions?"

"Those guys, yeah."

Glenn stared at him. "How is it you know about apostilles but not about cryptocurrency?"

Carter was gone from USPIS before they dealt with it in-depth, but he couldn't see the point of explaining that now. He said, "We need to focus on the situation at hand, all right?"

"Fine. But if you were bluffing about the transfer, how are we going to get the money to them?"

"We're not. I told you. It's a trap. They have no intention of making a trade."

"What about Abby?"

"What about her?"

"How are we going to rescue her if we don't pay the money?"

"You should eat," Carter said. "We need to get moving soon."

"Eat? While you sit there telling me we're walking into a trap? I mean, how can you even know that?"

"Stands to reason. Whoever's calling the shots nixed the idea of doing a big-dollar trade for Rachel and Abby. Which means they have a higher calling. Which means at least for now they need Rachel alive and under their control because of Stella Wolford, and they need Abby alive to keep Rachel cooperating. Our conditions have been rejected from on high. That doesn't mean Finn doesn't want the money. He's not an idiot."

"You think the guy who has Abby told Finn about the $10 million you offered him?"

"Hundred percent."

"Why?"

"He'll see it as a win-win proposition. Get the money and kill us, or more to the point, me. And maybe kill Finn if he's feeling greedy. But he knows he can't do it alone. Kill me, I mean."

"Why not?"

Carter adjusted the rim of his ball cap. "Because I've demonstrated the unlikelihood of him surviving such an encounter by himself."

"So what's your plan?"

"My plan is to make sure we don't get caught in a trap."

"But how?"

Carter told him.

"That's insane," Glenn said when he was finished. "You're crazy."

"Just do your part. And whatever you do, don't get out of the car when the time comes. No matter what happens. Do not get out of the car. That's very important." Before Glenn could reply, Carter moved into the back of the Suburban, found the duffel bag—the first one—with his change of clothes, and slipped into a green-and-blue patterned Hawaiian shirt, jeans, and red sneakers.

"What are you doing?"

"Be right back," Carter said, shutting the door and crossing the street.

"Everything okay?" the pizza lady said, recognition dawning on her harried face as Carter reentered in his new duds.

"Totally. Good pizza. Very tasty." He pointed at the help-wanted sign on the counter. "You still need a driver?"

"Like last week. You interested?"

"I'm interested."

"When can you start?"

"Right now."

The woman narrowed her eyes. She looked tired, hair askew, disheveled in worn jeans and a too-big Blackhawks sweatshirt. But she didn't look dumb. "Like, tonight?"

"Like, immediately."

She reached under the counter and retrieved a piece of paper. "Fill this out. Do you have a current driver's license?"

"Yes."

"Any felony convictions?"

"No."

Carter filled out the form to the best of his abilities.

"All right, Mr. Smith," the lady said, taking the paper from him. "Car's around the corner. Blue Honda Fit. Here's the keys." She slid them across the counter, walked to the oven, removed two pizzas, and boxed them. She put the boxes on the counter, slid them into an insulated bag, wrote something on a pad of paper, and handed the slip to Carter. "Two supremes. Tell him they're on the house because he had to wait so long. Don't speed if you can help it. About the signing bonus—"

"Keep it," Carter said, palming the keys, taking the pizzas, and walking out of the shop.

Carter and Glenn traveled in tandem to the park. Well, first to the apartment building half a mile in the other direction to deliver the two supremes. Good thing Carter had eaten already because even tucked inside their warmer, the smell of the pizzas filled the interior of the

Honda. Which Carter figured out pretty quickly was the car of the lady behind the counter based on the picture of her and a pint-sized boy in a Cubs uniform stuck to the dashboard.

The displeasure on the face of the mustachioed guy who answered the apartment door faded when Carter told him the pizzas were free, and he even managed to get over himself long enough to slip Carter a ten as a tip. Carter tucked the bill into his wallet, returned to the car, and slipped his Beretta into the warmer. He rolled down the window, gave Glenn the thumbs up, and then followed two or three car lengths behind the Suburban, sometimes letting a car edge in between them, sometimes not. It wasn't like Glenn would lose track of him with the lighted, two-foot-long Corrigan's Chicago-Style Pizza sign clamped with a magnet to the Fit's roof.

As Carter watched the Suburban disappear into the dark park, he found himself wishing he knew Chicago better. Problem was, he knew the basics, but not the details, which meant he could only back-of-the-envelope the amount of time it would take Finn to arrive to spring the trap. Assuming he hadn't already shown up and that Carter had just sent Glenn to his death. Which was also a possibility.

A moment later his phone buzzed with a text from Abby's phone.

Get out of the car with your hands where I can see them.

Gaunt Guy, thinking Carter was in the Suburban. Which meant Glenn was in place.

But not Finn.

Show me Abby, Carter texted.

You first.

Offer goes down $1 million every 10 seconds I don't see Abby. Your call.

Just over ten seconds later Carter's phone buzzed again. This time a text from Glenn from the burner phone Carter left with him.

I see her.

Do not get out of the car, Carter texted, and put the Fit into drive.

# NINETEEN

*Returning to duty had never been in question. As in, it wasn't happening. Even though, eighteen months on, Carter had made remarkable progress, his diagnosis—"gunshot-induced TBI"—and the accompanying medical records documenting his treatment weren't going to pass muster in the agency's Washington HR bureaucracy. That, plus the unofficial but ironclad determination by his superiors that he'd crossed a professional line going to Tony's bar that night and thus set the tragic events in motion, all but sealed his fate.*

*Carter summoned up as much indignation as he could muster when he was asked about it, by fellow inspectors, by the few college friends he kept in touch with, even by Tomeka Sims, the attractive and brainy accountant up the street now doing his taxes. What he left out of those explanations was an unspoken sense of, if not relief, inevitability. Having entered the service out of respect for an agency that pursued justice on behalf of his father, he understood instinctively that the personal betrayal he encountered in the form of Earl Madden, along with the feeling that he had done the right thing by going to Tony's, and would do it again, muted any desire to carry a badge again.*

*That, along with the deeply buried and never-voiced belief that it would be easier to hunt Madden on his own, unburdened by the strictures of administrative rules and regs.*

*Of course, that left the question of his livelihood. His medical bills were covered and he had a small pension. Thanks to Tomeka he kept his head above water. But that wasn't going to cut it in the long run.*

*In fact, it was Tomeka, sitting between him and his uncle at a Red Wings game he'd invited her and her teenage sons to (an invitation which, to his surprise, she quickly accepted), who suggested the idea of taking his life in a new, though familiar, direction.*

"Your father was a mailman. Why not you? I'm sure they'd take you on."

Carter considered the question, but not for long. "I'm not sure how my mom would feel about that."

"Well, they're not the only game in town. What about FedEx? UPS? Amazon?"

Carter waited for the Mud Hens centerfielder to nab a fly ball before replying.

"I don't think it's my vibe. I liked what I did at USPIS, even though I can't go back."

"Liked going after bad guys, you mean?"

Carter shrugged. "I liked the feeling of doing the right thing whether people appreciated it or not. Even when people were in my way."

He paused.

"Especially when they were in my way."

"A do-gooder, huh?"

"More like . . ." He thought about it for a second. He pointed toward home plate. "More like the way a backstop keeps bad things from happening to the people sitting behind it."

"Okay, then," Tomeka said with a laugh. "Let's check Monster.com for 'Human backstop.'"

That might have been that. The game went on. The Red Wings lost. Tomeka invited him to a church picnic the following week and he said why not.

Then his uncle called him four days later.

"What do you know about French bulldogs?"

*Carter thought about it. "Aren't those the ones that started out as English toy bulldogs and were bred with French ratters? They have those crazy ears? Other than that, not much."*

*A pause on the other end of the line. "Well, it also turns out they're valuable. A puppy can go for two-thousand bucks."*

*"Wow."*

*"They're valuable enough that people steal them. I mean, like at gunpoint. Look it up. It's happened several times."*

*"That's unfortunate. Why are you telling me this?"*

*"This woman at work. Her sister bought one from some lady in Erie. A breeder, I mean."*

*"Erie, Pennsylvania?"*

*"That's right. Problem is, she's afraid to pick it up. The sister, that is. She's a little, well, fragile."*

*"Sorry to hear that."*

*"Anyway, she's looking for someone to go get it. And she'll pay."*

*"How much."*

*"Five hundred dollars."*

*Carter's turn to pause.*

*"Five hundred dollars to drive to Erie and pick up a dog?"*

*"You got it. Interested?"*

*"Me?"*

*"Yeah, you. I was thinking about what that lady, Tomeka, was saying at the game the other day. She's cute, by the way."*

*"I guess."*

*"Actually, I was thinking more about your response."*

*"Which was?"*

*"How you said you liked the feeling of doing the right thing whether people appreciate it or not. Even when people were in your way."*

"*So?*"

"*So there might be people who want to get in the way of this lady picking up a $2,000 puppy.*"

*There weren't—that time, anyway. But Carter found the job, when he got around to deciding to take it, not half bad. Before the accident—before the shooting—he'd never liked driving long distances. Now, for whatever reason, he didn't mind at all. It relaxed him. He put his dented brain on autopilot and went. He made the round trip in six hours and fifteen minutes without incident, and happily pocketed the $500.*

*He was studying online job postings two days later—no sign of human backstop—when a man identifying himself as the French bulldog owner's second cousin called.*

"*I hear you deliver stuff. And that you have a gun.*"

"*Well—*"

"*Thing is, my grandfather just died.*"

"*Sorry to hear that.*"

"*He was what you call an Anglophile. Loved the Brits. Me, I don't get the attraction, but he was a great guy otherwise. Anyway, I was cleaning out his attic and came across a bunch of Sherlock Holmes stories. From something called* The Strand. *I did some checking and found out they're worth a lot. They're originals, apparently. I found a bookstore in Manhattan that'll buy them. Thirty-thousand dollars upon delivery.*"

"*Thirty-thousand dollars,*" *Carter said.*

"*No way in hell I'm shipping them. I'm not dealing with NYC traffic. And I've been reading stuff about rare book thieves. So how about this? I'll pay you $1,000 plus mileage for door-to-door delivery.*"

"*You said $1,000?*"

"*That's right.*"

Okay. NYC, here I come.

*On it went. In bits and pieces at first, then more regularly. An oil portrait—a family heirloom that needed shielding from an estranged and partially unhinged uncle—from Cleveland to Nashville. A laptop hiding compromising photos returned to a grateful woman before her jealous ex could upload them. Another bulldog, with Carter's Beretta—the display of it, anyway—coming in handy this time. Carter got busy enough that his uncle, a dispatcher for a trucking company, began moonlighting as his stationary backup and assistant.*

*All interesting, though not quite the backstop Carter was looking for.*

*Then came the call that changed his mind.*

*"Do you ever deliver people?"*

Carter turned off the Fit's lights, drove two hundred yards down the park road, and stopped. He climbed out, left the car door ajar, and crept the rest of the way on foot until he could see what was unfolding by the waterfront. It was even worse than he feared.

On one side of the parking lot sat a red Jeep. Gaunt Guy stood a few feet in front, illuminated by the Jeep's lights. Kneeling before him was a terrified Abby, her head yanked back and throat exposed from Gaunt Guy's left-handed grip on her black ponytail. His right hand held a gun jammed against the back of the girl's neck.

Approaching them, hands up, was Glenn.

He'd gotten out of the Suburban.

Except, seeing the look on Glenn's face as he saw his daughter's condition, Carter couldn't really blame him.

"Stop," he heard Gaunt Guy say.

Glenn stopped.

"Where the fuck is the mailman?"

To his credit, Glenn just stood there, speechless.

Carter turned and ran back to the Fit. He climbed in, started the engine, and drove the rest of the way into the parking lot. He drove slowly, like a student taking a first lesson behind the wheel. As Gaunt Guy stared in disbelief, Carter circled the lot, doing a wide sweep around the standoff, as if a man holding a girl with a gun to her head in a dark parking lot with the gray vastness of Lake Michigan pooling toward a blank horizon on their left was the kind of thing you saw every day on a pizza delivery. Because: Chicago.

Carter finished the circuit, an oblong three-sixty, and stopped the Fit so its position formed an isosceles triangle with the Jeep and the Suburban. He swapped his Red Wings cap for a Corrigan's Chicago-Style Pizza hat he found in the passenger footwell, pulled the brim below his forehead, reached for the insulated warmer, stepped out of the car, and faced Gaunt Guy and Abby.

"Hey—either of you guys order a pizza? Sausage and mushroom, extra cheese? Not sure if I've got the right address. Kinda pretty down here, though."

The shot would be tough, Carter thought, peeking at the pair from beneath the ball cap. Even an involuntary twitch by Gaunt Guy could cause the gun held to Abby's neck to discharge.

The gunman nailed Carter with a thousand-yard stare. "Wrong address, asshole."

Carter exhaled. Gaunt Guy hadn't recognized him.

"You sure? This is the place I was told."

"Put the warmer on the ground and walk toward me. Slowly." As Gaunt Guy spoke, he moved the gun off Abby's neck by an inch.

An inch was good. Better than nothing. But was it enough?

"No problem," Carter said, stepping forward. "You making a movie or something?"

"I said, put the warmer down."

"Like, here?" Carter said, taking another step. He was pretty certain he could do an inch. Relatively certain.

"Yes, there."

"Like on the ground?" Carter took another step. Still an inch. What was it with this guy?

"I said—"

Carter decided to risk it. But before he managed to fire, Abby lunged for the gun in Gaunt Guy's hands. *What the heck.* The man swore, pulling his hand free, and sighted the gun on Abby. The weapon was less than an inch from Abby's neck. Carter fired anyway, the discharge shredding the insulated warmer.

Abby screamed at the sound of the gunshot and rolled to her right as Gaunt Guy staggered back, blood blooming from the upper left side of his chest. He tried raising his gun but Carter shot him again, this time square in the chest. He dropped to his side but to Carter's amazement moved his gun arm once more. Before Carter could fire a third time Abby stood and stamped on Gaunt Guy's wrist like someone trying to extinguish an errant campfire flame. Carter pulled his Beretta free of the demolished pizza warmer and glanced over at Glenn.

"Don't move."

Carter looked back. Abby had spoken. She was facing him, Gaunt Guy's gun in her hands, which trembled as she pointed the barrel in Carter's direction.

"Easy now," Carter said.

On the ground, Gaunt Guy moaned as blood pumped from his chest, each spasm slower than the last.

"Put your gun down or I'll shoot. I mean it."

"Glenn," Carter said.

Abby's father spoke a second later, his voice catching. "It's all right, Abby. He's with me. He's on our side."

Abby didn't move. She held her position with the gun aimed at Carter. He appreciated her determination, as well as the skepticism in her eyes. In the abstract, anyway.

"What's going on?" Abby said. "Where's Rachel?"

Gaunt Guy gasped, a wet rattle in his throat.

Carter said, "We're looking for her. But we don't have much time. The quicker we get going the better chance we have of finding her."

"Put your gun down first."

Carter took a breath. He adjusted the brim of the Corrigan's Chicago-Style Pizza cap. He knelt and placed the gun on the ground.

"Like I said, we don't have much time."

"Abby," Glenn said.

Abby stumbled forward, a step at a time, nearly tripping, and ran into her father's arms.

Carter walked over and removed Gaunt Guy's gun from Abby's right hand where it rested inadvertently against the small of her father's back. She didn't notice; she was crying too hard. He walked over to Gaunt Guy, who stared at him through dull, glassy eyes. Carter pulled a pair of blue latex gloves from his jeans' back pocket, put them on, and patted Gaunt Guy down. After a moment he found his phone and his wallet, which was jammed with cash. The money that Glenn transferred to Abby's account. He counted it quickly. Three thousand dollars and change. He pocketed the money and examined the phone, reading the text message on the screen.

7 minutes off.

From Finn. Sent two minutes ago.

Carter pressed Gaunt Guy's right thumb on the phone until it opened. He maneuvered his way through the settings and removed the screen lock. He scrolled through the messages. A lot of back and forth involving Abby and Rachel and "the mailman guy" and somebody named Jason and some kind of package.

Jason—the shot caller?

And what was the package?

He took another minute and scrolled through the photos. He stopped at one in particular and studied it in confusion. Puzzled, he texted the picture to himself and walked over to Abby and Glenn. She had stopped crying but still clung to her father.

"What can you tell me about this guy?" Carter said, pointing at Gaunt Guy.

"Jesus Christ," Glenn said. "Give her a goddamn second."

"Not an option. Not if we're going to keep Rachel alive."

"Keep her alive? I thought we were rescuing her."

Carter ignored him and repeated his question to Abby. Glenn protested again. To Carter's relief, Abby pulled herself free and met his eyes.

"Vlad the Asshole."

"What's that, now?"

"The guy." She nodded at the dying man on the ground without looking at him. "What I called him. In my head."

"His name's Vlad?"

She nodded.

"Did he hurt you?"

She bit her lip and shook her head.

"Sure about that?"

"The other guy twisted my arm kind of hard."

The other guy. Blue Eyes.

"Did you get his name?"

"I think it's Stone."

**7 minutes off.**

Sent four minutes ago.

"Vlad and Stone. Okay. You did good, Abby. Really good. Just one more thing. Did either of them say anything about where they were going or anything about someone named Stella Wolford?"

She shook her head again.

"What about a place called Danville?"

"Not that I remember. They didn't talk a whole lot. Stone found me in the lobby of the theater and told me there'd been an accident with my parents and I had to come with him. As soon as I got outside I knew something wasn't right. But it was too late." Looking at Glenn, she said, "He told me he'd kill you and Rachel if I so much as whispered. He had me in the Jeep with Vlad the Asshole like two minutes later."

Carter said, "Did either of them mention anything about numbers? Like twenty-two seven?"

"Nothing like that. Just the cash that Dad sent. And a couple times I heard Vlad say, 'Fuck Jason.' Whatever that means."

Carter thought of the name he'd seen in the text messages.

**7 minutes off.**

Sent five minutes ago.

Across from them, Vlad gasped a last time and went still.

"Let's go," Carter said, directing Glenn and Abby to the Suburban. "Follow me back—"

"Oh, and Lobo."

"Lobo?"

"I heard Stone say it. It means wolf in Spanish, so it caught my attention. Something about whether Lobo sent some guy pretending to be a mailman after them. They both said they'd kill the mailman on sight if they saw him again."

Carter exchanged glances with Glenn.

"Lobo?"

"Not a clue," Glenn said. He'd released Abby from a hug but still stood with his left arm around her.

"Nothing else about who Lobo was?"

Abby shook her head. "Do you know who the mailman is they were talking about?"

"That's me."

"You?" Abby's brown eyes widened. "You're the fake mailman? They hate your guts."

"I'm not a fake mailman. I deliver packages. It's how I make my living."

**7 minutes off.**

Sent six minutes ago.

"We really need to go," Carter said.

"Where?" Glenn said.

Carter typed a number into the message window on his phone, linked the photo he'd transferred from Vlad's phone—the odd one of a string of numbers—and sent a text to Finn.

**Found this on Vlad's phone. Hand over Rachel and maybe I'll delete it.**

Satisfied the message went through, Carter looked at Abby and her father.

"To Danville."

# TWENTY

They circled back to Corrigan's Chicago-Style Pizza, Carter driving the Fit with Glenn and Abby trailing in the Suburban. Vlad's cell phone rested in a lower left-hand pocket in Carter's utility vest. Which he had back on. Vlad's wallet with an ID identifying him as Edgar Handel of Batavia, New York was in a right-hand pocket. Vlad's gun, a Taurus G2c with a seventeen-round magazine, was at the bottom of Lake Michigan. Carter's arms were still heavy from Paddy and all, but he had managed a solid outfield-to-home plate throw nonetheless.

"Took you long enough," the pizza lady said when Carter stepped inside the restaurant.

"Had to take a detour."

"Detours? Listen, we don't do detours. I've got two more deliveries sitting there. Pick it up, why don't you."

"Apologies," Carter said, placing the Fit's keys beside the Lion's Club vision care donation bowl. "I'm not able to continue in the position."

The woman's tired face flared into life, anger in her eyes. "Jesus Christ. Seriously? One delivery? For fuck's sake. Maybe my dad's right. Nobody wants to work anymore."

She looked ready to continue yelling but went silent as Carter placed a pile of bills on the counter and pushed them toward her.

"For your troubles. Three thousand dollars. And change. It's not stolen or anything, so don't worry about that. I'm sorry for the inconvenience. Oh, and you're going to need a new warmer."

She stared at him, eyes wide. Before she could reply he dug into his wallet.

"Almost forgot. From the guy who got the free supremes."

Carter placed the ten-dollar bill on the counter beside the other bills, offered the gaping woman an apologetic half smile, and headed to the door.

"Hey mister."

Carter turned around.

"Could I get my hat back? It was a custom job."

Back behind the wheel of the Suburban, Carter drove around the corner and parked on a side street. Abby ate a slice of pizza from the second box, tugging at the red flannel blanket draped over her shoulders that Carter offered from the supply he kept next to his medical kit. Glenn kept his eyes glued to his daughter as if afraid she would vanish into thin air.

"A thought," Carter said.

Abby and Glenn looked up.

"The thing is, I feel like the ball's back in our court. Figuratively speaking. We've evened out the odds. For now. I still need to make my delivery to Rachel. But."

"Delivery?" Abby said.

"But?" Glenn said.

"Before we go to Danville we have a decision to make. Well, you two do."

"Which is?" Glenn said.

"Whether you want to go along for the ride. I obviously didn't expect things to go this way. It's been an interesting evening, to say the least. Unfortunately, it's probably going to get more interesting. Maybe it's best if you take a break at this point. You've both been through a lot."

"What about Rachel?" Abby said.

"Don't worry about Rachel for the moment. Worry about yourselves. Starting with, it's probably best to fix your problem before it gets any worse. The fact that you're missing, I mean." He glanced at Abby's phone, which had buzzed nonstop with texts and calls since they left the park. "I've bought us a little time. I can circle back, drop you downtown. You'll have to do a lot of talking." This comment directed at Glenn. "You'll still have the problem of what happened at Art Wheeler's to deal with. I can't do anything about that. But at least you can call off the search for Abby."

"What about Rachel?" Abby repeated. "What happens to her?"

"I find her. I make my delivery. I go home. Well, actually to Louisville. You know what I mean."

"You make your delivery and rescue her, you mean."

"There are a lot of people looking for you right now," Carter said, ignoring the comment. "We need to address that issue first. Whatever you decide."

"What about the police? Or the FBI or CSI or something? Shouldn't we be calling them?"

Carter glanced at Glenn, who met his gaze and then dropped his eyes.

"We can definitely do that. We can for sure get those folks involved. Calling them doesn't change the fact that I still need to make the delivery. But it's an option, one hundred percent. I just think we need to deal with that first." He looked again at Abby's phone, which buzzed with another call.

"The second pizza."

Carter and Abby both looked at Glenn.

"Dad?"

"You ordered two pizzas," Glenn said to Carter. He was having difficulty speaking again. Carter realized it was probably time for more pain meds.

"What are you talking about?" Abby said.

"He ordered two pizzas. Before we went to the park. I couldn't understand why. It was just him and me. I mean, it seemed crazy to get pizza at all. It turned out to be a good idea because I didn't realize how hungry I was. We were just fixing dinner when . . . well, when everything happened. But I didn't understand the point of the second pizza."

"Dad—"

"It was for you. He knew he'd rescue you. He knew you'd be hungry." Glenn looked at Carter. "Isn't that right?"

Abby's phone buzzed again.

"It's Mrs. Patterson. The head. It's the third time she's called."

"Who the hell are you?" Glenn said to Carter. "Who the hell's so confident in a situation like that, that he orders a second pizza for the hostage he hasn't saved yet?"

Abby lifted her phone to her ear.

"Hello? Yes. Yes, I'm so, so sorry. I'm fine. No—I can explain. Actually, can you talk to my dad? Yes, he's right here."

Abby placed the phone on her right leg. She stared at her father.

"I want Rachel back."


To his credit, Glenn did well. Well for anyone, and especially for someone in his condition. It sounded as if he had learned something from the screwup calling Art Wheeler. He manufactured a complicated story. More complicated than Carter would have gone for. But beggars, choosers, etc. An unexpected business trip to the city. A decision to surprise Abby. An ill-conceived plan to intercept her at the theater for a late dinner. A misunderstanding about what time the show was. A second misunderstanding about who was supposed to alert Abby's teachers. Glenn traded the phone back and forth with Abby several times.

At one point, Glenn conducted a tense conversation with a police officer and Carter figured the gig was up. Still more apologies. Somehow, no reference to what happened at the Wheelers', which was a little surprising but on further review perhaps not. Carter assumed it would take the Chicago cops responding to the brownstone situation a while to figure out why they couldn't reach Rachel and even more time to find Glenn. At some point they'd find out about the explosion at their house in Indy, but maybe not for a little while yet.

Carter could tell Mrs. Patterson wasn't happy about the last piece of the puzzle. That Glenn would drop Abby off first thing in the morning, before class, since it was a long drive this time of night to Bellbrook from his downtown hotel. But after nearly thirty minutes, Abby disconnected the phone for the last time and plugged it into the charger cord Carter handed her.

"Well?" Carter said.

Abby blew out a dismissive breath. "They're pissed. *Pissed.* That was my last field trip ever, guaranteed. I might get suspended. And forget about Winter Ball. Also, I'm pretty sure Haawo knows I'm lying. But anyway, they bought it. They're not looking for me anymore."

"Who's Haawo?" Glenn said.

"She's—"

"How old are you?" Carter said to Abby.

She blinked at the interruption. "Sixteen. Why?"

Carter glanced at his phone, at the texts and missed call from the number he knew belonged to Finn. The gist clear from the first text.

**Let's talk.**

Carter said, "Can you drive?"

"Sure. I got my license this summer."

"Ever driven a car this big?"

"Not really. I got a Forester for my birthday. But it's small by comparison. So's Rachel's Kia. Your Jeep's kinda large," she said to her father. "Not like this, though."

"That's good enough." Carter moved into the passenger seat. "I need you to take the wheel for an hour or so. Your dad needs to rest and I need to shut my eyes. It's highways all the way. Just stick to the speed limit and you'll be fine."

"Um, I'm not allowed to drive at night."

"I appreciate that, but we've got bigger fish to fry right now. Plus, you look old for your age."

"No," Glenn mumbled. "I don't want her driving."

Instead of replying, Carter instructed Abby to open the black metal medical box and retrieve a bottle of Tylenol. She gave Glenn two more pills and handed him a bottle of water. On her own, she made him retreat to the rear seat and lay down. She covered him with a second red flannel blanket.

"Is he going to be all right?" she said, returning to the front and taking the wheel.

"He needs a doctor, sooner rather than later," Carter said. Understatement, but he didn't elaborate. "He's fine for now. Head north to the light, and take a left."

As Abby put the Suburban in drive and started out, Carter told his phone to call Dispatch. He kept it on speaker so Abby could see the GPS directions spiraling up the phone screen.

"Merc?"

Carter explained the situation.

"Thank God the girl's okay. How are you?"

"I'm running late. We're headed to Danville. Best guess Finn and Stone are going there now with Rachel."

"Stone?"

Carter looked over at Abby. She was staring intently at the road ahead of her, focusing on the task at hand.

"One of the guys who grabbed Abby at the theater. Big guy, blue eyes, shaved head. Like if Home Depot sold Vikings. He was with someone called Vlad. Vlad the Asshole, though I don't think that's his real last name."

Abby snorted but kept her eyes on the road.

"Also, Stone and Vlad—and maybe Finn—seem to think someone named Lobo sicced me on them. And there's somebody named Jason in the mix. Possible he or Lobo is the shot caller. Oh, also."

"Yes?"

"Vlad isn't in the picture anymore."

A pause. "Got it. I'll check them out. I'm still working on Danville. Isn't that where Dick Van Dyke is from?"

"And Donald O'Connor. Oh, and Bobby Short and Gene Hackman too. Why?"

"No reason. Call you back?"

"Give me ninety minutes. I'm getting some shut-eye."

"Glenn's driving?"

"Abby," Carter said, and cut the call.

"Dispatch?" Abby said. "Who's that?"

Carter glanced at the road map spooling forth on his phone. "Someone who helps me."

Abby arched her dark brows. "Helps you deliver stuff?"

"Something like that."

"He sounds just like you. Is he your father?"

Carter hesitated. "He's my uncle."

"Your uncle helps you deliver stuff?"

"That's right."

"That's cool, I guess. Does your father help too?"

"No."

"Why not?"

Carter looked ahead and saw the signs for I-90 West.

"My father's dead."

# TWENTY-ONE

"**D**o you ever deliver people?"

In fact, Carter decided, digesting the details, he did.

The job: Escorting a woman named Jenna and her three-year-old daughter, Kelsey. He met them in a parking lot outside Syracuse before dawn. No amount of makeup could disguise the bruises on Jenna's face. Or on Kelsey's left arm. The woman who dropped them off, wearing all black and sunglasses even at that time of day, assured Carter privately that those were just the bruises he could see.

The destination: a farm in Indiana. Carter's destination, anyway. He understood it was the first stop of many for Jenna on the way to a new life.

"You have a gun, right?" the woman in black asked Carter when Jenna and Kelsey were safely inside the Suburban, his upgrade from the Taurus that no longer served the needs of the job.

"Will I need it?"

"He's not going to let her go easily. This is a man used to getting his way, regardless of the outcome."

Carter told her he understood. And he did. He'd already laid down one, and only one, rule for this trip. No cell phones. No electronic devices of any kind. His years at USPIS had taught him plenty about tracking capabilities. The woman in black had agreed on Jenna's behalf. Given her word.

So it was on Carter that he didn't bother double-checking before starting out beyond a cursory search of Jenna's purse and Kelsey's backpack. As a result, *it wasn't until north of Martinsville, Indiana, that Carter finally made the tail. Blue van, always two, three cars back.*

How could he have been so stupid.

*"Jenna."*

*The woman stirred. The girl looked over in interest from her car seat, hearing her mother's name.*

*"Jenna," Carter repeated.*

*"Mmm," the woman said, lifting her head and opening her eyes.*

*"Are you awake?"*

*"Yes." She sat up straight. "Is everything all right?"*

*"Do you have a cell phone on you?"*

*She hesitated. Carter watched her glance at Kelsey, then look outside at the countryside rushing past in the dark.*

*"I—"*

*"Yes or no."*

*Another pause. Carter raised his eyes, finding the van trailing them in the near distance. Never far behind. Steady as she goes.*

*"Yes," Jenna said, face tightening.*

*"Is it yours? Or a loaner?"*

*"Mine," she said after a moment.*

*Though it was too late, Carter removed the battery anyway and snapped the phone in half after Jenna reluctantly removed it from her bra and handed it forward. He didn't chastise her, figuring she'd been through enough already. Instead, eyeing the van, he focused on what Jenna's chaperone said that morning.*

"He's not going to let her go easily. This is a man used to getting his way, regardless of the outcome."

*Well, Carter was used to getting his way, too. Like he told Tomeka at the Red Wings game. He liked doing the right thing. Especially when people were in his way.*

*Something else occurred to him. Since picking up that French bulldog in Erie, he'd undertaken several deliveries. So far, he'd been successful every time. He didn't like the idea of breaking that streak.*

*Ten minutes later, Carter exited Route 37, drove up the road, and pulled into the last parking space on the right outside the Hoosier Cafe, an all-night diner attached to a truck stop. Moths danced like swirling ash around sodium lights turning night into day. It wasn't perfect but it would have to do.*

*"What's happening?"*

*"Slight change of plans," Carter said. "We're going to take a dinner break."*

*"I thought we weren't supposed to stop, except for gas."*

*"Change of plans, like I said."*

*"Why? What's going on?"*

*"Nothing I can't handle. Let's go."*

*Carter asked for the last booth on the left. He took the wall seat and seated Jenna and Kelsey with their backs to the door. Two men entered just as the server took Carter and Jenna's order. They glanced down the aisle at Carter. He asked Jenna to turn around, making sure they saw her.*

*He said, "Do you recognize those men?"*

*"No."*

*"You're sure?"*

*"Positive. Why?"*

*"They recognize you."*

*"Oh God. What's going on?"*

*Instead of answering her question, Carter rose and said, "Wait here. Don't get up, under any circumstances."*

*He picked up his cup of coffee, walked the length of the diner, arrived at the men's table, and slid in beside the bigger of the two.*

*"Gentleman," he said. "I believe you have a little problem."*

"Anything?" Finn said.

"Not yet. It's hard on a phone."

*It's also hard when you're fucking typing with one hand and eating with another*, Finn thought, watching Stone start on his second cheeseburger. With at least two to go. Stone didn't consume so much as ingest, like an old-fashioned stove absorbing chunk after chunk of shoveled-in coal. Or a Norseman methodically tearing apart a haunch of mutton. But Finn didn't say anything. Not yet. Stone was slow to anger. Very slow. The look on his face when he awoke after Finn found him in the grass outside Rachel Stanfield's house was possibly the angriest he'd ever seen him. By contrast, Stone might have been staring at a crushed pop can for all the emotion he showed when they rolled up on the remains of Vlad an hour ago. In hindsight, a mistake not driving to the park together. But that was life. Or in this case, death.

The thing about Stone was that once he did lose his cool, an over-caffeinated Hulk on amphetamines better look out. Finn figured he'd need that version of Stone sooner rather than later. For now, the way this job was going, no point in jabbing sleeping grizzlies.

"Worth calling Jason?" Stone said, mouth full of burger, bread, and cheese. "He's the one with the setup."

"Not yet. See what you can find first."

What Finn didn't say: what a colossally bad idea. He had enough on his plate trying to assure Jason they were still on track. That everything was fine. That the package—the knowledge of it—hadn't been compromised. The last thing he needed Jason to know was that, in fact, they were on a wild goose chase to some nowhere burg called Danville because they still didn't know Stella Wolford's location because some shrimpy, interfering, lying fuckwad named Mercury Carter had shown up—maybe sent by Lobo, maybe not—not once, not twice, but three times now, and thrown a wrench into the middle of fucking everything.

Yeah, call Jason, and while they're at it, explain how the decision to side-door their way into the money that Jason turned down—$20 million fucking dollars—ended with Vlad, who came specially recommended by Jason, lying in congealing pools of his own blood.

Oh, and maybe also tell him that Carter knows about the numbers.

Because Carter had enough sense to look at Vlad's phone.

And even if he didn't know what the numbers were, Carter had correctly guessed the risk of those numbers getting out was enough of a bargaining chip to keep Rachel Stanfield alive.

For now.

Speaking of which. Behind him, she groaned through her gag.

"She's probably hungry," Stone said between bites.

"I figured that out, thanks. Anything?"

"Not yet. It might be good to feed her."

"I'm not running a fucking restaurant here."

Stone trained his blue eyes on Finn, his expression giving nothing away. It was like staring into chips of blue-tinged granite chiseled from a gravestone.

"Vets say it's fine to feed pets before euthanasia. Makes them comfortable. Their owners, too. Helps the process go more smoothly."

Rachel went quiet.

"Just saying," Stone said, returning to his phone and to his cheeseburger.

After a long few seconds, Finn shifted to the rear seat and removed Rachel's gag. He dipped into the Burger King takeout bag, removed a bag of limp French fries and a soggy Whopper, and dumped them in Rachel's lap.

"Not a fucking word." He returned to his seat and looked up and down the street, eyes peeled for cops.

Behind him, Rachel stifled a sob.

And began to eat.

Carter awoke with a start. He sat up and rubbed his eyes. He had slept without dreaming, as he always did, until right before awakening. Then the dreams flooded in at the last second. As they always did. Came and then vanished as quickly as taillights around a corner taken too fast.

"What's happening?" He eyed the stopped car in front of them.

"Traffic jam," Abby said. She stifled a yawn. "We haven't moved in forty-five minutes. I'm guessing an accident but it's hard to tell. Traffic's moving fine on the other side."

"What time is it?"

"Just past four. Your, um, phone's buzzed a couple times. 'Dispatch.'"

"Where are we?"

"Not totally sure. I saw a sign for Kankakee a few miles back. We're still on the highway."

Carter picked up his phone and checked the directions. Not even halfway there. Not good. But if they were delayed, Finn was delayed. Assuming he traveled the same route. Once again, he chastised himself for slashing the tires on Finn's van. What was he thinking?

"How's your dad?" Carter said.

"Still sleeping. I heard him moan once or twice. You're sure he's going to be all right?"

"I'm sure," Carter said, not sure. He put the phone to his ear and dialed his uncle. Despite the hour he answered almost immediately.

"Everything okay? You haven't moved for more than an hour."

Carter explained about the traffic jam. "Find anything?"

"I think so. Looks like Danville, Illinois, is where Stella Wolford is from originally. Her parents are Kenneth and Diane Madison. They're divorced, but they both still live there. Same last name as far as I can tell. I texted you his address. I'm still looking for hers. You think maybe their daughter's holed up with one of them?"

"No idea. But Art Wheeler gave the city up for some reason. If his firm did due diligence defending Summa ProHealth against the lawsuit, it's a no-brainer they ran a background check on Stella Wolford. Wheeler may have seen the Danville reference."

"Gotcha. Name Kevin Wolford come up yet? That's Stella's husband."

"No." Curious that it hadn't, come to think of it. "Anything on the other stuff?"

"Not yet. What's your move, with the traffic?"

Carter glanced at Abby. "We'll have to ride it out for now. Hope Finn's stuck in it too. Once we're free, we'll head to Kenneth Madison's house. Take it from there."

"Sounds like a plan. Oh, before I go. I assume there's nothing connecting you to what happened at that waterfront park?"

"No," Carter said. "There's not."

He disconnected and turned to Abby. "I can take the wheel."

"I'm fine," she said, and yawned again.

"Wasn't a question. You did good. You got us this far. I'll probably shut my eyes again anyway. I just want to be in place when traffic starts moving. You need sleep. You need to be rested for whatever comes next."

She looked as if she might protest, then yawned once more. A moment later Carter squeezed himself into the rear to give her room to trade places. He settled himself on the driver's side, adjusted the seat, and buckled up.

"Mr. Carter?"

"You can call me Merc."

She studied him. "That man, the one you shot. Vlad."

"Vlad the Asshole? What about him?"

She didn't smile. "He was going to kill you."

"I know. He was also going to kill you and your father."

"That's not what he said. He told me you were a bad man and he was just trying to get me back to my dad. After that, he'd make sure you didn't do bad things again."

"He told you I was a bad man after we got him that cash?"

"He said it was a trick."

"You believed him?"

"I didn't know what to believe. It was all a blur."

"Is that why you went for his gun?"

"I know it was stupid. I just figured if I didn't do something, he or you would kill me."

"Me, or a pizza delivery guy in the wrong place at the wrong time?"

Several cars back, someone honked a horn. The traffic ahead of them didn't budge.

"I knew it was you. So, the first one."

"How'd you know it was me?"

Abby rolled her eyes, her patronizing look softened by the yawn that followed.

"Like someone would be delivering a pizza down there that time of night."

# TWENTY-TWO

*T*he man sitting across from Carter stared at him. *"The hell are you?"*

*Face like something carved from an oak stump, wide shoulders, hands that looked more than capable of doing some serious damage. Wearing a nondescript blue golf shirt and a chunky, complicated workout watch. The ex-military vibe was so strong Carter could practically smell it.*

*Carter said, "I'm no one of consequence. But, to cut to the chase, because I know you're busy men, what I need to know is, what will it take to make your problem go away?"*

*"What problem?"*

*"The one sitting in the booth at the back of the diner with her back to us."*

*Golf Shirt looked down the aisle.*

*"Go on."*

*"Thing is, I don't want any trouble. I wasn't expecting a complication. I just want to be on my way. I'm hoping there's something I can do to persuade you to let me do that."*

*"Are you threatening us?" the man beside Carter said. Same ex-military vibe, with a red goatee and a side of psychopath thrown in for good measure.*

*"Hardly," Carter said. "I'm not stupid. It's just me, and, well . . ." He spread his hands flat on the tabletop, palms up. He guessed each man had, at a minimum, fifty pounds and three inches on him.*

*"We don't want trouble either," Golf Shirt said. "I think you know what we want. The fact you're sitting here tells me that much."*

*"In that case, maybe we could reach a mutual understanding."*

"*Understanding?*"

"*I'm wondering if I could offer you an inducement to let us continue. I'm not sure I can match what you're being paid for this trip. But maybe I could make it worth your while.*"

"*To do what?*" Goatee said.

"*To turn around. Go home and forget about tonight.*"

"*How much?*" Golf Shirt said.

Carter told him.

Golf Shirt took a sip of coffee. "*That's not going to be possible.*"

"*Why not?*"

"*We have strict instructions. We can't return empty-handed. We face a penalty if that happens.*"

Goatee looked surprised by this. "*A penalty? You didn't say nothing about—*"

Golf Shirt waved him off. "*It doesn't matter because we're not taking his money.*" The last comment directed at Carter. "*Sorry, but it's not an option. We have a job to do, and it's getting done.*" He looked past Carter toward Jenna and Kelsey. "*Easier all around if we just transfer the cargo now.*"

Carter took a sip of his own coffee and considered his options. He had to admit there weren't many. After a moment, he said, "*In that case, could I offer a counterproposal? In the interest of none of us wanting any trouble.*"

"*I'm listening,*" Golf Shirt said.

He explained what he had in mind. The amount he desired.

Goatee's laugh sounded as if he were choking. "*You want us to pay you? The hell kind of deal is that? You know we can just take them, right?*"

"*I've no doubt. But I've incurred certain expenses. What I'm proposing makes both our jobs easier. Skips the rough-stuff part. A quick fix.*"

Goatee started to speak when Golf Shirt interrupted, naming a figure considerably less than Carter's original proposal. Carter counteroffered. Golf

*Shirt countered that. It went like that for another minute, the two of them speaking in hushed tones, the look of exasperation on Goatee's face growing by the moment.*

*Finally, they reached an agreement. Carter took another drink of coffee as Golf Shirt took out his wallet and handed him five bills. They discussed meeting places. Carter rejected the first two, listened to the description of the third option, and nodded.*

*"See you there," he said, standing up and returning to his booth. "Let's go."*

*"What?" Jenna said.*

*"We need to get on the road."*

*"She just brought our food."*

*"We have to leave it, I'm afraid."*

*"But why?"*

*Kelsey started to whine, face smeared with ketchup. Before Carter could respond Jenna grabbed her daughter's cheeseburger, wrapped it in napkins, and stuck it in her purse.*

*"What did they say? Those men?"*

*"Not much. I worked it out."*

*"The one opposite you handed you something. What was it?"*

*"Like I said, I worked it out."*

*"Worked out what?"*

*"A problem they had. Let's go." Carter placed a five-dollar bill under his coffee cup and walked behind them to the cash register. He added a to-go large coffee, paid in cash, and followed Jenna and the girl outside.*

*He filled the tank before driving out of the truck stop. He watched the men in the van do the same. A good thing, considering what lay ahead. He watched them turn onto 37 and followed a minute later. They headed south, past the turnoff for Martinsville, past a jumble of used car places and fast-food restaurants. In a mile or so the landscape returned to fields and rolling* hills. Two miles farther on, the van's right turn signal winked. Carter made the same turn.

"What are we doing?" Jenna said. "Is this it?"

"Almost," Carter said.

The country road narrowed and curved. Wisps of evening mist rising from a nearby creek drifted across the pavement. The van a couple hundred yards ahead, out of sight once or twice around a bend. Carter crested a hill and encountered a long, slow decline. Trees towered overhead on either side and farther out, fields stretched to what would have been the horizon during the day. The glow of town lights faded, replaced by a black sky full of stars. Three hundred yards up, the road T-boned at a gravel lane. Carter turned right and followed the cloud of dust ahead of him. Two minutes later he pulled into a drive dead-ending at an abandoned barn, the van parked beside it.

"What's going on?" Jenna whispered. Carter's stomach tensed at the fear in her voice, but he forced himself to set the feeling aside. Deliveries and hitches, he reminded himself. He unbuckled and turned off the engine.

"Oh my God," Jenna said, twisting in her seat.

"Relax," he said.

"You sold us out," she said.

"Stay calm. I'll be right back."

"Like hell—"

Before she could finish, Carter grabbed the large coffee, hopped out quickly, and hit the fob to lock the Suburban's doors. The child-safety locks were set, though he didn't need the car's meep-meep to tell him that. Jenna's scrabbling at the door handles and her pleas for mercy told him everything he needed to know.

Carter walked toward the men's van, stopping ten feet short. He nodded. Both doors opened and the two climbed out. Carter took two steps closer.

"Keys," Golf Shirt said. "We'll take it from here."

Behind him the muffled sounds of Jenna's sobs and the pounding of her fists on the windows of the Suburban. A moment later a keening from the girl joining the cacophony.

"Sure thing," Carter said, taking three steps forward and tossing the cup of coffee into Golf Shirt's face. He registered the scream as he reached into the pocket on the right side of his vest and swiftly withdrew the knife. He hesitated briefly, conjured an image of his father, and then Earl Madden, and in one swift motion, like a teacher drawing a parabola on a chalkboard, drove the blade up and deep into Golf Shirt's thick neck. Carter jerked the knife back and forth as the blood gushed, cutting through tendons and cartilage and bone, letting the deep serrations along both edges of the blade do their work.

"The fuck," Goatee said, raising the semiautomatic in his right hand.

Carter tugged the blade free and whipped it across Goatee's wrist, ignoring the guttural gasps of Golf Shirt collapsing to his knees beside him. Goatee yelped in pain, dropped the gun, and took a step back. Carter stepped forward, clamped his left hand onto Goatee's right shoulder, and thrust the knife into his belly, just below his sternum. Ignoring the man's surprised grunt, Carter held the shoulder tight as he pushed the knife in deep, jerked it up, once, twice, a third time, hard, feeling the warm spray of blood on his hands.

"Oh," Goatee said.

Carter withdrew the knife, stepped back, and waited for the man to join his colleague on the ground. It didn't take long. Carter caught his breath, taking in what he'd done with a blink of surprise. As if to convince himself what just happened was real, he glanced over at the Suburban. He saw Jenna staring out the rear window, hands pressed against the glass, eyes wide, face as white as a birthday balloon.

Twenty minutes later, the men's bodies and their van dealt with, Carter returned to the Suburban.

"Please," Jenna said, reaching for her daughter as Carter opened the door. "Please don't hurt us."

"No one's going to hurt you," Carter said, starting the car and pulling away just as the fireball erupted behind them, consuming the van. And what was in it.

After dropping Jenna and Kelsey off at a farm deep in the southern Indiana hills, Carter turned around and made it as far as a rest stop on I-70 east of Dayton, where he dozed for a couple hours before finishing the trip. Late the next afternoon, back home in Rochester, he awoke to see Tomeka on the other side of the bedroom, quietly changing out of her work clothes. He checked the nightstand clock. Almost five P.M.

"There you are, sleepyhead. How'd it go?"

Carter waited a moment while he awakened fully.

"Not bad. Little rough."

"You okay?"

Carter thought about it.

"Yeah. Nothing I couldn't handle."

"Good to hear," Tomeka said. "Spaghetti tonight. My mom'll be here at six. You still okay to make the sauce?"

"Why not," Carter said.

# TWENTY-THREE

R achel stirred awake. She chastised herself for dropping off. But the combination of the much-needed food, as cold and greasy as it was, the rhythm of the van back on the road, and her bone-deep exhaustion from everything that had happened since that horrible moment in their kitchen, proved to be too much.

She realized she'd been dreaming of Chad Setterlin again. Dreaming of the day she first received notice of her representation. Of the awful facts the case presented, and her determination to look beyond them and to do her job. Tonight of all nights. Yet maybe that made sense.

Eleven-year-old Hannah Slater. Vanished one afternoon while walking to the corner convenience store to buy a package of powdered donuts for her grandmother. The grandma, Mary Blanton, four hundred pounds if she were an ounce. Assigned the job of watching Hannah after school while Hannah's mother, Sissy Slater, worked the four-to-midnight shift at Speedway. Grandma's idea of keeping an eye on Hannah was to plead with her in that skin-crawling singsongy little girl voice to run up to the store for more donuts, *won't you be a good child now.*

Hannah, string-bean skinny and dutiful as the day was long, always went, even if two-thirds of the time she had to use her own hard-earned babysitting money to buy the snacks. Five minutes to the corner, turn left, five minutes to the next corner, turn right, one minute to Green's Carryout. Up and back twenty-five minutes or less, depending on how many customers were in the store.

Except one day she didn't return.

And Mary Blanton, wheezing in her armchair in front of *Ellen*, waited more than ninety minutes to notify anyone.

A police canvass found Hannah's unclothed body late that night in a vacant lot two streets over.

Indy police arrested Chad Setterlin the next day. Easy pickings. Seen talking to Hannah right before she entered the store. Two priors for molestation, including a three-year-old niece, and a neighborhood history of indecent exposure. Open-and-shut case, with Rachel's chief job as his public defender trying to avoid a death sentence.

Except Setterlin hadn't done it. He admitted to talking to Hannah, maybe even talking dirty to her. But two minutes later he walked in the opposite direction from the store. He struck up a conversation with a thin-as-a-rake heroin addict named La'Donna Rogers, negotiating a blow job in exchange for half a bottle of Oxys he bought off a second cousin with a bad back. Police sure as hell weren't taking Rogers's word for anything. But security video from a camera on an auto parts warehouse across the street captured the whole incident, including the twenty minutes Setterlin was inside the one-room pigsty Rogers worked out of. According to the coroner, by the time Setterlin emerged from the crumbling brick house with a daffy grin on his face, Hannah—who wasn't as lucky when it came to security footage—had already been taken and was likely dead or dying.

It was Rachel's relentless digging that turned up the video. The warehouse security manager had insisted the cameras were inoperative, were only for show. What he didn't realize was that his boss, an operations supervisor, actually ran the cameras 24/7 to keep an eye on the comings and goings of employees, some of whom he suspected of clocking out early. Including the warehouse security manager.

No matter. Rachel had the video. Jurors were convinced. Justice for Chad Setterlin.

Though not for Hannah Slater.

"This is it."

Rachel tilted her head at Finn's voice.

A moment later, the ticking of a turn signal.

"How much longer?" The man called Stone, his voice low and guttural, like large rocks being dragged across concrete.

"Forty minutes. Plenty of time."

A moment after that, they were off the interstate. Still moving, but no longer at highway speeds.

*Going where?* Rachel thought.

*With plenty of time for what?*

By midnight, Rosa Jimenez finally thought she'd worked it out.

Stella Wolford, the girl fired by Summa ProHealth, was a drug addict and alcoholic. At least according to Gail Wheeler, who agreed to a short interview once it appeared her husband was out of immediate danger. Sedated up the wazoo and not going anywhere tonight, but stabilized after emergency angioplasty.

The lead bad guy—the one who left the Wheelers' brownstone alive, anyway—was hell-bent on finding Wolford. He didn't tell the Wheelers why, except to claim he wasn't her drug dealer. Who knows if that was true. How can you tell when a dealer is lying? When he opens his mouth.

So, some kind of home invasion-slash-retaliation-slash-kidnapping mission by a possibly aggrieved dealer. Solid enough.

By one A.M., Jimenez was back to square one.

Rachel Stanfield wasn't answering her phone. No surprise there. She could rightly be counted a hostage of some kind if she was still alive. Hostage, or accomplice, since Gail claimed she appeared tense but not in thrall to the Bad Guy. Maybe a Patty Hearst/Stockholm Syndrome dealio.

Problem was, Stanfield's husband wasn't answering his phone either. And oddly, when the husband called Art Wheeler earlier in the evening—according to Gail—he hadn't given any indication of a problem. Like, you know, someone kidnapping his wife to force an entry past the Wheelers' front door. Somehow that hadn't come up. So next step, Jimenez got the locals involved. Asked for a welfare check, despite the hour. And that's when things got weird.

"Say that again?" Jimenez said to the sleepy-sounding township cop who called her back.

"I said, their house is gone. Well, a chunk of it. Fire department saved half, maybe. Neighbors heard an explosion, so we're thinking gas line. No bodies so far."

By two A.M., Jimenez was doing her best not to think about her bed as she reviewed the situation with the Indianapolis FBI agent on duty, who sounded only slightly less sleepy than the township cop.

By three A.M., eyes swimming as Jimenez glanced at other mayhem the night had brought—a triple shooting on the South Side, a car crash where both victims had gunshot wounds, a body found at a lakeshore park, also shot—she called it a night. A BOLO was out for Rachel Stanfield. The hospital agreed to extra security for the wing where Art Wheeler lay in twilight sleep. The associate general counsel for Summa ProHealth, when Jimenez finally reached her, consented to an interview first thing in the morning.

It had been a long night, Jimenez thought, cutting down to North Avenue on the twenty-five-minute drive home. Hope to God the dog hadn't lost its mind with her working so late. A crazy case, but she'd done what she could. She'd made progress. She connected some bizarre shit—a house fire in an Indy suburb, a home invasion in Lincoln Park—in not much time.

But still. Jimenez kept coming back to the big question mark. The black hole in this confusing galaxy of facts.

She knew about the alleged dealer. She had Art and Gail Wheeler. And Rachel Stanfield and her husband, Glenn. The body of the red-haired giant in the backyard, of course. And somebody named Stella Wolford.

Who she still didn't have was the slight guy with the baseball cap who saved the day and then disappeared. That's who she really needed, Jimenez thought. And she wasn't remotely close to finding him.

Plenty of time . . . for what?

Blindfolded, Rachel had no way of gauging the hour. But even in the sensory blackout of her captivity, she sensed that something was about to happen. And it probably wasn't good.

Because things had changed. Finn's mood had grown fouler, if that were possible, since the terrifying moment in the Trader Joe's parking lot when Rachel realized Abby was nearby. They'd driven somewhere else, and after they arrived, Rachel heard a lot of swearing and furtive talking between Finn and Stone. After a few moments, the pair got back in the van and they raced off. As they did, Finn turned and claimed to Rachel that they still had Abby.

Rachel didn't think so. She thought Finn was bluffing. She could hear it in his voice.

The only question now was whether Abby was dead, or safe.

Rachel thought of Mercury Carter and his surprise appearance in Art Wheeler's condo. How the hell had he managed that?

*Now you're the one being hunted.*

Safe, Rachel decided. She was going with safe.

Time passed. She dozed again. She awoke abruptly as the van turned, rolled down a street, turned again, and once more, and came to an abrupt stop.

Nothing happened for a moment. Then the driver's and passenger's front doors opened simultaneously. A couple of seconds later she heard voices in the near distance. The low rumble of masculine conversation. The speakers indistinguishable as individuals. One thing was certain: more people than Finn and Stone were present.

Rachel had just processed this realization when things went quiet. A moment later the van door rolled open. Cool night air perfumed with diesel and the odor of cut grass filled the interior. A pair of hands grabbed her arms and pulled her forward without comment. She smelled the combination of woodsy cologne and BO she'd come to identify with Stone. Panicked, she tried reaching into her waistband for the nail. But it was too late. As Stone pinioned her arms to her chest, she felt her stomach flip as a second pair of arms, thick and strong as bridge cables, grabbed her legs and swung them into the air. She groaned loudly as Stone and the other captor toted her like furniture movers carting a couch.

"Shut up."

Finn.

It was the normal volume that terrified Rachel more than his tone.

He didn't need to lower his voice because there was no one around to hear him.

"It's time to part ways," Finn said. "You're going with some friends of mine. They have their instructions on how to treat you. Be a good girl and you'll be fine. Emphasis on good. Focus on the price you'll pay for misbehaving. Her name is Abby."

He was lying. Rachel knew it in her heart. Forced herself to believe it.

She stopped struggling to convey cooperation. She would play along. Her reward was being tossed unceremoniously onto a cold, hard metallic floor. She no sooner tried to get her bearings—her left hip on fire from the landing—than she felt straps pulled around her feet and chest, heard the clicking of metallic clasps, and despaired as an engine roared into life and her new prison—another vehicle—quickly pulled away.

# TWENTY-FOUR

Carter gave it a minute and knocked on the bungalow's door again. He wasn't optimistic. It was hard to believe, given the volume and duration of the barking inside, that anyone upright and sentient wouldn't be alerted to the presence of a visitor by now. He counted two dogs at least, and big ones, to judge by the decibel level and the way the door rattled from their efforts to get out.

Either no one was home or . . .

Or Finn had gotten here first.

Except Carter didn't think so. Rochester Red Wings cap in place and padded manila envelope in hand, he circled the house casually—just a delivery type going about his day—and didn't see signs of forced entry. So Carter's bad luck: Kenneth Madison was at work or on some kind of early morning errand. At least he wasn't in the clutches of Finn and Stone.

Yet.

They had arrived in Danville twenty minutes earlier. Carter circled the block three times, reconnoitering, before parking across the street. Abby woke up as the engine cut off. He explained what he was doing, exchanged a couple of texts with his uncle—nothing new—and walked to the door. And knocked to no avail.

Carter was standing on Kenneth Madison's porch steps, phone in hand, about to call his uncle, when he heard a voice.

"Help you?"

A woman, standing on the stoop of the house next door. Older, with short white hair and wearing matching light blue activewear pants and zip-up top. A baby cradled in her arms: a grandchild she was no doubt watching for the day. Until Carter realized it wasn't an infant at all but a dog, one of the miniaturized breeds, something small and brown and fuzzy clutched against the woman's bosom. Dressed in a matching blue outfit. Carter glanced at his Suburban, locking eyes with Abby in the passenger seat. Glenn still passed out in the rear.

"Ma'am." Carter touched the brim of his cap and lifted the envelope. "Just looking for Mr. Madison."

"Not home. Saw him pull out a while ago."

"Any idea when he might be back? Or where he is—work, maybe?"

"I can take that, if you'd like." She gestured greedily at the envelope.

"Much obliged. But I need his John Hancock. Rules and regs." Carter shook his head to indicate the idiocy of bureaucracy. "He work around here, by any chance?"

"Over in Crawfordsville," the woman said, raising an elbow to indicate the direction. "Does maintenance at Wabash College. Thought this was his day off, but maybe not."

Carter did the math, pulling up an Indiana map in his head. Minimum forty-five-minute drive, assuming they didn't hit traffic. He didn't relish the thought, especially after the hours-long tie-up that ended only with the coming of dawn when responders finally cleared up a nasty three-car crash.

Carter said, "I'm in the clear if a family member signs for it. Maybe his wife or"—he made a show of consulting the blank screen of his phone—"his daughter? Stella?"

"Stella? Haven't seen her around for a while. Good riddance, pardon my French. Though it's God's honest truth. Nothing but trouble from high school on. Half the reason for the divorce, maybe more, you ask me. And don't get me started on that boy she married. Kenny and Diane deserved better, I can tell you that much. Sure I can't take that? I'm practically family, living so close."

"Much obliged, but I'm sure. Speaking of Diane, any chance she's, you know, close by?"

"Got an apartment someplace off Vermillion. Kenny offered her the house, I'll give him that. For whatever reason she didn't want it."

Behind Carter the barking of the dogs inside Madison's house intensified.

"Easy, Princess," the woman said as the teacup dog squirmed in her arms.

Carter said, "Any idea where off Vermillion?"

"Someplace by the park, I think. But you might have better luck at Meijer."

"Meijer?"

"Diane works at the garden center. Early bird shift, last I heard."

"Hopefully, this won't take long." Carter opened his door after parking in the Meijer lot halfway between the store and the shopping plaza's service road.

"Crap," Abby said, staring at her phone.

"What?"

She punched out a text. "It's Haawo. She's wondering where I am."

"Haawo. A classmate?" Carter recalled the name from the night before.

"Like, my only friend there. What should I tell her? My first class starts in twenty minutes. Dad told the head he'd drop me off early."

Carter glanced at Glenn asleep in the back seat. This was a fire he needed put out quickly. After considering their options, he said, "Make

something up. Blame it on your father. Tell her you got delayed. A
traffic jam. Heck, that's close to the truth. Whatever you do, don't tell
her where you are."

"She'll suspect something. She's super smart."

"So are you. Figure it out."

He left the SUV, dissatisfied with his response but hoping Abby,
who'd already demonstrated her mettle ten times over, could improvise
better than her father. He entered the store and headed for the garden
center. It wasn't hard to find Diane Madison. Just past eight o'clock on a
weekday morning, only two people were working in plants and flowers
and one was a slope-shouldered twenty-something guy who barely
looked awake as he studied his phone in the enclosed cashier's booth.

"Mrs. Madison?"

She looked up, suspicion in her eyes. She turned off the hose she
was using to water pots of purple asters.

"Yeah?"

"You have a minute?"

"For what?"

"I'm trying to locate your daughter, Stella."

"Stella? What's she done now? Are you a cop?" She was a large
woman with hardly any chin, her shoulder-length black hair threaded
with gray lying flat against her head. Tired brown eyes looked past
Carter, scanning the outdoor shop to see if he was alone.

"She hasn't done anything. And I'm not a cop. If you have a second
I could explain?"

"Explain what? Why are you asking about her? If she owes you
money you've come to the wrong place." Madison reached into her jeans
pocket, pulled out her phone, and examined the screen.

"I just have a few questions for her."

Madison glanced at the kid in the cashier's booth. Still checking his phone, oblivious to them.

"What kind of questions?"

Carter plunged right in. Usually the best tactic. "Thing is, I'm a kind of mailman. Independent, like. I was trying to deliver a package yesterday evening to an attorney named Rachel Stanfield in Indianapolis. Ms. Stanfield has had some dealings with Stella, related to Stella's being fired from her job." He hoped Diane was aware of that development, but if not, it wasn't anything he could worry about now. When Diane didn't say anything, he continued.

"While I was at Stanfield's house, I happened to meet some individuals who are trying to find Stella. Objectively speaking, I'd say they don't have her best interests at heart. It's probably better if I locate her first."

"What individuals?"

"Four men. Insistent on finding her."

"Shit. This is about Kevin, isn't it? He owes them money, right? Or you?"

"Her husband? No. It's not about money. Why would you say that?"

"You have to ask, you don't know Kevin. He—well, wait a second."

Carter followed her gaze to the cashier shed, where the twenty-something guy was suddenly doing a lousy job of eavesdropping. Without speaking Madison turned and walked down an aisle, past shelves stacked with coiled-up hoses, bags of fertilizer, and green herbicide spray bottles. It was darker at the back, the morning sun not yet extending to the far corner.

"Start over," she said. "And make it quick. Who are you again?"

"Mercury Carter. Merc for short."

"And you're a mailman?"

"That's right. A freelance courier." He handed her a card. She looked at it and handed it back.

"If you're a cop, you have to tell me that, right?"

"I don't—that's an urban myth. But not to worry, because I'm not a cop. I'm just a guy trying to make a delivery."

"Why's a mailman so interested in finding my daughter?"

"Freelance mailman," he corrected. "Fair question. It's a little complicated, but it boils down to the fact that I can't make my delivery to Rachel Stanfield until I find Stella and make sure she's okay. Sort of a procedural thing."

"What kind of delivery?"

"A legal issue. That part doesn't matter."

"No offense, but you got any ID on you? Anybody can print a card."

"No problem at all." He produced a driver's license.

"Rochester, huh?" she said after studying it a moment. "Long way from home."

"Well, I deliver anywhere."

She handed his license back but there was no disguising the skepticism in her eyes. "I don't know. You got a manager or somebody I could call?"

"Not really. And with all due respect, it's time-sensitive that I find her. Stella, I mean."

"Why?"

"Let's just say it would be good if I located her before these gentlemen I mentioned. The ones I met in Indianapolis."

Mrs. Madison shifted her weight from her left foot to her right. "Well, you're out of luck. I haven't seen Stella in a couple of weeks and I've got no idea where she is." She said it defensively, and in anger, but Carter saw her hooded eyes brighten for a moment.

"You mentioned something about Stella's husband? Could her disappearance be related to him?"

"Kevin." She practically spat the name. "If she's in trouble it's because of him. Guarantee it."

"Why do you say that?"

Carter watched a debate play out on her face as she struggled with continuing the conversation or walking away. After a moment she relaxed and said, "Because there's nothing good to say about him. Barely works, high as a kite half the day, and drunk the rest. Won't lift a finger around the house, even when it was Stella with the job and him doing jack shit. She's had her own problems with drugs and booze, I admit it. But he just laughed anytime she tried to get help. Now you're telling me somebody bad is looking for her? That's on Kevin, no question." Madison was almost shaking as she spoke, she appeared so upset.

"I'm sorry to hear that. He doesn't sound like a good person. You're sure you don't know where they might have gone?"

"We thought the lottery thing might help," Madison said, as if she hadn't heard. "Kenny and me. He's my ex—Stella's father. At least get them out of debt, especially after Stella got fired. But things seemed to get worse after that." She barked a short, harsh laugh. "Only Kevin could fuck up a windfall."

"Lottery thing?"

"Thirty thousand dollars. Normal people, that's your ticket out. A new start. Not Kevin, though." She looked away from Carter. "Or Stella, if I'm being honest about it."

Something occurred to Carter. "Kevin won thirty thousand dollars from a lottery ticket?"

"What I said."

"When was this?"

"Month ago. Six weeks, maybe."

"Do you happen to remember the exact date?"

"No idea. It was—well, hold on." She pulled her phone out again and tapped at the screen. "Why do you want to know? Is it connected to these men?"

"I'm not sure," Carter said, being honest. He pulled out his own phone. He saw a text from Abby. She said the head at Bellbrook had texted her, wondering where she was.

Stall, Carter texted in return. Next, he scrolled to the photo of a string of numbers he'd retrieved from Vlad the Asshole's phone. The one he'd texted Finn, and which seemed to get his attention based on his sudden calls and texts—Let's talk—all of which Carter had ignored. Six pairs of digits. Looked a lot like lottery numbers to him.

"August 5," Mrs. Madison said.

"Excuse me?"

She raised her phone. "Stella texted me August 5 to tell me about the ticket. I'd been riding her pretty hard, especially after I heard she lost her job. I think she wanted me to feel like she'd be okay. Or at least get me off her back."

Six weeks ago. But before or after the deposition that Stella gave in her wrongful dismissal lawsuit?

"You said things got worse after that, not better?"

"Maybe not worse financially. I don't actually know. Kenny and me, we cut them off last year. Told them flat-out we weren't giving them any more money. About the only thing we agreed on after we split up. They bitched and moaned about it, Kevin especially, but we stuck to our guns. They finally stopped asking. They'd still drive over, mooch off me or Kenny for dinner, but that was about it."

"They lived in Champaign?"

Madison narrowed her eyes. "Urbana. Last I heard, anyway. How'd you know that?"

"Google, I think. You were saying you cut them off?"

"We didn't want to. We figured with all that money they'd turn things around. Maybe take us out to eat for a change. No such luck. After that, last text I had from Stella was about a month ago."

"Which was?"

She held up her phone to show him.

**Going away for a while. Bunch of crazy stuff happening. Don't look for me.**

"Any idea what she meant?"

"At the time, no, other than I figured they were back on drugs. Probably snorted or smoked up all the money. Then I found out her attorney died and I didn't know what to think."

"I'm sorry?" Carter said.

She fiddled with her phone again. After a few seconds, she tilted the screen toward Carter. He read the headline above the news item she was showing him.

LOCAL ATTORNEY DEAD AFTER FIERY ONE-CAR CRASH

"May I?"

She frowned but agreed to let him hold her phone and read the article. He skimmed it, taking in a barebones account of the death of attorney Jay Blanton in an accident late at night on a country road a few miles outside Champaign-Urbana, his sedan found wrapped around an oak tree at a treacherous curve. Police speculated he'd been speeding and said they couldn't rule out alcohol as a factor because of unnamed evidence found in the car, though toxicology hadn't come back yet. If it came back. The fire hadn't left much of his remains.

Carter checked the date. Two days before Stella's text to her mother. **Bunch of crazy stuff happening.**

Carter said, "You think this was related to Stella and Kevin dropping off the radar?"

"I don't know what to think," Madison said. "It's a damn shame, I'll tell you that much. Even though they were paying him, he was about the only one left trying to help Stella."

"She doesn't have any friends around, someone who might know where she is?"

"Stella burned a lot of bridges over the years. Not too many friends left."

Carter's phone buzzed with a text from Abby.

**It's not working.**

"What about Kevin? Was he tight with anybody?"

Madison's eyes strayed up the aisle. Carter turned and saw a heavyset man his uncle's age struggling to free a coil of hose from the shelf.

"Listen," Madison said. "I need to get going. I've already said too much."

"Friend of Kevin? Somebody that could point me his or Stella's way? Could help me help them? Help Stella?"

"Tell me again why in the world you want to help my daughter? Somebody you've never met?"

"Like I said, the sooner I find her, the sooner I can make my delivery."

"That's the only reason? To help yourself?"

"If I find Stella and keep her safe, does it matter?"

She shook her head. "You're a selfish little dude, whoever you are."

Carter shrugged. Not the first insult he'd heard along those lines since starting his new life.

Madison's turn to shrug. "It probably doesn't matter at this point. Kevin has a friend named Jon Stanley. High school buddy. Lives down by Terre Haute. Nothing but trouble. We both warned Stella to steer clear of him. Then, of course, I heard Stella mention him a couple times, that he and Kevin had been talking."

"Talking about what?"

"How would I know? Those two, though, it probably wasn't good."

"Got an address? In Terre Haute?"

"Afraid not. Listen, I need to get going."

"Know anyone who does?"

"Does what?"

"Have an address for Jon Stanley?"

Madison hesitated, mind elsewhere, and for a moment Carter didn't think she was going to reply. She broke her silence as she brushed past him and lumbered up the aisle.

"Kenny does. My ex. He might know."

"Thanks," Carter called after her. "He's over in Crawfordsville working, right?" When she looked at him in surprise, he explained about stopping at his house first.

"Good ol' Mrs. Mankins. Count on her to flap her jaw about Kenny's business to a total stranger. Well, she was right about one thing. Today's his day off. Not sure where he's at in that case."

"Thanks. I really appreciate it."

"Okay, I guess." She continued on to the man fumbling with the hose, then turned once more. "Listen, if you are a cop, you've got it wrong about Stella's attorney. Big surprise there."

"What do you mean?"

"That bullcrap about alcohol being a factor in his accident? Guy was a reformed alkie. One of the reasons he offered to take Stella's case. Hadn't had a drink in twenty years."

# TWENTY-FIVE

Glenn was awake when Carter returned to the Suburban. Carter was still thinking about Diane Madison's accusatory last comment.

"What's going on?" Glenn's voice sounded clearer, less laced with pain. Carter started the car and pulled out of their parking space.

He explained his reason for being at the Meijer and his conversation with Diane without going into details. He said, "We're going back to Kenny Madison's house, just for a second. Then we're going to Terre Haute."

Glenn started to ask why but Abby interrupted.

"What am I supposed to do about school? The head keeps calling and Haawo's freaking out. She knows something's up."

"That's all we need. Can't you put her off?" Glenn said.

"She's like my best friend, Dad. Like my only friend there. And—"

"And what?"

"Nothing. I'll tell her something."

As Abby's head dipped over her phone, Carter turned onto Vermillion and drove back toward Kenny's. He told his phone to call Dispatch.

"Merc?"

Carter explained what he learned from Diane Madison about Kevin Wolford, a $30,000 lottery ticket, and someone named Jon Stanley in Terre Haute.

"On it," his uncle said.

"The head," Abby said, shaking her phone at Carter. "She's calling again."

Carter kept to the speed limit, despite the urge to floor it. *Good ol' Mrs. Mankins. Count on her to flap her jaw about Kenny's business to a total stranger.*

"Don't answer. But listen. Here's my suggestion." The comment directed at Glenn. An idea had finally come to Carter.

"For what?" Glenn said.

"For what to say when you call her back."

"Which is?"

"The truth. A version of it, anyway. Tell her about your house. I'm sure it's been on the news. There's no disguising the fact. She can look it up herself. Who knows—maybe she's already heard. Tell her you intended to drop Abby off but you got a call in the middle of the night about the fire. That the two of you are on your way home."

"What about Rachel?"

"What about her?"

"What if she asks where Rachel is? Like, do I know if she's safe? From the fire, I mean. Rachel, well, she generally has more contact with the school than I do." Glenn looked guiltily at Abby.

"Tell her she's fine. That she's traveling separately."

"I can't keep lying. She'll suspect something. She probably already does."

"None of that stuff about Rachel is a lie."

"Really? I know that she's fine?"

Carter thought about the photo from Vlad's phone. The story of Kevin Wolford's lottery winnings. Finn's reaction, his desire to talk when he realized Carter had the picture. Like a man caught cheating on his wife and wanting very much to keep the discovery quiet.

"She's fine for now," Carter said. "With any luck, we'll see her in a couple hours."

"How?"

"She's calling again," Abby said.

"You ready?" Carter said to Glenn. "It's either this or we go to the police. Well, you go. Understandable if that's your call. But you need to decide."

Glenn looked like a man preparing to tell his kids their puppy was just run over by a car.

"Dad?" Abby said.

"I'm ready," Glenn said, reaching for her phone.


"Kenny's a popular guy today." Mrs. Mankins was back outside, without Princess this time.

"Why do you say that?" Carter said.

"Right after you left, two other men showed up. Knocked at his door, just like you did. One of them did, anyway."

"What did he look like? The one that knocked, I mean."

"Big. Ex-football player, I'm guessing."

"Only he knocked?"

"Only he went to the door. They both went as far as the steps. The other one turned around when he heard the dogs. Can't say as I blame him. Makes me nervous, dogs that big next door. Kenny likes them because he's never around. I asked him why he didn't just install an alarm and he said it cost too much. Tell you what, dogs that size aren't cheap."

"They didn't go inside?"

"Not at first."

"What do you mean?"

"Kenny showed up as they were about to leave. I was right about it being his day off. He was out getting coffee."

Carter glanced at Madison's front door. "Then they went inside?"

"Once Kenny put the dogs out back."

"Out back?"

She pointed a bony forefinger toward the rear of Madison's property, as if she were about to conjure a vision. "There's a shed in the yard. Kenny converted it into a dog house."

"Did the men come back out?"

Mrs. Mankins smiled with pride, beaming at how much she knew.

"Not three minutes later."

"Good thing you were paying attention."

Mrs. Mankins's smile turned to a frown. "My side window happened to be open."

Carter looked at his Suburban. Glenn was holding Abby's phone to his ear, deep in conversation. He thought about the headline on Diane Madison's phone.

Local attorney dead after fiery one-car crash

Jon Stanley, Kevin's nothing-but-trouble friend in Terre Haute.

*We both warned Stella to steer clear of him.*

Carter thanked Mrs. Mankins and climbed the steps to Madison's door. Resisting the urge to sprint, just as he'd resisted the urge to speed back here. Maybe a mistake. He tried the door; locked. He knocked once, three loud taps, as he debated whether to kick the door down or run around the house and hope for an open window.

"Yeah?"

Carter hid his surprise at the sight of the large, pasty-faced man standing before him with the patchy stubble of a guy on his day off. In build and stature, he might have been Diane's twin brother instead of ex-husband. Rough around the edges but not roughed-up.

"Kenneth Madison?"

"That's me."

Carter looked over Madison's shoulder. No one in sight behind him. Then, the second surprise. A dog appeared at Madison's side, a hound of some kind, head ensconced in a cone.

Carter did his spiel. Straightforward. Freelance mailman, package for Rachel Stanfield, Stella. Left out talking to Kenny's ex at the Meijer garden center for now.

Madison gave him a funny look. "How come you're asking the same things those other guys did?"

Carter glanced at the dog. "Pardon the question, but did they threaten you?"

"What business is that of yours?"

"I've had some dealings with them, is all."

"I thought you said you were a mailman."

"I am. But I've seen a, well, tough side to those guys."

Madison scratched his left arm, reached down and scratched the neck of the dog behind the cone.

"Tell you the truth, they did come on a little strong. Had some bullshit story about needing to talk to Stella about her lawsuit. The one she filed after she got fired."

"What'd you tell them?"

"Told 'em the truth. Last I heard they were over in Urbana but we haven't had much contact. Can't understand why she's so popular all of a sudden. She came into some money recently but I guarantee that's in the wind. If that's what this is really about, that is." He stared hard at Carter.

"I'm not interested in Stella's money. I just need to talk to her. Also, I'm glad you're okay."

"Since you seem to know so much, guess I'm glad I'm okay, too. Just for a minute there, I kinda regretted putting the dogs out before inviting them two inside. They were starting to make me nervous."

"What about him?" Carter pointed at the hound.

"Her. Dolly. She was in the bedroom sleeping. I only put the other two out because they're so damn loud. Tell you what, they changed their tune when she wandered in. Well, the one guy did."

"Changed his tune how?"

"Scared of dogs. You could see it in his face. Dolly wouldn't hurt a fly on crutches, but no need to tell him that."

"That guy have a scar on his left cheek?"

"Ugly one, yeah. Way he responded to Dolly, made me wonder how he got it."

Carter thought back to the change he'd seen in Finn's demeanor when Carter entered the Wheelers' living room behind the limping schnauzer.

"I appreciate your time, Mr. Madison." Carter turned as if to go. At the last second he stopped.

"They didn't by chance ask about Jon Stanley, did they? Friend of Kevin's?"

"Why are you asking about Jon?"

"No reason. Just wondering if his name came up. I heard he was tight with Kevin. Lives in Terre Haute. Troublemaker?"

"You got a lot of funny questions for a mailman."

"Some of my deliveries can be a little tricky."

"I think we're done here. I've had about enough of you people today. For the record, though, they didn't ask about Jon."

"All right then," Carter said. "I appreciate—"

"I talked to them, if it helps."

Carter turned around. Mrs. Mankins was standing on the second-to-top stair of the steps leading to Kenny Madison's porch. Princess back in her arms, snoring like a morning-after drunk.

"I'm sorry?" Carter said.

"After they left Kenny's. I just happened to be outside. The one man saw me and asked if I knew where Stella was. I said, 'Well, what did Kenny tell you?'"—looking up at Kenny as she spoke—"and they said something about you not being sure."

"You just happened to be outside," Madison said.

"Did they say anything else?" Carter said, wondering why she hadn't bothered telling him this after they pulled up the second time.

"Not a thing. No offense, Kenny, but they could tell I didn't think much of the situation Stella's got herself in. All three of them, I said. Stella, Kevin, Jon Stanley. I feel for you, Kenny. I really do."

## TWENTY-SIX

"Keep trying," Carter said.

"I am," Abby said. "It just goes straight to voicemail. I texted, too."

Carter pushed it a little, watching the fields of yellowing alfalfa and brown feed-corn stalks rush past as he drove. By his count Finn and Stone had a minimum fifteen-minute head start. Almost double that depending on how soon they arrived at Kenny Madison's house after Carter drove to Meijer. Neither Kenny nor Mrs. Mankins was entirely sure of the time frame. Only thing Mrs. Mankins was sure of was mentioning Jon Stanley to the two strangers in the same breath as Kevin and Stella.

At least Carter had Stanley's Terre Haute address and cell number, courtesy of Carter's uncle. A few hours earlier, Carter would have considered this an advantage. But that was before Finn turned down $20 million and Carter surmised someone above Finn was pulling the strings. Someone so mission-driven they'd pass on a fortune just to find Stella Wolford. Someone that on-task would either inspire Finn and Stone to find Jon Stanley's address no matter what or ensure that they got it.

That Finn, for all his bravado, was only a lieutenant, was a useful discovery despite the questions it raised. Almost as useful as the suggestion that Finn might not be partial to dogs. But who was Finn reporting to? Jason? Lobo? Someone else entirely? Carter was reminded of a science show he watched once with Tomeka, about astronomers' hunt for distant planets. How subtle changes in stars' lights or movements could indicate the presence of an orb without disclosing the orb itself.

Who or what was spinning around Finn?

"Hang on," Abby said.

"What?"

"I think I found Stanley's girlfriend. I'm pretty sure this is her on Instagram. I'm messaging her now."

Carter glanced at Abby as her fingers flew over her phone's keyboard. He was once again impressed with the girl. But there was no point in growing attached to her or to her smarts. If Carter didn't find Rachel soon, he'd need to park Abby and Glenn someplace safe. Up until now, they'd been lucky. Glenn had stabilized since the trauma of his beating and near torture, if his performance speaking to the head of Bellbrook Academy just now was any indication.

Carter was wrong: the head hadn't heard about the explosion and fire at the Indianapolis house. She looked it up online as they spoke and, according to Glenn, changed her tune immediately. So far, so good. Of course, the wild card was what would happen when news leaked that Rachel was present during the home invasion at the Wheelers' brownstone. That would be a lot harder to explain away.

"What should I tell her?" Abby said.

"What kinds of things does she post?"

"Mainly pictures of snakes. Some lizards. They might be like breeders or something? It's cool in a disgusting way. Should I warn her or what?"

Carter looked at his phone. Twenty-seven minutes to Terre Haute.

"See if they'll meet us someplace. Tell them we're buyers. We've got a zoo. We pay good money. Just get them out of their house."

"She can see I'm only a kid. My posts are just of me and Haawo and gross Bellbrook food"

Carter thought for a second. "Tell her—tell her your dad's the buyer. That he's not on social media. You have to do everything for him."

Two minutes passed.

"Well?"

"I think she bought it. I'm guessing she's not as into the snakes as he is. The problem is she's at work right now. In a hospital or something. She can't just leave. She said she'll try to reach Jon."

"What's her name?"

"Emilee."

"She knows for sure he's at home?"

"I guess." Abby looked at her phone. "He works second shift or something. She said he's usually asleep this time of day."

Carter groaned as he came up on a slow-moving truck. He made to pass, even though the line was double yellow, but pulled back at the sight of two school buses headed from the other direction. Time for evasive action. He tried Finn's number. No answer. Which could mean a number of things, starting with Finn believing that whatever he learned in Danville had given him the upper hand.

Carter tried to pass again. Now there was a third school bus. And a fourth.

"For the love of Mike," Carter said.

Glenn spoke from the rear of the Suburban. "Why don't we call the police and ask them to do a welfare check at Stanley's address? We don't have to explain everything. Just say we're concerned. You can disguise the call, right? Or your uncle can?"

"It's not a bad idea," Carter said. "But I'm not sure there's enough time. Welfare checks are on the low end of a department's priority list.

Below porch pirates, depending on the circumstances or the time of day. Maybe we should just call 911—"

"Why not SWAT him?" Abby said.

"What?" Carter and Glenn said at the same time.

"Fake a 911 call. People do it all the time. Call in a fake emergency so police will show up at their house." A funny look crept over her face. "These two Bellbrook guys? They got expelled last year for SWAT-ing a kid they were doing some online game with. They were the ones who . . ."

"Who what?" Glenn said.

She paused. "They picked on Haawo a lot. Her and the other Muslim kids. I thought it would get better after they left, but—"

"Isn't that illegal?" Glenn said.

"Bullying? I wish."

"No, I mean SWAT-ing."

Carter registered the hurt in Abby's eyes at her father's interruption and segue away from whatever Abby's Muslim friend had endured at Bellbrook. The thought occurred to him that this seemed like a family with a lot of therapy in its future, assuming they made it through the next few hours.

Instead of reacting to Glenn's comment, Abby looked at Carter and said, "Didn't you spoof my dad's number when he texted me last night? What's the difference?"

LOCAL ATTORNEY DEAD AFTER FIERY ONE-CAR CRASH

Something so important that someone told Finn to turn down $20 million.

Glenn said, "Abby, I'm not sure this is—"

"Call 'Dispatch,'" Carter said to his phone.

# TWENTY-SEVEN

C arter hadn't anticipated so many police cars. Apparently, a 911 call about a home invasion in progress was nothing to sneeze at. But if Carter's suspicions were correct, it's not like the call was that far from the truth.

Jon and Emilee lived in a complex of faded, side-by-side redbrick apartments, the units spread along a series of winding streets that looped this way and that like a jumble of electrical cords someone gave up trying to sort out and just dropped in a drawer. Parking a block away from Stanley's unit, Carter instructed Glenn and Abby to stay put, got out, and approached a crowd of gawkers.

"What's going on?" he said, sidling up to a woman his mom's age in a blue Indiana State sweatshirt and pajama pants.

"Not exactly sure," she said, eyeing Carter. "Cops came barreling in, lights and sirens, and a bunch ran inside. They came out after a few minutes and just been standing there ever since." She nodded at the knot of officers clustered in the duplex's tiny front yard. "You live here?"

"Just moved in. Other side though. Hope it's not always like this."

"Normally it's pretty quiet. These days, though, anything could happen."

"Isn't that the truth. So nobody hurt?"

"Sounds like nobody was home."

Carter climbed back into the Suburban a minute later.

"I think we're too late." He explained what he learned.

Abby looked stricken. "You think Finn and Stone got here first?"

"We have to assume so. Can you ask Emilee what kind of car Jon drives? Tell her we're here and we want to be sure he's home."

Abby looked skeptical but sent the message. "Red Ford pickup," she said after a few seconds had passed.

"Yeah, they beat us here. That truck's sitting out front."

"So what now?" Glenn said.

Carter thought about it. "Now we find Emilee, try to talk to her."

"What about Stanley?"

"I'm not sure there's anything we can do for him at this point. It's possible Emilee might know something that would help."

Just to be sure, Carter tried Finn again. Still no answer. He had to assume, given what happened to both Paddy and Vlad, that Finn could no longer see the advantage of speaking to Carter. On a hunch, he re-texted Finn the photo of numbers from Vlad's phone. Still nothing. Finally, he texted a message.

**Give us Jon Stanley or I'm showing those numbers to the police.**
Still nothing.

The hospital where Emilee worked occupied three blocks off the downtown square. Carter wondered how they were going to connect with Emilee inside a big medical facility without attracting attention. But it turned out she quickly agreed to meet them in the visitors' parking lot.

"I'm freaking out here," she said, staring at the three of them. She couldn't take her eyes off the bandage on Glenn's face. Her own face sported four different blue zirconia studs that matched her scrubs.

"Why's that?" Carter said politely.

"Well, one second you get ahold of me, the next I've got my neighbors texting me that the cops are in our apartment. I can't reach Jon.

And I can't get off to go over there." She looked furtively over her shoulder, pulled a cigarette from her purse. Before she could dig for a light Carter retrieved a lighter from a lower right-hand pocket on his utility vest and did the honors. Two parking spaces away, a sign declared the entire hospital property a smoking-free zone.

Carter checked his phone. Still nothing.

Emilee took a drag and said, "Who are you people, anyway?"

Carter went ahead and told Emilee his name and gave her the spiel. A version of the spiel. Focusing on trying to find Stella Wolford. Explaining they heard that Stella's husband Kevin was tight with Jon. That they were hoping to talk to him, see if he knew where Stella was.

"I want to talk to him too." Emilee jiggled her right foot as if stamping a sidewalk ant hill as she finished her cigarette and fished for a second one. "I don't know why he's not calling me back."

"So you don't know where Stella and Kevin might be?"

"No. He wouldn't tell me."

"Who wouldn't?"

"Jon. He said they were keeping a low profile."

"Stella and Kevin?"

"Maybe I should just go over there, you know?" Staring into the distance, talking to herself. "What are they going to do, fire me? They're already down five LPNs. They caught this one girl doing it with another nurse in the bathroom with the patient in bed right outside and they didn't do anything to them."

"Jon talked to them? Stella and Kevin?"

"They stayed with us one night. It was this big secret thing." Emilee gave Carter a look as if she'd already told him this three times. "We couldn't even go out. I said we had all this money, why not, but no way."

"Money?" Abby said.

Emilee stared at Abby as if seeing her for the first time. "Is that what this is about? You know about the ticket? That stuff about buying snakes—was that all bullshit?"

"Did you say ticket?" Carter said.

"I didn't say nothing," Emilee said, defiance freezing her face. "Listen, I need to go."

Carter took a shot in the dark. "Did Jon win money in the lottery? That kind of ticket? Like Kevin? Because Kevin won $30,000. You'd think that was a good thing. But apparently not. Stella's mother said it made things worse. She couldn't understand why."

Emilee didn't say anything. Carter pressed on.

"If Jon did win something, it could be the reason he's not answering his phone."

"What are you talking about?"

"Just that I'd like to know if Jon won something in the lottery. It might explain some things. It might help figure out what's going on. Maybe help find him."

"Nothing's going on."

"Then why can't you reach him?"

Emilee dropped her second cigarette and stubbed it out on the remains of the imaginary ant hill she'd now crushed into oblivion. Carter put her in her late twenties, but the dark smudges under her eyes and worry lines creasing her pale forehead like fork tines dragged across rising dough made her look far older.

She said, "You said Kevin won $30,000?"

"According to Stella's mom."

The day was mild but Emilee crossed her arms as if a chill was in the air.

"A few months ago Jon won $21,000 off a ticket. It was a little sur-prising, to tell you the truth."

"Because he won so much?"

"Because he never played the lottery. He always said it was a waste of money. Then this one day he went to the store and next thing I know, he's got an official lottery check. It helped, too. Those snakes aren't cheap."

Carter checked his phone. Still nothing from Finn.

He said, "Do you happen to remember if that was before or after August 5? That he hit the lottery, I mean."

She thought about it. "Before. Second week of July. I remember because my birthday's on July 27 and after Jon won, he said I could have anything I wanted. I said Taylor Swift tickets because she was in Chicago that weekend. He wasn't too happy about it when he found out how much the scalpers wanted, but he got them. I'll give him that."

"So Jon won $21,000 in the lottery the second week of July, and his friend Kevin won $30,000 on August 5."

"If you say so."

"Seems like a funny coincidence."

"Not really, now that I'm thinking about it."

"What do you mean?" Abby said.

"Like I told you, it was out of character for Jon. He always said the fix was in with the lottery. That it just ripped off poor people. Then for some reason he did it anyway. Now you're telling me Kevin won a bunch of money right after that. So I'm thinking maybe Kevin decided to go for it after Jon won."

Carter thought: A guy who never plays the lottery because the fix is in suddenly decides to play and wins $21,000. Three weeks later, give or take, a buddy he's tight with—a guy with documented money problems—wins $30,000.

Tomeka was the one with the head for numbers. No question. But even Carter had a feeling something wasn't adding up.

He said, "When Stella and Kevin visited, you said 'it was this big secret thing.' Any idea why?"

She shook her head. "Jon wouldn't tell me, except to say we had to stay put. I was pissed we couldn't go out to dinner. We were sitting on close to seven thou at that point and we had to DoorDash Red Lobster."

Before Carter could ask his next question, Abby said, "Did Jon or Kevin ever say anything about somebody named *Lobo*?"

"Lobo?"

"Lobo, yeah. Like the day you were all together. The big secret thing."

"Abby . . ." Glenn said.

"I don't remember any Lobo," Emilee said, ignoring the interruption. "Jon and Kevin were off talking to themselves that night. Down in the basement. I tried asking Stella what was going on, but she wasn't too friendly. She was a bitch, to be honest about it. We ended up on our phones on opposite sides of the living room while the guys were downstairs. Jon never did tell me what the big deal was."

"The day they visited," Carter said. "Was that before August 5? Could that have been the day Kevin heard about Jon and the lottery and decided to try it? Maybe that was the secret?"

Emilee's phone buzzed with a text. She stared hungrily at the message, only to shake her head a moment later.

"Jesus Christ."

"What?" Abby said.

"Code Brown. I've gotta go."

"Code Brown?"

"Patient missed their bedpan. This'll be fun. Love this fucking job."

As she started to leave, Carter shifted to his right and positioned himself in front of her.

"Excuse me?" Emilee said, taken aback.

"Sorry. This is really important. Did Stella and Kevin pay this big-deal visit before or after August 5?"

"I don't know. Who cares?"

"You might, because it might help us find Jon."

"How?"

"Yes or no?"

Emilee's phone buzzed again. The same look of disappointment crossed her face. But to Carter's relief, she tapped on the screen and scrolled here and there.

"After. August 12, looks like."

"You're sure?"

"Totally. Remember I told you about going out to eat, how Jon said we couldn't? We had all this money and we couldn't do anything with it? We got in a big fight about it. I was like, 'You didn't have a problem with Taylor Swift tickets. And that was only a couple weeks ago.' That's how I remember." She got a funny look as she ignored a third text.

"What?" Carter said.

"Nothing, I guess. I forgot about it until just now."

"Forgot what?"

"Something Jon said during our fight. He laughed it off afterward, said he was just kidding. But after today . . ."

"Said what?"

"After I reminded him about Taylor Swift, he looked at me and said, 'Things are different now. Are you trying to get us killed, or what?'"

# TWENTY-EIGHT

The four of them stood there a few seconds, no one saying anything. Carter was wondering if their luck had finally run out when Abby said, "I just thought of something."

"What?" Carter said.

"Could I see your phone?" The question directed at Emilee.

"I really need to go."

"It'll only take a second. I promise."

Reluctantly, Emilee handed her phone to Abby. Carter watched curiously as Abby maneuvered her way across the screen.

"There."

"There what?" Glenn said.

"Jon's phone. It's here." She played with the phone a moment more and her own phone buzzed with a text. She asked Carter his number, and a second later his phone buzzed as well. "Okay. You should have his location now."

Carter pulled up the map and showed it to Emilee. "Any idea why he'd be there?"

"How'd you do that?" Emilee said.

"The Find My app," Abby said. "It's detecting his phone."

"Really?"

"Didn't you activate it?"

"No idea. Jon bought these after he hit the lottery. He set it up for me."

Patiently, Carter said, "That place? Any thoughts?"

Emilee studied the screen. "I'm not sure. That's the old Buck-Fields quarry." She looked at Carter, her face clouded with anguish. "Why would his phone be there? That's not a place you just go."

"I'm not sure," Carter lied. "But we're going to find out."

"I don't know what to do," Emilee said. Her phone had buzzed with at least two more texts. She stared blankly at the entrance to the hospital. She looked about to cry.

Carter thought briefly of inviting her to accompany them to the quarry. Then he recalled the mess he encountered in Glenn and Rachel's basement. The bag of tools on the floor. The bomb around Glenn. The lengths that Finn and company had been willing to go to find Stella Wolford and secondarily to gain access to Glenn's mysterious fortune.

He said, "You should leave. Drive to your apartment. Talk to the police. Show them your phone."

"But what about . . ." She looked at the hospital.

"Don't worry about that. You said yourself they're understaffed. You've got a personal situation to deal with. They'll understand."

Emilee hugged herself. For just a moment she now looked much younger, almost like a girl Abby's age.

"All right. That's what I'm going to do. When you get there, will you . . . ?"

"We'll do everything we can," Carter said.


They found the entrance to the Buck-Fields quarry off Route 46 three miles outside of town. Carter driving, Abby navigating, Glenn in the back. Carter studied Glenn's face in his rearview mirror from time to time, unable to read what he was thinking. He realized that in the rush to rescue Abby the night before, he never got an explanation of why

Glenn had access to $20 million he couldn't tell the police about. He'd have to get to the bottom of that, and soon. Just not now.

Fast food and retail sprawl gave way to tract housing gave way to more fields of browning feed-corn stalks, and then they were there.

"That way." Abby pointed down a gravel road. "It says eight hundred feet."

"Thanks," Carter said, setting his mind to figuring out why, if Finn and Stone had grabbed Stanley and brought him here to . . . well, why they wouldn't have destroyed or at least disabled his phone. Finn might not have cottoned on to the GPS tracker Carter stuck on his van back in Indy. But he had to be asking himself how Carter found him at Art Wheeler's brownstone. After that, and after what happened to Paddy and Vlad, he'd be taking precautions.

"Hunch down," Carter ordered as the gravel road neared a blind turn, tall bushes crowding either side.

"Why?" Glenn said.

"Do it."

His passengers safely out of sight, Carter slowed to a crawl as he took the turn. He looked left and right and left again, scanning for threats. None, as far as he could see, but with the undergrowth that told him exactly nothing. The road curved back to the right and fifty feet ahead dead-ended at a grassy turnaround. A gate attached to a chain-link fence blocked further passage. A gate hanging slightly ajar.

Carter opened the storage compartment between the driver's and passenger's seats and retrieved his Beretta.

"Where's the phone?"

"Here," Abby said. "Somewhere here, I mean. It's not that precise. Not like the movies. It could be anywhere in a fifty-foot radius."

"Okay. Stay here."

"What are you doing?" Glenn said.

"Stay here, and stay down."

Carter hopped out of the Suburban, eyes darting back and forth. He skirted the edge of the bushes on the left and confirmed there wasn't room to conceal a car within. A quick reconnaissance on the other side confirmed the same. If Finn and Stone brought Stanley here, they'd already finished the job and left.

Cautiously, Carter approached the open gate. Leaning to retrieve a small branch, he hooked it into a gap in the chain link and pulled. The gate moved toward him with a creak. Something rustled in the undergrowth. Carter moved back, weapon out and sighted. A moment later a groundhog so fat it looked incapable of ever seeing its shadow waddled past. Carter stood his ground until his breathing evened out and then proceeded through the gate.

The vista opened up here. Below him pooled a dark expanse of water, perhaps two football fields in size and who knew how deep, surrounded on four sides by limestone walls bearing the gouges of mechanical scarring. The drop to the water looked a hundred feet if it was an inch. Across the quarry a blue September Indiana sky filled the horizon, wisps of clouds feathering the prospect. A hawk wheeled overhead, crying as it rode a breeze high above the dark water. Carter took a step forward, and another, and looked down.

He tried to understand what he was seeing. Maybe a vagary in construction. An engineering failure that necessitated a temporary delay that for whatever reason turned permanent. Perhaps the last-minute cancellation of a contract—a building in New York or Chicago or Minneapolis was no longer in need of limestone cladding. The construction a victim of a recession or the pandemic or who knew what. For whatever reason, a shelf of unmined limestone jutted out from the wall twenty feet below, interrupting the sheer face of the manmade cliff. An outcropping that had not been cleft into building material. Instead, it provided a ledge about thirty feet long and ten feet deep. Just big enough to arrest the motion of a falling body. But one that jumped or was pushed? Not that it mattered, in the end. The result was the same.

Carter knelt and studied the form on the ledge below him. Limbs askew, body frozen in a grotesque parody of an old-school disco dancer. The man—Stanley?—wore sneakers and jeans and what looked like a black concert T-shirt, though Carter couldn't make out the band name or the tour dates. He thought about Emilee's recollection of their fight before Stella and Kevin had shown up. *Are you trying to get us killed, or what?*

A footfall behind him. Carter rolled to his left, popping up a second later in a commando-crawling shooter's posture with the Beretta extended out and up. After a second he swallowed and lowered the gun.

"I told you to stay in the car."

Abby.

Instead of speaking, she raised her right hand. She was holding a cell phone.

"I found it over there." She nodded at a bush. "And something else."

Carter pulled a handkerchief from his cargo shorts' front pocket and wiped the phone. "Fingerprints," he explained.

"Sorry. I didn't think."

"It's okay." He looked at the phone. The background picture was a thin man with shaggy brown hair, whom Carter assumed was Jon Stanley, standing beside Emilee. He glanced toward the edge of the cliff. No question the body on the shelf was the same person. He looked back at the phone. The two were holding some kind of large lizard—an iguana? The screen was locked. But he saw two missed calls and a text message, all from the same person. Carter took his own phone and snapped a picture of the screen.

"Thank you for finding this," Carter said.

Abby nodded and tried to move past him, toward the edge of the quarry. He reached out and put a hand on her shoulder.

"It's him. It's not pretty. Why don't you stay with me?"

"Oh my God."

"Something else," Carter said, hoping to distract her.

"What?"

"You said you found something else."

"Oh yeah. It's weird. It might be nothing . . ."

"Show me."

Reluctantly, Abby turned and walked through the gate.

"It's over here. It was a few feet from the phone. Back in the bushes."

Carter followed the girl to the grassy turnaround. For the first time since the events of the previous evening, he looked at her outfit and fully processed the fact she was wearing a long-sleeved purple tunic, black leggings, and high-top red Chuck Taylors. Dressed up for a girl her age. Exactly what you'd wear to the theater. Not driving across the Midwest looking for your kidnapped stepmother.

"Here," she said, crouching.

"Abby." Glenn, approaching from the van. "What are you doing?"

Carter crouched beside her. Before he could see what she was pointing at, she asked him for his handkerchief. She took it, reached into the leafy shadows, and a moment later pulled out a snake, which she held by the tail without a hint of revulsion. Carter studied the animal. It was like nothing he'd seen before, except maybe in a zoo. Sandy brown, patterned skin, spade-shaped head that suggested a venomous snake. Maybe as long as a garter snake, tops, though thicker. Like a miniaturized rattler or copperhead. It was also as dead as Jon Stanley, its head flat, its fangs jutting out in unnatural fashion, as if plastic drinking straws had been jammed through its crushed jaw.

"What in God's name?" Glenn said.

"One of their snakes?" Abby said. "Jon and Emilee's, I mean?"

"As good a guess as any," Carter said. "But why is it here?"

"Maybe he had it when those guys came in? Or grabbed it, somehow?"

"Maybe."

As curious as the find was, Carter's mind wasn't on the snake. It was on the body on the ledge and the missed calls and the text he'd seen on Stanley's phone. A new name. Someone who appeared in a hurry to reach Stanley. Terry Kientz. He Googled the name. He clicked on a LinkedIn profile he found. He frowned as he read the result. The information only added to the mystery. And now, as a result, he had something hard to do. Very hard.

"Hang on," he said, stepping away from Abby and Glenn. Overhead, the hawk cried again. He found Emilee's number from the text Abby sent with the pin of the quarry address and pressed the call icon. He didn't want to bother her again, not now, but he had to ask about Terry Kientz. There was no getting around it. As he raised the phone to his ear he heard a sound and saw Abby running toward the gate.

"Stop." Carter cut the call and jogged after her.

She was through the gate and standing at the quarry edge before he could reach her.

"What are you—"

"He's alive," Abby said.

"What?"

"I heard him call out, just now. Look."

Carter peered down at the incongruous limestone shelf. Sure enough, the corpse flattened on the hard surface had become a man lying on his side, moaning. Carter felt his phone buzzing. He looked and saw it was Emilee calling back after he'd killed his own call. He disconnected.

"Let's go. We don't have much time."

"Go where?"

Carter pushed the girl ahead of him, forcing her to jog through the gate, past Glenn, and back to the Suburban. Carter opened the SUV's side door and pulled out the metal locker he kept beneath the middle seat. He worked the combination lock, opened the locker, and pulled out a clear plastic box. He opened that and retrieved a burner phone. One of several. He powered it up and pressed 911.

After the dispatcher answered and asked him what his emergency was, Carter said: "The police are looking for a possible kidnap victim. Name of Jon Stanley. He's alive but you need to send someone quickly to rescue him. They'll need ropes and a portable extendable ladder. A long one—at least twenty feet, I'd say." He gave the woman the location and repeated the need to hurry.

"What's your name?"

"Hurry," Carter said and cut the call.

# TWENTY-NINE

It was risky but Carter had Abby drive. If a cop was half a mile away on Route 46 in either direction from the quarry and picked up the 911 call and location they were all but doomed. Yet he needed them in motion and he needed to talk on the phone without the distraction of driving. And Abby had demonstrated her prowess on the overnight trek. And in a million other ways. When they reached the highway, Carter thought about what he read on Terry Kientz's LinkedIn profile and instructed her to drive west, back toward town.

"Hello?"

Emilee, picking up as Carter called her back.

"It's Mercury Carter. We found Jon. He's hurt but I think he'll be okay." Carter hoped this was true. "Where are you?"

"Oh my God. Hurt how?"

"Hurt badly. Help is on the way. Are you home?"

"I just parked down the street. I can't get near my apartment."

"I need to ask you one last question. Do you know a Terry Kientz? It looks like he was trying to reach Jon."

Emilee's voice changed. She was breathing hard. Carter imagined her rushing down the sidewalk in her blue scrubs toward home.

"What about Terry?"

Carter repeated the question.

"What the hell's Terry got to do with any of this?"

"So it sounds like you know him?"

"He went to high school with Jon. Listen, I gotta go. I see the cops. I need to talk to them."

"Do you have Terry's number? Do you know where he lives? It's very—"

"Who the hell are you?"

"I'm sorry?"

"I mean, what the fuck. You barge in and know all this stuff about Jon and Kevin and Stella, and now Jon's hurt and the cops are here and I may lose my job, and well, shit. I mean, who the fuck are you people, anyway?"

"Look, I know it's hard to believe. But we're trying to help."

"Goddamn right, it's hard to believe."

"Terry Kientz's number?"

"Go to hell, asshole," she said, cutting the call.

As they approached the outskirts of Terre Haute, an ambulance and a fire truck raced past them in the opposite direction. Carter glanced at Abby. She might have been driving up to the corner store for a gallon of milk for all the concern her expression betrayed. He was impressed yet again. Then something occurred to him.

"Emilee can identify you," Carter said. "I just realized it. Because you reached out to her on Instagram. And texted the quarry address to our phones."

"Oh shit. I didn't think."

"For God's sake," Glenn said.

"Should we . . ." Abby looked stricken, as if a surgeon had just informed her that removing her left arm in the next five minutes was the only way to save her life. "Should we ditch my phone?"

Carter thought about it. "Hang on." He raised his cell and called his uncle.

"Merc? I was getting worried."

Carter filled him in, ending with Terry Kientz.

"Stay on the line."

While he waited, Carter gave Abby driving instructions, telling her based on a hunch to head north, out of the city.

"What are we doing?" Glenn said. "What about Rachel?"

Carter checked his messages. Still nothing back from Finn. Was that string of presumed lottery numbers important to him, or not?

"We're getting close," Carter said.

"How in the world could you possibly know that?"

"Merc?" his uncle said.

"I'm here."

He put the phone on speaker while his uncle went over what he found. Some of it Carter already knew, some of it he didn't. Terry Kientz lived in Champaign, Illinois. He was the assistant IT director for something called the Intra-Continental Lottery Association, or ICLA for short. Other than LinkedIn, his social media was locked down. His uncle couldn't find any online confirmation of a connection to Jon Stanley or Kevin Wolford. But he was able to provide a home address and a cell phone.

"Thanks," Carter said when he was finished.

"What are you going to do?"

"We need to reach this guy and warn him. Odds are fifty-fifty Finn and Stone know who he is, based on what we found at the quarry."

"Only fifty-fifty?"

"The fact Stanley's phone was in the bushes and not in the bottom of the quarry was a wild card in our favor. That and the snake. Either way, we need to get to him." He explained about Jon Stanley's $21,000 lottery ticket and Kevin Wolford's $30,000 ticket. "A guy who never plays the lottery because he distrusts the government and a guy who's chronically broke both win big—one after the other—and in the middle of this is a guy who does lottery IT for a living? No way that's a coincidence. We need to connect the dots. And make sure he's okay."

His uncle said, "Time to involve the authorities? Things are getting more complicated by the second."

Carter's phone buzzed with a text. He examined the number.

"Maybe. Gonna call you back."

"Watch yourself."

He read the text and examined the photo that came with it. He'd finally heard back from Finn.

**Those numbers leave your phone I'll cut her up piece by piece and send you the video.**

Carter adjusted his ball cap as he studied the photo Finn sent. The lighting wasn't great and the image was slightly blurred. No matter. The gist was clear. The numbers mattered to Finn.

In the photo, Rachel Stanfield faced the camera, blindfolded, bound and gagged, locked inside a large wire-mesh cage.


Rosa Jimenez sat back, frustrated. Lawyers. Why did it always have to be so hard?

"I get that Stella Wolford was a 'minor plaintiff,' as you call her," she told the Summa ProHealth associate general counsel, throwing the phrase back at her. "That doesn't mean she isn't important to somebody. Somebody willing to threaten your boss."

A little past ten the following morning. Sitting in a conference room on the eighth floor of a gleaming, dark green–windowed skyscraper two blocks off La Salle and four long, windy blocks down from the Board of Trade. One of five floors occupied by the Summa ProHealth corporate headquarters. At the far end of a long table sat Kendra Ritter, Summa ProHealth's associate general counsel, who gave off an Olivia Pope "Don't fuck with me" vibe with her blue power suit and pearls despite the worry creasing her forehead like the mother of all migraines. Hunched over in the seat beside her, a young, pale woman—Andi—introduced as Ritter's executive assistant. Last, and maybe least, an older guy—Clay Crowder—with buzzed steel-gray hair and a soft middle like a deflating tire, shifted uncomfortably in a chair opposite the women. Crowder was head of Summa ProHealth security and a former UI Chicago police department deputy chief. Jimenez had nodded in recognition of that last detail in hopes of keeping things pleasant.

"I'm sorry," Ritter said. "I didn't mean—"

"It's all right. Let's not get distracted. The point is, she's of enough interest to somebody that they home-invaded Mr. Wheeler's brownstone and looked ready to do just about anything to get information about her. The question is, is there anything about her lawsuit that would explain what happened last night?"

Ritter lifted a tablet from the conference room table and studied it. "Like I said, there's not a whole lot to work with. Stella Wolford was terminated as a data entry clerk after several warnings and meetings with her supervisor. We even put her on a PIP, though we weren't required to because of her job classification."

"PIP?"

"Performance improvement plan. We outlined a series of benchmarks. She'd do okay for a few days, then backslide. It was a pattern."

"That was here?"

Ritter shook her head. "A data center outside Urbana. Pre-pandemic, it was your typical office. More recently we permitted a hybrid situation. It worked for a lot of people. But not Stella Wolford."

Jimenez thought back to her brief conversation with Gail Wheeler. She said, "Terminated for on-the-job drug abuse, correct?"

"That's right. We maintain that her subpar performance was due to her drug addictions combined with alcohol abuse. We have a fully documented file of our efforts to work with her before her termination." She consulted the tablet again and looked at Andi, who handed her a sheet of paper. "We're confident we would have prevailed. This was nothing but a frivolous lawsuit, in our judgment."

"What was her argument?"

"That her addiction placed her in a protected class under the Americans with Disabilities Act, and therefore her termination was wrongful."

"From what I know of the ADA, that sounds opportunistic. But not necessarily frivolous."

"That isn't our view," Ritter said, frost in her voice.

"Be that as it may, no idea why somebody would want to find her so badly?"

"None."

"What about Wolford's lawyer? Where's she in all this?"

"He," Ritter said. "He's . . . well, tragically, he died in a car accident recently. I just learned of it this morning."

"He's dead?"

"That's right."

Jimenez frowned. She recalled something she was told when she first made detective. Something that struck her as hyperbole initially but over the years had proved its worth time and again. A twist on the old law enforcement saw of "When in doubt, ask all about."

*Always count the bodies*, she was instructed. *Not just the ones at the scene.*

She asked Ritter for the attorney's name and did a quick search on her phone. She studied the result that popped up.

LOCAL ATTORNEY DEAD AFTER FIERY ONE-CAR CRASH

"That's interesting."

"How so?" Crowder said.

"Well, let's see. Somebody is so bent on finding Stella Wolford that they home-invade Mr. Wheeler's brownstone. To complicate matters, they apparently have his co-counsel in the lawsuit along for the ride, a person who is now in the wind and presumed to be under the control of the home invaders. That is, unless you've heard from Rachel Stanfield in the past twelve hours?"

Ritter shook her head.

"Meanwhile, Stanfield's Indianapolis house was reduced to rubble yesterday evening in a mysterious explosion. Now you're telling me, on top of all that, that Stella Wolford's attorney is dead? Yeah, I'd say it's interesting."

After what felt like a commercial break-length pause, Ritter said, "I see. And is there a conclusion you're drawing?"

"Only that I hate coincidences," Jimenez said. When Ritter didn't respond, she said, "Look, my only priority is figuring out who broke into the Wheelers' brownstone. Find out who wished them harm and take those people into custody." She left out the body of the redheaded giant with the garden hose around his neck for now. "It seems like there's a lot of puzzle pieces here. Speaking of which."

She gave Ritter Mrs. Wheeler's description of the slight guy in the baseball cap who saved the day and then vanished into thin air.

"I have no idea who that would be."

Jimenez turned to Crowder. "Somebody on your side of the street, maybe? Assigned to keep an eye on Wheeler on the down-low? I'm guessing the top lawyer for a health insurance outfit isn't the most popular guy in the room. Especially these days."

"I'm not at liberty to discuss security assets. But I can say for sure he wasn't one of our guys. Starting with, we don't hire shrimps."

"Got it." Jimenez was inclined to believe him, despite the fact that his sullen response to the question suggested, based on her experience, that he probably discussed Summa ProHealth's security assets at length from his perch on a barstool each and every night.

She said, "That leaves us with the same question our home invader had: Where is Stella Wolford?"

"She's not in Urbana?" Ritter said.

"We're checking on that. Initial indications are negative."

"That's the only address we had."

"Nothing secondary?"

"Not that I'm aware of."

"Anything else? Anything that might help me understand what happened last night?"

Jimenez watched as glances were exchanged around the room. Despite Ritter's lawyerly reserve, Crowder's blue-line-of-suspicion stone face, and Andi's secretarial cool, the message was clear. Nobody here had a clue either.

Increasingly, it felt like the only people with answers were Stella Wolford herself and a slight guy with a baseball cap and some unorthodox skills. Neither of which Jimenez was even one millimeter closer to finding than when she woke up that morning with a sleep-deprivation headache and realized she was out of Café Bustelo and that the dog had gacked all over the kitchen floor.

Which was par for this case so far. That was for damn sure.

# THIRTY

"Oh sweet Jesus," Glenn said. "Jesus God."

For her part, Abby simply wept.

Carter was back behind the wheel. They were headed north on Route 63, halfway back toward Danville, maybe an hour out from Champaign-Urbana. Cruise control locked and loaded at seventy-one MPH. Carter itching to blast it past eighty but knowing full well they couldn't risk a cop at this point. He'd get there. He always did.

He waited until Glenn stopped rocking in the rear passenger seat and Abby's tears slowed to the occasional sniffle. It might have been a mistake to show them Finn's photo of the captive Rachel, along with the warning. But despite their anguished response, he didn't think so.

"Listen up."

The interior of the Suburban fell silent.

"I know it looks bad. It is. I'm not going to sugarcoat it."

"Looks bad? They're going to kill her," Glenn said. "If they haven't already."

"That remains to be seen."

"For God's sake, how can you—"

Patiently, Carter said, "Let's add some things up here, and I'll explain."

"Fuck that. We need to face reality. It's over."

Abby turned a tear-stained face to Carter. "What kind of things?"

Carter took a moment to organize his thoughts. There was a lot riding on this, on assuaging their fears. The same ones he had, as a matter of fact.

After a moment, he said, "Point one. Rachel is stationary. She's no longer on the move. That's good."

"How can you possibly know that?" Glenn said. "They could have switched cars—put her in a cargo van or something."

"To transport her, sure. But not to hold her. The photo's the give-away. Finn thought he was being cute, showing us that. Making us feel helpless. Well, he did, initially. But look at the picture again. Right-hand side, one half of a three-prong electrical outlet is visible. Above that, there's a small gouge."

"So?" Glenn said.

"That's a crack in painted sheetrock. That's not vehicle siding. That's a wall."

"That makes it even worse," Glenn said. "That means she could be anywhere."

"Just the opposite," Carter said. "She's somewhere now. In a car or van, moving place to place, she's God knows where. Hard to trace. But locked away? She's someplace with an address. And addresses can be tracked."

"That could be literally anywhere in the world."

Carter maneuvered the Suburban into the passing lane to move around a sedan with its left turn signal stuck on. "Again, with all due respect, just the opposite. We had eyes on Rachel last night. We know Finn and Stone were in Terre Haute this morning to grab Jon Stanley. Rachel was dropped off someplace in between during that time. It's a small radius. Probably less than one hundred and fifty miles."

When Glenn didn't respond, Carter said, "Also, there's an SKU."

"A what?"

"It's hard to make out. On the left side of the cage, on the left support strut, there's a label. On the label is a code, a jumble of numbers and letters. It's called a stock keeping unit. It's how retailers track their inventory. Everybody uses them now."

"So?" Glenn said again.

"So purchased or stolen or whatever, that cage came from somewhere. I've got my uncle working on it. Tracking that SKU could narrow things down."

"Unless they stole it from California."

"It's a good point." Carter thought for a moment. He said, "But stealing a cage to imprison a hostage implies intent. It means they had to think about it, even for a day or two. Go through the steps to acquire it. But based on everything we know"—he glanced at Abby, debated, realized he had no choice—"they weren't expecting to have passengers with them after visiting your house."

He paused to let the implications of that hit home. Abby sniffed, dried her eyes, and looked back at her father.

Glenn said, "Even assuming that's true, that the SKU can be tracked, that'll take time. Time we don't have."

"That brings me to point two. Sorry, three, after the SKU."

"Which is?" Glenn said, unable to disguise his impatience.

"Jon Stanley did us a favor. He bought us some of that time."

"What are you talking about?"

"The snake," Abby said.

Carter nodded. "That's right."

"I'm not following," Glenn said.

"Remember what Emilee told us? What Jon said when they had the fight about going out to dinner? He said, 'Are you trying to get us killed, or what?' Jon knew something was up. That they might be in danger. Which means he was being careful. Taking precautions. When Finn and Stone showed up he was armed, so to speak."

"With a dwarf adder," Abby said.

Carter looked at her curiously. "Go on."

She held up her phone. "Full name, Namaqua dwarf adder. I did a Google Image search. World's smallest viper. Native to southern Africa. Its bite is toxic, though not usually fatal. But it can be nasty."

Carter thought about it. "Nasty is probably the key. The question is why they went to the quarry. It's possible Finn and Stone took him there, figuring it was the closest place on the fly they could interrogate him without anyone hearing."

"Or maybe Jon tricked them," Abby said. "Told them he could take them to Stella."

"That's what I'm thinking. Then, when they got there, Stanley turned the tables on them. He unleashed the snake. Based on its condition, I'm wagering it bit one of them, Finn or Stone. That changed everything. Maybe Stanley tried to bullshit them, trade his life for the antivenom. Maybe they freaked and he tried to bolt. Regardless, he opened a window."

"There's a website that says the antivenom isn't effective," Abby said. "And usually not required."

"I'm guessing Finn and Stone don't know that, though. In the heat of the moment, looks like Stanley made a run for it and went over the quarry edge himself or with their help. One of them killed the snake, obviously. The main thing is, Stanley was able to ditch his phone first, which leads us to point four."

"Which is?" Glenn said.

"It's possible they don't know about Terry Kientz."

A few minutes later they were clear of Danville and headed west on I-74.

Glenn said, "You think he tossed his phone before they saw those messages?"

"There's a good chance, yes."

"How can you know that?"

"Think about it. We got to the quarry around eleven A.M. We were fifteen, twenty minutes behind. The missed calls and the text came in at ten forty-five. It's a possibility."

"But how could Finn not know about Terry Kientz to begin with? Or Jon Stanley, for that matter?"

Before Carter could answer, Abby said, "Shoot."

"What?" Carter and Glenn both said.

"It's Haawo." Abby's fingers flew over her phone's keypad. "She knows where we are. Ugh. I should have guessed she'd do that."

"Do what?" Glenn said.

"That Find My app we used to track Jon to the quarry? I forgot we have each other's phones on it. In case . . . well, just in case."

"Can you turn it off?" Glenn said.

"I did, back there. But she already pinpointed me. She's asking me why I was in Terre Haute."

"You need to do something about her before she ruins everything."

Abby's face twisted in anger at her father's comment. "Do something about my best friend? My only friend?"

"Don't be so melodramatic. You have plenty of friends."

"Don't pretend like you know anything about me. I have zero friends, at least at Bellbrook. Except for Haawo. And I'm—"

"And you're what?"

"I'm *her* only friend. Because the kids there are trash. The way they treat her is trash. Just because she's Muslim and goes to a mosque. They don't even try to get to know her.

"I'm sorry to hear that. But now's not the—"

Carter cleared his throat. Glenn and Abby glared at each other, then looked at the mailman.

"I think we can all agree it's not ideal that Haawo knows something's fishy," Carter said.

"That's putting it mildly," Glenn said.

"That said, if you're each other's best friends, maybe you can put her off for a while. At least ask her to give you time to explain before she outs you. Hopefully, you'll be back in school by tomorrow anyway."

"Oh joy."

"Abby," her dad said.

"What do you think?" Carter said.

"I'll do my best," Abby mumbled, returning to her phone.

"Okay," Carter said. "Back to Terry Kientz."

"What about him?" Glenn said.

"How Finn couldn't have known about him is a good question. It's confusing. But here's a theory."

They were back to the land of cornfields stretching over what appeared to be literal leagues toward a distant horizon, the vista broken only by rows of giant wind turbines, blades rotating as lazily as county fair Ferris wheels.

"Which is?" Glenn said.

"It goes back to what we figured out last night. The fact there's a shot caller who's not Finn."

"Assuming that's even true, so what?"

Carter ignored Glenn's skepticism. "Someone who's in a position to turn down $20 million probably has some pretty big fish to fry. Which means he likely operates on a need-to-know basis."

"So what?"

"So, in this scenario, all Finn needed to know was the importance of locating Stella Wolford and figuring out what she or anybody else knew about this 'twenty-two seven' thing. Finn had leeway to follow that trail wherever it led. But his primary mission, without explanation, was Stella. The best analogy might be the way terror cells operate."

"Wait a sec," Abby said. "Where'd this $20 million come from?"

The car went quiet. Carter looked at Glenn and waited for him to respond. When Abby's father stayed silent, Carter said, "That was the ransom for you and Rachel."

Abby stared at Carter. "You have $20 million?"

The look of shame that came over Glenn's face nearly rivaled his horror at seeing the photo of Rachel in the cage.

"I had access to $20 million," Carter said, deciding they didn't have time for a fuller explanation—the one Abby deserved—right now. "It obviously didn't matter in the end."

Studying Abby's face, he could tell she wasn't fully buying it. But before anyone spoke she unbuckled and moved into the rear.

"Dad? Are you all right?"

"I'm not sure," Glenn said. "I'm not feeling great all of a sudden."

"Fever?" Carter said.

Abby rested her hand on her father's cheek. "I don't think so. It's a little hard to tell."

Carter instructed her on where to find a thermometer in his medical supplies box.

"Ninety-seven point eight," Abby said three minutes later.

She followed Carter's directions on checking for infection around Glenn's facial wound and using a flashlight to examine his pupils.

"Sounds like a mild concussion," Carter said after considering everything. "Either from the blow to your head or the explosion. You should probably see a doctor."

"We don't have time for that," Glenn said. "Not after . . ."

Not after the photo of Rachel in the cage. Carter figured as much. He knew it would come down to this eventually. Finn hadn't just been threatening them. He'd been testing their resolve. Finn had gambled that the image would disrupt their momentum. Counter the advantage the photo of the lottery numbers gave them. Cause them to rethink their strategies. It had certainly done all that, beginning with Glenn's reluctance to seek medical assistance.

But there was something else. Finn had unknowingly shown his hand. Because unless Carter was wrong about the timing of Rachel's imprisonment—and he was pretty sure he wasn't—Finn had been hanging on to that photo for several hours as a trump card. A last resort. Then he played it after the screwup at the quarry. Which spoke to an undisciplined lashing out. The notion that circumstances beyond his control had caused Finn to push back.

None of which negated the fact that Glenn was right. They didn't have time for a detour. Not at this point.

"I thought of something else," Glenn said, his voice close to a whisper.

"What?" Carter said.

"It's only a matter of time before the cops trace Abby's messages back to her, and then me. What then?"

"We deal with it."

"How? It could change everything for the worse."

"Maybe," Carter said. "But let's not get ahead of ourselves. It's not like TV. It's going to take them a while to put the pieces together. Assuming Jon Stanley is alive, he's their first point of contact. They'll want to know what he can tell them. And even if they do identify us, so what? It's not like they can find us." Carter paused. "Unless you want them to."

Glenn didn't say anything.

Abby said, "If the cops get involved, and Finn finds out, will they kill Rachel?"

"I don't know," Carter said. Thinking: *It's a good question.* Thinking: *A girl this young shouldn't be forced to ask that kind of question.* He wondered if he was doing the right thing, keeping Abby in the mix. He knew what his uncle would say. He also wondered if he had any choice after everything that had happened.

"Well, one thing?" Abby said.

"Yes."

"I just deleted my Instagram account. That should slow them down a little, right?"

"A little," Carter said. "Thanks. I appreciate that. I'm guessing that wasn't easy."

"It's easier than losing Rachel."

"Fair enough. Now, if it's all right, I need you to do one more thing."

"Which is?"

"I need you to make your dad comfortable for the next thirty-five minutes."

"That's a little specific," she said uncertainly. "What then?"

"Then we'll know exactly how much time Jon Stanley bought us."

# THIRTY-ONE

Finn drove until he was sure they weren't being followed. Who might do that, other than cops, he wasn't exactly sure, but he wouldn't put it past Carter. Not after the shit that guy pulled in the last twelve hours. The random driving back and forth across Terre Haute made for a tense hour, what with Stone slumped white-faced in the back seat, bare chested after he'd stripped in a panic to expose the puncture wounds in his neck where the snake had sunk its fangs with savage speed. The creature appearing seemingly from nowhere after they stopped the van by the edge of the quarry. Bringing back not a few unpleasant memories for Finn involving a different kind of beast.

The fuck was it with this job? First Paddy, then Vlad, now Stone?

Finn feared the worst the first time Stone threw up. Not out of any sympathy for Stone, but in the same way a man fears the loss of a dependable field weapon. At this level, replacement parts were hard to come by. Between the beating Carter managed to inflict on Stone the day before and now this, things weren't looking good. A shame, but asset disposal was an occasionally necessary if inconvenient aspect of mission ops.

There was nothing to do now but wait. Wait for Stone to stop gasping and moaning and breathe his last in the parking lot of a brick Baptist church in southern Indiana or to beat the odds and pull out of it.

One thing was certain. No matter what happened to Stone, Carter was going to pay. Finn would make sure of that. *The hunter becoming the hunted, my fucking foot*, he thought. He hadn't come all this way, set aside his reservations about working with someone like Jason—*never trust an idealist* had always been Finn's rule, even if you affirm their ideals—gotten so close to finding Stella Wolford and shutting down that potential information breach at its source, just to let Carter win the day. To let some flat-affect, smart-aleck, wannabe mercenary masquerading as a mail carrier—a mail carrier!—get the upper hand. Fuck Jason and his warmongering blather and the "package" Jason was poised to deliver in a day or two. It was the principle of the thing at this point.

*No*, Finn thought, glancing back at Stone, prone in the back seat, eyes shut, massive chest slowly rising and falling. *Not a chance.*

Carter was going to pay. Pay until he was begging Finn to put him out of his misery for good. Pleading for the pain to stop. Beseeching him for mercy as his bowels loosened and his mouth foamed and his eyes rolled in agony.

But no clemency would come. Because Carter was going to regret, all the way to the end of his miserable life, the day he rang the bell at Rachel Stanfield's house.

Access to Terry Kientz was going to be a problem. Carter could see that right away.

The subdivision that Kientz lived in was nondescript in all the usual ways, including the lack of privacy. This wasn't the exurban realm of McMansions that he encountered trying to make his delivery to Rachel, each house floating on expansive turf and tree and mulch islands. This was a compact neighborhood crowded with dozens of cookie-cutter houses with attached garages and minimal side yard offsets. Residents or passersby would spy derring-do a mile off. So there was that. Then, add to the mix the guy on lookout duty out front.

The *Illinois Insulation* sign on the side of the van he was sitting in was a professional job but fooling nobody.

Not Carter, anyway.

"What are we going to do?" Abby said after Carter explained the situation.

"I need to get inside. Try to talk to Kientz. If . . ."

"If he's alive?"

"If I can," Carter said firmly.

"What about me?"

"I need you to get your dad checked out."

"Like in a hospital?"

"Too risky. Better to take him to a pharmacy with a walk-in clinic—CVS, Walgreens, whatever. My uncle can help find a place." He thought for a moment. "How about this? Tell them he fell off a ladder yesterday but insisted on bringing you here for your U of I college visit, which is today and can't be rescheduled. Explain that he cut his cheek in the fall. Play it however you want. Just keep your eyes open. Any indication they're not buying it, excuse yourselves, say you're late for your tour, and leave. Can you handle that?"

"Will it help us rescue Rachel?"

*A good question*, Carter thought. But what he said was "Yes."

"In that case, gimme the keys."


Carter ran through the usual scenarios, considered meter reader, debated cable salesman, ultimately settled on census taker, mainly because that clipboard was his sturdiest.

He approached from the west, walking up behind the guy sitting in the Illinois Insulation truck. Carter had no doubt the man made him in his rearview mirror as soon as he neared the house, but suspicion wouldn't set in right away. Carter was guessing the guy had already pegged his fair share of dog walkers and joggers and maybe even real mailmen in the past hour alone. You couldn't react to every one of them. So he did his best to blend into the scenery until he pulled even with the truck. Then he walked into the yard, strolled past a fiery red Japanese maple, bounded lightly up the front steps, approached Kientz's door, and knocked twice, sharp but friendly. Inside, a TV boomed, a game or a gameshow of some kind.

A second later he heard the truck's door open.

"Hey. Nobody's home."

The man, already headed toward Carter.

Carter knocked again and stepped back. He checked his watch and looked around like a potential homebuyer taking in the neighborhood. Seeing the Illinois Insulation man, he gave a friendly wave as if acknowledging a fellow solicitor before turning around to face the door.

The big question: One guy on lookout meant how many inside?

Carter recalled the undercount of men at Rachel Stanfield's that Stone tried to slip past him. Best to assume at least two. More than that could be tough. Not that he had any choice.

Now the man was on the porch and tapping his shoulder.

"Hey pal—did you hear me? I said nobody's home."

Carter detected the flat vowels of Chicagoland in the man's voice. Interesting. He knocked a third time.

"Are you deaf or what? Do yourself a favor and move on."

Not a gameshow on the TV inside. Definitely a game. Didn't sound like baseball—too bad—and it was too early in the week, and too early in the afternoon, for a college match unless these guys were really into club rugby. Probably soccer, Carter guessed. A FIFA match from someplace. Tomeka was a big fan of the sport, rarely missing an MCC women's game back in Rochester if she could help it. Carter, not so much. Hard to get excited over a game where so many people have so much trouble putting a small ball into a big net.

"Hey—are you listening?"

Carter turned and examined the man. Heavyset, sprouting short black bristles on his chin, wearing a gold link chain necklace thick enough to lock a mountain bike with, and sporting a Gabriel Iglesias 2022 tour shirt. Arms like pony kegs, chest like a barrel, if the barrel held rapidly setting cement. His tightly cinched cargo shorts sagged a bit, no doubt because of the large caliber handgun Carter guessed was tucked in the rear of his waistband.

Carter made as if to shield his eyes from the afternoon sun and said, "I mean, you can hear the TV, is all. Like someone's inside."

"They probably just left it on."

Carter gave a friendly laugh. "Really? Who does that? I mean, the way electric bills are going."

"Forget electric bills. You need to take a hike."

"There—you hear that?" The TV had suddenly gone quiet.

Carter turned and knocked a fourth time. "I'm sure there's someone here." He tapped his clipboard optimistically. "Hopefully, it's my lucky day."

The man narrowed his eyes as if he couldn't believe what he was hearing.

"This is the last time I'm going to tell you—"

Before he could finish Carter heard the click of a deadbolt. The door opened no wider than the length of a credit card.

"We're not interested." A man's voice, his Windy City accent mirroring that of the Illinois Insulation guy.

"It'll only take a minute." Carter once again tapped the clipboard.

"I said—"

You couldn't take things for granted. It was true when he carried a USPIS badge and it was true now. Off-the-shelf pepper spray, for example. It didn't always work as advertised. Maybe it would deter an arthritic bear, maybe not. To achieve the result he won the evening before with Stone outside Rachel Stanfield's house, you had to special order. Same went with stainless steel clipboards. They tended to be a giveaway. Like, who outside a Chevy plant manager carries something like that around? But cover it, both sides, with self-adhesive wood grain wallpaper? That's more like it. You came off as an anthropology graduate student researching urban norms and mores. Or a census taker. Carter raised the clipboard to demonstrate his good intentions to the man inside, inserted one end into the narrow door crack, and twisted it with a sharp jerk. The man cursed as the metal edge scraped his fingers and tried to slam the door, but steel trumps wood every time.

Carter moved fast, gliding through the opening and jabbing the clipboard's short edge against the man's windpipe jutting out above his white ribbed wifebeater. Hard and fast, like shoving home a loose brick in a wall. The man stumbled backward, nearly tripping on the red recliner parked in front of the room's widescreen TV—yup, soccer—hands rising to his throat, gagging for air that wouldn't come. Carter pulled the door all the way open and brought the clipboard down hard onto Wifebeater's head, stepping to the side as the man dropped to his knees beside the recliner, knocking the remote to the floor—*huh-huh-huh*-ing the entire time—and collapsed.

The wide-open door was counterintuitive. But it had the desired effect. Gold Chain hesitated just a moment before rushing inside, glancing at the street to see if anyone had seen what happened. Confirmation to Carter that the man's marching orders included instructions not to attract attention. The delay meant that Carter had just enough time to slam the clipboard on Gold Chain's right hand as it rose, gun firmly in his grasp. The man howled as the top of the board's metal clip—filed to a razor edge by Carter before stowing it aboard the Suburban, standard operating procedure—raked the top of his hand like a knife drawn across raw chicken. As the gun dropped with a thud and the man's thumb and pointer finger bloomed red, Carter jerked the clipboard up and slammed it into the underside of his attacker's chin with the force of a man violently throwing up a window sash. No sooner did the man's teeth click at the impact than Carter reached out, grasped the gold dog collar with his left hand, and spun him around. Yanking at the chain in a single smooth motion he slammed the man's head against the edge of the open door. As Gold Chain's eyes rolled into the back of his skull, Carter brought the clipboard down on the top of his head and stood back as the man dropped to the floor, limbs splayed like the aftermath of a sledding accident gone very bad.

Satisfied that both men were temporarily down for the count, Carter shut the front door, carefully and slowly, no hurry at all, as if he were reluctantly bidding farewell to a departing lover. And then dove behind the recliner one second after hearing a floorboard creak on the opposite side of the room and one second before hearing the metallic penny-dropped-in-a-can clicks of two sound-suppressed shots.

At least two guys had been inside. Good to know. And they'd figured a workaround for the risk of gunshots. Not so good. Memories of Carter's backyard on a cold, snowy February night flashed before him.

Carter unholstered his Beretta. He only had one move. It wasn't a good one. You took what you could get, he guessed. He breathed in, raised the remote he'd whisked off the floor, and clicked to unmute the TV. The sound of a man speaking Spanish in a loud, exuberant baritone filled the room. But was it loud enough? Carter glanced around the edge of the chair in time to see the second man divert his attention away from Carter by a split second as he startled at the unexpected noise.

Carter's Beretta roared a second later, just as the crowd on the TV also roared.

# THIRTY-TWO

C arter found Kientz in the basement. He hadn't been as lucky as Jon Stanley. Garroted, if Carter had to guess. Slumped on the floor beside a black chair on rollers, blood pooling around his throat. Above him, a desk containing multiple computer monitors and a sickly house plant, its leaves blue tinged from the small grower's light it sat beneath. Carter knelt and examined Kientz. Bruises on his face suggested he'd been struck hard several times before he died. Interrogated by one or both of the inside men, no doubt. Based on available evidence, Carter guessed he was one, maybe two hours too late.

But what had the men wanted? The basement, thoroughly ransacked, looked like a tornado had touched down; they'd been searching for something. The location of Stella Wolford? Is that why Kientz—or one of these men, masquerading as him—tried calling and texting Stanley that morning? If it had been Kientz, had he died possessing information that might lead Carter to Rachel Stanfield?

Carter pulled a pair of latex gloves from his utility vest, snapped them on, did a quick reconnaissance, and collected some supplies. Back upstairs, he used the rolls of duct tape he found along with a length of nylon line to supplement the zip ties currently binding the hands and feet of Gold Chain and Wifebeater. He did a makeshift hogtie for both men just to be sure. Although they were coming around, they weren't going anywhere anytime soon.

There was no need to secure the man he shot. The man with not one but two teardrop tattoos below his left eye.

Before returning to the basement, Carter called Abby.

"They're examining him now. They also changed his bandage."

"Any sign of infection?"

"Nope. The lady says whoever dressed the wound was obviously a professional. She asked what hospital did it. I fudged and said Methodist. Was it you?"

"I'm glad it's not infected. Any word on a concussion?"

"They're getting to that. What about the guy you were looking for?"

"I found him. Give me ten minutes and I'll start walking in your direction."

"What'd he say?"

"Ten minutes, all right?"

Back in the basement, Carter tapped at Kientz's keyboard and pushed his mouse back and forth to wake the monitors. They were password protected and locked down. No surprise for equipment used by the IT director of a multi-state lottery association. Not counting napkins from take-out meals, there wasn't much paper anywhere that Carter could see, which meant that anything important was locked away on hard drives or sitting in the cloud. Either way, about as accessible as files stored in a moon crater. Carter searched every inch of Kientz's desk anyway. Looking for anything that might tie Kientz to Kevin Wolford and Jon Stanley and explain the coincidence that both men won large lottery prizes in quick succession.

On the surface, it looked as if Kientz had figured out a way to game the system. Best guess: how to tinker with software to steer winning tickets to his friends. Graft as American as apple pie. All well and good. Except for the wild card in the scenario. A psychopath named

Finn. Why was he in the picture and so interested in learning the location of Kevin's wife, Stella? Furthermore, how did Finn's relentless quest and Kientz's lottery scheme relate to one guy named Lobo and another named Jason? And how was any of this going to help Carter find Rachel?

A sound overhead. Faint thuds. Carter sighed and went back upstairs. Gold Chain and Wifebeater stilled as he entered the living room, but it was obvious they'd rolled off their original positions. The look in their eyes made it clear they'd flay Carter alive in an instant if given the chance. Carter took the opportunity to tighten their bindings and add new ones. He found their phones, waved them in front of their faces to unlock them, and examined the text messages and recently called numbers. No names. Interesting. Everything by digits. All Chicago exchanges. No mention of Kevin Wolford or Rachel Stanfield or Finn. No reference to Lobo.

Pulling a kitchen chair into the room, Carter sat and said, "Either one of you happen to have a phone number for a guy named Kevin Wolford?"

They shot him murderous looks, the kind suggesting that not just flaying but disembowelment would be the least of Carter's future problems.

Although unlike the guy cooling on the carpet, their faces were tattoo free.

Carter sighed, and said, "I don't have time to play the heavy here, so I'll make it simple. The way I tied you up, you're not going anywhere. Take my word for it or wear yourself out trying, but I'm being straight with you. Meanwhile, it's possible a welfare check might get called in to this address if no one hears from Kientz for a day or two. Or maybe not. If he has stuff up and running, automatic updates and all that, it could be more. Seventy-two hours. Ninety-six. It's a long time. You hear these miracle stories about babies pulled from earthquake rubble after a week, but that's the exception to the rule. No food or water that long—it's a tough way to go. So, I'll repeat the question: A number for Kevin Wolford?"

The same murderous looks, accompanied by the frisson of something else. Fear. As if giving that information away carried a price heavier than they were willing to pay.

While he waited, Carter took photos of the recent call logs on two of the three phones. Try as he might, he couldn't get the phone of the man he'd shot to open. Facial recognition had its mortal limits, apparently. Finished, Carter pocketed the phones and returned to the basement for one more sweep. He was struck again that the only paper present was take-out napkins. Lots and lots of napkins. He idly flipped through the pile. He made it to the last and was about to set them down when he noticed the outline of writing on the back of the last napkin. Lines from the pressure of a pen. He flipped the napkin over. He found himself looking at a ten-digit number scrawled in pen. Sloppily, as if written in a hurry. Flipped over and buried as if Kientz knew to be careful with it.

The exchange was local. Champaign-Urbana. Carter plugged the number into his phone and dialed. It rang three times. Four. Five. Six. Carter was waiting for voicemail to kick in when he heard the click of a connection.

"Terry?"

Carter hesitated only a second.

"Kevin."

"What the hell, man," Kevin Wolford said. "I've been trying to reach you."

# THIRTY-THREE

Rachel went still, hearing a sound. Not in the room where she was being held. Outside it—outside the building, in fact. A car door slamming. Another. Two more. The sound of engines. She stayed motionless—like she had any choice. The cage or whatever the hell she was jammed inside was too small to do much but lay quietly.

Her left side ached from the hours of captivity and her inability to shift more than a couple of inches at a time. They'd at least given her access to a bathroom before pushing her inside the chamber, but who knew how much longer she could hold it. For a long time she listened in the dark to the sound of men's voices, first in the room, and later outside, in what she guessed was a hallway. Indiscriminate murmurs. Nothing she could make out except that the voices exuded menace and foreboding. All the time dreading the interrogation she'd been promised upon her arrival. The implication that she'd have been better off talking to Finn than experiencing what lay ahead at the hands of someone called Jason, whoever he was.

But so far, that hadn't happened. Now, hearing the sound of departing cars outside, Rachel doubled down on her efforts to gauge her surroundings. Counting the exact number of captors was impossible but she'd determined there had to be at least four, based on the pair she heard inside the room and what she was pretty sure were two other distinct voices in the hallway at the same time. But was there a fifth? Or a sixth? Regardless of that, how many left just now? She was guessing they wouldn't leave her here alone unless they were about to torch the place or blow it up. But several minutes had now passed without that happening. Of course, it was possible someone was here, was in fact sitting in this room, frozen like a statue while he watched their captive. Even if she was alone, that didn't negate the possibility of cameras streaming her every move. Either way, though, the time had come. She had to risk it. The departures outside signaled that something was going on, something she might be able to use to her advantage.

Slowly, ever so slowly, she pushed her hands into her waistband and fished for the nail.

She'd given up once. She wasn't going to do it again.

Rachel had been sitting at her desk, reviewing mitigation strategy for Craig Wiseman's death penalty trial, when the front desk buzzed her. Almost two years ago to this very day.

"Rachel? Um, Cindy Chen's here."

Rachel picked up on the receptionist's puzzled tone. "Like, *here* here?"

"In the lobby. She's asking if you're available."

Rachel grabbed her cell to see if she'd missed texts from Cindy. But the only messages so far that morning were a question about the deck installation from Glenn and a reminder of her ob-gyn appointment the next day. She checked her online calendar to see if she'd blanked on a meeting; also nothing. Cindy wasn't the prosecutor on Wiseman and Rachel couldn't think of any other cases they were both currently involved with. Nothing since Chad Setterlin and the security video that hamstrung his rape-murder prosecution, and that was months ago. Odd.

"Okay. Send her back."

Rachel waited in her doorway until she saw the Marion County assistant prosecutor round the corner.

"Everything okay? I wasn't expecting you—unless I forgot something?"

"No, this is on me. I apologize for just showing up. I wanted to come in person."

"That doesn't sound good."

"Someplace we can talk in private?"

"Sure." Rachel gestured at her office.

Inside, it seemed for a moment as if Cindy wanted to stand. She relented and took the hard plastic chair Rachel offered. It was difficult to read her expression. Even harder to determine why she'd shown up wearing an Indy Mini Marathon pullover, jeans, and running shoes, her gray-streaked hair in a ponytail.

"Is that pullover part of your undercover vibe?" Rachel said, trying to keep it light.

"Sorry. It's my day off—I should have changed. Except, well, I only just heard."

"Heard what?"

Cindy took a breath. "Late yesterday afternoon a girl was jogging on the towpath. There's a place where it curves by a bunch of woods, big cottonwoods on both sides. Just as she got there, someone grabbed her."

"Okay," Rachel said, try to stay calm but immediately thinking of Abby, who often went for runs around their house. With a tinge of panic, she remembered that Abby slept over at a friend's the night before and planned to go straight to school this morning. But that was miles away, on the other side of town. Nowhere close. And Abby was under strict instructions to run only when it was light out and stick to main routes. Rachel fought the impulse to check her phone for texts from her stepdaughter since yesterday.

Cindy said, "The guy starts dragging her into the trees. Fortunately, she screamed and fought like hell. Guy ends up with a face raked raw from her nails and she gets away."

"Thank goodness," Rachel said, stomach on fire.

"She's a Butler freshman, but before she started she took a self-defense class through her church. Tough girl."

"Great." Rachel fought unsuccessfully to hide her relief.

Cindy shifted uncomfortably in her chair. "Anyway, she's got her phone with her and calls 911, but she's not the only one. Couple other people heard her screaming. Cops flood the scene and they find the guy in his car two blocks away. Girl makes the initial ID." She paused. "It was Chad Setterlin."

"Jesus. You're kidding."

"I wish I were. Anyway, they took him into custody and got a search warrant for the car. And that's why I'm here."

"Okay." Something definitely didn't feel right; in her seven years in the public defender's office, Rachel couldn't recall a prosecutor making an unannounced personal visit like this. Even Cindy, who, while maybe not a friend, was someone she'd gone out for drinks with on a few occasions. Shared a bit of personal stuff with, on both sides, though it was mainly shop talk. That had been the case even after they faced off over Setterlin, even after his acquittal two years earlier.

"I mean, I wouldn't normally do this," Cindy said, adding to Rachel's apprehension. "But you've always been fair. I've appreciated working with you."

"Cindy, what the hell is going on?"

Cindy leaned back and folded her arms. "We found Hannah Slater's bracelet in the trunk of Setterlin's car. And one of her sneakers. And her T-shirt. And . . . her underwear."

"Oh God."

"And what was left of La'Donna Rogers. Which wasn't much. Because it turns out we were right all along. Chad Setterlin is one sick fuck."

It took Rachel a second. Rogers—the prostitute who provided Setterlin's alibi in the form of a blow job–for–Oxys trade around the time of Hannah's disappearance.

"But—Hannah's things were never found. After he was arrested."

"Near as we can tell he had a hidey-hole someplace. We're tearing the neighborhood apart as we speak. It's possible there are other victims."

Rachel had always thought *speechless* was, well, a figure of speech. Not a real thing. Now she sat frozen, unable to make a sound.

"I'm sorry, Rachel."

Except Cindy didn't sound very sorry. At least as far as Rachel was concerned.

She laid it out straightforwardly. Setterlin claimed the police planted the clothing items in his car out of frustration at his acquittal. But in addition to being a bunch of low-life BS, that was a non-starter because nothing was ever located in the neighborhood canvass before Hannah's body was recovered. There was nothing to find. The killer left no trace of her anywhere except for her corpse.

Then yesterday, as detectives picked through the trunk of Setterlin's beater, they found a blood-covered used condom rolled up in Hannah's underwear. Police were confident the blood would return as Hannah's and the semen as Setterlin's. Best guess, he'd already grabbed Hannah and stashed her in a shed before he entered La'Donna Roger's apartment.

Rachel gasped, unable to help herself.

"Is there anything—can we—"

"Oh, we'll fry him, trust me. Double jeopardy means Hannah's out for us"—she held Rachel's gaze as she said this—"but we're talking to the feds about maybe going that route. Plus there's La'Donna and whatever other bodies we turn up. Course, be a lot easier if we'd nailed him the first time."

*This can't be happening,* Rachel thought.

But what she said was, "You're sure it was him?"

"It's airtight. He lied to everyone. Including you." She paused again. "Especially you."

Cindy stood, and as she did, glanced at the Craig Wiseman case file. "Least we know that fuckwad's guilty."

"Cindy, I—"

"I wanted you to hear it from me. I felt I owed you that much." She walked out of the office without another word.

After that, Rachel went through the motions with Wiseman's case. Cindy was right: no question of guilt there. The white supremacist had live streamed himself gunning down two elderly members of a synagogue followed by two Black shoppers at a nearby Kroger. Only the intervention of an armed Kroger security guard kept Wiseman from his final destination, a mosque three blocks away. He ended up receiving the death penalty despite Rachel's best efforts at exposing his brutal childhood at the hands of a violent, alcoholic Hells Angels father.

One week after Wiseman's sentence was pronounced, over the protests of everyone from her boss to her parents to Glenn, Rachel handed in her resignation. After a month off, she started at Donavan, Crabtree and Hamilton, making it clear she was only interested in corporate litigation. Nothing else. Absolutely no criminal work of any kind.

Ever.

<br>

Rachel spaced out her movements in ten count intervals. One thousand one, one thousand two . . . dragging the sharp end of the nail across her plastic binding. One slash at a time. At one thousand ten she stopped, clutched the nail, and lowered her hands to her waist. And waited. And listened. And counted to ten. And started anew.

Beginning on the fourth round, she intentionally tapped the head of the nail against one of the cage bars, the resulting ping filling the void like a gong. She held her breath. Nothing happened. She continued for two more rounds of scraping and pausing, scraping and pausing. Still nothing. She relaxed a little. It was hard to believe that someone keeping watch in the room would have missed the sound or the fumbling of her hands. After three more rounds, she decided she also was in the clear when it came to cameras. She went back to work with renewed energy.

She knew she was on a trip of no return. If she was able to free herself—a huge if—she had to be ready to follow up with the consequences of that action. To flee or to fight or to hide. How, she wasn't sure at this point. The lack of certitude might have scared her once. Rattled her. After all, it was her absolute conviction that Chad Setterlin was innocent, that he was being railroaded, that had driven her, kept her up at night, forestalled any nagging doubts that maybe something wasn't quite right with his story.

But that was in the past. That was in a world that twenty-four hours earlier ceased to exist. A life she could never return to. A way of looking at things that was permanently taken from her. Now was the time to embrace the unknown. Celebrate the extra hours and minutes of life she'd been granted not once but twice by the strange man with the baseball cap who saved both her and Glenn when things were darkest. She put aside thoughts of Glenn for now and the ongoing mystery of the gun they found that Glenn didn't disavow, along with the bizarre reference to a fortune.

She also forced herself not to think about Abby, about the fate of their daughter. Hardest of all, she blocked consideration of the child she was finally carrying after the miscarriages. She had to stay focused. One thing at a time.

One thousand one. One thousand two. Scrape. Scrape.

Now was the time to walk to the edge of the hole, stare into the abyss, and finally find out what was down there.

# THIRTY-FOUR

After explaining who he was to Kevin Wolford, Carter said, "The thing is, I'm in a position to help you. But we don't have a lot of time."

"Fuck that shit. Tell me where Terry is."

"Terry's dead. I'm looking at his body right now. I can send you a picture if you don't believe me. What's more, Jon Stanley nearly died this morning. I'm guessing you already know about Stella's attorney and the car crash. I'm told they're blaming alcohol, which is kind of funny given that he didn't drink."

Silence filled the air so long that Carter worried Kevin had hung up.

"Terry's dead?"

"Murdered, to be precise. I'm in his basement now."

"Jesus. Who did it?"

Carter thought about the man with the teardrop tattoos upstairs. "Someone you don't have to worry about. But he wasn't alone. Which is why I'm offering to help."

"Who are you? Are you a cop?"

"Just a deliveryman. I'm trying to get a package to someone. You don't know her. But you might be able to help me find her. In return, I might be able to get you out of whatever mess Terry got you and Stella into."

"What the hell do you know about Terry?"

"For starters, I'm guessing he was running a software scam. You and Jon Stanley both won big lottery tickets over the summer. Doesn't sound like a coincidence to me."

"That's none—"

"I don't care about that. You can game the system all day long for all I care. Nail the Powerball and move to Saint Lucia. My only interest is in how this scam relates to a guy named Finn, who's hell-bent on finding you, by the way. You and Stella."

"Finding us? Why?"

"Not sure. Figuring out why could help me complete my delivery. That's where I need your help. Once I connect the dots, hopefully I can help you."

Another pause, though not as long.

"This guy. Finn. He's still after us?"

"As far as I know. But his numbers have been reduced."

"What's that supposed to mean?"

Carter flashed back to the Red Wings–Mud Hens game where everything started over for him. He said, "It means I'm motivated to make my deliveries and I do what I have to when things get in my way."

"That sounds like a threat."

"Don't take it that way. But let me say this. Finn is also motivated. He's been tasked with finding Stella and he's willing to go to great lengths to do so. Right at the moment it appears he's hit a roadblock. That he's at an impasse. Thanks in large part to Jon Stanley."

"What do you mean?"

"I'll get to that. In the meantime, you know that old saying about sharks? How they have to keep moving or they'll die? It's not entirely true. Except in Finn's case. He's a shark that has to keep moving. Not to avoid dying. To keep killing."

Kevin got quiet again. At last he said, "How do I know you're not actually Finn? That this whole thing isn't a setup?"

It was a good question. Carter hadn't thought about that angle. He pondered it for a second. Considered all the different people he'd encountered over the past day who could have vouched for him, from Art and Gail Wheeler to the lady at Corrigan's Chicago-Style Pizza to Kevin's own in-laws. The problem was the same every time. None of them knew him or Finn from Adam. They could have been impersonating each other for all they knew. He didn't have a work-around handy. He decided to bluff.

"Fair enough," Carter said. "You raise a good point. I can't actually prove that. So I'm going to let you go. I appreciate you talking to me. Just be careful, all right? Pay attention to the news. Find out what you can about Terry and Jon and a Chicago break-in involving a guy named Art Wheeler. You'll figure out what Finn's been doing. And remember, you're next. If I found you, even over the phone, Finn will too. Only he's not interested in helping you out of a jam. Anyway, be careful and—"

"Wait."

Carter waited. He heard a woman's voice in the background.

"Hang on."

Carter hung on impatiently. He'd already put Abby off twice, telling her to circle the block.

"Okay," Kevin said.

"Okay, what?"

"I just talked to Stella. Jon's girlfriend messaged her earlier. I told Stella to ignore her but she wouldn't listen."

"Emilee messaged her?"

"She wanted to know what the fuck was going on. She told her about Jon and about somebody who met her outside the hospital. Who were you with?"

"A teenage girl and her father."

"What's the girl's name?"

Carter told him.

"Is she Mexican?"

"She's American."

"Hang on," Kevin said again.

Carter hung on again.

Kevin said, "Okay. Emilee was able to talk to Jon briefly. At the hospital. He told her what happened. Who grabbed him."

"All right."

"It doesn't sound like you."

"That's because it wasn't."

"So what do you want?"

"I just need a little information. And then—"

"Where are you?"

"I told you. I'm at Terry's house."

"You said you could help me with . . . help me get out of this?"

"Yes."

"Can you come in person?"

"If you want."

"Can you bring food?"

"Food?"

"Hell yes, food. We're starving. We've been holed up a while and everything's running out."

Carter found a market near the U of I campus and picked up bread and cheese and cold cuts and pop and fruit and a few other staples, grabbed sacks of burgers and fries at Merry Ann's, and headed back east on I-74.

"How do we know this isn't a trap?" Glenn said. "That Finn wasn't sitting there with a gun to Kevin's head the whole time?"

He slumped in the front seat as he stared out the window, looking wan and exhausted after his checkup at the pharmacy. But the expression of defeat Carter saw earlier when he showed him the picture of his wife in a cage was, if not gone, greatly diminished. So that was good.

"It's a fair question. We have to take that risk. For what it's worth, I don't think Finn and Stone knew about Terry, thanks to the business with the dwarf adder. They're following the same trail of breadcrumbs we are, only they missed one. If I had to guess, they're regrouping, especially if that snake bit one of them. Also—"

"Yes?"

"As it happens, I've spoken to people with guns to their heads. Kevin didn't sound like those people did."

Glenn turned to Carter with a wary look. "Not to harp on this, but why in the world would a freelance mailman be in a position to talk to someone with a gun to his head?"

Carter glanced at Glenn. He hated to do this, but it was long overdue. Also, he was running out of patience. He said, "Before I answer that, maybe I should ask why a lawyer for a pharmaceutical company has access to $20 million he can't tell the police about."

"What?" Abby said from the back seat.

"Nothing," Glenn said sharply, glaring at Carter.

"I thought you had the $20 million," Abby said to Carter. Then to her father: "It's yours?"

"For Chrissake. Thanks a lot," Glenn said to Carter. He faced his daughter. "Pretend you didn't hear that."

"Pretend I didn't hear you have $20 million? Are you kidding?" After a moment she added, "Does Rachel know?"

Carter watched as Glenn's silence gave Abby her answer.

"Dad, what's going on?"

"Nothing. I mean, it's complicated. It's—"

"Is that what's behind this? The fact you have all this money?"

"No. This has nothing to do with that."

"Then what?"

"It's none of your business, Abby. It's just a work thing. We don't have time—"

"The trials," Carter said.

Glenn and Abby both looked at him.

"What trials?" Abby said.

Carter put on his turn signal and merged onto the highway going east. He glanced at the GPS on the phone, at the address Kevin Wolford gave him. Twenty minutes off.

"The addiction vaccine trials. Possibly the greatest medical breakthrough this century if it works. Right?"

"It's very preliminary," Glenn objected.

"Worth billions if successful, from what I read," Carter said. "That might be a low estimate. Twenty million is a drop in the bucket by comparison. But not insubstantial. Which has me wondering if that's what we're talking about. And if so, why you can't tell the police."

"Can we not do this in front of her?"

"No."

"Jesus." Glenn looked out the window, refusing to make eye contact with Abby. "Well, like I said, it's complicated."

"I would tend to disagree," Carter said. "Shareholder meetings and proxy statements and performance tables are complicated. Plus stuff like cryptocurrency, whatever that is. Having $20 million you can't tell the police about isn't complicated. It's pretty simple, actually. It implies illegality."

Once again, Glenn didn't say anything right away.

"Dad?"

Before Glenn could respond, Carter's phone rang. His uncle.

"Status?"

Carter went over his encounters at Terry Kientz's house. Leaving out some details with Glenn and Abby listening in.

"You think those guys worked for Finn?"

"I'm not sure. Either way, my working theory is they have something to do with this Lobo we've heard about. Or this Jason guy." In the distance, a bank of nimbus clouds piled up at the horizon, edges smudged with gray like ash drifting onto campfire marshmallows. There was more to his theory but, as with the nitty-gritty of events at Kientz's house, he didn't share it aloud. Instead, he said, "You saw the numbers I texted you?"

"I'm running them down now. I do have something small, though."

"Okay."

"I matched the SKU. That's the good news. It connects to a company out of Oklahoma City. Fencing Solutions. They service construction sites, county jails, municipal impound lots, storage units. Places like that. Oh, and kennels."

"Kennels."

"Like dog pounds. Maybe bigger breeders, too. I can check on that, since I'm trying to identify shipments next."

"Good idea." Carter recalled the photo of the caged Rachel Stanfield.

"You sure it's smart to go to Kevin Wolford in person? Could be a trap."

"I don't think so. But might be a good thing if it is."

"Point taken. Be careful. I'll get back to you on the SKU. And the kennels."

After Carter cut the call Glenn looked over at him.

"How could this being a trap possibly be a good thing?"

"Because it gives us the chance to end things. Find Rachel, I make my delivery, we all go home."

"You make it sound easy."

"I didn't mean to. It will be anything but."

# THIRTY-FIVE

C arter took the next exit. Eleven minutes from the address Kevin provided. He thought about the portion of his working theory that he left out when speaking to his uncle and pushed the Suburban to fifty-seven, two miles over the road's posted limit. The part he didn't want Abby and Glenn to hear. The part that didn't take a position on who the men who killed Terry Kientz worked for. Because chain of command wasn't his concern right now. What mattered was timing.

If Terry Kientz figured out a way to manipulate state lottery commissions' algorithms, to tip the scales toward whomever he chose, that was a big deal. That would be of value to someone. And it had been, apparently, because something spooked both Kevin Wolford and Jon Stanley about the endeavor. *Are you trying to get us killed, or what?* Yet during this same time period, Kientz stayed alive. Even when Wolford and Stanley were taking precautions, Kientz remained aboveground. He continued to have value.

Then something changed. Stella Wolford's lawyer was dead. Stella was as good as dead if Finn found her. Art Wheeler and Jon Stanley should be dead. Terry Kientz was as dead as they came. Rachel was being kept alive for some reason, but who knew when that might change? As all this was playing out, someone above Finn—Lobo? Jason?—turned down the chance for $20 million. There was no question in Carter's mind what this sequence of events conjured up. A ticking clock.

Something was about to happen; Carter was sure of it. A deadline was nearing. Loose ends were being tied up. Dominoes were falling. Even players with demonstrable worth, like Terry Kientz, were no longer needed.

And if it was time to eliminate someone like Kientz, who could summon up riches with the click of a mouse, what hope was there for Rachel?

The abandoned farmhouse where Kevin supposedly went to ground sat a hundred yards down the end of a gravel lane studded with weeds. A large, towering maple on the left and a stand of shaggy firs on the right blocked much of the structure from view except for a glimpse of a boarded-up window and a partially collapsed gable. Even after Carter drove past the property, it was difficult to make out the house from a glance in his rearview mirror. Let alone determine if any cars were parked out front. If Finn or one of the other players managed to track Kevin and Stella here and invade and do their worst, and then lay in wait, no one passing by would ever know.

Weighing all this, Carter turned into a Circle K a mile down the road.

"What's going on?" Glenn said.

Carter explained the situation.

When he was finished, Glenn said, "But if it's a trap, and you don't, well—"

"If I don't make it."

"Well, yes. What about us?"

"Same as at Art Wheeler's. Give it twenty minutes. If you don't hear from me after that, call my uncle. He'll take it from there."

"What about Rachel?"

"We'll have to hope for the best at that point."

"That's it?"

"It's worked so far."

"Her locked in a cage like a fucking dog, someplace we don't have a clue where it is? That's your idea of it working so far?"

Carter looked at him. "We need to get moving. We're wasting time."

"You didn't answer my question."

Before Carter could reply, Abby got out of the Suburban and walked around to the driver's seat, narrowing her eyes at her father as she went.

"Let's go," she said.

They drove past the farmhouse again, this time keeping it on their left. Carter instructed Abby to turn around a quarter mile down at the intersection of a county road. They let one car pass, then another, and when the road looked clear Abby turned right. After two hundred yards she slowed, pulled over, and Carter hopped out and disappeared into a cornfield.

He moved as quickly as he could through the stalks, which wasn't saying much: thickly planted, the corn ran in narrower rows than he expected. The browning leaves brushed against him as he passed, like sheaves of old newspaper unearthed from an attic trunk. He fought a rising sense of panic, patted the holstered Beretta to reassure himself, and continued on.

Finally even with the house, Carter hid within the the field while he examined his surroundings. This close, he saw that the structure was not just abandoned but crumbling. Wind and rain and sleet and snow over who knew how many seasons had stripped off all but a few swatches of white paint, leaving warped and gray boards behind. The porch was collapsing into itself. A hole the size of a kitchen sink gaped on one side of the bowed roof. Weeds carpeted what had once been a gravel turnaround.

He figured an approach from the rear was his best option. He jogged a few dozen yards farther down and was rewarded with the sight of a blue pickup truck parked by the side of the house. Someone had propped uprooted cornstalks around it as a makeshift blind. Behind the truck crouched a man, shotgun in his arms, eyeing the driveway. Carter stepped two rows back and withdrew a tiny foldable pair of binoculars from an inside pocket on the left side of his utility vest.

In the last picture Carter saw of Kevin Wolford, a screenshot from Facebook, Kevin was sporting three or four days of stubble, tops. By contrast, the man behind the truck had close to a full beard. The smirk from the social media photo was gone, replaced by a hungry, hunted expression. But there was no question it was the same person. Was Kevin taking the kind of precautions normal for any hungry, hunted individual? Or was he a player—or a pawn—in a bigger game?

Carter moved farther down the field, a few steps at a time before freezing for a count of ten to be sure he wasn't seen or heard. In another minute he glimpsed the rear of the house, which loomed about a hundred feet up from the remains of a barn, the latter structure nothing more than a heap of wood beams and roof remnants. No other cars. Carter checked his watch. Eight minutes had passed. He thought about the body of Terry Kientz, of Rachel in the cage, of the ticking clock.

He left the cornfield just below the remains of the barn and crept up behind the ruins, keeping them on his left as he circled. Glancing left and right, he paused a moment before dashing to the farmhouse's back door. No good. Locked or jammed or who knew what. Fortunately, the open window beside it missing all its glass was an easy fit for someone his size.

Inside, crouched on a kitchen floor littered with dead leaves, Carter stayed low, caught his breath, and listened. The only sound was passing traffic up on the road.

He unholstered the Beretta, tiptoed out of the kitchen, eased through the empty dining room, and stepped into the living room. Also empty. No one downstairs. So where was Stella?

His answer came a moment later in the form of a creaking floorboard overhead. Made sense. Assuming that was Stella, he was guessing Kevin positioned her as a lookout from above. What Kevin was thinking would happen if someone who wasn't Carter came barreling down the driveway with no time for Stella to make it downstairs, let alone jump in the blue pickup, he wasn't sure. Not his problem at the moment. His challenge was getting up those stairs without everything going to hell.

He decided to keep it simple. He didn't dash up like a man trying to save someone from a fire, nor did he soft-shoe it like a burglar. He walked up normally, one step at a time. Well, as normally as you could in a crumbling pile of a farmhouse sheltering a couple on the run from a band of hired killers. The wooden treads shifted and creaked as he climbed, announcing his presence as surely as if he'd whistled loudly. No matter. Sometimes the element of surprise was the lack of surprise.

Sure enough, as he reached the top, he heard movement in the first room to his left and paused as a shadow approached the door.

"What are you doing up here? I thought we had a signal—"

Carter stepped forward, lowered his right hand, the one holding the Beretta, and used the base of his left palm to punch Stella Wolford in the face. He didn't want to. The gun she held in her right hand gave him no choice. It didn't matter that, based on the way she was holding it loosely by her side, you could have told a decent knock-knock joke in the amount of time it would have taken her to swing into action. You couldn't take this kind of thing for granted.

"The fuck," she gasped, raising her left hand to her face, which gave Carter the opening to grab the hand, twist the young woman around, and drive her to the floor, knees first. By the time she remembered the gun it was in Carter's hand and then behind him on the floor. He holstered the Beretta, retrieved a mini-flashlight from his vest, and pressed the battery end against the base of Stella's neck.

"Don't move and don't speak. Do you understand?"

Moaning softly, she nodded.

"Are you Stella Wolford?"

Another nod.

"Is that your husband Kevin outside? With the beard?"

A whispered yes. Then, voice husky and raw, "Please don't kill me."

He kept the pressure on her neck with the flashlight. "I'm not going to kill you unless you give me a reason to. I'm the guy trying to help you. The one who talked to Emilee earlier today. First question. Is there anyone else in the house? Or nearby?"

Stella Wolford shook her head.

"Are there any weapons in the house besides your gun and the shotgun Kevin has?"

She struggled, attempting to throw Carter off her back. He held firm and pushed the flashlight harder against her neck. After a moment she gasped and went still.

"Other weapons?"

"The truck," she grunted.

"What about it?"

"Hunting rifle. In the rack."

"That's it?"

She sniffed as her nose streamed red, nodded.

An in-and-out-of-recovery alcoholic drug addict and her schlumpy bearded husband armed with a handgun, a shotgun, and an inaccessible hunting rifle. Versus Finn and Stone. Carter was thinking it was a good thing he arrived when he did.

"Don't take this personally," Carter said, and then gagged her with a length of black electrical tape he pulled from his vest. After satisfying himself that she could breathe through her bloodied nose, he bound her hands.

"Let's go," he said, helping her stand. He used a handkerchief to wipe blood from her face. "Are you getting enough air?"

"Uck ou," she said through the gag.

"I'll take that as a yes."

He guided her across the hall and down the stairs. She was wearing jeans and a gray sweatshirt. Her skin was unnaturally pale, as if she'd lived not days but weeks indoors. Her light brown hair was pulled into a tight ponytail held in place with a rubber band. From the sheen of her hair and the stink of her BO it didn't seem as if she'd showered in a few days. She carried the same extra weight as her mother, though she seemed frailer than the woman Carter talked to in the Meijer garden center. Like a person at the end of her rope.

In the living room, Carter approached a cracked window and looked outside. The yard was clear; the driveway empty. He decided a frontal approach was safer. He didn't like the idea of coming up behind Kevin. He directed Stella Wolford to the front door, which hung loose on an upper hinge. He maneuvered them outside and down the remaining steps of the collapsed porch.

"Kevin," Carter called out. "It's Mercury Carter. The guy who called you. I need you to put the gun down and come over here. To the front of the house."

Silence.

"I've got Stella. I also have a gun. I'm not going to use it unless I have to. I'm here to help. But I can't do anything until you show yourself. Without the shotgun."

"Let her go."

"As soon as I see you, unarmed, I'm going to send a text to someone. About five minutes after that, a car is going to pull down that driveway loaded with groceries, plus hamburgers that I'm pretty sure are still warm. After that we can talk about what we're going to do next. But before any of that happens, I need to see you and your hands."

"You grab my wife and expect me to just give up?"

"I'm on a bit of a deadline here, Kevin."

"Walk toward me with your hands up, then we'll talk."

Carter sighed. At the sound, Stella swiveled her head toward him. Her eyes were bright and bloodshot. Her nose was swollen. Streaks of red ran down her cheeks. Her breathing was raspy. She looked ready to kill someone, or pass out, or both in quick succession. Carter looked around. The only signs of life were two small birds dive-bombing a hawk high overhead. He thought about it. At this point, it was as good a play as any. He reached into a pocket on the right side of his vest, removed the utility knife, and cut Stella's gag.

"Let her go," Kevin said.

Carter waited.

Stella cleared her throat and said, "Jesus Christ, Kevin. Put down the goddamn gun and get the fuck over here."

# THIRTY-SIX

They spread out in the living room. Carter sat Stella in the sturdiest of the farmhouse's remaining chairs while he reset her nose and cleaned her face. He made Glenn lie on the floor on a tarp he brought from the Suburban, propping his head on an inflatable pillow he kept in the SUV near the life preservers. He directed Abby onto the couch, its mildewy stuffing spilling from a dozen holes, and asked her to keep an eye out the front window while she ate. Kevin sat on the floor devouring a hamburger, eyeing Carter warily. When Carter was finished with Stella, he made her drink half a vanilla milkshake, then handed her a bottle of water and a hamburger.

"First things first," Carter said. "Everyone getting enough to eat?"

"Any reason you couldn't have brought pizza instead?" Stella said.

"They were fresh out. Here's the deal."

Keeping to the bare minimum, Carter outlined the events that brought them to the farmhouse.

"So," Carter said when he finished. He looked from Stella to Kevin and back. "Either of you have any idea why this guy Finn is trying to find you?"

"None," Stella said. "I ain't never heard of the guy before."

"Does the phrase *twenty-two seven* mean anything to you?"

Kevin and Stella looked at each other

"Nothing," Kevin said. "What is it?"

"That's what I'm trying to find out."

Glenn cleared his throat. "Finn kept asking my wife about it. When he was . . . when they were at our house. She didn't know either. Our impression was Finn thought you did."

"Well I fucking don't," Stella said.

Carter looked at Kevin. "The lottery tickets you and Jon Stanley won. How'd that work?"

"I don't know what you're talking about."

Carter squeezed his eyes shut and open. It occurred to him that had things not been turned upside down the way they were, not only would he have concluded both his delivery to Rachel Stanfield in Indianapolis and to the other party in Louisville, he would have been back home in Rochester in time for dinner out with Tomeka. *Oh well.*

Carter glanced at Abby, her eyes glued to the window as she ate. What the heck. She knew most of it anyway.

He said to Kevin, "About this time yesterday, Finn and his men had Glenn over there and his pregnant wife Rachel tied to chairs. They were ready to chop fingers off one by one to get the information they needed. For starters. They find you, they'll do the same or worse. Then there's the little matter of Stella's attorney dying in the car crash, plus what happened to Jon Stanley. Right now, I'm the only thing standing between you and a similar fate. Does that help you understand my question?"

"Fuck you," Kevin said, but his bravado was gone.

Carter returned to the wobbly chair he was sitting in. "Lottery tickets."

Kevin looked over at Stella. She shrugged.

"Okay, okay."

"Okay, what?"

"Jon told me he had this surefire thing. He knew this guy who would give us a set of lottery numbers to play on a specific day at a specific store. Guaranteed we'd hit it. Only catch is the guy collects twenty percent. But we keep the rest."

"The guy—Terry Kientz?"

Kevin nodded.

"You didn't know him before?"

"Never heard of him until this summer. He was Jon's friend, not mine."

"So easy money."

"Hell yes."

"A good thing since you were broke, right?"

Kevin went silent.

"Answer the question, goddammit," Glenn said. "We're running out of time."

"Yes, fine. I was broke."

"Okay," Carter said. "That's a solid chunk of change. Which is why I don't understand what happened next. It seems like things got worse, not better. According to your mom, anyway." The comment directed at Stella. "Then all of a sudden you're on the run. Why?"

"Because my husband's a fucking douchebag, is why."

Carter looked at Stella, who had spoken with a mouth full of hamburger.

"I'm the douchebag?" Kevin said. "Who's the one who was drinking away our money?"

"My money. I'm the one with the job."

"Until you got fired."

"Enough," Glenn shouted. "Why did things get bad?"

Stella shook her head, swallowed, and took another bite of burger. "You might as well tell them, Kevin. It's not like we've got much choice at this point. Thanks to you."

"Tell us what?" Carter said.

Kevin lowered his head, almost as if he had nodded off. "I owed some money."

Stella snorted. "Some money?"

"It wasn't my fault." Kevin's voice pitched up slightly. "Nobody believed me when I said I'd pay them back. My car was gonna get repo'ed and we got an eviction notice. I had to do something."

"*It wasn't my fault*," Stella mocked.

Carter said, "How much did you owe?"

He hesitated. "Ten thousand. But like I said, it wasn't my fault." Kevin glared at his wife.

"So what happened?"

"What happened is I borrowed it."

"Borrowed from who?"

"This guy," he said, looking away from Carter. "Somebody I met at a bar gave me a number to call. That guy heard me out and gave me another number. It took like a day to set up. The next day I drove to Chicago. I had to go into this basement in this house on the South Side. It was fucking scary. But I finally got the money."

"A loan shark," Carter said.

"I guess. Yeah."

"What was the vig?"

"The what?"

"The interest. What were the loan conditions?"

"They sucked, is what they were. Ten percent for a week, then fifteen percent every week after that. Until I hit a month, at which point I owed double the original amount."

"Did you pay him back?"

"Not right away. I didn't have any money—that's how I got into this mess. I wasn't sure what I was going to do. Then I was talking to Jon and sort of explained what was up, and the next thing you know, I had the money from the lottery deal and paid off the loan."

"You were in the clear. With the loan shark."

"I just told you that."

Carter glanced at a long, Finland-shaped hole in the living room wall and the exposed rotted lath and crumbling horsehair plaster it revealed. "If you made good with this guy, why are you holed up here?"

From her chair, Stella said, "Yeah, Kevin. Why are we here? Tell him what happened next."

"Shut up."

"Tell us. Now," Glenn said.

For the first time, Carter saw what appeared to be fear in Kevin's eyes. "A couple of days later, these two guys show up at our door. I recognized them from my meeting in Chicago. They said their boss wanted to know how I got so much cash to pay him off. I told him I won the lottery. But . . ."

"But what?"

"They didn't believe me. They said I didn't seem like a guy who could come up with that kind of money in a hurry."

*No argument there*, Carter thought. But what he said was: "What'd you tell them?"

Kevin sighed and shook his head. "I made something up. They didn't believe me. And then—"

"Then they threatened to kill us unless he told them the truth," Stella said.

The room fell silent. Abby reached out a hand and touched Stella's shoulder. Stella jerked away, anger flashing across her face. Abby shrank back.

"And?" Carter said.

"I told them the truth," Kevin said. "They left. The next thing I heard, from Jon, is that Terry wasn't working his ticket deal for himself anymore. He was working it for the guy."

"For the loan shark."

"Yeah."

"Was Terry getting anything out of it at that point?"

Kevin gave a weak laugh. "Other than keeping his head on? I don't think so. They had him over a barrel. They told him they'd kill him if he said a word. But even if he did, if he somehow got free of them and told the cops, he was looking at prison time. He was jammed up bad."

"You still ran, though. After that."

Stella said, "We came home one night and one of the neighbors said someone had walked up to our house and then was sitting in a van for a long time. We left that night. I wasn't going through that again."

Kevin said, "And right after that, we heard about Jay."

Jay Blanton, Stella's lawyer.

LOCAL ATTORNEY DEAD AFTER FIERY ONE-CAR CRASH.

Carter considered the information. *Someone had walked up to our house.* Finn? Or one of his men?

Kevin had been smart to run.

Carter leaned back cautiously, aware the rickety chair he was sitting in might give way at any moment. He processed the information. Terry Kientz's lottery scam hijacked by a loan shark. A perfect revenue source. He thought about the photos he found on Vlad the Asshole's phone. Pictures of lottery numbers; had to be. The time that texting those to Finn had bought them. Which means they had value. So did that make Finn the loan shark?

But if the fix was in on Terry, if his scam had been hijacked, why was Finn still looking for Stella? To tie up loose ends?

Carter said, "The loan shark. What's his name?"

"I have no idea," Kevin said.

"What did he look like?"

"I don't know. Mean. Black hair. Maybe Hispanic."

Carter interrupted and described Finn, Stone, Paddy, and Vlad.

"Any of those guys sound familiar?"

"They're all white?"

"That's right."

Kevin shook his head. "I didn't see anybody like that."

Next, Carter described the men he saw at Terry Kientz's house.

"The big guy you mentioned. The one with the gold chain. He was at our house. He's the guy who threatened to kill us."

Carter thought about this. Something wasn't adding up. He said, "You have no idea what the name of the guy you dealt with is?"

"I told you, no. I tried asking but they made it clear that wasn't happening."

"Lobo."

The heads in the room turned in unison to look at Abby.

"Why?" Carter said.

"Think about it," Abby said. "Who else could it be? Vlad kept talking about him when I was in his car. A couple times he said 'here,' like here in Chicago. It makes sense."

Lobo. Wolf. A hunter.

Was this the person looking for Stella Wolford? Was he the man Finn was working for? The shot caller?

The man who might know the location of the building where Rachel Stanfield was being held in a cage?

A sound overhead. The skittering of an animal in the cracked ceiling. Carter turned to Kevin.

"How'd you end up here? This house, I mean."

"We used to party here. When I was in college. We'd sneak out on the weekends." Kevin looked around the room. "It wasn't this bad back then."

"You graduated from U of I?"

"I went there for a few months. My grades weren't great."

Stella snorted again.

"The guys you partied with. Are you in touch with them?"

"A couple. Why?"

"Like I said over the phone. If I found you, Finn's going to find you. Or this Lobo. If people you hung out with know about this place, it'll come out. You're going to have to move."

Stella spoke up. "Where? There's no place left for us to go."

Carter saw her point. He also wondered if it was his responsibility anymore. He had enough to worry about with Glenn and Abby. And finding Rachel. Stella and Kevin had served their purpose by filling in another piece of the puzzle in the shape of a loan shark nicknamed Lobo. It was that guy Carter needed to focus on now. Not these two.

Except that Kevin and Stella, like those photos of the lottery numbers he texted Finn, still had value. And would, until their whereabouts were divulged.

His phone buzzed. His uncle. Carter stood and left the room.

"Any luck?"

"I found a shipping manifest. An order of kennel cages. Several locations between Oklahoma City and northern Illinois."

"Addresses?"

"They're coded and linked to internal documentation. So they don't show up right away. It's part of a delivery system. All we've got is cities right now."

"Which ones?"

"Five. Springfield, Missouri. St. Louis. Terre Haute. Greencastle. And Fort Wayne."

Carter thought about it. He crossed off Springfield and St. Louis right away. Both were too far from Chicago for the time frame they were looking at. Fort Wayne not likely either. Terre Haute was definitely in the running, as was Greencastle.

"Okay. Let me know as soon as you have addresses. Any luck with those numbers from Terry Kientz's phone?"

"All burners as far as I can tell."

"Any of them linked to someone named Lobo?"

"Not that I could find. What are you going to do now?"

"I'm going to find Lobo. Looks like he's the one in charge."

"What about this Jason guy?"

"I need to work with what I've got."

"What are you going to tell this Lobo, assuming you reach him?"

Carter looked into the living room. At Kevin and Stella, glaring at each other with sullen, dead expressions.

"I'm going to see what he's willing to trade for Rachel Stanfield."

"What he'll trade?" Carter's uncle said.

"What," Carter said. "Or who."

# THIRTY-SEVEN

R achel froze.

At first, she wasn't sure she heard anything. Perhaps she imagined it, or extrapolated something from the sound, however small, she made as she worked on her bindings. Or the noise produced as she shifted painfully in the cage, trying to gain purchase as she worked. An echo of some kind. Maybe the HVAC system or some other building mechanicals. She listened so long that she gave up, figuring her mind was playing tricks out of fear of being caught the closer she came to freeing herself.

Then she heard it again.

Something between a creak and a whimper. Definitely not mechanical, whatever it was. Nothing for about ten seconds. Then again. This time much closer to a whimper. No question about it now.

She wasn't alone.

But who? Another captive, like herself? Also gagged, making communication impossible? She considered tapping the nail on her cage's bars as she had at the outset of her escape attempt, seeing if whoever it was would respond in kind. Or attempting the best guttural cry she could manage through her own gag.

She decided against both options. She couldn't rule out a trick. The possibility that someone in the room was messing with her. Someone who may or may not be aware of her efforts to free herself but posed a danger regardless. Someone not on her side. Instead, she counted out a full minute, hearing the noise twice during the interim. Irregular—no pattern involved. She didn't respond either time. After the minute passed she went back to work. Scrape. Scrape. Scrape. One nick at a time. Why bother stopping now? Alone or not, what did she have to lose?

It took Carter ten tries. Not that he was surprised. The cell phones he lifted from the men in Terry Kientz's house held a lot of numbers. When he finally reached someone who heard what he had to say it wasn't Lobo. Nor was the person he spoke to after that. It was the person after that who turned out to be the man he needed to reach.

"Who is this?"

"Someone you need to talk to."

"How'd you get this number?"

"It was on a phone."

"What phone?"

"One of two, actually. Phones carried by men who were at Terry Kientz's house in Champaign."

Silence filled the connection.

"What do you want?"

"I want the location of Rachel Stanfield."

"Who?"

"Please don't play it like that. I just want Rachel. That's all. No questions asked. I'm a reasonable guy. Tell me what you want in return. Hopefully, we can work something out."

"Listen up, *bolillo*. I have no idea who or what you're talking about. But if something happened to the men with those phones, and you had something to do with it, I guarantee you'll regret the day you were born."

The man, with yet another Chicagoland accent, spoke in a soft voice so threatening in its calm that an image of one of Carter's baby pictures popped unbidden into his mind. He couldn't tell if the man was bluffing. He wondered if it mattered.

"Apologies—I left a couple of things out," Carter said. "I know all about Terry Kientz and the lottery scam and Kevin Wolford and the loan you gave him and your right-hand man Finn. I think that information would be interesting to certain people. But none of that matters to me. I just need to know where Rachel Stanfield is."

"What did you say?"

The voice no louder than a knife slicing through a cut of tough beef.

"Which part?"

"The part about a man named Finn."

"I said I know all about you and him."

"You're lying."

Impatiently, Carter tapped his right foot. "I assure you, I'm not."

"You are. Because Finn is not my right-hand man. He is my worst enemy. He is a man I would gut like a fish and feed him his own intestines if I ever see him. Right before I move on to you."

The feeling that overtook Carter in that moment was as if he'd been bustling down stairs, missed the last step, and nearly tripped and fell.

Lobo wasn't in league with Finn?

Lobo and Finn were at odds with each other?

What the hey?

Carter said, "How do you know Finn? If he's not working for you?"

"What happened to the men in Champaign?"

"They encountered unexpected complications. Tell me about Finn. Then I'll fill you in."

"Return him to me."

"Finn? I have no idea where he is. That's part of the problem."

"Not Finn. You know who I mean."

For the first time, the voice that succeeded in lowering the temperature in Carter's veins to well below freezing sounded different. There was still anger there, yes. But something else.

Fear.

Carter said, "I don't know who you mean."

"Why would you lie about something like this? Why?"

Once again, Carter felt confused, as if his GPS led him left when he was supposed to go right.

"Let me start from the beginning. I'll make it quick. Try and get us on the same page."

"Maybe you can start by telling me who you are. So I'll have a name to whisper into your ear as I cut you into pieces."

"My name doesn't matter," Carter said. But then, he told him anyway. Something told him he needed Lobo on his side. He explained about his arrival at Rachel and Glenn's house the night before, about the mess he encountered there. He walked Lobo through the subsequent events: the trip to Chicago, the trip to Danville, the trip to Terre Haute and to Champaign-Urbana. He left out a few details. But he tried to make the point that despite all the moving parts, and there were many, in the end the only thing that mattered was Carter's ability to make his delivery to Rachel and go home.

When he was finished, Lobo said, "Freelance? What does that mean?"

Carter explained.

"I'm not following. You're either a mailman, or you're not."

Carter tried and failed again. He was worrying about the time once more. About Rachel in the cage, and about the friends Kevin Wolford had who knew about this house. Something occurred to him. He stepped around the corner and called to Abby. She left her lookout on the couch and came over.

"What's up?"

"I'm talking to Lobo. I need you to explain something to him. The fact I'm freelance—independent. Explain in Spanish, I mean. His English is excellent, but I think there's a slight language issue on this one. It might help us if he appreciates the concept that I'm not, you know, with the government."

"You're not, are you?"

He looked at her. "What do you think?"

After a moment she nodded. He put the phone on speaker and listened as Abby spoke, though he understood very little. A couple of phrases and words here and there. *Por cuenta propia. Independiente.*

Carter also knew a few other phrases. Ones that Abby said several times.

*Por favor. La esposa de mi padre. Como mi madre propia.*

Finally, Abby nodded. Carter took the phone off speaker.

"Do you understand now?"

"Why are you with a Mexican girl? Did you kidnap her too?"

"Kidnap who?"

"The girl. Did you kidnap her like him?"

Carter felt unmoored for a third time during the call. A sensation like biting into a familiar, favorite food and tasting something rancid instead.

*Did you kidnap her like him.*

*Return him to me.*

As Abby turned to go, Carter raised his finger. She stopped. A second later, Carter placed the phone back on speaker mode.

He said, "This man. Finn. He doesn't work for you."

"Are you kidding me? I just told you—"

"Finn has something of yours." A pause. "Someone."

No response. That was good enough for Carter.

"If I have this right, you and I have something in common. Finn has someone I care about, and it sounds like he has someone you care about, too. We both want them back. Am I correct?"

Several seconds passed. "Who are you?"

"I already told you. My name's Mercury Carter. I'm a freelance delivery person as . . . as my friend here explained. I need to hand something to Rachel Stanfield to complete a job. Unfortunately, Finn has stashed"—he glanced at Abby—"has *taken* Rachel someplace. I'm closing in on where she is. What I'm starting to wonder is whether this location, wherever it is, might be of mutual interest."

"Mutual interest."

"You heard me."

"What evidence do you have that this lady, Rachel Stanfield, is even alive?" The soft, almost childish voice that Lobo spoke with at first, the one that so chilled Carter, had deepened now, taking on sharper, raspier edges as if a heavy cold were settling in.

Carter looked once more at Abby. "I've let Finn know that I know about the lottery numbers. That's helping keep Rachel safe. That and the fact they still don't know Stella Wolford's whereabouts." He thought about the falling dominoes of the past few hours. Signs that a deadline was approaching. "But time is running out. As I think you know."

"Are you proposing something? Or are you just going to talk all day?"

"I'm thinking."

"I am too. I'm thinking I'd like to meet in person and tear you limb from limb until you tell me the truth."

"Meet where?"

"Here. Where else? I'm not coming to you."

Here. Chicago. Two and a half hours drive, minimum. Out of the question. There wasn't enough time.

Carter knew what he had to do. He didn't like it, but it was the only solution to the communication problem given their time constraints. An emissary had to be appointed. Someone who could vouch for Carter in person, act as a go-between with him and Lobo short of Carter driving all the way back to Chicago. For better or worse, Carter had the perfect person in mind.

Two people, in fact.

# THIRTY-EIGHT

C arter returned to the living room, camera open on his phone. Right on cue, Stella tried to muck things up. Flat-out refused to be photographed. Said it was the stupidest fucking idea she'd ever heard. Carter asked her to please watch her mouth around Abby. Even Glenn, in his weakened state, grinned at that.

Carter was adamant. "This isn't optional. Do you remember what I told you about Rachel and Glenn's house? What I saw there?" The questions directed at Kevin. He nodded, most of the sulk in his eyes gone now.

"Finn is not a stone-unturned kind of guy," Carter said. "He'll only rest when the job is done. You two are the job."

"So kill us," Stella said.

"What?" Kevin said.

"You know what I mean. Fake it. You already banged me up bad enough," she said to Carter. "Squirt some ketchup on us. Send him that picture and maybe he'll leave us alone."

"I can't do that."

"Why not? I thought you were trying to help us."

"The reason I can't do that is—"

"He can't do that because if Finn thinks you're dead he'll kill Rachel."

Carter regretted hearing Abby voice aloud the conclusion he'd already reached. But he wasn't surprised she figured it out. She seemed like that kind of kid.

He stood them against the wall, away from the Finland-shaped hole, and staged it there. He had Kevin hold up Abby's phone, the wallpaper switched to a generic artsy blur, so the time and date were visible. He studied the results. Perfect. It was time to propose the transaction he mentioned to his uncle.

He texted the photo.

But not to Lobo.

To Finn.

"Done," Carter said.

What he didn't tell them about was the text message he sent to accompany the photo.

**Trade?**

After Kevin and Stella collected their meager belongings Carter shepherded everyone into the Suburban. Kevin asked about their guns. Carter told them they were hidden safely away.

"What if we need them?"

"If we get to a point where the two of you need guns, we'll be as good as dead anyway."

"Easy for you to say."

"Yes it is, as a matter of fact."

And with that, Carter started the car and headed back into town, back to Terry Kientz's cookie-cutter house in a cookie-cutter subdivision with a fiery Japanese maple in the front yard.

Finn stared at the photo, a dozen thoughts crowding into his brain.

Starting with, *The fuck was it with this Carter guy?*

"What?" Stone said.

After deliberating a moment, Finn showed him the picture that Carter had texted him, of Stella and Kevin Wolford. He didn't tell him about the one-word question that accompanied the photo.

"So what now?"

"Hang on." Finn had a lot to think about. Problem was, he didn't have a lot of time to do it in.

First thought: relief that Stone wasn't dead. Relief mainly because he was going to need Stone for at least another four hours, and because he'd been calculating weight and dimensions and issues of leverage and wondering exactly how he was going to make him disappear by himself if the snake bite ended up doing its job.

Second thought: concern that, despite his recovery, Stone appeared to be at about seventy percent. He'd stopped vomiting and the sweats and nausea were gone, but he still looked as pale as a real-life Viking after four months of near-total Nordic darkness. Finn was going to need one hundred percent for what came next.

Third thought: Jason was pissing him off. Assigning him a task, one he was good at and that he enjoyed—finding luckless individuals and slowly extracting information from them—and then calling it quits. Telling him it was time to cut their losses and move on. The package had to be delivered. As if everything Finn went through since rolling up the drive to Rachel Stanfield's house yesterday was of no consequence. Move on, according to Jason, because too many fires were burning.

One, literally, at Rachel and Glenn's house. Two others, figuratively speaking. One in Chicago involving the cops crawling over Art Wheeler's brownstone. Another in Terre Haute involving the cops rappelling up and down a quarry. Implying that Finn had colored outside the box of the job specifications one too many times. Like any of that was his fault. He was no more blameworthy than his much younger self was for breaking into that house one night not knowing the owner kept an untethered and hungry pit bull for protection . . .

Enough of that. Talk about water under the bridge. Fourth and final thought: Jason might have good reason to pull the plug and complete his own job. One, despite his current dissatisfactions, that Finn wholeheartedly agreed with. Because if you didn't draw a line, send a message, who in this fucked-up country would? But that conclusion didn't mean Finn was done. He had a score to settle. And the path to doing so had just been laid out for him.

He lifted his phone and found the text chain with Carter. He was about to respond when he paused, recalling his interaction with Rachel Stanfield outside Art Wheeler's brownstone.

*You're scared of that guy.*

*Bullshit, I'm scared*, Finn thought.

*I see it in your eyes.*

Total bullshit.

*Now you're the one being hunted.*

"Bullshit," Finn said, loudly enough that he startled Stone. He didn't hesitate as he responded to Carter's suggestion.

*Trade?*

Sure

The men in Terry Kientz's living room had done an admirable job of rolling back and forth across the floor, knocking down a lamp and overturning a chair in the process, while somehow keeping clear of the blood pooling from their slain companion. They lay back-to-back, nearly to the dining room, hands unsuccessfully scrabbling at each other's bindings like the hired muscle version of two warring bucks ensnared in each other's antlers. They went still as Carter entered through the front door as casually as a man returning home from a long day at the office, Kevin and Stella trailing behind him.

"Holy shit," Kevin said, taking in the scene.

"No way," Stella said.

"On the couch," Carter said.

After they complied, grumbling and swearing, Carter walked to the pair on the floor, pulled out his phone, dialed a number, and set the phone on speaker.

"Sí."

Carter held the phone in his left hand and loosely handled the Beretta in his right.

"I'm here," Carter said. "English, remember."

"What about the girl? She could translate."

Carter glanced at the dead man, at the blood congealing around him.

"I don't want her seeing this."

Oddly, the answer seemed to satisfy Lobo. A moment later, he began speaking. He started by asking a one-word question: "Who?" Gold Chain responded just as succinctly: "Me and Carlos."

"Gracias a Dios," Lobo said. Something in his tone kept Carter from objecting.

From there, Lobo gave instructions to the pair. Orders that, based on their reactions, puzzled them at first and then aggravated them to no end. Finally, they gave their word to their boss and to Carter. Satisfied, Carter set the phone down, retrieved the knife from his vest, and sliced through the bindings. The pair didn't get up right away but instead remained in fetal positions as they rubbed their wrists and ankles. After a minute they sat up but remained on the floor. Each hesitated, then gratefully snatched the water bottles Carter handed them, downing them in a few seconds. They shuffled to the bathroom, one by one, before returning and sitting warily on a pair of dining room chairs.

"¿Listos?" Lobo said.

"Sí." Gold Chain said.

"It began about two months ago," Lobo said to Carter.

"Go on," Carter said.

"I knew I'd found a gold mine with Kientz. He oversaw software for six states. The first week alone I made $50,000."

Carter said, "You took over his operation."

"Mateo ran it. But yes, I took control."

"Mateo?"

Gold Chain tapped two fingers to his chest.

"My brother," Lobo said.

Gold Chain was Mateo, Lobo's brother. No wonder Lobo had thanked God. Carter glanced at the body of the third man, the one with the teardrop tattoos. Considered how everything might be unfolding differently in this moment had he shot a different man in the chaos of entering the house.

"Are you there?"

"Sorry," Carter said. "Fifty thousand. Good money."

"Yes."

"But something happened."

A pause. "Yes."

Carter waited. After a moment, Mateo spoke.

"This man, Finn, showed up one day. He told us he wanted in on our loan operation. He proposed a fifty-fifty split."

"And?"

"We told him to go to hell, of course. We thought that was it. Two days later, Miguel disappeared."

"Miguel?"

"One of my *primos*," Lobo said. "My cousin. They dumped his body in my backyard. What was left of it. Later that day, Finn made contact again. This time by phone. He told us they knew about the lottery thing and wanted in on that too."

"They knew about the lottery because Miguel told them." Carter thought about the tools he saw in Glenn and Rachel's basement. The instruments Vlad intended to use against them.

"The information was taken from him, yes."

"Was that when they infiltrated?"

Mateo grunted. "That's when we started hunting them. To punish them for what they did to Miguel."

Lobo said, "He was an innocent in this. He worked a desk job downtown. His only crime was overhearing the wrong conversation at a family barbecue."

Carter said, "I take it you didn't find the men who killed him?"

The phone went quiet and no one in the room spoke for a moment. Then Lobo said, "Tell him."

Mateo said, "We told Finn to go to hell. No way we were cooperating. Especially after Miguel. Two days later, Gabriel went missing. He never came home from school."

"Who's Gabriel?"

"My son," Mateo said. "He's eight years old."

Carter weighed the information. "Finn took him."

"Yes."

"Police?"

"That evening, a package was left on the front stoop of my house. It contained one of Miguel's fingers. The message was clear. Tell anyone and the same fate awaited Gabriel."

"You had to cooperate."

Mateo nodded. "They told us if we complied, we'd have him back safely. That he was simply collateral."

"Collateral? For what?"

"For time."

For time. For a deadline. The clock was ticking.

"We looked," Lobo said from the phone. "Trust me. We looked everywhere. He was nowhere to be found. We had no choice. We had to let them in. It didn't stop us from continuing the search. But . . ."

Carter thought about the scene he encountered in Terry Kientz's basement earlier in the day.

"So Finn weaseled his way in. Made money off your operation."

"That's right." Lobo's voice cold and steely.

"Something changed," Carter said. "Mateo and Carlos and"—a glance at the carpet—"an associate ended up down here. Why?"

Mateo and Carlos looked at each other but neither spoke.

Lobo said, "Last night, we were told that Terry knew Gabriel's exact location. That if we wanted him back, we had to get it from him."

"From Terry?" That seemed improbable to Carter. But he thought he saw where this was going.

"That's what we were told," Mateo said.

"I take it he didn't know."

"Not that we could determine." Carlos spoke for the first time.

"Terry didn't know," Carter said.

"How do you know that?" said Lobo.

"Because time is running out. They're on a deadline. They're tying up loose ends. Terry was one of them. Finn lied to you when he said Terry knew where Gabriel was. He knew what you would do."

"It wasn't Finn," Lobo said.

"What do you mean?"

"It wasn't Finn who told us to go to Terry. It was that Nazi Jason. The one who started everything."

# THIRTY-NINE

"Jason," Carter said.

Mateo nodded, his bruised face purpling with rage.

"Nazi Jason. Is that an expression?"

"What do you mean?" Lobo said.

"You know. Like Shithead Jason or Asswipe Jason. Like that."

"It's not an expression. He is a Nazi. White power, white rights, whatever. Just like that guy who shot up the El Paso Walmart. And the one who killed the women at the spas in Atlanta. And the one who murdered all those people at the mosque in New Zealand. It doesn't matter what they're called. They're all the same. Nazis."

"Does this Jason have a last name?"

Lobo told him.

Carter paused and texted the information to his uncle.

Then, to Lobo, he said, "Excuse me for speaking candidly. I just want to be sure I understand correctly."

"Go ahead."

"You run a moneylending operation. Not passing judgment; just stating a fact. When you learned through one of your customers, Kevin Wolford, what Terry Kientz was up to, you saw a fresh revenue opportunity. You took it. I get it. Then, out of the blue, Jason shows up looking for his own revenue source. He makes a move to muscle in on your loan operation, using Finn for the dirty work. After Miguel was grabbed, Jason learns about the lottery. He realizes there's even more money to be made. He gives you no choice by kidnapping Gabriel. A few weeks pass?"

"A month."

"A month, okay. In that time, did you get any idea what Jason wanted this money for?"

"None. He kept telling us it wouldn't be much longer. He sent us photos from time to time, proving Gabriel was still alive."

Patient. While a white supremacist is holding your eight-year-old nephew hostage under threat of death.

Carter said, "Then out of the blue, Jason tells you Terry knows where Gabriel is."

"Except he didn't, according to you," Lobo said.

"Like I told you, he's wrapping things up for some reason. He used you again, this time to silence Terry."

"Everything you've said about me is correct. I'll have to take your word about Jason and Terry. But we still have a problem."

"Which is?"

"I still don't know why I should trust you. Especially after what you did to Germán."

Germán. The gunner Carter took out. He considered the man's fate. It was difficult to feel much sympathy after what he saw in the basement, and what Germán's tattoos said about his background. But still. Bad guy or not, Germán struck him as another casualty of Jason's lies.

"Hey. What about us?"

Stella, on the couch. Squirming with frustration. And probably the DTs. Talk about someone Carter was having difficulty feeling sympathy for.

He was about to wave her into silence when his phone buzzed with an incoming call. His uncle. He told Lobo he would call him right back.

"Thanks for the text," Carter's uncle said. "I have three things for you, if you have a second."

"I have a second."

"First, it's not Jason Norris. That's an alias. But it helped me find the real name. Your man is someone named Jason Wegner."

"Jason Wegner," Carter said, raising his voice so Mateo and Carlos could hear.

"Second thing. Thanks to the name, I figured out twenty-two seven."

"Some kind of white supremacist group?"

"You knew?"

"I just now worked it out. But only generally. Go on."

"It's a date. I should have guessed that. I'm sorry for not getting it earlier. It's written European style—day, then month. For us, it's the opposite. We'd say it *seven twenty-two*. July 22. It refers to the 2011 massacre in Oslo and on Utøya, the island where the white supremacist shooter killed all those youth camp children. Wegner is the leader of something called the 22/7 Brigade. He's a piece of work, from what I can see."

"Indeed. You said there's a third thing."

"Oh yeah. I almost forgot. I finally found it."

"It?"

"The address where that cage was shipped to."

Carter left Stella and Kevin in Kientz's living room. The fit that Stella threw was about what Carter expected. Out of earshot of Mateo and Carlos, he told her they had no choice.

"There's an X through this house now. Wegner knows Kientz is dead. If he knows, there's a good chance Finn knows, which means he'll cross this off his list of places to look for you. It's the safest place. Hiding in plain sight."

**Trade?**

**Sure**

"But we can't stay here with, well—" Stella's eyes strayed to Germán's body on the living room floor.

"There are other rooms in the house. There's food in the refrigerator. There's a working bathroom. I'd advise not going into the basement, but other than that it's nicer than where you've been."

"How long are we supposed to wait?"

Carter thought about it. He looked at his phone. Almost four o'clock. Five in Indiana.

"If you haven't heard from me by this time tomorrow, call this number."

Carter handed her a card containing nothing but his uncle's cell phone.

"We have to wait until tomorrow?" Kevin said.

"Tomorrow. Explain the situation, follow his instructions, and prepare for a long few days."

"We'll be arrested," Stella whined.

"Probably. But consider the alternative."

"Which is?"

Carter gestured at the remains of Germán and headed for the front door.

On the sidewalk, Mateo tugged at Carter's elbow, gestured at his own phone, and said, "Hang on. He's sending reinforcements. He wants us to wait."

"Who?"

"My brother. He doesn't want anything to go wrong. He says it's safer this way, for Gabriel. I agree."

Carter shook his head. "It's a three-hour drive from Chicago to where we're going, minimum, assuming no traffic."

"Even so. He was clear."

"The other thing is, you don't just send reinforcements. First, you make a bunch of calls and send a bunch of texts, then those people make their own calls and send their own texts, and eventually after a ton of running around you hit the road. At the absolute earliest, it could be ten o'clock by the time they get there. If we're lucky. Right now, we're less than two hours off. We need to move."

"We? Meaning you, me, and Carlos? Against who knows how many? You're trying to get my son killed, is what you're doing."

Carter glanced down the street and saw the Suburban round the corner and head in his direction, Abby at the wheel. He fought the frustration he was feeling, the need to act on the information his uncle dug up.

"I understand your perspective," he said. "Your brother is probably right. We don't know what we're walking into. What we do know is that Finn is closer to your son than these reinforcements. He's the one we have to worry about. Him and Jason. Jason's up to something. There's a reason he's tying up loose ends. My priority is to find Rachel Stanfield, sooner rather than later at this point. So that's what I'm going to do. While I'm doing that I'll help your son if I can. I promise. As far as you and Carlos are concerned, I can't advise you on the best course of action. But I'll suggest you don't have as much time as you think you do."

As Carter finished speaking the Suburban pulled up alongside. He nodded at Abby. She stayed inside but scooted over to the passenger seat. Carter glanced at Terry Kientz's house.

"I need to make arrangements to rescue Rachel Stanfield," he told Mateo. "It means adding a couple passengers. But I have to leave right now. The clock's running, and we lose an hour in the direction we're going. I hope you can understand."

Mateo followed Carter's glance.

"I understand."

Three minutes later, passengers aboard, Carter pulled away and headed east toward a building on the outskirts of Greencastle, Indiana.

Glenn let ten minutes pass, taking in what he knew about their destination. Maybe their final destination—in so many ways. Then he looked at Carter and said, "They fudged the trials."

Carter nodded but didn't say anything. Glenn glanced at Abby, who was watching him from the front passenger seat. Now or never, Glenn supposed.

In the way back, the two passengers the mailman brought along listened intently.

"The vaccine trials," Carter said.

"That's right."

"What about them?"

"It doesn't work. The vaccine, I mean."

"Doesn't work? Like, not at all?"

Glenn breathed out slowly. "Haphazard at best. Not statistically significant. And the side effects—they're bad. There's evidence that . . ."

Carter didn't say anything.

"It's possible it could worsen an addiction," Glenn said. "Or make someone who isn't normally susceptible to compulsion, well, suddenly vulnerable."

"It could create addicts?" Carter said.

Glenn nodded.

"And no one saw it coming?"

"We rushed things."

"Why?" Abby demanded.

Glenn thought about chastising his daughter. He realized how absurd the idea was under the conditions, and said, "We thought we had to."

"Why?" Abby said again, her voice more agitated.

Glenn's shoulders sank a little. He said, "One of our competitors launched a weight-loss drug two years ago. It had an unexpected off-label outcome of reducing other compulsive behavior, which in some patients translated to a cessation of addictive cravings. It made an already successful product even more lucrative."

"So what happened?" Abby said.

"Our strategy to match them was to isolate the anti-addictive element and market that component alone. There was, well, a lot of pressure to do it quickly. And like I said, it didn't achieve the anticipated outcome."

Carter said, "Where's the $20 million come in?"

Glenn took a deep breath. He looked at the passing countryside and spied a series of grain silos in the distance, fat and squat against the horizon. "Two of the executive vice presidents started offshoring funds," he said. "They said it was part of an investment strategy. It might have been, at first. Xeneconn has a lot of irons in a lot of fires. I helped with the paperwork. By the time I figured out what was happening, it was too late."

"What was happening?" Abby said.

"Golden parachutes," Carter said. "But not the legal kind. If I'm hearing you correctly."

"You are," Glenn said.

"Golden what?" Abby said.

*What a fool I've been*, Glenn thought. *What a fucking goddamn fool. And now it's too late to do anything about it.*

He said, "It's a strategy for executives to stockpile money in case they get fired. A lot of boards are cracking down on the legal version. In this case, it wouldn't have mattered. Because these VPs aren't planning to stick around. They have the money set to go the moment news breaks about the, well, the fudging."

"Flight funds," Carter said. "Gold plated, so to speak."

"Exactly."

"Funds you helped set up. To facilitate their ability to escape."

Glenn nodded, lowering his head.

"Dad?"

"I've destroyed everything I cared about. And for what?"

"Is it really too late?" Carter said. "No chance to back out?"

Glenn thought about the last few days before the home invasion. The threats from the VPs when he insinuated that he'd had enough. The hang-up calls from unfamiliar numbers on his cell that always rang busy if he tried calling back. His reactive fear, maybe misplaced, maybe not, that led him to buy the gun. Given all that, could he be blamed for thinking Finn was after him, not Rachel?

Rachel. The gun he didn't tell her about. Rachel, who looked past his divorce from Maria and happily agreed to take on the title of stepmom. Who soldiered on after her professional meltdown, continuing to support him and do all she could to show her love for Abby. Rachel, who insisted they keep trying for their own child, that she was fine, even after the nightmares of the miscarriages and the toll it took on them.

"It's too late," Glenn whispered, glancing at the farm fields rushing past, at the towering banks of clouds overhead, at the patches of blue sky that ought to signal hope but instead brought to mind bottomless reflecting pools he deserved to slowly drown in. "I've destroyed everything. For nothing."

"Almost nothing," Carter said.

Glenn looked at him. "What?"

"The apostille."

"What about it?"

"Think back to what Vlad told us last night. We had five minutes to prove we had access to $20 million. Otherwise, he couldn't make any promises about Abby."

Glenn looked guiltily at his daughter, at the pain in her eyes at the mention of all that had happened.

"What are you saying?"

"I'm saying that relatively speaking, it turned out to be a good thing that you're in this mess," Carter said. "If you hadn't filed that document, if you hadn't done paperwork for those VPs, we wouldn't have had anything to show Vlad. And if we hadn't had that . . ."

"No," Glenn said, seeing red. "Stop. That's insane. That's not how the world works."

"Maybe not. Probably not. Except last night it did."

Glenn squeezed his eyes shut, ruing the day he was born.

"Dad?"

"Oh Abby," he said, reaching for her.

# FORTY

They crossed the Indiana line forty minutes later. An hour to their destination, according to the GPS. Carter thought about what he knew. Which wasn't much. But, maybe, just enough.

According to his uncle, the SKU on the cage holding Rachel indicated the crate was shipped five years ago to the Putnam County Humane Association Impound Center on the edge of Greencastle. One of several crates the center ordered. Funny thing was, the center had moved since then. Set up in newer, bigger, shinier digs across town. Where it received a second, bigger cage delivery a year ago. Meaning the cage holding Rachel hadn't moved with the center. Meaning if she was in the original cage, there was a good chance it was in a building that no one—well, hardly anyone—would have reason to visit.

Carter ticked the speedometer up to seventy-six miles per hour. Seventy-seven. Seventy-eight. Time was running out.

"It's time."

Rachel focused on keeping her breath even and controlled. She recalled the exercises she learned in yoga. In the class she took over the summer as she neared the end of the first trimester and the doctor gave her the green light. Concentrating both on her breath but also her hands. She clamped her wrists together as tightly as possible, praying the gesture would maintain the illusion of intact bindings. Thank God the plastic ties hadn't fallen off when she sliced through them just seconds before the door to the room opened. As she compressed her wrists, she simultaneously squeezed her right hand, feeling the nail tucked between her first finger joints and the top of her palm.

"It's time," the man outside the cage repeated, this time with a hint of derision in his voice.

Disaster nearly struck almost immediately. As she heard the lock snap open and the cage door swing wide with a metallic creak, a hand grasped her elbow and yanked. If she hadn't been so intensely focused on her hands they might have separated. The deceit would have been detected. But her luck held. As a distraction, she protested loudly through her gag. When she felt his grip loosen, just for a second, she swung her feet out, indicating compliance. A second later her insides froze as she heard the click of a knife. A moment after that she felt her feet separate and realized the man had freed her legs. She could walk. At least for a little while.

Upright for the first time in hours, Rachel swayed a bit, nearly losing her balance in the process.

The man said, "You don't want to keep Jason waiting."

She lowered her head toward her left leg, numb with inactivity, and shifted it slightly. Trying to say it had fallen asleep. Somewhat.

"Not my problem. Move."

He had her by the right elbow, his hold an iron grip. She stumbled, bumping into him. She was almost certain this man was new; not Finn, and not one of his henchmen. Whoever it was, she expected him—she wanted him—to stink of enough body odor and cigarette smoke and halitosis to drop a moose. Instead, he smelled pleasantly of wintergreen and Febreze.

"Jesus. Would you knock it off?" He paused, adjusting his grasp after her near tumble.

Adjusting his grasp because he'd almost lost control of her.

"Last time I'm telling you. Move it."

Rachel moved it. One step, another. Step by step. Feeling returned to her leg. Once she was sure she had her equilibrium back, she closed her already blindfolded eyes. The time had come.

She pictured Glenn, Abby, the baby inside her, and let her dead weight take over. She felt herself slip down. She bent her knees. The sensation like playing a game of trust in middle school. Except without the promise of supporting hands awaiting your plunge backward.

"Oh, for fuck's sake."

She twisted her left arm free as her descending bulk momentarily overcame the strength in the man's hand. As she dropped she used her left hand to grab ahold of the duct tape binding her eyes. She gave a yelp at the shock of pain as she ripped the tape off. She pivoted to her right, looked up, and saw a man wearing a ball cap with unfamiliar lettering, his face pinched with fury, leaning to grab her. Their eyes met. His were as flat and cold as a February sidewalk.

Rachel hesitated, but only for a second. Hesitated because it was an unnatural move; a gesture that, for all the fight-or-flight blah blah you read about, human instinct recoiled from. But she had no choice. She understood she only had one chance. That everything that had happened since yesterday evening, when the men walked off Glenn and Rachel's pandemic-project deck and into their kitchen, led to this moment.

She drew her right arm back and drove the nail protruding from the bottom of her right fist into the man's left eye.

His screech was not as loud as Rachel expected. She was imagining something cinematic. Agony that would turn her stomach. Instead, he cried out no more stridently than if he'd been slapped on the cheek, staggered back, righted himself, and with disbelief etching his face raised his left hand to the source of the pain. Rachel summoned an image of her tormentors—the scar-faced torturer, the red-headed brute, Stone, and above all Finn. She took a deep breath—fuck instinct—and punched the top of his left hand with the palm of her right, driving the nail deep into the socket.

This time he didn't yell at all. He simply gave a grunt, quivered like a man touching an electric fence on a dare, and collapsed.

Rachel trembled, seeing what she'd done. All the blood.

Then she took off in a shuffle as fast as she could go, tearing off her gag as she went, and headed for the door at the end of the long dark room full of empty kennels.

Empty except for one.


"You can't just leave us," Abby said. "Not when we're so close."

"I understand how you feel," Carter said. "But it's too dangerous."

"More dangerous than going to the quarry?"

"That was different. That was an emergency. We were trying to save a life. Which we did, as far as I can tell. But I have to go alone from here."

They were on College Avenue parked outside Marvin's Restaurant. Dusk was falling. By Carter's estimate it was almost twenty-four hours to the minute since he'd walked up to Rachel Stanfield's door outside of Indianapolis and rung the bell. Three times. Which was a lot in his experience. A day since Finn opened the door, setting off Carter's inner alarm. Triggering his first headache in a while.

Abby said, "Saving Rachel isn't an emergency?"

"It's a different kind of emergency."

"Right."

Carter knew she had a point. He just wasn't going to acknowledge it.

He examined the burner phone in his hand one last time. The one he tinkered with, thinking about the coming confrontation, just in case.

Satisfied with his handiwork, he disconnected it from the laptop, put the computer away, and pocketed the phone.

He said, "You'll be safe inside. No one's going to try anything. With any luck, we'll be back soon and join you. I hear the burgers are great."

The first thing Rachel did when she reached the door at the front of the room was punch the handle lock and throw the dead bolt. A heavy-duty door; maybe required by code for a building like this. Either way, she was grateful for the reinforced steel and for the door's sheet-of-paper-sized window crosshatched with safety wire. A window that would make it difficult to see much inside. A difficult-to-breach window on a strong door that was excellent for preventing people inside the room from leaving. But also for keeping people out. She wondered idly if her captors had considered that.

She looked around and spied a sturdy-looking metal desk. She grabbed the edge and pulled. It moved barely an inch. She tried again—gasped—and got two inches. She took a breath and kept at it. Another inch. Two. Three. Slowly, slowly, she dragged the desk across the room, pausing each time she felt the screech of metal on polished concrete was too loud, that it was impossible no one could hear. After several minutes' effort, she shoved the desk against the door. It was a decent barrier. The desk was heavy. It wouldn't hold forever. But it was a start.

Satisfied no one was coming, yet, she hobbled to the cage where the small figure lay. The figure making the sounds she'd heard. Bound, gagged, and blindfolded like her. But a child, not an adult; no question. She lifted the fastened brass lock and let it drop back down. The figure inside tensed but made no sound.

"Hang on," she whispered.

Rachel limped the length of the room to the body of the man with the nail in his eye and the cap—with its indecipherable acronym, *RWDS*—still on his head. She kneeled, swallowed her revulsion, and searched his pockets until she found his phone. She moved that aside and looked until she located the keys. She rose with difficulty and returned to the cage. It took a minute to open the lock because her hands were shaking so badly.

"It's all right," she said once the door was open. She reached out and carefully loosened the child's gag. Next, she gently peeled off the duct tape blindfold. Finished, she found herself looking into a pair of large, brown eyes, bright with fear. A boy—young. Seven or eight at the most. He looked as if he were going to cry out. Before he could, she covered his mouth with her hand.

"Shhh. No noise until I get help. Okay?"

After a moment he nodded.

Rachel returned to the man on the floor, found his knife, and ignoring the boy's look of fear at the blade, used it to cut the remainder of his bindings. She extended her arms, pulled him out, and folded him into her. A moment later he hugged her back. She held him for almost a minute. When she felt he was ready—when they were both ready—she said, "Follow me."

Holding his small hand, she led him to the opposite end of the room, away from the door. She settled him in a corner. She raised her fingers to her lips to underscore the need for quiet. He nodded solemnly. She rose and at that moment saw what she missed before. The room had another door. This one blocked by a file cabinet. She limped to it. Judging by the exit sign above it, the door led outside. She tried to move the cabinet but it was too heavy. She tugged at the drawers but they were locked. Except for the middle one. She pulled it out. A stack of manila folders lay inside.

She lifted the top one, opened the cover, and examined the photo on top. She puzzled over it a moment, picked up the papers beneath it, and studied them. She wasn't exactly sure what she was looking at. Well, she knew what they were. Just not why they were in the file cabinet. She tried pulling the drawer all the way out. It wouldn't slide free. She tried again and gave up and pushed it shut. She peered around the cabinet at the door. *Alarm Will Sound*, a sign said. Could she risk it, even assuming she could somehow move the file cabinet? Who knew what was on the other side of that door? Or who?

Rachel stepped back. She walked the length of the room to the desk she had pushed against the main door. She listened for sounds in the hallway outside. Nothing so far. Assuming someone else was in or near the building—this Jason, for example?—how long would it take them to miss the man whose blood was currently draining onto the polished concrete floor?

She went back to the dead man and retrieved his phone. The device was basic; a burner, she was guessing. Many of the clients she defended used them. Chad Setterlin among them. He had many, it turned out. She pressed the keypad. Locked. No touchscreen. Shit. But there was still 911. She had pressed *9* and *1* when she stopped. She heard Finn's voice in her ear as they stood on the sidewalk outside Art Wheeler's brownstone.

*Stone and Vlad have their instructions, and they're clear. If they don't hear from me in regular intervals, or there's even the faintest hint the cops have been called, they'll kill Abby. They won't ask for permission. They'll just do it.*

Just do it. Could she risk it?

She was pretty sure they didn't still have Abby. That something happened in Chicago to thwart their plans.

But could she be positive?

Was the gamble worth it?

She stopped herself. If not the police, who else? Carter? She didn't have his number, obviously. What about Glenn? She recalled her shock at learning from the mailman inside Art Wheeler's brownstone that he was alive.

*This doesn't seem like the kind of neighborhood where you need a gun. What's it for?*

*I have money. Lots of it. Millions.*

Irrationally, Rachel punched Glenn's number in. But the locked screen was blank. Frustrated, she nearly flung the phone to the floor. As she raised her arm, the face of Chad Setterlin floated before her. His aggrieved expression in the weeks leading up to trial as he insisted on his innocence.

Then another face. Cindy Chen. A night they'd gone for drinks together. Months before the Setterlin debacle. A dismissive comment Cindy made about defendants in a case she was prosecuting. *Stupid mopes thought these burner phones were their ticket to freedom. Maybe try an original passcode for a change.*

Rachel dialed Glenn's number again. A passcode prompt popped up. Four dashes. Four digits. She held her breath and punched in four numbers. 1-2-3-4.

The screen unlocked.

She called Glenn's number. It went immediately to voicemail. A sure sign the phone was dead or destroyed. Her heart sank, and the minor euphoria she felt the night before at Art Wheeler's upon learning he was alive vanished. Who else? Her parents? She dismissed the thought immediately. Not with her dad's heart. Her sister? Good idea, especially if she had her number memorized. That had been a New Year's resolution, actually. Commit more family members' and friends' cell phone numbers to memory. Something Glenn was always after her about: memorizing the important stuff. As it was, she knew by heart only three outside of her office number: her parents, Glenn, and . . .

Abby.

Heart pounding, Rachel cycled through the scenarios.

As with Glenn, the phone going straight to voicemail. Absent other information, confirmation of the worst possible outcome. That Rachel was wrong—that Abby hadn't been freed. That . . .

Or maybe, by some miracle, Abby was alive and somehow answered, but in her excitement giving away the fact that Rachel was no longer in captivity. *They won't ask for permission. They'll just do it.*

The far more likely scenario: Finn or one of the other men with Abby's phone, seeing it was Rachel calling. Same outcome.

But no. That wasn't right. The stress and exhaustion of the past twenty-four hours were taking their toll. Rachel wasn't calling from her phone. She was calling from the phone of the man on the kennel floor. The man with a nail through his left eye. A completely different number. One her captors would or wouldn't recognize. If not, all the better. If so—she'd deal with that in the moment. Deepen her voice. Hang up. All she needed was the tiniest bit of information. If Abby was safe, Rachel's path lay clear as day ahead of her, starting with phoning for help.

Forefinger trembling as if she had palsy, Rachel slowly tapped in the number. When she was finished, the digits laid out on the screen before her, she stared until they blurred before her eyes, then pressed the green call button.

One ring.

No automatic cut to voicemail.

Two rings.

In Finn's control—him reaching for it, puzzling at the number?

Three rings. Deciding it was spam and ignoring it?

Four—

"Hello?"

Rachel couldn't help herself.

"Abby?" she shouted.

# FORTY-ONE

"Rachel? Oh my God."

Abby. Alive.

"Abby," Rachel said. "Oh, Abby."

"Rachel—are you all right?"

"I'm . . ." She glanced around the room. "I'm okay, I guess. I don't know where I am. And I'm not sure how much time I have."

"Don't worry. Merc's on his way. He's going to get you out of there."

"Merc?"

"The mailman guy. Mercury Carter. He knows where you are. I mean, we all do."

"You do? How?"

Before Abby could respond, Rachel heard the first sign of life outside her prison since the man lying dead on the floor entered the room and dragged her from her cage. Men's voices. Loud and urgent. Shouting a name. The scrape of boots on concrete. A moment later, the sound of the door handle turning and the door shifting in its frame as someone tried to shove it open.

"Abby. Someone's coming." Whispering now, even though she was on the opposite side of the room.

"What?"

"Someone's trying to get in."

"In where?"

"Into the"—she looked around—"into the room I'm in. The door's locked and I blocked it. I don't know how long I can . . . how long I have. I need to call the police, Abby. Now that I know you're all right."

"I'm fine. And like I said, Merc's on his way. It won't be long now."

A boom echoed through the room. Someone was kicking at the door. It was steel-reinforced with a serious deadbolt. But it wouldn't hold forever.

"I have to go. I love you."

*Boom.*

"Rachel, wait—"

Another boom, and then the call disconnected as suddenly and completely as someone pausing a streaming song mid-lyric. Rachel wasn't sure if she'd accidentally hung up or if something happened to Abby. But at least she reached her. At least she knew she was alive and, as far as she could tell, out of Finn's control. That was all that mattered. Glenn's daughter—their daughter—was safe.

*Boom.*

Hands trembling, Rachel dialed 911.

Nothing happened.

*Boom.*

She tried again. Still nothing. Desperate, she tried Abby's number once more. Now that wasn't working either. *What the hell?* Something was wrong. She couldn't get a signal. She thought briefly of the panic she experienced the day before when her internet went down as, gun to her head, she tried to retrieve Stella Wolford's deposition. She glanced at the boy cowering in the corner, his eyes seeking solace from her that she realized she couldn't give. Now or maybe ever.

"Shit. Shit. Shit."

She tried 911 again, and again, and again.

Nothing.

*Boom. Boom. Boom.*

"I thought we had a deal," Finn said on the other end of the line.

"We do have a deal," Carter replied, keeping an eye on the road ahead of him. "I'm just not making it with you."

"What are you talking about?"

"I just told you. If Jason Wegner wants Kevin and Stella so badly, and I think he does based on what they know, on what they might say, he's the guy that's taking delivery. Not some second banana. I only deal with top dogs."

A moment of silence as Finn took in the significance of Carter knowing Jason's full name, or so Carter guessed.

Then: "Fuck you, you son of a bitch."

"Sticks and stones. I'm three minutes off. Have Jason have Rachel ready. Tit for tat, we make the switcheroo, and we both move on."

"Listen—"

The connection died before Finn could finish. As if a switch had been flipped. Odd. No matter. The die was cast at this point.

Carter glanced in his rearview mirror at his passengers, silent as they processed what they heard. Working out the details of what came next. It was a cold calculus, offering to serve up Kevin and Stella in exchange for Rachel after he spent so long trying to find them to help them. But desperate times, etc.

Carter saw the turn-in up ahead. As soon as he made the left into the light industrial park he killed the Suburban's lights. A small gesture, given they knew he was coming. But no point advertising it more than he had to. Slowing to fifteen miles per hour, Carter saw right away what a good setup this was. Several of the prefab buildings sported for-lease signs. Two of the streetlights lining the service drive were out. A box truck blocking a loading dock lacked a license plate. The site wasn't completely abandoned, with after-hours interior lights on in a couple facilities. But the park had seen better days to be sure.

After a quarter mile or so the road doglegged to the right. Now it was even quieter. No vehicles sat in front of the long two-story warehouses lining the road on either side, with weeds smothering a few of the drives. Past those buildings, thick woods crept up to a chain-link fence on the left side, while an empty lot stretched out on the right, filled with high grass and here-and-there piles of construction debris. A hundred yards farther on, sitting by itself, cloaked in darkness, encroached by bushes, loomed the former Putnam County Humane Association Impound Center.

Carter stopped several yards back, giving himself a panoramic view of the building, including the multiple vehicles parked out front. On the far left, a box truck. Beside it, a blue van. On the other side of the entryway, a pickup truck and two large SUVs. Carter turned around and fixed his eyes on his passengers, both sitting upright, their faces a mix of apprehension and expectation.

"Ready?"

Mateo and Carlos nodded.

"Let's go."

*Boom.*

Two chairs. A mop and a bucket. Three fifty-pound bags of kibble tucked in a corner and covered with dust and cobwebs. The idea ridiculous but Rachel went ahead anyway. Nothing to lose at this point. She tossed the chairs and cleaning equipment onto the desktop. Straining, she added the kibble one bag at a time. Anything to up the amount of weight atop the barrier. To make it that much harder to push the desk away when the inevitable happened and the door gave. She was under no illusions it would hold for long. But what choice did she have?

As she labored with the last bag, Rachel looked up and saw a face through the door's small window. Just a glimpse. But enough to stop her in her tracks. No question about it. The big man—the largest of the four who walked in off their deck yesterday evening. The one who hit Glenn in the head with the gun. The one called Stone. And now he was here. As she stared, momentarily transfixed, something else appeared in the window beside his face. The barrel of a gun. Next she heard his voice, low and coarse, like the throb of an engine revving through a cracked muffler.

"Open the fucking door. *Now*."

A gun. Of course. How could she have been so stupid?

She abandoned the table and limp-jogged back to the corpse on the floor. She patted down his clothes, first his flannel shirt, then his jeans. Wincing, she dug under his body. She found it in his waistband. Struggling with his dead weight, she finally freed it. She stared at it. It was . . . a handgun. She had no idea what kind. The one and only time she'd fired a weapon was during law school, when her criminal law professor arranged an optional outing to a shooting range. The woman told the students it was important for anyone considering a career in public law—regardless of which side of the courtroom they planned to sit on—to have at least handled a gun. Rachel wasn't so sure but went along anyway. And left the range convinced she never wanted to repeat the experience.

She limped back to the boy in the corner. She sat beside him. She held the gun in her right hand. It was heavier than she expected. She raised it in the direction of the door. She placed her finger on the trigger, removed it. Placed it there once more. The weapon wasn't much. Especially against the kind of men just outside the door. She knew that. But it was all she had left.

*Boom.*

*Boom.*

*Screek.*

A sliver of light appeared along the edge of the breached door as it bounced against the edge of the barricading desk.


Carter figured on a waiting party, hidden from view but close, and he wasn't far off. He made out movement behind two of the vehicles parked to the right of the entrance to the impound center. The truck and one of the SUVs. Hard to say how many men back there.

"One o'clock," he whispered.

"Got them," Mateo said.

Carter lowered the driver's side window, opened the door, crouched, and fired four times, shattering windows on each of the vehicles. Silence for a moment. Then return fire from the rear of the truck. Then nothing. Then more gunfire, this time from the right side of the building. Where Mateo positioned himself, darting there during Carter's covering fire. Carter held his breath, waiting. A moment later he saw Mateo move forward, bent low, approaching the rear of the truck. A second later, more gunfire. Mateo emerged after a few seconds, held up two fingers indicating the number of men, made a throat-slashing gesture. Carter didn't respond. He was distracted by the sight of Carlos appearing from a thicket of shrubs to the right of the building, holding a man before him. A man with a knife through his throat. Carlos moved his knife hand up and down twice as if pumping a fist in celebration, before lowering the man's quivering body to the ground. It brought back a memory which Carter considered briefly before dismissing it.

Carter counted to five and dashed across the cracked asphalt lot to the blue van parked to the left of the main door beside the box truck. He lowered himself onto the parking lot surface, rested his chin on the cool asphalt, sighted a pair of boots visible through the undercarriage of the box truck—their owner creeping quietly forward—and fired twice, each shot hitting an individual boot. The man cried out as he fell, crippled in both legs. To his credit, he still returned fire beneath the van. An admirable move but also a mistake, since his gun hand was out of position when Carter strode up and fired a third and final shot that just missed the swastika tattooed in the middle of the man's forehead. But not by much.

Checking that the shooter was dead—he was—Carter knelt, examined the undercarriage of the box truck, and recalled the mistake he made slashing the tires of Finn's van. He reached into a utility vest pocket, retrieved the item inside, and completed a quick task. Finished, Carter stepped back into the parking lot. He hand-signaled Mateo and Carlos to hold their positions. They waited a full minute. Satisfied no one else was coming, he edged himself to the front door and snuck a glance through the glass. The lobby inside was dark, though Carter saw lights on deeper in. He tried the door. Locked—no surprise. There was always the back entrance. The greeting party had to have come from somewhere. He gestured to the others his intentions to head that way when they stopped in their tracks.

A gunshot. From inside.

Carter moved quickly but not as fast as Mateo. Before Carter could react, Mateo waved Carter and Carlos back and fired three shots into the door, the punch of the shots spiderwebbing the glass. So much for entering undetected. Mateo reared back, kicked the glass in, reached through and unbolted the door. A moment later they were inside and running for the back.

"Get your boy," Carter said. "Don't worry about anyone else."

The layout was simple enough. Lobby up front. A hallway with small, windowless rooms on either side—examination rooms, Carter guessed. What looked like a supply room, although the assault rifles stacked on one of the tables didn't seem like standard humane society issue. Next to the guns, some kind of radio contraption. It registered in Carter's brain as he rushed past. Similar to one he saw on the wooden console table in Rachel and Glenn's living room. He remembered the weird way his call to Finn disconnected a few minutes earlier. He was pretty sure he knew what the gizmo was.

He reached the door just behind Carlos and Mateo. He caught the glint of metal inside. The shiny bars of cages. Heard voices, chief among them a crying child and a woman, begging for her life.

Never missed a delivery.

Carter hadn't yet.

He barreled through the door.

# FORTY-TWO

Carter stopped, gun up, processing the scene before him. Beside him Mateo and Carlos, both breathing hard.

The room held four men. Three of them alive. The fourth, incongruously, lay dead, his face covered in blood, a ball cap beside his corpse. The remaining three stood against a far wall. On Carter's right: Stone, his massive left arm around the neck of a young boy, to whose head he held a gun. On the left, Finn, holding his own gun against the head of Rachel Stanfield. Between them, a stranger, smiling like a man seeing family again after a long flight.

"One step," the man said. "One step, and *pop*."

Carter didn't lower his gun. But he didn't take a step, either. His eyes flitted from Stone to Finn and back. He said, "Jason."

"You know my name. And I think I know yours. Mercury Carter."

Carter did the math. Considered the angles. Calculated lines of sight and bullet trajectories. Not good.

Carter said, "We meet at last. Whatever. Key thing at this point, I'm not out to make any trouble. You've got your thing and I've got mine. I just need Rachel. I have something to give to her. That's all. I'll finish my job and be on my way."

Wegner's eyes shifted in the direction of Finn and his captive.

"The Wolfords."

"I'm sorry?"

"You promised us Kevin and Stella in exchange for Rachel. Where are they?"

"Someplace safe."

"Not here, though. Which was the deal."

"I don't make deals with people who kidnap children."

"So you lied. And cheated."

"If you say so. Either way, back to Rachel. You hand her over, no harm, no foul."

Wegner shook his head with a smile. "I should trust you why?"

"Because I'm not your chief concern. I'm just a guy trying to do his job. Not interfere with yours."

"Ah yes. 'Do his job.' Like I believe that."

"Believe what you want. It's the truth."

"The truth? My understanding"—glancing at Finn—"is that you've been promulgating this charade for hours now. For more than a day, in fact. You keep claiming you won't get in anyone's way, that you just need to accomplish a task, yet somehow you keep turning up, over and over, not unlike the proverbial bad penny. Which makes me curious. What in the world do you have for Ms. Stanfield that's so important?"

Carter had heard some distinct voices in the past day. Stone's gravel slurry of a growl. Stella's raspy whine. Lobo's chilling half falsetto. Wegner was plain vanilla by comparison, which might have been scariest of all. An ordinary voice coming from the mouth of an ordinary-looking man. The timbre of a property-casualty salesman from Omaha on a swing through the Great Lakes states. Possibly six foot, though that was probably a stretch. Neither thin nor fat. Prematurely white hair, receding off the forehead, cut short but not buzzed. Tortoiseshell eyeglasses and a scholar's neatly trimmed white beard which, in combination with his white, button-down long-sleeve Oxford, hinted at academic pursuits. That look belied by cargo pants and what appeared to be a new pair of casual hiking boots—metro park worthy, but not Appalachian Trail. An insurance salesman on a Saturday primed to run some errands, starting with Target.

"None of your business." Carter looked at Rachel, whose pale face and exhausted-looking eyes, dark as cave holes, suggested she might be near the end of her rope.

"I would beg to disagree."

"Your problem, not mine."

"In that case, how about this? You give me the package and I give you Rachel."

"Sorry. Delivery only goes to the name on the invoice."

"Really? Surely she's more important than a possession."

"Rules are rules."

Wegner seemed amused by this. "I admire your standards, Mercury Carter. With that in mind, I'll up the ante. What about Rachel and the boy for the package?"

"Same rules apply."

Carter heard Mateo inhale beside him.

"You'd sacrifice both their lives in the name of your precious delivery."

"You're the one sacrificing lives."

Carter did more math. Thought about the outcome. Didn't like the conclusion he reached.

Wegner said, "I'd suggest you're splitting hairs, and also that you have thirty seconds to make a decision. After that, we're walking out of here. Whether these two accompany us alive is up to you."

Carter exhaled in disgust. *Why did it have to come down to this?* Reluctantly, he weighed his options a final time. From this distance, he could probably take Stone and save the boy. Or take Finn and save Rachel. Fifty-fifty he could take both, possibly with help from Mateo and Carlos, but he'd never been a gambler. No—he knew what he had to do. He heard his uncle's voice whispering it in his ear like a whining mosquito. The angel on both shoulders. The choice was obvious. It's just that he had a code. Perfection meant something. His father never missed a delivery. Until his last day on the job, which was also his last day on earth. To fail was to tarnish that legacy. To hand Rachel's delivery over to Jason bordered on sacrilege. But maybe that was how it had to be.

"All right."

"All right what?"

"It's a deal. The package is yours."

Mateo exhaled loudly.

"A wise decision. Tell me where it is and we'll take our leave."

"It's in a pocket in my utility vest." Carter lowered his eyes to indicate where. "I'm going to reach in, take it out, and slide it to you."

"One wrong move," Wegner said.

"Understood."

Carter raised his left hand, reached over, unsnapped the pocket, and removed the phone. Just as slowly he knelt, then pushed it down the polished concrete floor. It skidded a dozen yards and stopped after a half rotation. Wegner traded glances with Finn and Stone. They further tightened their grip on their captives. Wegner leaned over and picked it up.

"Interesting." Wegner looked quizzically at Carter. "All this for a phone?"

"What can I say. I'm only the deliveryman."

"An overambitious one, I'd wager."

Wegner studied the phone a moment longer, seeking its importance in its exterior. He turned it over. Wegner adjusted his glasses onto his nose and brought the phone closer to his face. He studied it further. A puzzled look on his face, he turned to Rachel.

"Who's this from?"

Her reply was indistinct.

"Answer the question."

She looked to be summoning her remaining strength to respond. "I have no idea. I told you yesterday"—nodding wearily at Finn—"I don't know anything about a delivery."

"Would you be offended if I said that I think you're lying? Just like Mr. Carter here?"

"I'm . . . not . . . lying."

Wegner studied the phone a moment longer. Carter held his breath. Wegner leaned over, slipped the phone into Finn's left-hand pants pocket, and said, "Take her outside and figure out what—"

A sound in the hallway. Thudding feet. Gasping. Carter glanced behind him.

A figure in the doorway.

"Rachel!"

Oh, no.

Abby.

# FORTY-THREE

"Down!" Carter shouted at the girl as he fired, hitting Stone in the left shoulder and spinning him away from the boy. A second later Carter dove to his right, fingers extended as he sought the light switch by the room's entryway. The room plunged into darkness. He fired again, but aimlessly, to create a target, and threw himself at the slow-moving Abby, ignoring her cry of pain as she collapsed under his weight. His feint with the random shot worked as someone—Finn?—returned fire in that direction. But no one was there. To judge by the sounds Carter heard, Mateo and Carlos were already on the move, working their way down the room. More shots, the flashes' illumination exposing the sight of Rachel on the floor, a jumble of shadows that might have been Finn and Jason, a lumbering hulk that had to be Stone, and no sign of the boy.

Hearing Abby groan beneath him, Carter struggled to his feet, just as a boom sounded at the far end of the room followed by the klaxon of an alarm and a glimpse of light as a door opened to the outside. Carter made out three figures stepping over a file cabinet and stumbling outside. Just before the door shut and the room went dark again—*whoop-whoop-whoop* went the alarm—he saw Mateo and Carlos next to the boy, his eyes glinting in the light. A few feet away, Rachel was trying to push herself up.

Gabriel and Rachel.

Safe. Alive.

Outside, the sound of engines revving.

As Carter flicked the lights back on, Abby ran across the room and half-skidded, half-fell into Rachel's arms. They lay on the floor sobbing. For a second they appeared to be a single distraught, delirious being, their individual bodies tough to distinguish. A few feet away, Mateo, legs splayed before him, embraced his son, who sat on his lap, head against his chest. Carlos stood beside them, repeatedly pressing the keypad on his phone. After half a minute he held it up in frustration as if trying to find a signal.

Carter spun, left the room through the main entry door, and walked up the hall. He found the widget on the table in the supply room beside the assault rifles. He studied it. He was almost certain what it was. That it wasn't an explosive device. He knew what those looked like, generally. He felt eighty, eighty-five percent sure that this was some kind of signal jammer. He looked around, settled on a broom in the corner, and picked it up. Eighty percent, without question. He brought the broom's handle down on the machine once, twice, a third time, until it lay in pieces on the tabletop. Satisfied, he returned to the kennel room. Across the way, Carlos, on the phone, gave Carter a thumbs up.

Carter walked over to the Abby-Rachel pile and said, "Abby. Where's your father?"

Abby reluctantly released Rachel, wiped tears off her cheeks, and partially sat up.

"At the restaurant."

"How'd you get here?"

"I Ubered."

Carter shook his head at that. "Where's the driver?"

"She left."

"How'd you know to come here?"

"I saw the address on your GPS before you dropped us off."

"I told you to stay put. Coming here was dangerous. You could have been . . . . What were you thinking?"

Carter waited. "Abby?"

"I needed to know if Rachel was okay," she said. "Maybe it wasn't smart, but I figured it would be safe because . . ."

"Because why?"

Abby folded her arms. "Because you were inside. And I'd already seen what you could do."

Carter was so taken aback he didn't respond. By the time a reply formed in his head, Rachel spoke.

"It's on me. I called her."

Carter leaned over, offered her his hand, and helped her to stand. A moment later Abby rose and wrapped her arms around her stepmother.

Rachel said, "I had to know if she was alive. Then I was going to call the police. But I couldn't—something went wrong with the signal. Before I could do anything else they got through the door. I had a gun, but I don't really know how to use one. I aimed it and it just went off . . ."

"You couldn't call out because they jammed the phone signals," Carter said. "They did the same at your house and probably at Art Wheeler's. An electronic cell jammer. I'm guessing they had it ready to go in case of this exact scenario. Precautionary deal. They probably activated it as soon as they realized you'd escaped. I assume you escaped?" He glanced at an open cage on the other side of the room, then at the body of the man with the blood on his face. He kneeled and examined the initials on the man's ball cap. He Googled them. And frowned.

"Yes," Rachel said, answering Carter's question. She seemed about to say something else, then stopped. "The papers. My God. I almost forgot."

"Papers?"

She pulled free from Abby and hobbled to the cabinet lying on its side. She tugged the middle door free, pulled out the manila folder, and handed it to Carter.

Carter stared at the photo in his hand. At the picture of a mosque. New looking, a contemporary design that combined classic minarets with a Midwestern barn vibe. Something to admire under different circumstances. He thought about the box truck he'd seen outside. Considered what his uncle learned about Jason Wegner. The 22/7 Brigade. Wegner's move on Lobo, first for his loan-sharking business, then the more lucrative lottery scam. His need for money. But a need that was finite. So time limited that he turned down $20 million. Because a clock was ticking. Dominoes were falling.

He looked up at the sound of Abby's phone ringing. She answered and a second later burst into tears.

"No, I'm fine. It's all right. It's going to be okay."

"Abby," Carter said.

"One sec."

"Who is that?"

She sniffed. "Sorry. It's Haawo. She finally got her phone back. They took it away because she was on it so much before, texting me. It's like the first time all day I've been able to talk to her. I thought it would be okay if, I mean, if I just let her know I was all right and stuff?" She frowned. "I'm glad I did, since her Friday is shot and she's kind of upset."

"Shot how?"

"Without her phone, she couldn't arrange a ride to Friday afternoon prayers like she usually does. And there was supposed to be a teen thing afterward. At her mosque, I mean. She was looking forward to it."

Carter nodded, ready to move on. Then he processed what Abby just said.

*Mosque. Prayers. Afterward.*

Dominoes falling.

"Mercury?"

"Hang on."

Carter took a picture of the mosque and texted it to his uncle. As soon as it went through he called.

"Merc? You okay?"

"More or less. That picture. Where is that?"

"Hang on. Got it. One sec."

Carter used the next minute to flip through the remaining pages in the folder. Examining them one by one, he was struck by the detailed drawings of entryways and exits, roads into and out of the building's parking lot.

"Merc? That's the Islamic Center for Greater Indianapolis. What's going on? Is this related to Wegner?"

"How far is it from Greencastle?"

"Checking." A few seconds passed. "It's on the far west side of Indy, so only about forty minutes."

"You see a calendar of events? Anything happening there tonight—Friday?"

"Let me look." Carter glanced at Abby's puzzled face without saying anything. "There's a community meal thing. 'Dinner With Your Muslim Neighbor.' Looks like a big deal from the picture of the dining hall."

*No. No, No.*

Carter walked over to Mateo and Carlos. As he went he told his uncle what to do. Who to call. Emphasized they had very little time.

"Wait a minute," he said to his uncle. "Hey, Mateo."

The man looked up, arms still around Gabriel.

"I need to go. I don't have time to drop you back in Champaign. Can you manage?"

Mateo narrowed his eyes and stared at Carter. "Reinforcements will be here shortly."

Carter nodded and turned around.

"Hey."

"Yes?"

"Gracias," Mateo said, bobbing his chin at his son.

Carter nodded again and called out to Abby and Rachel.

"Let's go. Time's running out."

"What do you mean?" Rachel said.

Carter looked at his phone. At the Google results for the initials on the dead man's cap.

RWDS.

Right-Wing Death Squad.

"I mean we really need to go."

# FORTY-FOUR

Rosa Jimenez made a face. It wasn't the worst cup of joe she'd ever had. Hands down, that would be at St. John the Baptist's after Mass on the twice-yearly pilgrimage she made to placate her mother. Brown crayon water was better than that swill. But this was close. Wasn't hospital food supposed to be good now? Apparently, word hadn't gotten around. Up on the cardiac unit, anyway.

She checked her phone. Ten minutes to go until the attending physician promised her another sit-down with Art Wheeler. Once again, it would have to be brief. Until then, she was serving time in a waiting room with walls covered by framed art consisting of blobs and swirls that brought to mind some of the more graphic blood spatters she'd seen in the past couple of years.

She set the phone on her thigh and picked it up immediately as it buzzed with a call.

"Yeah."

"Sorry to interrupt."

"It's okay. What's up?"

"There's a guy on the other line says he needs to speak to you right away."

"What's he want?"

"He just said it's important."

"Always is. Take a message. I'll be free in about thirty."

"The thing is—"

"What?"

"He didn't ask for you by name. He said he needed to speak to the person handling the Art Wheeler home invasion where the dog was injured."

Jimenz paused. "He mentioned the dog?"

"Yeah. Little gray schnauzer?"

That had not been in any reports.

"Detective?"

"Yeah."

"He also mentioned something about a garden hose."

Jimenez stood.

"Put him through."


Carter kept well back. It took some doing because the box truck was traveling at exactly one mile per hour faster than the posted speed limit, no more, no less, and the rush of cars exceeding that pace and blowing past on the left was relentless. But he had to take precautions. It wouldn't do to have anyone make him at this point. He was also worried about the fact he didn't see the blue van. The fact that the three musketeers—Wegner, Finn, and Stone—left the impound center in two vehicles rather than stay and fight it out should have been a relief. Instead, it added to the sense of vulnerability and impending doom that Carter felt.

Beside him, he heard Rachel talking to someone on the phone. Something to do with the call he had her place as they left the impound center and headed for the highway. Using Abby's phone to get someone to go to Marvin's burger joint to get Glenn to a hospital to be more thoroughly checked out.

"Hang on," Carter said to the Chicago detective. He half-turned his head toward Rachel. "All set?"

"He's on his way to the ER. They think he's going to be okay."

"Good to hear." To Jimenez, he said, "All right, sorry."

"Listen, Mer—what's your name again?"

"Mercury. Call me Merc."

"Okay, Merc. Either way, you're not making a whole lot of sense here. It'd be better if we could meet."

"We don't have time to meet. Like I said, I need you to call whoever it is you alert about something like this. The Islamic Center for Greater Indianapolis. Everyone there is in danger. I'm guessing a bomb."

"You know you're calling Chicago."

"Of course. But I'm figuring you've been on the phone several times with your counterparts in Indy because of what happened at Rachel Stanfield and Glenn Vaughn's house. I need you to call them back and rally the troops. Like ASAP."

"Why in the world should I believe anything you say?"

"I can think of a few hundred reasons," Carter said, fighting off impatience. "Those being, from my limited understanding, the average number of attendees at an Eid celebration at a bigger-than-average mosque. Like I said, I-74 East, white box truck." He gave her the license plate.

"How in the world do you know that?"

"Hundreds," Carter said, and hung up.

"How do you know that?" Rachel, seated in the Suburban's front passenger seat, echoed Jimenez's question.

"Know what?"

"Know where the truck is? I can't see it."

"Tracking device. I stuck it on the undercarriage just before going inside the kennel."

Rachels' eyes widened into saucers. "How did you . . . I mean, what made you think that truck was important?"

"Box trucks are always important. In my experience."

"But what if you guessed wrong? What if that's not what we think it is?"

"You saw the documents and the photos in the file cabinet. You know who Wegner is now. You tell me."

She didn't say anything for a moment, instead looking through the window at the traffic in front of her. He pointed out the truck four car lengths ahead. She nodded.

"Mercury?"

"Yes."

"Thank you for what you did back there. And for everything. You saved my life. Our lives. Over and over again. I'm sorry about the delivery. I know it's a priority thing." She offered a small smile, as if slightly embarrassed for him. "I'm a little biased but I'm glad you relented in the end."

"Right. Thanks for reminding me." Carter reached over and opened the compartment between the seats. He found the envelope and handed it to Rachel.

"What's this?"

"It's the package I was hired to deliver to you. The real package. Sorry for the delay."

"What are you talking about? I thought you gave it to Jason, back there. The phone. The one he handed to Finn. That wasn't it?"

He shook his head. "Rules are rules."

Rachel stared, speechless. "You mean you—"

She stopped midsentence as the Suburban shuddered, something slamming hard against the rear bumper.

Abby screamed while Carter fought to control the car. He yelled at her and Rachel to get down just before the second blow came. He looked in the mirror. The blue panel van from the impound center, its lights turned off. A perfect maneuver. He hadn't seen it coming in the heavy traffic. Distracted by Rachel's efforts to get help for Glenn and the revelation about Rachel's package. Stupid. The van had been trailing him while he trailed the box truck. He should have—

The van rammed a third time, pushing him across the right-hand-side rumble strip and onto the gravel berm.

"Hang on," Carter shouted.

He kept his line true, resisting the urge to whip the wheel to the left, and almost made it.

He hadn't counted on the culvert just ahead. His front right tire caught the edge of the drop-off and the Suburban careened down a sharp embankment. Carter tried to right the SUV but it was too late. It rolled right—*bang*—flipped over, and over again—*bang, bang*—before coming to a rest on its top.

# FORTY-FIVE

Carter came to after a second or so, smelling burned rubber. He reached out and touched the side airbag. He was hanging upside down. He heard the rush of traffic and a tractor trailer's rough downshift and the sound of whimpering beside and behind him. Two distinct voices. So that was good. Trying to clear his head, he located the belt lock, depressed it, and eased himself free, dropping to the inverted ceiling of the Suburban. He righted himself, winced at a pain in his left shoulder, turned around, and made out the shadowy bulk of a vehicle behind them. The blue van, its brights suddenly on, pulling in behind and blocking his view. He had what, maybe one minute?

He tried the door. Nothing. The Suburban's top was wedged into the grass below the berm from the force of the impact or it had been damaged by the rollover. Either way, it wasn't budging. His head thick, struggling to react, he reached for his keys, still in the starter. It felt unnatural, pulling them out upside down. He managed it, just barely. He found the emergency window punch on his keychain. He jabbed it hard against the window's upper left corner. Nothing. He tried a second time and the window exploded. He eased through feet first, rolled to his belly, rolled to his left, and came up Beretta in hand.

Stone appeared first, his massive frame silhouetted by the brights of the van. He was moving slowly. His left shoulder drooped from where Carter had shot him as he held Gabriel in the kennel room. Stone raised the assault rifle he cradled in his arms and Carter shot him in the chest. He kept moving. Carter fired again, rolled once, twice, fired once more, and ducked into the woods bordering the edge of the interstate. Stone followed Carter's movements, tracking him into the woods, raised the rifle, and stood as still as if saluting a flag. Then his knees buckled, he dropped to the grassy ground, and he fell to his side.

Carter shifted deeper into the woods. He scanned the space around the van for Finn. He waited. He tightened his grip on the Beretta. Only a matter of time. It would have been just like Finn to send Stone—beaten up, snake bitten, shot—to provide cover for Finn's fatal assault on Carter. He waited. Almost too long.

At that moment, like something out of a dark fairy tale, Stone groaned and pushed himself onto his knees. And half stood, rifle still in hand. He looked around like a man who'd heard his name called on a playing field but was uncertain the direction the sound was coming from. Carter was raising his gun to fire when Stone groaned once more and fell to his left. As he did, his bulk blocked the van's brights for just a second. Long enough for Carter to make out the figure striding toward the overturned Suburban. Not to the side where Carter fought his way free. To the other side, where Rachel and Abby remained suspended upside down, still trapped in their belts, unable to move. Sitting—hanging—ducks. Finn passed the rear of the Suburban, cutting off Carter's only line of fire. He didn't have time to roust himself from his position in the woods and stop Finn. Who was also the type of person to take out a helpless woman and her stepdaughter first before turning his weapon on his tormentor. Carter had maybe six seconds.

Carter dug in his utility vest for his phone. Found it. Two seconds. Punched in the passcode. Two more seconds. Dialed the preprogrammed number. Two seconds . . .

"You had your chance," Finn shouted at Rachel.

"No," Carter yelled.

"I warned—"

The phone in Finn's pants pocket went off. The one Carter slid down the floor of the kennel. The one that Jason tucked into Finn's pocket.

*Yarf-yarf-yarf!*

The one he'd outfitted with a barking dog ringtone.

*Yarf-yarf-yarf!*

Carter was pretty sure from the start he knew where the Iowa-shaped scar on Finn's left cheek came from.

*Yarf-yarf-yarf!*

Carter scrambled around the corner of the Suburban. Finn was clawing wildly at his pants, maddened by the sound. Scrabbling for his pocket. Raking the fabric to find the source of the noise. The manic gesture caused him to lower his rifle by approximately two inches. More or less. Still even with the pale, terrified faces of Rachel and Abby. Finn looked over as he heard the snap of a twig. He tried swinging the rifle around. He wasn't fast enough. Carter fired. Once. Twice. Finn fell to his side, the phone still ringing, the recorded barking maybe the last thing he heard.

Carter walked to Finn, leaned over, pulled the rifle from his hands, and tossed it in the grass. He knelt and stared at Finn. It didn't take long. You could see it in Finn's eyes, which met his but reflected absolutely nothing. When Carter was certain, he hustled back to the Suburban and saw to Rachel and Abby.

They were bruised and scared and confused but okay. He used the window punch twice more, clearing pathways for them. Once they were out of the SUV and on the grass and sipping bottles of water, Carter called his uncle, and then placed a 911 call. Probably not necessary given the slowing traffic and all the rubbernecking. After another couple of minutes, he heard the first siren.

Shortly after that, to the east, a large flash of light arced across the night sky, followed a few seconds later by a loud percussive thump.

# FORTY-SIX

Rachel wasn't sure what was coming next, for her or for Glenn. And obviously, for the two of them together. She also knew that right at the moment, she didn't care.

"It's okay," she said once more.

"Of course it's not okay." Glenn lowered his head. "It's a disaster. And it's only going to get worse. All thanks to me."

"You don't know that. Plus, look what we just went through. Could it be as bad as that?"

His head dipped even lower.

Rachel tried to keep an even keel. Which meant not reaching out a comforting hand, but not storming from the hotel room either. Not that anyone would blame her if she did. To wake up, alive, after everything, to be holding Abby and Glenn in her arms again, to understand that her baby was going to be all right. And now this. Learning about the secret Glenn kept from her. The botched vaccine trials, the fudged results, the offshoring, the golden parachutes, the mysterious threats Glenn received. The reason he bought the gun.

*Oh, Glenn.*

If they hadn't both nearly died, she might consider killing him.

A knock at the door of the adjoining hotel room. Rachel heard it open, followed by the sound of a man's voice. A moment later Abby poked her head through the door linking the rooms. Their home for now.

"Um, the guy's here?"

"Guy?" Rachel said.

Abby looked at the card in her hand. "Brad Barbin?"

"Right. Have him come in," Rachel said. "We'll be there in a second."

Barbin—the attorney who agreed to represent Glenn as he sought to extricate himself from the vaccine trials debacle. One of his attorneys. It was a big debacle.

"Okay," Abby said. She raised her phone. "Also, Haawo says hi. Says she's glad you're okay."

"That's kind of her," Rachel said.

Abby started through the adjoining door and stopped.

"Dad?"

"Yes."

"Never mind."

"No. What is it?"

"It's just." She hesitated, leaning against the doorjamb. "I wanted you to know that . . . well, my grades."

"What about them?" Glenn said.

"It was because of Haawo. All the bullying she went through. I stopped caring about a place that would allow that. I'm sorry. But it's the truth."

Glenn nodded but didn't speak.

"Oh, honey," Rachel said.

Their daughter turned to let the lawyer in.

Glenn slowly straightened up. "So what now?"

"Now, I guess we both have some big decisions to make."

"Really?"

Rachel gave a harsh laugh. "Yeah, I'd say so."

"Sorry, that's not what I meant. I mean, I know I have a lot of stuff to think about. But is your decision really that hard?"

"Of course it . . ." She stopped. She watched him studying her. After all they'd gone through, after the secret he kept from her, he was still the one who knew her better than almost anyone else in her life.

It hadn't been until last night that Rachel was able to focus on the package that Carter delivered. To reflect on it. The small parcel that made such a big impact. A flash drive, of all things. Barely two inches long. On it, hundreds of documents. The court case of Lamont Buchler. A death row inmate in Ohio, sentenced to die for killing and dismembering a young couple in a drug-house slaying. A consistent claim of innocence, despite his own history of drug dealing, his presence in the house earlier that day, and a Swiss cheese alibi from a dopehead girlfriend.

Deep within the flash drive's folder, a secretly recorded prison cell phone video of another inmate—a gang leader—confessing to the killing and laughing about framing Buchler.

"Please help me," read the handwritten note wrapped around the flash drive. "No one else will take my case."

When Rachel pressed Carter, the mailman was vague on the subject of how he came to be delivering such an unusual package. He simply said, "You'd be surprised at the weird things people ship with me." Rachel thought the conversation was over. Then, he added, "Feels like it was the right move, in hindsight."

Despite everything, Rachel laughed. "You think?"

Glenn knew the gist of what happened next. How she spoke briefly with her supervisor at Donavan, Crabtree and Hamilton. Explained that she needed some time off. That she couldn't say exactly when she'd return.

What she hadn't told Glenn yet. She wasn't going back. She was putting her public defender's hat back on. She was taking Buchler's case. Not because she should. Because she wanted to. What was it she threw in Glenn's face the evening they argued in their kitchen? An event that felt so long ago but was barely seventy-two hours old? *You shouldn't have implied that I'm successful but not happy.*

Glenn, who knew her so well.

She reached for him.

Time to start over.

Again.

# FORTY-SEVEN

Three blocks away, the detective shook her head, drilled Carter with her brown eyes, and said, "You still haven't explained about the garden hose."

"Sorry. I thought I went over that. That I noticed it before I went inside."

"Did you also notice it was around the guy's neck?"

Detective Rosa Jimenez. Carter had slid her card into his wallet after she handed it to him. As she escorted him into the room on the fifth floor of the US Attorney's Office in Indianapolis. He'd been there once, years before, his USPIS inspector's hat on.

"I'll admit, you don't see that every day."

"Someone throttled to death with a garden hose? Yeah, you don't. So how'd you do it?"

"I beg your pardon?"

"You heard me. How'd a guy your size manage to strangle a thug like that? I bet he had seventy-five pounds on you, easy."

"I'm not sure I can help you there."

"You're refusing to answer the question? Is that it?"

Carter scratched his head. He felt exposed without his Red Wings cap on. But he had removed it out of respect for the detective.

"I don't think that's the case," he said, weighing his words carefully. "I answered your questions about Finn and the Wheelers. I'm just a little stymied on this one."

"Really? Maybe the Wheelers' backyard security video would improve your memory."

"Possibly."

"Good to hear. You ready to tell me what happened?"

Carter straightened his back, placed his hands palms down on his thighs, and said, "I'm ready for you to show me the Wheelers' backyard security video."

Jimenez crossed her arms. Carter stifled a yawn. It had been a long twenty-four hours. He had spoken to a lot of detectives. There was a great deal of interest in what happened. For starters, how he figured out what Wegner was up to. Then, how he was able to pass on the box truck's coordinates as it sped toward the Islamic Center for Greater Indianapolis. Finally, what he thought was going through Wegner's head when the truck hit the first set of road spikes laid out by police and the leader of the 22/7 Brigade decided to detonate the explosives then and there, even though he was a good quarter mile from the mosque. Carter answered everything to the best of his abilities. Except for the last one, about Wegner's state of mind. He really didn't know.

Carter looked up and realized Jimenez was staring at him wordlessly. He glanced at the conference room door and said, "Is that video something we watch in here? Or another office?"

"Why? You in a hurry?"

"Sort of, actually."

"How come?"

"I'm two days overdue on a delivery in Louisville. It doesn't look good."

"Delivery of what?"

"A package."

"What kind of package?"

"I'm not at liberty to divulge that."

"Who's it going to?"

"Same answer. So—the video?"

He watched the detective wrestle with her response. She seemed to be waging an internal debate with herself. Finally, she said, "If I didn't know better, I'd say you're confident there's no security video of what happened to that man in Art Wheeler's backyard."

"There isn't?"

"I didn't say that."

"Okay." He looked at his watch. "Can we get it over with?"

A staring match for another few seconds. Then Jimenez uncrossed her arms and said, "Look, Mr. Carter. I get it. You saved the day. You saved Rachel and Glenn and Abby and the Wheelers and Kevin and Stella Wolford and a whole bunch of people at the Islamic Center. What you did was amazing, especially given the fact you claim to be 'just' a mailman."

"Five hundred and seven."

"I beg your pardon?"

"There were 507 people at the mosque that night."

"I'm aware of the exact number, thank you very much," Jimenez snapped. "But the thing is, I drove all the way down here to talk to you because I've got a dead body in a backyard. That guy didn't trip and end up with a hose around his neck. I can't ignore a murder just because he's a bad guy. You were a federal agent once. You get that, right?"

Hands on his thighs, Carter calculated the drive time to Louisville. He thought about the body of Germán in Terry Kientz's house and the bodies of the gunners outside the abandoned humane society impound center and the body of Vlad the Asshole in the parking lot of the lakeside park.

He said, "I can appreciate that, yes."

"Oh really? It's not 'the ends justify the means' for you?"

"I couldn't say." He glanced once more at his watch, faced the detective, and raised his eyebrows. "So, the video?"

"You're a hell of a cold customer, Carter. Anybody ever tell you that?"

"To be honest, you wouldn't be the first."

"I bet."

Instead of responding, Carter stayed still for a few more seconds, then slowly rose from his seat, gauging the detective's reaction. When Jimenez didn't object, he said, "You have my number. You'll call if you find it? The video, I mean? Also—"

"What?"

"I deliver to and from Chicago. If you ever need."

Jimenez shook her head in disbelief.

"Just an FYI," Carter said, and headed for the door.

Outside, Carter walked to the garage where his rental was parked. The Suburban probably totaled, but he was trying to stay optimistic. He checked his watch. Louisville by three, three-thirty at the latest. Maybe three forty-five.

He was driving down the garage ramp, approaching the exit, credit card in hand, when his phone rang. Dispatch.

"I'm clearing Indy," Carter told his uncle. "Finally back on schedule."

"You're alone?"

"Yes. What's up?"

"Your mom just called. Wanted to check with me first. Wasn't sure how busy you were."

Carter fought back a moment of panic. "Everything all right?"

"Sort of. She just got off the phone with Marcus Washington. She's a little rattled."

"What he'd want?" Carter had stayed in touch with the USPIS inspector who investigated his father's death, but hadn't spoken to him recently.

"Ever heard of Lynn, Massachusetts?"

"Sure. First baseball game under lights was played there. Nineteen twenty-seven, I think."

His uncle paused. "Right. Anyway, house went up in flames there two days ago. Firefighters found a body in the basement. Evidence points to it being Earl Madden."

Carter gripped the steering wheel. "What kind of evidence?"

"Random documents, old driver's license, some newspaper clips about your dad."

"Okay." Carter felt his heart racing. "What about fingerprints, or DNA?"

"I don't think they've got that. At least not yet. The body was badly burned."

Carter relaxed a little. "Sounds dicey. Just for the heck of it, though, any idea how far Lynn is from Louisville?"

"Figured you'd ask. Fifteen hours, give or take."

The driver of the car ahead of Carter paid her fare, waited for the gate to open, and passed through. Carter rolled his window down. Inserted the parking ticket. Twelve dollars owed. Could be worse.

"Long way," Carter said, inserting his card into the machine. "But I have to go through Rochester, anyway."

"What the map says."

"Right," Carter said, taking his card, waiting for the bar to rise, then pulling onto the street.

"What are you going to do?"

"Well, first I'm going to call Tomeka. Then I'm going to Louisville. Then I'm driving home." Carter slowed, approaching a light. "And then I'm going to Lynn."

# ACKNOWLEDGMENTS

I'm grateful to the many people who helped me bring Mercury Carter to literary life.

For starters, a big thanks to writer and editor Michael Bracken, who published the first-ever appearance of Mercury Carter—a short story also titled "The Mailman"—in *Mickey Finn: 21st Century Noir, Volume 1*, in 2020, and bought another Carter story for the third Mickey Finn volume in 2022. If you're not familiar with this anthology series, surf on over to Down & Out Books to order all the volumes available so far. I'm similarly grateful to the appropriately named Kerry Carter, editor of *Mystery Magazine*—another must-read for crime fiction fans—who published three Mailman stories.

Phil Gentile, a US Postal Inspection Service inspector and supervisor, spoke with me at length about his agency and answered several questions about the life of a USPIS trainee and agent. Once again, retired Indiana police detective Bill Parker corrected law enforcement errors I'd allowed to creep into an early draft; any leftover mistakes are mine alone. I'm also thankful to Hayleigh Colombo, who helped me get my Indianapolis running trail and park geography correct, and to Adam Henkels for assisting with a question about Chicago police hierarchy.

A big shout-out to the team at Mysterious Press, including founder and CEO Otto Penzler, publisher Charles Perry, and publicist Julia O'Connell. A special tip of the hat to Mysterious Press editor-in-chief Luisa Cruz Smith for her edits and suggestions that made *The Mailman* so much stronger. Thanks also to my agent, Victoria Skurnick of LGR

Literary, for guiding me on my writing journey in general and specifically inspiring me to create a much-needed backstory for Carter.

Finally, eternal gratitude to my wife, Pam, who has now been my first reader for more than forty years and still never fails to improve what I write. The least I can do is to deliver, Mercury Carter–like (but without the gunplay), a heartfelt note of love and appreciation for her.